THE DARK
FANTASTIC

ED GORMAN

LEISURE BOOKS NEW YORK CITY

A LEISURE BOOK®

January 2001

Published by

Dorchester Publishing Co., Inc.
276 Fifth Avenue
New York, NY 10001

ISBN 0-8439-4819-1

The name "Leisure Books" and the stylized "L" with design are trademarks of Dorchester Publishing Co., Inc.

Printed in the United States of America.

Visit us on the web at www.dorchesterpub.com.

To Don D'Auria

In memory of Susan Carrithers

TABLE OF CONTENTS

THE DARK
FANTASTIC

Introduction

By Bentley Little

Ed Gorman is a writer's writer. Which is to say that he is one of those authors whom other writers make a concerted effort to read, one of those authors respected, admired and envied by his peers, one of those authors the rest of us look to for inspiration and . . . well, to find out how to better hone our craft.

But that's not enough. Sure, it's an ego boost to be highly acclaimed, to win awards, to be mentioned as an influence by novelists both big and small. And it makes those of us who read him feel privileged and special, part of a club, more hip and intelligent than the great unwashed who have yet to discover the pleasures of his fiction.

But Ed Gorman deserves better. Ed Gorman deserves more.

13

He deserves to be a household name.

Why?

You hold in your hand twelve compelling reasons.

A confession: I have not read all of the stories in this volume. But I don't need to in order to unreservedly recommend the book. The quality of Gorman's writing is that consistent. I *have* read eight of them, and they are everything I have come to expect: powerful, literate and wholly original. Equally at home with mysteries, Westerns, horror, suspense and science fiction, comfortable at novel, novella and short-story lengths, Gorman has always shifted easily between genres and forms. The man's nothing if not versatile.

Witness this collection.

"The Face" is an existential horror story that takes place during the Civil War. "Junior" is a hard-edged Western in which an infamous killer's family is treated like royalty by the cowed citizens of a frontier town. In "Different Kinds of Dead," a traveling salesman on a snowy Nebraska highway meets a sultry, mysterious woman who forces him to confront a sad truth about himself.

"Yesterday's Dreams" could have come from the pages of *Black Mask* or one of the other magazines that published Raymond Chandler, Jim Thompson and their ilk. The story of a burned-out ex-cop and a beautiful blind woman with mysterious powers, it takes place now but has the sensibility and un-put-downable narrative thrust of the very best forties pulp fiction. "The Broker" is both a scathing social commentary and a noirish horror story about a shallow and shady man who obtains goods and services for the very rich.

The horror of "Cages" takes place in a dystopian future with a poverty-stricken population devastated by a drug known as dreamdust. Dreamdust figures prominently in "Survival" as well, an even bleaker science fiction tale that takes place in a world nearly destroyed by nuclear and biological weapons unleashed by fascist Christians.

In "The Long Sunset," a young man, his best buddy and the female friend who loves one but is loved by the other grow up and apart even as a miracle appears in their midst. It is an aching elegy for lost love, dead dreams and lives that did not work out quite the way they should have.

As you can tell, this is not a "theme" collection . . . but in a way it is. For while the settings and plot points of these stories are all over the map, they are remarkably consistent in both tone and thematic content. There are recurring motifs: beautiful young women who offer redemption to lost souls; emotionally barren middle-aged men bereft of their families. Like any artist worth his salt, Gorman addresses a unified set of concerns through his work, and he approaches them from a variety of angles, creating a remarkably varied literary canon in the process.

This range of style and subject matter is impressive, of course. But, for me, Gorman's finest talent is his ability to evoke melancholy, that subtle mood of sweet sadness that is the most difficult of all emotions to conjure. There are numerous authors who can elicit laughs, who can summon scares, who can create heart-pounding, sweaty-palmed tension. But there are precious few who have the talent to make a reader feel the sublime sorrow and poignant regret of melancholia.

Ed Gorman

Ed Gorman is among that elite group.

Nearly all of his stories are imbued with a sense of loss; nearly all of his main characters are forced to struggle with death and estrangement and loneliness. It is this knowledge of alienation and emotional isolation that marks Gorman as a thoroughly modern writer—whether his fiction takes place in the past, the present or the future—and it is what lifts his work above that of most of his peers.

But enough joy and good cheer!

Read these stories and enjoy them. For beneath the doom and gloom (or on top of them, perhaps), these are clever and entertaining tales that should delight and satisfy readers of all stripes. A writer's writer he may be, but there's no reason for Ed Gorman to be relegated to cult status, and if there is any justice in the world, this collection will introduce his work to a wider mainstream audience.

Not that I don't enjoy being a member of that hip, smart club, mind you.

But it's high time for the rest of the world to catch on.

Ed Gorman deserves no less.

Foreword

The horror story was my first literary love. While I'd end up primarily a writer of suspense novels, horror was my first—and in some respects most lasting—influence.

Now, when I say horror, I also mean science fiction, because most of my favorite "horror" writers frequently combined the two forms.

Edgar Allan Poe, Henry Kuttner, C. L. Moore, Ray Bradbury, Theodore Sturgeon, Robert Bloch, Charles Beaumont, Philip K. Dick, and many, many others did a lot of what I call "fusion" fiction. Today, Dean Koontz and Stephen King also combine these forms.

The same with great horror movies. *Alien, The Dead Zone, The Brood*, and much earlier, *The Black Cat* and the British *Quatermass* series—all are excellent horror-sf films.

This is a very special collection for me because it's

going home again. Where I came from spiritually (I can still remember the emotional impact of first reading Bradbury in seventh grade and literally hanging out at newsstands, eager for the new sf-horror magazines to come in.

A very special collection for me, and, I hope, a good read for you.

Ed Gorman
9 December 1999

Yesterday's Dreams

ONE

1

There was a little boy up here one day, a soft and fertile spring day, and he said to his mother *listen to the singing, listen to the singing* and she said that's the wind in the trees, honey, that's not singing. But I agreed silently with the little boy. On this slope of hill, when the wind passes through the trees just right, it really does sound like singing, a sweet sad song, and sometimes I imagine that it sings the names of those I come here to see, my wife Susan and my daughters Cindy and Anne.

There was no singing today, not a Chicago hot and Chicago humid August day like this one, August 29 to be exact, Anne's twelfth birthday, or would have been if it all hadn't happened, if the three of them hadn't died.

I brought a few garden tools so I could clean everything up around the headstone, and I brought sunflowers, which Anne had always liked especially.

I started out the way I usually do, saying prayers, Hail Marys and Our Fathers, but then just sort of talking to them in my mind, and telling them how it's been going since I took early retirement on my 48th birthday, and how the rest of the family is doing, all the aunts and uncles and cousins who had loved her so much.

I stayed a couple of hours, spending the last twenty minutes or so watching a bright red family of cardinals building a nest on a low-slung branch nearby.

After I left, I drove over by Wrigley Park, where Susan lived when I first started dating her back in the early '60s, past the theaters where we used to see the romance movies she liked so much, you know with Sandra Dee and Troy Donahue and people like that, and the dance hall where we saw a very young Jimi Hendrix, long before anybody had ever heard of him, or before anybody knew what to make of him, either.

Then I stopped in a bar and had a couple of Lites, me having started to lose that old boyish figure of mine, and then I stopped by a video rental store and picked up three episodes of "Maverick," James Garner being just about my favorite actor. I'd seen this particular batch before but I never seem to get tired of them.

2

I was supposed to eat dinner at my brother's that night but I canceled because he warned me that his wife Liz had invited one of her church friends along so we could meet. Don't get me wrong. Liz is a nice woman. I like her. But her friends don't appeal to me. They're a lot like Liz, big and purposeful and sure of themselves in ways that aren't always attractive. But then I'm probably not being fair to them. I always end up comparing them to Susan and not many women can stand up to that.

Anyway, I canceled dinner saying I had a sore throat and headache. Liz sounded irritated, and as if she didn't believe me—and she shouldn't have; hell, I was lying—but she finally forced herself to sound civil and say she hoped I got to feeling better.

So here I was at the microwave when the knock on the door came. I was having the Hungry Man minute steak dinner. When you eat enough of these jobbies, you get to know how to kill the worst of the taste on each particular dinner. For instance, the chicken dinner can be pretty well covered up with a little mustard on the breast, whereas the beans and franks takes a whole lot of ketchup. As yet I haven't figured out what to do with the fish dinner. No matter what you put on it, and I've tried just about everything, it tastes like it came direct from Lake Erie back when they found all those strange sad sea creatures floating dead on it.

The knock.

I transferred the dinner from the microwave to the

plate I had waiting on the table and then I went to the front door.

Funny thing was, when I got the inside door opened, I didn't see anybody, just a purple dusk through the dusty screened-in-porch.

Then I heard the sniffle.

"I'm real scared, Mr. Flannery."

She was somewhere between six and eight, a raggedy little white girl in scruffy shirt and jeans. She smelled hot and teary. Her mussed blonde hair looked sweaty.

I looked down and said, "What's the matter, honey?"

"People said you was a cop."

"I used to be a cop, honey."

"Somebody kilt my Daddy."

Being a cop is a little like being a doctor. You have to resist panic not only for your sake but the sake of the others.

"Where is he, sweetheart?"

"Down'n the garage. Somebody shot him. Right here." She tapped her thin little chest and started crying again.

"C'mon, honey, we'll go see."

I grabbed the flashlight I keep next to the front door in the little hutch next to the statue of the Virgin Mary Cindy made me when she was in fourth grade. At first I wasn't sure what it was but she was only too eager to tell me. "It's the Blessed Mother, Dad," sounding as if she had just suspected for the very first time that ole Dad might be a dunce. "Oh, yeah, sure," I said. "That's just what I thought it was." I can still see her smile that day, and how she held her arms out to me.

All these years later, I bent down and picked up a different little girl. But this one wasn't smiling. I held her tight as we went out the door, and just as the screen door slammed she started crying hot and hard into my neck.

3

In the moonlight and the heat, in the smell of hot car oil and dried dog droppings, the alley was a silver gravel path past neat rows of garbage cans and plump brown plastic bags of garbage for the city trucks come Thursday.

"That one?" I'd say, nodding to the girl I was carrying, who was still crying, and she'd just shake her head and say no not that garage.

We ran nearly to the end of the alley to a small beaten garage that could fit maybe one compact, and she just went hysterical on me, sobbing and kicking her hard little shoes against my legs. "He's in there! He's in there!"

I took her back down two garages and set her on moonlit grass still warm from the afternoon and said you stay there honey right there and don't move all right, and then went back to the little garage at the end of the block and got my flashlight going and found her daddy, who was dead all right, indeed.

I never got used to corpses. In detective stories cops always tell jokes around stiffs because according to the writers this is the only way cops can deal with it all. But I never told jokes and neither did the cops I worked with. If you found kids who were dead, you got mad and wanted to kill somebody right back; but if they were adults you got scared because you saw yourself down there. Like an Irish wake, I guess, the person you're really mourning is yourself.

Whoever shot him must've really hated him.

He had a bullet hole in his trachea, in his shoulder, in his chest and in his groin, most likely his balls.

He wore a white shirt that was soaked with pinkish blood, and dark slacks that smelled of where his bowels had let go. In life he'd probably been a decent enough looking blond guy—dishwater blond, I guess they call it, like his daughter—working class probably, like most of the people in the neighborhood, cheap little wedding ring on his left little finger and a messy dragon tattoo of red and blue on his inside right forearm at the base of his dirty rolled-up sleeve.

I didn't touch him. I didn't even go into the garage where he was propped up against the back bumper of one of the old Kaisers that that crazy millionaire had manufactured right after World War II.

I went back to the girl and said, "Honey, what's your name?"

She looked up and said, "He's dead, isn't he?"

"Honey, we'll talk about that later. But now I need to know your name and where you live."

"Somebody killed him."

I bent down and touched her cheek. "Honey, what's your name?"

"Sandy."

"What's your last name?"

"Myles."

"What's your Dad's name?"

"David."

"Where do you live?"

She raised a tiny pale arm and pointed. "Over

there." She pointed to a house across the alley and two doors down.

"See that house behind us?"

She turned and looked. "Uh-huh."

"I'm going to run in there and call the police and then I'll come right back out. I'll take you in with me if you want to."

"He's dead," she said, and started crying again.

I reached down and scooped her up and carried her up to the house. An old and frightened Polish woman came to the door and opened up only after I told her six different times that I really was Nick Flannery, the ex-cop from down the street, and I really did need to use her phone.

4

A male-female team of uniforms showed up first. I didn't recognize them and vice-versa. They were very young, probably no more than a year out of the Academy.

They reached the garage before I did. Sandy had started crying so hard that she'd thrown up. I'd stayed with her to get her washed and give her a couple of sips of the strawberry pop the old widow offered her.

I left Sandy inside and went out to the alley and when I got to the garage I saw the female inside with her flashlight and the male standing out on the gravel looking at me.

"You're Mr. Flannery?"

"Right."

"You called in about the murdered man?"

"Yes."

"Dispatcher said the body was in the garage."

"Right. It is."

He gave me a quizzical cop look—the same kind of look I'd given hundreds of drunks, fakers and lunatics during my own career—and said, "Maybe you'd like to show us where the body is then."

"It's not in the garage?"

"Not that we can see."

I took my flashlight and walked into the garage. Several old tires hung on the wall, laced up with silver cobwebbing. You could smell rain and sweet rot in the old wood.

The female officer had stacked three crates on top of each other and was exploring an attic-like shelf made from plywood sheeting.

"Nothing," she said. And then sneezed from the dust.

Heavy tires popped gravel outside. Car doors opened and slammed. I heard the young cop say, "Nothing here. No body we can find."

A familiar voice said, "Like we don't have enough to do already."

I went out and let him see me and he was just as surprised as I figured he'd be.

"Hey," he said, "what're you doing here?"

"I called it in."

"The dead guy?"

"Yeah."

"Then where is he?"

"I don't know."

Hodiak and I had started out as rookies together. I spent my nights with my kids and Hodiak, unmarried, spent his at night school. He got his BA then his Masters in Criminology. He made detective about seven years before I retired. I hadn't seen him in a while, not since his hair had turned white.

"Let's go in and talk to the little girl," I said.

5

Hodiak spent fifteen minutes with Sandy in the kitchen. By this time, the old woman had fixed her up with more strawberry pop and a small dish of ice cream, at least half of which was white and sticky on her face and pink little hands.

She said that she and her Daddy had been walking home from the grocery store, taking the alley as they usually did, when this man appeared and started arguing with her daddy, saying he owed him money and everything, and then the guy got real mad and took out a gun and shot her daddy several times, and then the guy took off running. She cried and cried but she couldn't get her daddy to wake up. He'd managed to crawl into the garage but now he wasn't moving. And that's when she remembered that a cop named Flannery lived down the street—people always told her to run to my place if she ever got in any trouble—and that's how we met.

Hodiak left her in the kitchen and walked me back outside. He took his own flashlight and we went over the garage again.

"There's a lot of blood."

"There sure is," I said.

"So we know he was at least wounded pretty bad."

"He was more than wounded. He was dead."

"Then if he was dead—and believe me, a cop like you, he'd know a dead guy when he saw one—but if he was dead, then where the hell is he?"

I shook my head again.

Ed Gorman

"No offense, Flannery, but if he was dead then he'd still be here."

"Somebody moved him."

"Who?"

"I don't know."

"And why?"

"I don't know that, either."

The uniformed cop came up. His female counterpart was sitting with her car door open filling out a couple forms. "I canceled everything. The ambulance and all."

"Thanks," Hodiak said. "You two start by checking that house over there, where the little girl lives. Then start looking around the neighborhood. He couldn't have gone very far if he was shot up so bad."

The male cop nodded then walked back to the car to tell his partner their instructions.

"No body," Hodiak said. He sounded tired. "It never ends."

I'd been thinking the same thing. "No, it doesn't."

Hodiak shrugged. "Well, there are eight million stories in the Naked City, compadre, and this has been one of them." He clapped me on the back. "You get my note, about the funeral?"

"Yeah. Appreciated it."

"Sorry I couldn't make it. Some police convention in Arizona."

"Sounds like tough duty."

He smiled sadly. "Sorry about what happened, Flannery. You had one hell of a nice family. They ever nail anybody yet?"

"Not so far."

I walked him back to his car. The temperature had started to fall suddenly. You could see silver dew on the grass. There was a hint of fall in the air. September and its fiery leaves and harvest moons would be here soon enough.

"You doing all right with your leave and all, Flannery?"

"Pretty good. I do a little security work now and then. Gives me something to do."

He got in his car, started it, rolled the window down. His radio squawked with raspy dispatcher sounds. "I still get out to that old bowling alley couple times a month, see some of the old guys. You know. You should stop out there sometime."

"Maybe I will."

He nodded. "I'll keep you posted on all this. If we hear anything, I mean."

I smiled. "Yeah, if a dead guy checks himself into a hospital, be sure and let me know."

6

Over the next week, I walked back up the alley at least twice a day. Disappearing bodies were the stuff of mystery novels, not reality. The odd thing was, the blood tracks didn't leave the garage. He bled a lot while he was propped up against the Kaiser but when he left the garage—

All I could think of was that somebody had wrapped him up in tarpaulin and stashed him in a car trunk.

I suppose I enjoyed it, playing detective. Sure beat flat-footing it all over a busy Saturday afternoon mall in rubber-soled shoes and a uniform designed to look like a cop's. I went to Sandy's house several times, each time her neighbors telling me that Sandy was at her aunt's house, but she didn't know the aunt's name or address. Poor little kid, I wondered how she was doing.

Gradually, I gave it up. Hodiak phoned a few times to tell me that they'd had absolutely no leads, and to invite me out to the bowling alley again. And after skipping a few days, I walked to the garage again but found nothing helpful whatsoever.

Autumn came nine days following Sandy knocking on my door. You know how it is in the Midwest. The seasons rarely give warning. They sneak up on you and pounce. I drove to one of the piers and looked at Lake Michigan. When the sky is gray and the temperature face-numbing, there's a kind of bleak majesty to the big international freighters set against the line of horizon. At home, I turned on the heat and put the Lipton iced tea away and hauled out the Ovaltine.

On Tuesday of the following week, just at dusk, I saw Sandy. Or thought I did.

I was on my way back from the grocery store, making the six blocks afternoon walk, when I saw a little girl at the far end of the block. I called out for her and waved but instead of waving back, she seemed to recognize me, and then take off running.

After dinner, I went back up the alley with my flashlight. Checked out the garage. Noted where the blood trail ended. And then raised my eyes and looked at the back of Sandy's house, where a light shone in a small upstairs window, behind heavy drapes drawn tight.

I went over and knocked on the front door. The wind was up, a November wind in mid-September, and you could hear leaves scraping the sidewalk like a witch's fingernails on a blackboard, and hear the lone neighborhood owl cry out lonely in the chilly gloom. No answer. I looked at the curb. A red Honda sat there. I hadn't noticed it on my previous trips over here. I went out to the curb and opened the driver's door and rooted around until I found the registration. No help. Car belonged to one Jessica Williams. Sandy's last name was Myles, her father's name David.

I went around back and tried that. No answer there, either. I tried the doorknob. Locked.

I took a few steps back so I could get a better look up at the window where the light had shone. There was no light now. Somebody had turned it off. I sensed somebody watching me from upstairs.

I trained my light on the upstairs window. The curtains fluttered slightly.

Hide and seek. But whoever was up there sure wasn't about to come down. I stood there staring up at the window for a while, wondering who Jessica Williams might be, and where Sandy was and if she was all right.

After awhile I went home and made myself some Ovaltine and found a Randolph Scott Western on one of the cable stations and went to bed around midnight. I didn't sleep well. I was too excited about the coming day.

7

I was up at 5:30. I made some instant coffee in the microwave and took it out the door with me. It was overcast and cold enough for frost.

At 5:45 I parked six spaces down the street from Sandy's house. The red Honda was still there. A yellow rental trailer had been added. Sandy, a woman of about thirty and David Myles, the same man I'd seen dead in the garage, were carrying overloaded cardboard boxes from house to trailer.

I picked up my Smith and Wesson, the one I'd kept from my days in uniform, and got out of the car and walked up to the trailer. Sandy and the woman were inside. Myles was rearranging boxes in one corner of the trailer.

"I'd like to talk to you, Mr. Myles."

He jerked around as if he were going to clip my jaw with his elbow. He wore a shortsleeve shirt. His splotchy red and blue dragon tattoo was easy to see.

"Who the hell are you?"

"You want to talk out here or you want to go inside?"

"You didn't answer my question."

He came at me but he wasn't much good at violence. I grabbed him by the shoulder, turned him around and wrenched his tattooed arm into a hammerlock.

"You leave my daddy alone."

Sandy was back, scared. She pounded my hip with her tiny fists.

"I don't want to hurt him, honey. I just want to talk to him." I put more pressure on his arm. "Tell her, Myles."

He spoke through gritted teeth. "It'll be all right, sweetheart. You and Jessie just wait inside."

"Jessie's scared, daddy."

"Tell her I'm fine."

I let go of him. "We're just going to talk, honey. See?"

She looked sleepy as she glanced from her father to me. "You won't hurt him no more?"

"I won't, honey. I promise."

"Jessie, she's got a gun, Mr. Flannery, and she could shoot you."

I smiled. "Then I'll be sure to be real careful."

She watched us a little while longer, thinking things she didn't express, or maybe didn't know how to express, and then turned and ran fast back up the walk and steps and inside the house where she called, "Jessie! Jessie!"

"You've got a nice daughter."

"Cut the crap. What's this all about?"

He had the sullen dumb good looks of half the grifters you see in prison. "I want to know how you came back from the dead."

"Back from the dead? Gimme a break."

The street was awakening. Cars and trucks and motorcycles rumbled past on the ancient brick streets, and bass speakers announced the day. A boxy white milk truck, the kind you don't see very often any more, stopped on the far corner and a woman in a white uniform jumped down to the street, walking fast to an apartment house.

"The last time I saw you, Myles, you had four gunshot wounds."

"You're crazy."

"Sandy said she saw a man shoot you."

"Kids make things up."

"Am I making it up about seeing you with four bullet holes?"

"You got the wrong guy, mister. Do I look like somebody who's been shot four times recently?"

Not much I could say to that. I had no idea what I was dealing with here.

Jessie and Sandy came down the walk, both carrying boxes. Jessie slammed the door behind her. They got the boxes in the trailer then stood watching us. Jessie was pretty in a weary way.

"Who is he?" Jessie said to Myles.

"He's Mr. Flannery," Sandy said. "A cop."

Myles said, "You know what he's trying to tell me?"

"Huh-uh," Jessie said.

"He's trying to tell me that somebody shot me four times a couple of weeks ago."

I bent down to Sandy. "You saw somebody shoot your Dad, didn't you, sweetie?"

Sandy glanced up at Jessica then at Myles. She shook her head. "No."

Myles said, "You and Jessie get in the car now, honey."

He was leaving. I'd never find out what happened. As the ladies went around and got in the car, I grabbed Myles and said, "I've got your license number. I can get an APB put on you in five minutes."

"What the hell is your problem, man? I'm not hurting nobody. My girlfriend and I got jobs in another city and so we're moving. What's the big deal?"

"You coming back from the dead, that's the big problem. And I wasn't bluffing about that APB."

"Just walk away from him, David," Jessie called. "Just walk back here and get in the car and we'll drive away."

Myles looked confused and exasperated now. "I knew I couldn't get away clean from this."

He did kind of a James Dean thing where he hung

34

his head and kind of muttered to himself. "I told her this'd happen."

"Told who?"

He looked up. Leaned closer. "I gave her my word."

"I still don't know who 'her' is."

"The blind girl. 3117. That pink stucco apartment building halfway down the block."

"What's she got to do with all this?"

"What's she got to do with all this? Who do you think healed me?"

"So you were shot four times?"

He nodded. "Yeah, you got the right guy." He made a face. "It sounds crazy but it's the truth. This guy shot me point blank—I owed him a little bit of money—and then all of a sudden I can feel myself dying and then all of a sudden—Well, I woke up and there was this really pretty blind girl, probably eighteen, nineteen, somethin' like that, leaning over me and helping me to my feet."

"What about your wounds?"

He shrugged. "I know how it sounds, but they were all gone. I mean I still had blood all over me but the wounds were all healed. You couldn't even see any scarring. It was just like I'd never been shot."

"And this blind girl did it?"

He nodded. "I guess. I mean, I don't know who else it would've been. She made me promise not to tell anybody and I really feel bad, you know, even telling you. But I guess I didn't have much choice, huh?"

"No, you didn't."

He glanced back at his car. "We've got to get going. Our jobs start tomorrow and we'll be driving all night as it is. Plus I don't want this guy to find out I didn't die. He'd kill me again."

"You know I don't believe you."

He grinned. "That's what I told her, the blind girl. I said, even if I did tell anybody, who'd believe it? Just like you, man. You don't believe it."

He walked back to his car, started it up, the muffler needing some immediate repairs, and took off.

Without quite knowing why, I walked down the block to 3117, the pink stucco apartment house. A bald man in a blue work shirt and tan work pants came whistling out the front door. He swung his black lunch pail in time to a tune I couldn't hear.

I wanted to go over to him and ask him if there was a blind girl in the apartment house who could heal people the way Jesus used to. But I figured the guy would probably think I was just some drunk rambling past.

TWO

1

That day, I called Hodiak three times but he wasn't in and I left no message. In the afternoon, I raked leaves in the back yard and then cleaned out the west side of the garage. Every once in a while, I'd look over at the back of 3117, the rusty fire stairs that climbed four floors, and all the flower pots people had setting in their rear windows.

In the evening I drove over and parked several spaces away from 3117. I sat there until around 8:00

and then I gave it up and went home and had a Hungry Man I needed both catsup and mustard for. It was a new model and I hadn't figured out how to deal with it yet.

In the morning it rained, and I went back to my post at 3117. I spent three hours there, mostly listening to callers on a talk show arguing about all the new taxes.

I spent the first half of the afternoon at the library checking out more books on Chicago history. These days the past is a lot more restful to contemplate. Chicago was just as violent then as it is now, but even the atrocities of yesteryear have a glow about them. Even killers look kinder when you set them back a hundred years or so.

This time I was there twenty minutes when the blind girl came down the steps, her white cane leading the way. She was slender and pretty in a summery blue dress with a blue sweater over her shoulders. She moved with the jerky speed of blind people making their way through a dark universe filled with land mines and booby traps, the white cane her flicking antenna. When she reached the sidewalk, she turned right.

In the next half hour, a strange time when the sun would make an appearance in three-minute segments then disappear behind rolling black thunderheads, she went three places—the corner grocery store where she bought a small sack of groceries, the corner pharmacy where she bought something that fit into her grocery sack, and a large stone Catholic church built back in the early part of this century. She stayed in church fifteen minutes then walked back home.

I parked and got out of the car and was within ten

feet of her when a man in his thirties came out of the apartment house door and said, "I wondered where you went. You should've told me you were going somewhere." He had paint daubs all over his T-shirt and there were a few yellow streaks on his jeans. In his hand he held, with surprising delicacy, a paint brush. The kind Degas used; not the sort the Acme House Painting Co. prefers.

He met her halfway down the walk, took her in his arms and then, for the first time, became aware of me. He had good instincts. I could tell right away he was suspicious. He glared at me then turned away and walked the blind girl inside.

When I got back to my car, I noticed something curious. Four spaces back from where I'd parked was another car, a blue Saab. A man with a dress hat sat inside. He was pulling surveillance and I figured I knew which house he was watching. He caught me looking right away and pulled a paperback up over his face.

Apparently, I wasn't the only one who'd heard about the blind girl.

2

"You saw this man yourself?"

"Yes, Father, I did."

"And he was dead?"

"Definitely."

"You couldn't have made a mistake?"

"He'd been shot four times. Including a shot right here." I tapped my throat.

"And then you saw him a few weeks later?"

"Yes."

"And he was alive?"

I nodded.

"And there was no evidence of any wounds?"

"All I could see was his throat but it was clear. No sign of a wound at all."

"This is pretty strange, I sure have to say that."

He was a young priest, thirty-five at most, with the face of an earnest young altar boy who was suddenly old, sitting in a dusty den in a dusty rectory next to the same dusty church where my girls had been baptized and from which, too few years later, they'd been buried. I recalled the first time I'd ever been inside a rectory, how disillusioning it was. In my Catholic boy's mind I'd imagined that priests spent all their time praying and discussing urgent theological matters. But when I came inside that day, I must have been twelve, I saw a Cubs game on TV being watched by the Monsignor himself. He wore a T-shirt and smoked a cigar and had a can of Pabst Blue Ribbon balanced in his lap. This was a long way from Jesus and the twelve apostles.

"And the girl?"

"The blind girl," I said.

"You don't know anything about her?"

"No; nothing."

"But the man—Myles—he said she was the one who healed him?"

"That's what he said."

The priest thought for a long moment. "I guess you're asking me if it's possible?"

"Right. I mean, have you ever heard of this before, of healing like this?"

"Oh, sure, I've heard of it. But I've never witnessed it, if that's what you mean. And I have to say, Rome is very skeptical of things like this. Especially these days." He smiled sadly. "Between pedophile priests and the church going broke, we don't need to play a role in a hoax."

"Is that what you think this is?"

"I think it's a possibility."

"With four bullet wounds in him?"

"There have been hoaxes a lot more complex than something like this." The sad smile again. "I'm not being much help, am I?"

"I appreciate you being honest."

"Maybe it's better to just let this go."

"You mean forget it?"

The priest nodded. "You strike me as a man who needs to relax and forget about things for a while. I mean, it wasn't that long ago that your family—Well, you know what I mean."

I stood up, laughed. "I thought you'd call Rome and tell them that you had another Miracle of Fatima on your hands."

He stood up, shook his head. "There are people who say that was a hoax, too."

"Fatima? But hundreds of people said that they saw the Virgin."

"Mass hypnosis. It happens. Look at Hitler."

He walked me to the door. "You ever think of going on a vacation?"

"I've thought about it."

He grinned. "Well, think some more about it, all right?"

3

Twice that night I drove past 3117. The blue Saab was there both times. He might not be a master of disguise but he sure was dogged.

Later on, sleeping, I got all wound up in the covers and woke myself up. The girls were with me, and their mother, present in the dark room somehow. I had tears in my eyes and I was scared but I wasn't sure of what, and I was so lonely that I needed to be held like a child or a small scared animal. I got up and straightened the covers and laid back down. I slept but when I woke I wasn't rested at all.

At nine that morning, I sat at the kitchen window watching the bright autumn leaves in the gray autumn rain, and saw a tiny wren drenched on the sill, and then I got up, put on my fedora and my rain coat and walked up the soggy alley to the corner where I turned right and walked to the end of the next block.

The blue Saab sat just about where it had been last night. He had the engine running. Probably using his heater. It was cold enough.

I walked back to the alley then cut in the yard behind 3117. There was a rear door leading down five concrete steps to a laundry room. The air smelled of detergent and heat from the drier.

At the far end of the laundry were five more steps, these leading up to the apartment house proper. I checked the row of twelve mail boxes in the lobby. Everybody was Mr. and Mrs. somebody except for a Vic McRea and Jenny Conners. They lived on the third floor, to the back.

I was starting up the stairs when I heard a male

voice two floors above me. "Jenny, you think I like going out in the rain? You think I'd go if I didn't have to?"

The girl said something, but she spoke so softly I couldn't pick it up.

I hurried back to the basement where I stood in the shadows waiting for Vic to pass by.

His steps were heavy on the stairs. Halfway down, he paused. I heard the snick of a match head being struck. The heavy footsteps picked up again.

When he passed me, I saw he was the same young guy who'd given me the big glower yesterday afternoon.

He turned the collar up on his London Fog and went out into the rain.

I waited ten minutes and then I went upstairs and knocked on the door where the blonde girl lived.

"Yes?" she said from behind the closed door. The hallway carpet was worn to wood in places, and everything smelled of dust.

"There's been an accident, ma'am."

"What?" Panic fluted her voice already.

"A man named Vic McRea. Do you know him?"

"Know him? Why—"

Chains were unchained, locks unlocked.

She was much prettier close up, long blonde hair to her shoulders framing a face both lovely and eager, a child hoping to please. She had dark blue eyes and only when you studied them carefully did they reveal their blindness. She wore a white blouse and blue cardigan sweater, big enough that I suspected it was Vic's, and a pair of jeans that fit her well.

When I got inside the door, I said, "I'm sorry I had to do that to you."

"But you said Vic—"

"I was lying. I'm sorry."

She started to say something but then stopped herself. Then, "You're here to rob me, aren't you? Vic said someday somebody would trick me into opening that door."

"I'm not going to rob you, I just want to talk to you."

"About what?"

"About how you can heal people."

She waited a long time before she spoke again. "That's ridiculous, healing people, I mean. Nobody can heal people except God."

"How about if we sit down?"

"Who are you? You scare me."

"My name's Nick Flannery. I used to be a Chicago cop. There's no reason to be afraid of me."

She sighed. "I really have a headache. And anyway, I don't know anything about healing people."

"Please," I said. "Let's sit down."

We sat. She navigated the room quickly, moving over to a green couch as worn as the runner in the hallway.

I took a vinyl recliner that had a cigarette burn in the left arm and several cuts on the right one. The place had the personality of a decent motel that had been allowed to deteriorate badly. The air was filled with a kind of weary history. You could hear WWII couples in this room dancing to Glen Miller, and their eager bright offspring, long years later, toking up a joint and listening to Jefferson Airplane.

Jenny was too nervous to sit back. She stayed right on the edge of the couch, her fingers tearing at the edges of a magazine as she spoke. "Why did you come here?"

"I told you."

"The healing thing? But that's crazy."

"I know a man named David Myles. He said you healed him."

"I've never heard of him before."

"I can understand why you wouldn't want people to find out about you."

"I'm just a plain, ordinary person. I'm blind, as you can see, but that's the only difference between me and everybody else."

She tore the magazine edges with quiet fury.

"What happens, people find out about you and you have to run away?"

"What would they find out?"

I sighed. "Jenny, I'm not going to hurt you; I'm not even going to tell anybody about you. But I did see David Myles the night somebody shot him—and then I saw him several days later. There weren't even any scars. It was as if he was never shot."

"Do you really think that somebody could do that—heal somebody that way?"

"Well, somebody did. And the man who was healed said that you were the one who did it."

For the first time she sat back on the couch, as if she were exhausted. She dropped her head slightly and put her hands together in her lap.

After a long silence, I said, "Jenny."

"I wish you'd just leave."

"I want to know the truth, Jenny."

She raised her head. Her beautiful but blind eyes seemed to be looking directly at me. "Why is it so important to you?"

"I—I'm not sure I could explain it so that it'd make any sense."

She said nothing. Just stared.

"A while back, my wife and two daughters were murdered in a robbery. One of those wrong time-wrong place situations. They happened to be in this store buying some school clothes when this guy came in all coked up. He killed six people in the store." I snuffled up tears. "She was my partner, my wife I mean. I'd never had a partner before. And I really miss her."

"I'm sorry for you—and them. But I still don't see—"

"I'm not sure there's a higher power, Jenny. God or whatever you want to call it. I want to believe but I can't—not most of the time anyway. I kneel down and I close my eyes and I pray as hard as I can but—But then I get self-conscious and I hear my own prayers echo back at me and I think, Hell, I'm just repeating a bunch of mumbo-jumbo I heard when I was a kid. None of it's true. You're born and you die—that's all there is. And that's what I believe, most of the time."

Softly, she said, "That's not all there is. I know it's not, Mr. Flannery."

"That's what I mean, Jenny. Maybe if I could believe in you—well, maybe then I could believe in some kind of higher power—and believe that someday I'll see my wife and daughters again."

"Would you get me a diet Pepsi?"

"Sure," I said, standing up.

"In the kitchen. In the fridge. And—take your time."

"All right."

"I need some silence. Silence is good for people."

"Yeah—yeah it is."

I took my time getting her the diet Pepsi, finding a glass and dropping three cubes in it, and then stopping in the bathroom before returning to the living room.

I set glass and can on the coffee table in front of her and filled the glass with fizzing cola.

I went over and sat down. I was careful not to speak.

"I really can't talk to you without Vic being here, Mr. Flannery."

"Who is Vic exactly, anyway?"

"My fiancé."

"I see."

"The way you say that, I take it you don't approve of him."

"It's just that he doesn't look like the kind of guy you'd be with."

She smiled. "That's one thing you learn from being blind, Mr. Flannery. You have to learn to see inside because you can't see outside. I don't mean that I'm any kind of mind-reader or anything—but Vic isn't as rough as he seems. Not inside, anyway."

"He knows about your—ability?"

"He knows everything about me that matters, Mr. Flannery, including any special talents I might have." She brought her glass to her lips and sipped cola. "You seem like a very decent man, Mr. Flannery."

"Thank you."

"But I had a very different impression of you when you lied to me at the door," she said. "Vic isn't a bad man."

I laughed. "All right, Vic's an angel. You've convinced me."

"Hardly an angel. He's made mistakes—one very, very bad one in fact. It almost broke us up."

"Can you talk about it?"

She shrugged. "He doesn't have much money. He saw a way to make what he thought was a fortune and he took it." She shrugged again. "There was a man who had a very sick wife and Vic decided to—" She shook her head. "Vic wasn't a very honorable man in that situation."

"He wanted to charge the man money for what you do?"

"It doesn't matter any more. Vic learned his lesson. He's changed completely now."

"What time will he be back?"

"Probably around three."

"Why don't I call you around four then. All I want is to talk to you. Learn some things about you. It'll help me, I know it will."

I got up and went over to the couch and lifted her hand and held it in mine. "This is very important to me, Jenny."

"I know it is, Mr. Flannery, and I think if I approach Vic in the right way, he'll let me do it."

She brought her other hand over and covered mine. "I'll be waiting for your call."

4

But I wasn't the one who called.

Two hours later, my phone rang and I picked up and a harsh whiskey voice said, "You stay goddamn away from her, you understand?"

"Who is this?"
"Who is this my ass. You know who it is."
As of course I did.
"You understand me, jerk off?"
"Yeah," I said. "I understand."
"You'd better," he said, and slammed the phone.

5

That night, I watched a couple more "Mavericks" and had a Hungry Man that took a whole lot of mustard. But I was distracted. I just kept thinking about her sweet dignified little face and the great wise peace I felt within her. I wanted to go back and see her some more, ask her more questions about life beyond this one, but there would be Vic, and with Vic there would be a fight, and I would likely hurt him and then she'd never talk to me again, not the way she loved Vic she wouldn't.

A knock came at the door about the time the second "Maverick" ended. I went and opened the door and there she was.

She wore a transparent plastic rain scarf and a white rain coat that looked soaked. The rain had been pounding down for the past three hours. In her right hand, she clutched an umbrella, in her left her white cane.

"I decided to go for a walk," she said, and shrugged. "I just wanted to stop by and apologize for the way Vic talked to you." She started to say something else and then abruptly started crying. "He's got somebody on the side again—and I just needed to talk to somebody."

"C'mon in," I said, and took her around the shoulder and led her into the living room.

In the next fifteen minutes, I hung up her coat to dry, set her wet shoes in front of the small crackling fireplace, got us some Ovaltine and then listened to the problems she was having with Vic. She smelled of rain and perfume that made me sentimental.

She told me about Vic.

Seems every city they moved to, Vic found himself a new girlfriend. The pattern was pretty much the same. At first it would be just a kind of dalliance. But then gradually it would get more and more serious. Vic would start staying out later and later. Eventually, he'd start staying out all night. He always had the same excuse. Poker. But she'd never been aware of him winning or losing any appreciable amount so she had no reason to believe his story.

"But he always comes back to you?"

"In his way, I suppose."

"I'm not sure what you mean."

"He comes back and makes all kinds of promises but I don't think he means to keep them. He's just biding his time till his next girl."

"I'm sure you don't want to hear this, but maybe you'd be better off without him."

"I love him."

"Trust is a big part of love. For me, anyway. And it sure doesn't sound like you can trust him."

"He's only twenty-nine. Maybe he'll change someday. That's what I keep hoping anyway."

"How's the Ovaltine?"

She smiled. "I haven't had this since I was a little girl at the convent."

"The convent?"

"Well, actually, it was an orphanage but a very small one. There were more nuns than kids. So we always called it the convent."

"Your folks put you there?"

She shook her head, staring into the fireplace. I had to keep reminding myself that she was blind. "I don't know anything about my folks. Nothing at all. I was left with the nuns when I was six days old. That's why—well, that's why I don't know anything about my—gift. I just have it. I don't know how I got it or where it came from. It's just always been there. And maybe it'll go away some day."

"Have you ever talked to a doctor about it?"

"Right after I got out of high school, this was when I was living in New Mexico with a foster family, I went to visit a parapsychologist at the state university. He told me that there's a tradition of psychic healing in nearly every culture, dating back to earliest man and the shaman and the Babas of Africa. He told me there's a man named Dawson in Montana who can 'influence' the course of somebody's illness if not exactly 'heal' it. He also said that most of psychic healing is a fraud and that if I ever went public, the press would attack me and discredit me—and that if I ever demonstrated that God used me to heal others—well, I'd be a freak all my life and I'd never be left alone.

"The thing we talked about this afternoon, when Vic tried to 'rent' me to the rich man with the sick wife?"

"Right."

"That proved just what the parapsychologist told me. How they'd never let me alone. When I found out that Vic was asking the rich man for money, I got furious and told the rich man that I would try and help his wife but that I didn't want any money at all. Then Vic got curious."

"You helped her?"

She shook her head. "She was so sick. I just couldn't believe that Vic would do anything like that. I was able to help her. I thanked God I could do it. But it didn't end there. The rich man saw a way to get even richer. What if I worked for him and he sold my services to the highest bidder? That's what he wanted to do. Vic and I ran away. That was four months ago. The rich man probably has people looking for us. I just wanted to hide out when we got here. But six weeks ago, I saw a boy hit by a car and I went out and helped mend his leg. And his mother knew what I was doing. She started telling people around the neighborhood. The mother ran up here and told me about David Myles being shot."

"So what's next?"

A sad smile. "I guess I just wait for Vic to get over his latest crush."

There was no point in my railing about Vic again. She'd just get defensive. "How's the Ovaltine?"

"The Ovaltine's fine. But I sense that you're not."

"I'm all right."

"You mentioned your wife and daughters were killed."

"Yes."

"Why don't you come over and sit next to me?" This time the smile was bright. "I promise I won't make a pass at you."

"That wouldn't be the worst thing in the world, you know."

I went over and sat next to her on the couch. And I told her about my wife and kids, not their dying but

51

their living. How Susan had gone back and gotten her BA in English at night and had planned to get her teaching certificate; how we bought a horse for Cindy on her eighth birthday and kept "Lady" out in a stable in the farmlands; how Anne was a very gifted ballet dancer, and how her teachers talked of her going to New York to study when she reached ninth grade. And a lot of other things, too, the odds and ends that make up family life, the birthday parties when daddy dresses up in silly hats, the puppy who poops everywhere, the vacation to Yellowstone, the terrifying weekend when Susan found a lump on her breast but it proved to be nothing serious, the times when I found myself falling in love all over again with my wife, the life we planned for when the girls grew up and left home.

I must have talked for an hour. She spoke only rarely, and then little more than a word or two to indicate that she was still paying full attention. At first I tried to stop myself from crying but somehow with her I wasn't ashamed, and so when I was overcome by my terrible loss and the great sorrow that had followed, I cried, full and open.

During this time, we never touched, no consoling hands, no reassuring pats.

When I was done, I was exhausted. I put my head back and closed my eyes and she said, "Just stay like that. I want to help you."

I wasn't sure what she was talking about. No broken bones, no illness that I knew of, where I was concerned.

Out of the corner of my eye, I watched her situate herself pretty much as I had, leaning her head against the back of the couch, closing her eyes.

She felt around the open space between us until she found my hand.

"This will probably scare you a little bit at first but just give in to it, all right? Close your eyes now."

I closed my eyes.

There was a minute or two of absolute self-conscious silence. I felt the way I did when I prayed sometimes, that I was performing a charade, hurling pathetic words into the cosmic and uncaring darkness.

And then I felt it.

A few years ago, I had a hospital exam where the doctor gave me a shot of valium. I couldn't even count backwards from ten before a great roaring sense of well-being overcame me. The nervous, anxious person I was too often was gone, replaced by this beatific man of inner peace.

I felt this now, though a hundred times more, as I sat on the couch next to Jenny, and when I saw Susan and the kids I cried, yes, but they were tears of joy, celebrating all the sunny days and gentle nights and faithful love we'd shared for so many years.

I don't know how long it was before I felt Jenny's hand leave me, I just knew that I never wanted to come back to reality. I wanted to be in college again with Susan, and in the delivery room when Anne came along, and watching Cindy wobble down the block on her bike the day we took the training wheels off. So much to remember . . .

"I'm sorry," Jenny said. "I need to get back in case Vic gets home early."

"I don't know what you did there, on the couch I mean, but—"

She touched my cheek, her blind eyes seeming to

search my face. "You're a decent man. You should take comfort from that."

I stood up, helped her up. "I'm walking you back. And no arguments. This isn't the neighborhood it used to be. It's not real safe."

6

This late at night, ten o'clock, lights were out in most houses, and the night air smelled of cold rain.

For a time we walked without saying anything. Then I said, "How'd you learn to do that?"

"To make you feel better?"

"Uh-huh."

She wasn't using her cane. She had her arm tucked through mine. It felt good.

"A few years ago, I visited this friend of mine in the hospital. Down the hall from her was this man dying of cancer. He was very angry and very frightened. And he was very abusive to the nurses. When I passed by his door one day, I heard him weeping. I'd never heard anybody cry like that before. I went in to his room and went over and took his hand and I felt this—energy—I don't know how else to describe it—this great warm feeling in me that I was able to transfer to him simply by holding his hand. I didn't help him with his disease at all—he was in his early nineties and it was his time to go, I suppose— but I did comfort him. He died peacefully a few weeks later."

"And since then—?"

"Since then, when I sense that somebody's in great pain, I try to help them."

"You're quite a woman."

She laughed. "Oh, yes, I'm a regular role model. I'm blind and I'm broke and I have a fiance who keeps stepping out on me."

"But your gift. You—"

"Not 'my' gift. God's gift. You asked me if I believed there was some plane of reality beyond ours. Yes, I believe there is. I mean, I'm not sure it's 'God' as we think of him but there's something out there, a place where we survive what we think of as death. And whatever that force is, it's chosen to use me as one of its tools. I'm sure there are a lot more people like me in the world, all hiding out, all afraid of any exposure because they don't want to be treated like freaks."

We reached her corner.

"It smells so clean. The wind and the rain," she said.

I saw the blue Saab parked a few spaces from her apartment house. I thought of what she told me about the rich man trying to find her.

I took her arm a little tighter.

"Is everything all right? You seem tense all of a sudden."

"I just don't want you to get blown away in this wind."

The man in the Saab shrunk down some.

We reached her apartment house. By now I knew what I needed to do.

I walked her to the door.

"This is sort of like a date, isn't it? Walking me to the door, saying good night." She leaned forward and kissed me on the chin. She smiled. "I meant to kiss you on the cheek. Bad aim."

"I really want to thank you for—"

"I'm the one who should be grateful. I had a very nice time tonight."

She turned and opened the door. "Good night."

"Good night," I said.

I watched through the glass door as she climbed the steps, her white cane leading the way.

7

Ten minutes later I slid my car into the last space on Jenny's block. The blue Saab was still there. I wanted to see where he went after leaving here.

Thirty-five minutes later, his headlights came on and he drove away. I let him get to the corner and then I went after him, staying a half block away. With so little traffic at night, following him was not easy.

He took the Dan Ryan. If he was aware of me, he didn't let on. Fifteen minutes later, he took the exit he'd been looking for, and drove over to a motel that sat on the east edge of a grim little strip mall.

He pulled up to his room and went inside. The lights were already on. He stayed twenty minutes. When he came out, another man accompanied him. The man carried a small black leather doctor's bag.

I gave them ten minutes before I went up to the door and put some of my old Burglary knowledge to work. A cop picks up a lot of skills in the course of his career.

The room smelled of stale cigarette smoke and the moist walls of the shower stall. I used a flashlight to go through three different suitcases and a bureau full of drawers. The red eye of the answering machine blinked, signaling a message had been left. It must have come in between the time they left the room and I entered.

I went over and picked up the receiver and dialed the operator. "Yes?"

"There's a message for you, Mr. Banyon."

"Yes."

"From a man named Vic. He said things won't be ready till eleven. That's all he said."

"I appreciate that." According to my watch, it was 10:30. I had a terrible feeling that I knew what was going on here. I just hoped I wasn't too late.

8

Twenty-five minutes later, I pulled into the same space I'd used earlier that night.

The blue Saab was in place.

I saw Vic helping Jenny out the door.

She didn't know that anything was wrong. She loved Vic and trusted him and if he suggested that they go for a late-night stroll, or maybe plant themselves in the Chicago-style pizzeria around the block, why that would be just fine with her.

Vic led her to the sidewalk just as the two men were leaving the Saab. The second man had lost his black leather bag but he seemed to be carrying something with great delicacy in his black gloved fingers.

I had to move fast to reach them just as they reached Jenny and Vic. Cold mist whipped my face in the dark windy night.

When I reached them, I saw what the man held in his hand. A hypodermic needle. He was going to drug Jenny.

"Jenny!" I said.

They had been so intent on what they were doing that they didn't notice me until now.

"Who is this?" the man with the needle said. He spoke in a European accent, German maybe. Then, "Quickly, give me her arm!" he said to Vic.

Vic pushed Jenny forward.

I had my Smith and Wesson in hand and I said, "Stop right there. I mean everybody."

The man with the needle held Jenny's arm. He could easily jab her with the needle and accomplish his task. I put the gun barrel inside his ear.

"Drop the needle."

"You have no business here," said the other man, in an identical accent.

Both men looked at Vic.

"Who is this?" the man with the needle asked.

"Some clown; some ex-cop. He's nobody."

"Perhaps you haven't noticed, my friend," said the other man, "but he has a gun."

"He's no friend of yours, Jenny," Vic said. "You have to trust me. These men are going to help us."

"It's the rich man, isn't it? That's who they're working for."

"We just got off to a bad start, Jenny. With him, I mean. He wants to help us, put us in a nice new home and have some doctors study you—but privately, so nobody else will know."

Silently, she raised his hand, felt through the darkness for his face. When she found his cheek, she said, "They paid you to help them, didn't they, Vic?"

"I never claimed I was an angel, Jenny."

"No. But you did claim you loved me."

I was caught up enough in their words that I didn't hear the driver take two steps to my right and then bring down a black jack with considerable force on the back of my head.

I heard Jenny scream, and somebody clamp his hand over her mouth, and feet scuffle on the rainy sidewalk. I smelled autumn and cold and night; and then I just smelled darkness.

I didn't go all the way down, just to my knees, and I quickly started reviving myself, forcing myself to take deep breaths, forcing my eyes to focus. There was blood on the back of my neck but not much and not serious.

Car doors opened and slammed; the Saab, I knew. They'd left the motor running and when the doors opened I heard a Frank Sinatra song. Briefly.

Then they were gone.

9

I was starting the long and painful process of standing up when I heard somebody nearby moaning.

Vic was propped up against a tree. They must have hit him very hard in the seconds when I was unconscious. Blood streamed down his face from a wound on top of his skull.

I stood up and wobbled over to him.

"Where did they take her?"

"Can't you see I'm bleeding, man? Maybe I have a concussion or something."

I kicked him in the ribs, and a lot harder than was necessary, I suppose.

This time he didn't moan, he cried. "Shit, man, I just wanted a little money and the whole god damned thing went wrong." He looked up at me with puppy dog eyes. I wanted to kick him even harder. "They didn't even pay me, man. They didn't even keep their word."

I reached down and yanked him to his feet. It took me five good shoves to get him to my car. He started crying again when I opened the door and pushed him inside.

I got behind the wheel. "Where're we going?"

"You think I'm gonna tell you? They'll kill me, man."

"Yeah, well I'll kill you first so you'd better keep that in mind."

I gave him a hard slap directly across the mouth to make my point.

He started crying again. Only now did I realize he was all coked up. Everything was probably very crazy to him, fast and spooky. "You probably don't think I care about her, do you?"

"Vic, I want to know where they took her."

"I was gonna give her half the money. I really was. I mean, I really *like* Jenny. She's marriage material, man. It's just that right now I'm not ready—"

This slap cut his mouth so that blood trickled out. He put his head down and sobbed.

I didn't want to feel sorry for him but I couldn't help myself. "Vic, just tell me where they took her. This may come as a surprise, but I really don't enjoy slapping you."

He tilted his head in my direction and laughed. "You could've fooled me."

I laughed, too. "Vic, you're out of your league, don't you understand that?"

He shrugged, daubing at the blood in the corner of his mouth. "That's what Jenny always says. That I'm out of my league." He shook his head. "What a miserable bastard I am."

"Right now I wouldn't disagree."

He sighed. "They're taking her to their Lear jet. We'd better hurry."

I knew the airport he named.

10

On the way, he said, "Maybe she's an angel."

"What?"

I was driving fast but allowing for the wet streets.

"An angel. From heaven, you know. I mean, maybe that's what Jenny is. Maybe that's why she can heal people."

"Maybe," I said, having no idea what else to say, and being embarrassed by talking about angels.

The airport was toward Waukegan. The rain had started again and the dark rolling Midwestern night made the few lights on seem distant and frail, like desperate prayers no one hears.

"Or a Martian," Vic said. He had a handkerchief and he kept daubing his lips.

"A Martian?"

"Yeah, I don't mean from Mars necessarily but from outer space, anyway. I saw this 'Star Trek' deal once where they found this girl who could heal people. I think she was a Klingon."

"I thought Klingons were the bad guys," I said. "At least that's what my two daughters used to tell me."

"Yeah? Well, maybe there were some good Klingons they didn't know about."

What could I say?

* * *

In the rain and the gloom, the small airport had the look of a concentration camp about it. The cyclone fencing, the mercury vapor lights, the signs indicating that attack dogs were on the prowl—nice friendly place.

I pulled up to the gate and flashed the badge I knew I shouldn't be carrying.

"Some problem?" the uniformed guard said.

"Not sure yet."

"You'd better check in with the office before you do anything."

"Fine."

He nodded and waved me through.

I didn't check with the office. I drove straight out to the landing strip.

"There," he said.

The Lear jet was fired up and just getting ready to go. The passenger door was still open. Apparently not everybody was aboard.

I swung the car wide so that we came around from behind the graceful white plane.

I pulled around to the front, parking in front of the wheels, and got out. Vic was a few minutes behind me.

"I don't want to get in anything with guns 'n' shit, man. I mean, that's not my style."

"I just want to get Jenny away from them."

"They're bad dudes, man. They really are."

I saw the man with the doctor's bag walking across the tarmac to the Lear jet. We were hiding behind the car. I didn't think he saw us.

I moved fast, running toward him so that there was no chance for him to get away.

He tried, of course, turning around and running in a bulky way back toward the office.

I got him by the collar and spun him around. He smelled of expensive cologne.

"Let's go get Jenny."

"There are six people aboard that plane," he said in his European accent. "The odds aren't very good in your favor." He glared at Vic and shook his head. "And certainly this lounge lizard will be no help to you."

"Let's go," I said, putting the gun into his ribs.

The three of us walked to the plane.

We climbed the stairs and went inside where two men in black turtlenecks and black Levis held Mausers on us.

"I want Jenny," I said.

"Not going to happen, babe," said Mauser number one. "Hand over the doc and we'll let you go."

Vic said, "They got us, man. Just let them have the doc."

"Where's Jenny?" I said.

"Here," she said, and appeared in the doorway behind the Mauser twins.

"Are you all right?" I said.

"So far."

They hadn't drugged her, probably deciding they didn't need to. Her clothes were wrinkled and her hair was mussed. Her mouth was drawn tight. She was scared.

The doc made his move, then, and it was a bad move. He tried to jerk free of me and when he did, the Mauser twins, who had been trained for split-second action, opened fire, no doubt figuring they would hit me instead of him.

But they hit the doc, and several times, and right in the chest.

Vic dove left, I dove right.

After the first burst, the Mauser twins quit firing so they could assess the damage.

"Oh, God, babe," said one Mauser twin to the other, "we shot the doc."

"The old man is going to kill us," the second Mauser twin said.

By then, the shooting over, the pilot and co-pilot had drifted up to the front of the plane. So did the stake-out driver.

They all stood around and looked down at the doc. He was dying. He was already an ashen color, his breathing in tattered gasps.

"Man," said one Mauser twin to the other. "You really got our tit in the wringer."

"Me? Listen, babe, that was your bullet, not mine."

Jenny stepped forward, saying, "I would appreciate it if everybody would leave this plane."

"What's that supposed to mean?" said the first Mauser twin.

The stake-out driver said, "It means just what she said." With the doc down, he was apparently the man in charge. "I want everybody off this plane."

11

Took twenty minutes, during which all of us stood on the tarmac in the mist and fog. The Mauser Twins went and got coffee for everybody from a vending machine.

Vic, pacing around in little circles to stay warm, said, "She could make a lot of money."

"I thought you said she was an angel."

"Angels can't make money?"

I just shook my head.

The stake-out driver came over. He looked sad. "The doc, he's my cousin." He spoke with his cousin's accent.

"I see," I said.

"The girl," he said, "if she saves him, I'm going to let her go."

"That's the right thing to do."

"Do you understand any of this, the way she heals people?"

"Not a bit."

"I still say she's an angel," Vic said. "Or a Martian."

Just as he started to scowl at Vic, Jenny appeared in the passenger door. "You may come back now."

Five minutes later, we were feeding the doc some of the tepid vending machine coffee we'd had earlier.

I can't say he looked great—he was still very shaky and pale—but he was awake and talking.

He sat in one of the passenger seats, Jenny next to him.

"I wish you would let me learn about you," the doc said.

She sat there so pretty and sad and said, "I just accept it, Doctor. It's a gift and you don't question gifts."

I went over and said, "You look tired, Jenny, how about if I take you back?"

She stared up at me through her blindness and said, "Thank you. I really need to rest."

12

The three of us sat in the front seat. Vic had his arm around Jenny. I wanted my arm to be around Jenny. I wanted Vic to be on the other side of the world.

"We really owe you for this, man," Vic was saying. "I mean, you really came through for us."

"He's right," Jenny said gently, speaking above the hot blast of the car heater. "We really are very grateful."

"I'm gonna change, man. I really am. I'm taking this pledge right now. Vic McRea is a brand-new man. And I mean that, babe."

My God, I thought, is she really going to buy into this bilge?

When we reached their apartment house, I pulled over to the curb. I felt great sorrow and rage. I was losing her.

"Jenny, I—" I started to say.

But Vic already had the door open and was climbing out.

Jenny quickly took my hand and leaned over and kissed me on the cheek. "You're really a remarkable man, I hope you know that."

"C'mon, babe," Vic said from outside, "I'm freezing my tush."

And then they were gone.

13

I didn't sleep well. I had all the old bad dreams and then I had a new bad dream, that Jenny and Vic were on an airplane and flying away and I was standing on the tarmac feeling an icy emptiness and a kind of animal panic.

And then somebody was knocking at my door and I was looking at the sunlight in my bedroom window.

I got my robe on and answered the knock and there she was.

"I heard you were looking for a new partner," she said, "so I thought I'd apply for the job."

I kept my lips pressed tight so nothing of my morning mouth would escape and then I took her in my arms and held her right there in the doorway.

Inside, she said, "I told Vic goodbye this morning. He took it a lot better than I thought he would. Especially after I gave him my last $500."

"Good old Vic," I said.

"Yes, good ole Vic," she said. "Now how about some coffee?"

Different Kinds of Dead

Around eight that night, snow started drifting on the narrow Nebraska highway Ralph Sheridan was traveling. Already he could feel the rear end of the new Buick begin sliding around on the freezing surface of the asphalt, and could see that he would soon have to pull over and scrape the windshield. Snow was forming into gnarly bumps on the safety glass.

The small-town radio station he was listening to confirmed his worst suspicions: the weather bureau was predicting a genuine March blizzard, with eight to ten inches of snow and drifts up to several feet.

Sheridan sighed. A thirty-seven-year-old bachelor who made his living as a traveling computer sales-man—he worked especially hard at getting farmers to buy his wares—he spent most of the year on the road, putting up in the small shabby plains motels that from a distance always reminded him of doghouses. A

Ed Gorman

brother in Cleveland was all the family he had left, everybody else was dead. The only other people he stayed in touch with were the men he'd been in Vietnam with. There had been women, of course, but somehow it never worked out—this one wasn't his type, that one laughed too loudly, this one didn't have the same interests as he. And while his friends bloomed with mates and children, there was for Sheridan just the road, beers in bars with other salesmen, and nights alone in motel rooms with paper strips across the toilet seats.

The Buick pitched suddenly toward the ditch. An experienced driver and a calm man, Sheridan avoided the common mistake of slamming on the brakes. Instead, he took the steering wheel in both hands and guided the hurtling car along the edge of the ditch. While he had only a foot of earth keeping him from plunging into the gully on his right, he let the car find its own traction. Soon enough, the car was gently heading back onto the asphalt.

It was there, just when the headlights focused on the highway again, that he saw the woman.

At first, he tried sensibly enough to deny she was even there. His first impression was that she was an illusion, a mirage of some sort created by the whirling, whipping snow and the vast black night.

But no, there really was a beautiful, red-haired woman standing in the center of the highway. She wore a trench coat and black high-heeled shoes. She might have been one of the women on the covers of the private eye paperbacks he'd read back in the sixties.

This time, he did slam on the brakes; otherwise, he

would have run over her. He came to a skidding stop less than three feet from her.

His first reaction was gratitude. He dropped his head to the wheel and let out a long sigh. His whole body trembled. She could easily have been dead by now.

He was just raising his head when harsh wind and snow and cold blew into the car. The door on the passenger side had opened.

She got inside, saying nothing, closing the door when she was seated comfortably.

Sheridan looked over at her. Close up, she was even more beautiful. In the yellow glow of the dashboard, her features were so exquisite they had the refined loveliness of sculpture. Her tumbling, radiant hair only enhanced her face.

She turned to him finally and said, in a low, somewhat breathy voice, "You'd better not sit here in the middle of the highway long. It won't be safe."

He drove again. On either side of the highway he could make out little squares of light—the yellow windows of farmhouses lost in the furious gloom of the blizzard. The car heater warmed them nicely. The radio played some sexy jazz that somehow made the prairie and the snow and the weather alert go away.

All he could think of was those private eye novels he'd read as a teenager. This was what always happened to the Hammer himself, ending up with a woman like this.

"Do you mind?" she asked.

Before he had time to answer, she already had the long white cigarette between her full red lips and was lighting it. Then she tossed her head back and French inhaled. He hadn't seen anybody do that in years.

"Your car get ditched somewhere" he asked finally, realizing that these were his first words to her.

"Yes," she said, "somewhere."

"So you were walking to the nearest town?"

"Something like that."

"You were walking in the wrong direction." He paused. "And you're traveling alone?"

She glanced over at him again with her dark, lovely gaze. "Yes. Alone." Her voice was as smoky as her cigarette.

He drove some more, careful to keep both hands on the wheel, slowing down whenever the rear of the car started to slide.

He wasn't paying much attention to the music at this point—they were going up a particularly sleek and dangerous hill—but then the announcer's voice came on and said, "Looks like the police have really got their hands full tonight. Not only with the blizzard, but now with a murder. Local banker John T. Sloane was found murdered in his downtown apartment twenty minutes ago. Police report an eyewitness say he heard two gunshots and then saw a beautiful woman leaving Sloane's apartment. The eyewitness reportedly said that the woman strongly resembled Sloane's wife, Carlotta. But police note that that's impossible, given the fact that Carlotta died mysteriously last year in a boating accident. The eyewitness insists that the resemblance between the redheaded woman leaving Sloane's apartment tonight and the late Mrs. Sloane is uncanny. Now back to our musical program for the evening."

A bosso nova came on.

Beautiful. Redheaded. Stranded alone. Looking furtive. He started glancing at her, and she said, "I'll spare you the trouble. It's me. Carlotta Sloane."

"You? But the announcer said—"

She turned to him and smiled. "That I'm dead? Well, so I am."

Not until then did Sheridan realize how far out in the boonies he was. Or how lacerating the storm had become. Or how helpless he felt inside a car with a woman who claimed to be dead.

"Why don't you just relax?"

"Please don't patronize me, Mr. Sheridan."

"I'm not patroniz—Say, how did you know my name?"

"I know a lot of things."

"But I didn't tell you my name and there's no way you could read my registration from there and—"

She French inhaled—then exhaled—and said, "As I said, Mr. Sheridan, I know a lot of things." She shook her head. "I don't know how I got like this."

"Like what?"

"Dead."

"Oh."

"You still don't believe me, do you?"

He sighed. "We've got about eight miles to go. Then we'll be in Porterville. I'll let you out at the Greyhound depot there. Then you can go about your business and I can go about mine."

She touched his temple with long, lovely fingers. "That's why you're such a lonely man, Mr. Sheridan. You never take any chances. You never let yourself get involved with anybody."

He smiled thinly, "Especially with dead people."

"Maybe you're the one who's dead, Mr. Sheridan. Night after night alone in cheap little hotel rooms, listening to the country western music through the wall, and occasionally hearing people make love. No woman. No children. No real friends. It's not a very good life, is it, Mr. Sheridan?"

He said nothing. Drove.

"We're both dead, Mr. Sheridan. You know that?"

He still said nothing. Drove.

After a time, she said, "Do you want to know how tonight happened, Mr. Sheridan?"

"No."

"I made you mad, didn't I, Mr. Sheridan, when I reminded you of how lonely you are?"

"I don't see where it's any of your business."

Now it was her turn to be quiet. She stared out at the lashing snow. Then she said, "The last thing I could remember before tonight was John T. holding me under water till I drowned off the side of our boat. By the way, that's what all his friends called him. John T." She lit one cigarette off another. "Then earlier tonight I felt myself rise through darkness and suddenly I realized was taking form. I was rising from the grave and taking form. And there was just one place I wanted to go. The apartment he kept in town for his so-called business meetings. So I went there tonight and killed him."

"You won't die."

"I beg your pardon?"

"They won't execute you for doing it. You just tell them the same story you told me, and you'll get off with second degree. Maybe even not guilty by reason of insanity."

She laughed. "Maybe if you weren't so busy watching the road, you'd notice what's happening to me, Mr. Sheridan."

She was disappearing. Right there in his car. Where

her left arm had been was now just a smoldering red-tipped cigarette that seemed to be held up on invisible wires. A part of her face was starting to disappear, too.

"About a quarter mile down the highway, let me out if you would."

He laughed. "What's there? A graveyard?"

"As a matter of fact, yes."

By now her legs had started disappearing.

"You don't seem to believe it, Mr. Sheridan, but I'm actually trying to help you. Trying to tell you to go out and live while you're still alive. I wasted my life on my husband, sitting around at home while he ran around with other women, hoping against hope that someday he'd be faithful and we'd have a good life together. It never happened, Mr. Sheridan. I wasted my whole life."

"Sounds like you paid him back tonight. Two gunshots, the radio said."

Her remaining hand raised the cigarette to what was left of her mouth. She inhaled deeply. When she exhaled the smoke was a lovely gray color. "I was hoping there would be some satisfaction in it. There isn't. I'm as lonely as I ever was."

He wondered if that was a small, dry sob he heard in her voice.

"Right here," she said.

He had been cautiously braking the last minute and a half. He brought the car comfortably over to the side of the road. He put on his emergency flashers in case anybody was behind him.

Up on the hill to his right, he saw it. A graveyard. The tombstones looked like small children huddled against the whipping snow.

"After I killed him, I just started walking," she said. "Walking. Not even knowing where I was going. Then you came along." She stabbed the cigarette out in the ashtray. "Do something about your life, Mr. Sheridan. Don't waste it the way I have."

She got out of the car and leaned back in. "Goodbye, Mr. Sheridan."

He sat there, watching her disappear deep into the gully, then reappear on the other side and start walking up the slope of the hill.

By the time she was halfway there, she had nearly vanished altogether.

Then, moments later, she was gone utterly.

At the police station, he knew better than to tell the cops about the ghost business. He simply told them he'd seen a woman fitting the same description out on the highway about twenty minutes ago.

Grateful for his stopping in, four cops piled into two different cars and they set out under blood red flashers into the furious white night.

Mr. Sheridan found a motel—his usual one in this particular burg—and took his usual room. He stripped, as always, to his boxer shorts and T-shirt and got snug in bed beneath the covers and watched a rerun of an old sitcom.

He should have been laughing—at least all the people on the laugh track seemed to be having a good time—but instead he did something he rarely did. He began crying. Oh, not big wailing tears, but hard tiny silver ones. Then he shut off both TV and the lights and lay in the solitary darkness thinking of what she'd said to him.

No woman. No children. No love.

Only much later, when the wind near dawn died

and the snow near light subsided, only then did Sheridan sleep, his tears dried out but feeling colder than he ever had.

Lonely cold. Dead cold.

Of the Fog

David Huggins was pushing radio buttons to find a
decent song when he looked up and saw, there on the
edge of the interstate, there in the fog and light drizzle, there against a backdrop of deep green Iowa
countryside, one of the most beautiful young women
his thirty-four-year-old eyes had ever seen.

She was maybe a hundred yards away. She wore a
man's red windbreaker, jeans, and hiking boots. Her
short blond hair made her classically beautiful face
seem even younger. Her blue eyes were possessed of
a radiance that was almost alarming, even at this distance.

Only the mouth troubled him, and he instantly
knew why. It was Lavonne's mouth, full and insolent.
He'd gone with Lavonne for the first three years of
college. It took him all the way to his senior year to
learn just how unfaithful she was. He'd walked in on
her one day. She was in bed with one of his fraternity

brothers. Huggins had literally gotten sick, gone in the john, and thrown up. She'd treated him scornfully. It wasn't any big deal, she'd said. Being somebody's girlfriend wasn't like being his wife. All the time she'd talked, he just kept looking at her mouth. How much pleasure those erotic lips had given him over the past three years. But now they smirked at him.

This girl had the same mouth.

She held up her lone suitcase for him to see. GRIN-NELL, read a large Magic Marker sign on the front side of the suitcase. Huggins was on his way to Des Moines. He made the trip three times a month. He was a hospital supply salesman and covered this whole section of Iowa.

His right foot hovered three inches above the brake. A drizzle like this, a cold morning like this, he should be a gentleman and stop to pick her up. Though he didn't pick up hitchhikers as a rule, she didn't seem dangerous. A beautiful girl like her, she had more to fear than he did.

His black oxford descended another inch.

If he was going to stop, he'd better stop now.

This close, she was even better-looking. She leaned her face toward the car. She broke into a nice, girlish midwestern grin, all freckles and innocence.

His black oxford eased down the final inch, until it came in contact with the brake.

All he had to do was step down a little harder now, and the new Buick, for which the company paid half, would come to an easy stop.

She was still smiling at him. Anticipation gleamed in her startling blue eyes. Just another minute or so and she'd be out of this fog and drizzle.

All he had to do was stop.

She smiled, then, the young woman. Smiled, her full lips suddenly insolent, as if she had just appraised him and found him wanting somehow. All he could see was Lavonne smiling, that practiced, empty, deceitful smile.

He slammed his right foot on the gas pedal and started to fishtail away.

The young woman went into combat mode. She leaned even farther toward Huggins' car and then flipped him the finger. She called him several names, each of which challenged his right to call himself a man.

He watched her in his rearview. She kept her middle finger up straight and proud for him to see.

Her name was Marcia Quinn, and she was a Drake University junior from Chicago, and sixty miles ago she'd been pushed out of the car when she'd finally answered her boyfriend's question about whether she'd been faithful while he'd been studying in Rome this summer.

"You couldn't be goddamned faithful for two goddamned months?"

"It didn't mean anything, Todd. I mean, it was only a couple of nights. And I didn't fall in love with him or anything. I guess I was just bored or something."

Slam went the brakes. Open went the door.

Todd Bellamy, who was also a Drake junior, then pitched her suitcase out of the car and took off down the interstate, traveling fast and angry.

This was about an hour ago, just when the drizzle started.

If it hadn't been for the rain, she might have enjoyed hitchhiking. All her life she'd been told how dangerous this was. Especially now that the Highway Killer had taken the lives of four young women. Which just made the experience all the more exciting. Who knew what lay ahead—maybe later on, she'd take candy from a stranger. Or maybe she'd be picked up by the man who'd killed three young women on this interstate over the past fourteen months. He used a heavily serrated blade to kill his victims. Even after all this time, the police had no real clues. None they were admitting to, anyway.

Her mood started to be good again until the guy in the Buick came along.

If there was one thing Marcia Quinn wasn't used to it was being treated shabbily by men.

Men, most men, treated her with almost embarrassing deference. They wanted to go to bed with her. A young woman with her looks . . . men, most men, were trophy hunters. And she was indeed a trophy. Years from now, the men she'd shared a bed with would look back and recall how beautiful she was, and her beauty, in memory, would be even more astonishing.

Or so she'd been told by a professor she'd slept with last spring term. Todd'd really be pissed if he found out about *him*.

All of which was why she was so angry about the guy in the Buick.

Where the hell did he get off pretending that he was going to give her a ride . . . a girl so many men would have been happy to have in their cars . . . and then speeding off like she was some kind of leper or something?

She continued to hitchhike.

The fog was what made it so difficult.

Drivers couldn't see her until they were right upon her . . . and then it was unsafe to stop. A car in the fog behind them might slam right into their rear end. Happened all the time in conditions like these.

The longer she walked, the sorrier she felt for Todd. She shouldn't have slept with that guy this summer. All the temptations Todd had likely had in Rome . . . and he'd passed them all up because he loved her. The only reason she slept around was so she could say she'd cheated first. Her first few boyfriends had cheated on her . . . and she never wanted to go through that humiliation again. It became a point of honor to sleep around before your lover did. But Todd wasn't into sick love games like that. Todd was a decent guy. And she felt terrible now that she'd betrayed him. She was going to apologize to him as soon as she got a chance.

Todd was a keeper.

She didn't want to end up like her gorgeous older sister . . . three failed marriages by age thirty-two . . . her good looks a curse rather than a blessing.

She really did need to work things out with Todd.

Drizzle became rain now . . . hard, cold winter rain in late August . . . rain that hissed, rain that stung, rain that soaked.

She started thinking about the Buick again, and how much she hated the driver. Somehow he became symbolic of all her troubles.

She trudged on through the gray, foggy downpour.

Huggins wished he wasn't hungry. Though he worked out twice a week at a gym, he had put on twenty pounds over the past few years, pounds that resolutely refused to come off. For the first time in his life Huggins, who had been one of the skinniest kids in his high-school graduating class, began to think of himself as "overweight."

The café was up on a hill just east of where the off-ramp ended. He'd stopped there a few times before. The place was basically a greasy spoon where the people of the nearby small town came for breakfast and lunch. Truckers tended to use the truck stop thirty miles due west of there.

The café covered the ground floor of a two-story concrete block building that had the look and feel of the kind of construction done right after World War II, fast and cheap. This year, the place was painted pea green. There were three pickups and a few cars in the parking lot.

The moment Huggins opened the café's door, he heard a country and western singer whine plaintively, "You got custody of the kids, but who gets custody of my heart?"

The smells of cooking grease, cigarette smoke, and coffee mugged his olfactory nerves.

He regretted coming in here, but he was too self-conscious a person to turn around and walk out.

Three men in green John Deere caps sat at the counter, watching him. They didn't look impressed. Huggins wasn't an impressive guy. He'd always done moderately well with women but not with men. Men tended to ignore him. He wasn't tough or clever or even particularly interesting. He didn't even care much for sports. Men seemed to sense all these lackings instantly, and they avoided him.

The restaurant was laid out simply. The counter and the kitchen took up the west wall. Booths took up the east wall. The red vinyl was patched in many places with tan masking tape. The walls were hung with framed photographs of country and western singers. The photographs were signed.

Huggins was still getting used to the harsh and sour smells of the place.

He went to the counter and sat down on the last available stool. He'd just have a cup of coffee and get out of this place.

"You're wearin' that bra again, aren't you, Ellie?" said one of the men at the counter. The other men at the counter all smiled and laughed like schoolboys, filling their eyes with the considerable sight of Ellie.

Ellie was a big bottle-blond woman—big but not fat, just big—dressed in a pink polyester waitress's outfit. The pink allowed the black push-up bra beneath the polyester to be on full display. Huggins studied her a moment. She had a panther tattoo on her left forearm and she wore a teeny-tiny nose ring. The tattoo might be one of those press-on dealies. She couldn't be much more than twenty or so. Huggins filled her bio in with ruthless prejudice—high-school dropout, denizen of a trailer park. Cruel but probably true.

"I bought it with a gift certificate Charlene gave me," she said. Immediately Huggins saw the faces of the men change into hard, harsh masks.

Whoever Charlene was, she meant a lot not only to Ellie but also to these three men.

"That sonofabitch," Roy said. He had a white scar running down his right cheek.

"I just hope I'm the one to catch him," said the second man. He had a badly broken nose.

"I just hope you're the one who catches him, too, Phil," Ellie said, her eyes and voice overbrimming with sudden tears. "What he did to Charlene and all."

Roy put out a quick, strong hand and touched Ellie's arm. "They'll find him. Don't worry about that, Ellie."

"She was like my own sister," Ellie said, tears still strong in her eyes and voice. "My own sister."

The third man, the one closest to Huggins, leaned over and said, "Girl who used to work here, Charlene Tuttle, she was Ellie's best friend. That Highway Killer, they call him."

Ellie sniffled and said, "Sorry, mister, I forgot to wait on you."

"That's fine," Huggins said. "No hurry."

"You want coffee?"

Huggins nodded. And added, "You have any breakfast rolls left?"

"I think so."

"Good. I'll take one."

He hadn't been going to eat here, but now that he was actually sitting at the counter he felt a bit drowsy, tired. He liked the warmth of this place, and the man next to him seemed friendly enough. Wouldn't hurt to stay out of the downpour, either. He hadn't been in any major car accidents in his life. He didn't want to start now.

Ellie popped Huggins's breakfast roll in the microwave, then melted two pats of butter on top of it. Then she brought it over to him.

Huggins thanked her and started in on the roll. It was delicious.

Marcia Quinn's ride took her to the same café where Huggins's blue Buick sat in the parking lot.

The young farmer behind the wheel of the Chevrolet pickup pulled up to the edge of the lot and stopped.

"My farm's about ten miles from here," he said. "I've got to go home and see how the calving's going. Vet's been out there since early this morning." He nodded to the café. "There may be somebody inside there going to Des Moines. I'll probably be back myself. I usually pick up a sack of burgers here and bring them home for the wife and me."

Marcia thanked him for the ride, jumped down from the cab, and then yanked her suitcase to the ground.

The young farmer touched his hand to the bill of his Cubs cap in a kind of salute and then took off.

The parking lot was eerie with rolling fog and a slimy, cold mist. Marcia felt disoriented and vaguely frightened.

Maybe this'd be like a horror movie. She'd walk through the fog and get into the café, only to find it inhabited by ghouls and monsters. She envisioned Dracula and Frankenstein and the Wolf Man all sitting at the counter—Todd loved the Universal horror films from the forties, and by now she loved them, too—watching for her. Waiting for her.

Then she saw the blue Buick and got pissed all over again. She recalled the driver's angry face, the slight sneer of his lips as he floored his car and sped away from her.

Been intimidated by her looks. A lot of guys were like that. So they had to hurt her in some way. Some petty little sting just to prove to her—and to themselves—that they weren't under her lovely sway.

She thought about writing some obscenity on the

trunk of his car in lipstick. Then she thought about giving him a flat tire.

But they both sounded pretty juvenile. And, for that matter, not really much in the way of retaliation.

She started to walk toward the door of the café. Even lost in the fog, she could faintly hear the whine of the country and western music and smell the hot, tart scent of steaming lard.

Then she stopped and smiled.

And glanced back over her shoulder.

There in the fog she could see the outlines of the blue Buick.

Oh, he was going to pay, the bastard who'd sneered at her and passed her by.

He was going to pay real good.

Huggins had just returned from the rest room, had just seated himself at the counter again, when the front door of the café slammed open and the woman staggered inside.

Her jacket had been torn, her face was scuffed with dirt, her hair was a wild, soaked mess.

She made sounds that were half sobs, half moans.

"Oh, my Lord," Ellie said.

She hurried over to the young woman and caught her just as the woman was about to pitch face-first to the floor.

Everything in the little café came to a halt. The two other waitresses, who had been serving people in the booths, stopped what they were doing. The cook came out from the kitchen, wiping his hands on a grease-spattered white apron. A man who'd been about to deposit money for a phone call suddenly hung up the receiver.

Ellie half carried the young woman over to the only empty booth.

"Get me a clean towel and some hot water," she said to one of the other waitresses.

The woman hurried to the kitchen.

Ellie propped the young woman up against the wall, then set her legs up on the seat.

By now the three men at the counter had drifted over to the booth to inspect the young woman more carefully.

"What happened, hon?" Ellie said, sounding maternal, even though she was a couple of years younger than the woman she was caring for.

"He . . . he tried to rape me," the young woman said in a monotone. "And then he tried to kill me with his knife. But I . . . I jumped out of the car."

She looked up at Ellie with sorrowful eyes. "I don't remember much about . . . running. I guess I just . . . just ended up here."

Then she started crying.

She made almost no sound at all. Her shoulders trembled and her head shook back and forth but you could barely hear her. It was very moving.

The only thing that bothered Huggins was . . . how had all this happened to her in the time since he'd passed her on the highway?

This was definitely the same young woman who'd flipped him the bird. Not more than twenty, twenty-five minutes could have passed since that time. So how could all this have happened to her?

But maybe he was rationalizing, he realized.

Maybe by challenging the time frame of her story he was simply trying to put the blame on her instead of where it properly belonged.

On him.

Given the condition of her clothes and face, something had clearly happened to her.

And it *wouldn't* have happened to her if he'd picked her up and given her a ride.

He felt guilt and shame, sitting there so isolated at the counter, the other men gathered helpfully around the booth where the young woman was propped up.

He'd probably best get out of here. She was probably going to recognize him and probably going to tell everybody here what he'd done to her.

Passing up a woman in a downpour wasn't exactly a gentlemanly thing to do. The people in this little café, no matter how long he explained, were never going to understand about Lavonne and how she'd betrayed him back in college and how *this* young woman reminded him of Lavonne, which was why he'd passed her by. . . .

"What's your name, sweetheart?" Ellie said.

"M-Marcia Q-Quinn," she said, fighting more tears.

"Where you from, hon?"

"C-Chicago. I g-go to D-Drake."

No, they'd never understand why he hadn't given her a ride. . . .

Better to make his quiet way up to the cash register and leave money for his bill (plus enough for a nice tip) and get back in his Buick and finish the drive to Des Moines.

He didn't want these people to dislike him—all his life he'd desperately wanted people to like him—which they'd certainly not do if the woman recognized him.

He took out his wallet.

The bill was $1.87, bkfst rll and cff as Ellie's scribbling read on the green ticket.

He took three ones from his wallet, nice green crisp ones, and then stood up.

Nobody was even looking in his direction. They were all too concerned about the woman.

They were asking questions about when it happened, where it happened, what her assailant looked like.

Huggins was certain now that she'd get around to telling them about him. About the man who'd refused to give her a ride. About the man who had thus inadvertently caused her to be in this terrible situation.

He was just a few feet from the cash register when he heard the young woman say, "My God."

"What's wrong, hon?" Ellie said.

"That's him. Over there. By the cash register."

Now *everybody* was looking at him.

"Him? That guy?" Roy said, nodding to Huggins.

"H-He's the one, all right!" Marcia Quinn said.

"Hey!" Roy shouted. "You just freeze right where you are, mister."

"Damned right," said Phil-of-the-broken-nose.

They started walking toward him, moving slowly and carefully, as if he were a wild and dangerous animal who might attack them at any moment.

He tried to speak. But his throat was so dry he couldn't.

"Spread 'em, mister," Roy said.

Before Huggins could understand what was about to happen, Roy grabbed him and turned him around and hurled him so hard against the cash register that it wobbled the entire stand.

"You search him, Phil," Roy said. "I'll make sure the sumbitch don't try anything."

"Maybe introduce myself to him first," Phil said, "before I go feelin' him up 'n' all."

Huggins didn't know what he was talking about. Not until Phil drove a hard fist deep into Huggins' kidney was Phil's message clear.

Huggins felt all the strength go out of his knees . . . and indescribable pain radiate from his kidney all the way up under his armpit.

Now he knew how Phil had gotten his nose broken so many times. This was a guy who loved to fight. And who was good at it, too. He used his fists with fury and precision.

The punches sapped Huggins of all strength. He could do little more than cling to the checkout counter. He was afraid he was going to fall down.

As Phil started to pat him down—wasn't that what the cops always called it on TV cop shows?—a sense of unreality overcame Huggins.

A small, hick café in the middle of a vast ocean of rolling fog . . . perhaps this was a nightmare.

Had to be.

He hadn't done anything to the woman . . . and yet they were so eager to believe her.

Another punch slammed into his kidney.

This time he heard himself moan. Felt his knees start to weaken.

No, this was real. The fog . . . the café. So isolated and *unreal* . . . yet real.

Phil patted him down.

When he came to Huggins' crotch, he rapped him with his knuckles, sending shock and pain through Huggins' entire lower body.

"Nothin'," Phil said as he reached Huggins' ankle.

"Throw me his wallet," Roy said.

"Who died and made you fucking pope, huh, Roy?"

"Just throw me his goddamned wallet."

Huggins felt his wallet leave its familiar, warm place riding next to his right buttock.

"You're David Huggins?" Roy said as he went through the wallet.

"Yes."

"I can't hear you, asshole."

"Give it to him, Roy," Ellie said. "Give it to him real good."

"She's lying," Huggins said. "I didn't even let her in my car. I saw her but I passed her by."

"A real gentleman," Roy said.

"She never even got in my car, do you understand?"

"I asked you a question, asshole. Your name is David Huggins?"

"Call the law if you think I'm guilty. Get one of your deputies over here."

"We'll worry about the law, jerk-off," Roy said. "For now, I want you to answer my questions. Or Phil'll start in on your kidney again, you understand?"

"Do the bastard like he done them," Ellie said.

"You're David Huggins?"

"Yes."

"And you live at 393 Maple Lane in Cedar Rapids?"

"Yes."

Pause. "There're a couple of photographs in here. A good-looking woman and a little boy."

"My wife and son."

"What's your wife's name?"

"Cindy."

"How old is she?"

"Twenty-eight."

"What's your boy's name?"

"Brian."

"How old's he?"

"Four."

"Where's Cindy work?"

"I want you to call the law," Huggins said. "Right now. You don't have any right to do this."

Ellie snorted. "You just happen to be talking to an auxiliary policeman, asshole. And you're too dumb to even know it."

"Ask the woman there."

"Ask her what?" Roy said.

"Ask her if she's telling the truth."

"You seen her same as I did. All busted up that way," Roy said. "She sure as hell *is* telling the truth."

"Ask her."

"You're lyin', mister," Ellie said.

"Go on. Ask her."

"Hit the bastard, Phil."

Phil hit the bastard.

Apparently Phil had tired of hitting the bastard in the kidney. This time he hit the bastard in the side of the head.

Darkness was instant. Darkness and more pain.

Huggins felt his knees start to give way. His thighs were trembling the way they did when he and Cindy made love standing up. But now the trembling was not from pleasure.

"This could be fake ID," Roy said.

"With my picture on it?"

94

"Hell, yes. You can buy any kind of fake ID you want."

"Why would I have fake ID?"

"So nobody could trace you to where you really live."

"Why the hell would I do that?"

"So people wouldn't find out you're the one been killin' all those poor girls out on the highway."

"I'm really David Huggins."

"What's your phone number?" Roy said.

"In Cedar Rapids?"

"Yes."

"I really want you to call the law," Huggins said. His voice sounded funny to him now. Part of Phil's punch had landed on Huggins' ear. There was a kind of tinny, distant quality to his voice now.

"You want Phil to hit you again?" Roy said.

"No."

"Then tell me your phone number."

Huggins told him his phone number.

"I'm going to call that number right now. She be home?"

"She should be. Tell her to call the law."

Roy laughed. "Right. That's just what I'll do. I'll tell her to call the law."

Then Roy and his voice started to move. Huggins could hear the voice toward the back of the café now.

"If you're making up this number, I'm going to let Phil have himself a field day, mister."

"Kick his ass, Roy," Ellie said. "I just keep thinkin' about what he did to Charlene."

She had started to cry again.

"Ma'am, I'm not the man you're looking for," Huggins said. "I'm sorry what happened to your friend. But I didn't do it. I really didn't. Ask that woman if she's telling the truth. She was just pissed that I didn't give her a ride."

"She isn't makin' anythin' up," Ellie said. "If anybody's makin' anythin' up, it's you."

"Quiet now," Roy said.

Huggins angled his head toward the back of the café where Roy stood next to the pay phone.

The three kitchen men stood near the kitchen door, smoking cigarettes and watching everything without a word.

The coins were loud as they dropped down the pay phone.

Roy dialed, then glanced at Huggins. "You better not be makin' this up."

Huggins said nothing. What was there to say?

For the first time, he let his eyes drift to the front door. It was no more than ten, twelve feet away.

There was at least a chance of reaching the door, then running out into the fog. Weather like this, they'd have a hell of a time finding him. They'd probably have hunting dogs around to help them look . . . but by that time he'd have made his own contact with the law and told them what was going on . . . how the blonde had lied about him . . . about how Roy and Phil had become judge and jury and jailer.

Roy said, "Mrs. Huggins? Mrs. David Huggins?"

Silence.

"Is David home, ma'am?"

Silence.

"I see. On his way to Des Moines, then."

Silence.

"No, no, thank you, ma'am. No message. I'll just try him a little later tonight."

He didn't even think about it. He just did it.

One moment he was still spread-eagled in front of the cash register.

The next he was running toward the back, toward the pay phone, shouting, "I'm at the Bluebird Café, Cindy! Call the cops! Call the cops!"

But he wasn't fast enough.

He'd been able to blurt out only one or two words . . . when Roy hung up.

Huggins was sure that Cindy hadn't heard him at all.

He sensed—then heard—Phil coming up behind him.

Though he'd never been much of a fighter, Huggins spun around and went into a crouch just as Phil delivered a roundhouse right hand.

The punch missed by several inches.

Instinctively, Huggins took the moment and brought his knee straight up between Phil's legs.

Phil's scream had an alien, animal-like quality to it as he crumpled to the floor, grasping his crotch.

Huggins ran straight to the booth where Marcia Quinn sat. He pushed Ellie aside so he could get to Marcia better.

Marcia started to work herself backward in the booth, as if she might try to scale the wall. Her eyes showed her fear.

"Stop him! Stop him!" she screamed.

"Tell them the truth," Huggins said. "Tell them that I didn't even stop to pick you up."

But Marcia, never one to miss a dramatic moment, picked up her butter knife and waved it in front of Huggins as he leaned in to shout in her face.

"Stay back!" she said.

By now Ellie had regained her flat-footed strength and grabbed Huggins around the neck, getting him in a very effective choke hold.

She was big enough and strong enough to kill him. And nobody seemed inclined to stop her.

He didn't have any choice. She was a woman, true, but she was also one of his chief persecutors. There was only one way to stop her.

He knifed an elbow deep into her ribs and the side of her stomach.

Her grip didn't lessen at all.

He felt himself gasping for air, his entire body beginning to writhe as oxygen was being cut off.

He slammed his elbow into her ribs a second time, much harder.

He could instantly feel her arms loosen a bit as her brain registered the shock of his elbow.

She cursed him.

And redoubled her effort.

"Tole you that was one gal who could take care of herself," Phil said.

Roy laughed. "Guess you were right."

For them, this was professional wrestling, and the best sort of all—a big farm woman kicking the hell out of a small city fella.

This time, he gave her the double whammy: His elbow again found her ribs and stomach. And this time the heel of his shoe also found the center of her lower leg.

She cried out when the kick came.

Her grip loosened enough that he was able to wrench himself away from her and grab Marcia Quinn by the front of her red windbreaker.

"Tell them the truth!" he shouted. "The joke's over! You've paid me back enough!"

But Marcia just sat there staring at him. She said, very quietly, "You were going to rape me. You told me you were."

He sensed them coming up behind him again, Roy and Phil, and this time he decided *he'd* be the aggressor.

He turned around and smashed Phil in the face. Phil wasn't the one who cried out. Huggins was. From years of watching TV, he'd gotten the impression that slugging somebody else was pretty easy. All you did was take a swing and let go. What nobody had told him about was how your knuckles hurt—hell, your whole hand—when it came in contact with the solid bone of jaw.

Phil smiled. "You candy-ass."

Phil was a lot more used to be being hit than Huggins was to hitting.

Roy came for him now, too. "Just relax, Huggins. You're starting to get hysterical."

"I want you to call the law right now."

Roy said, "That's probably a good idea."

Phil looked sharply at his partner, as if Roy had just suggested something exceedingly stupid.

"We can take care of him," Phil said.

"Go call Rick Shay," Roy said.

Phil didn't look happy. But he walked to the back and made the call.

"I want her to give a sworn statement," Huggins said, "that I tried to hurt her in any way."

"Hard to prove," Roy said, sounding skeptical. "Your word against hers. And, friend, I'd take her word any day."

"If she was really in my car," Huggins said, "they'll be able to find footprints from her hiking boots and pieces of her hair and strands from her red jacket."

As he finished talking, he glanced at Marcia Quinn. "And she'll have to lie to an officer of the law. Then she'll be in a lot of trouble."

She just stared at him. Said nothing.

"I'd also advise you and your geek friend back there to keep your hands off me." He nodded to Ellie. "Same with you. You don't have any legal right to hurt me in any way. When your lawman gets here, you're all going to be in trouble."

"The fact is," Ellie said, "you're still the Highway Killer. Still the guy who stabbed Charlene and them other girls."

"No, I'm not," Huggins said. "I'm a salesman driving to Des Moines. I probably wasn't much of a gentleman to turn Marcia down for a ride. But that's all I'm guilty of."

One of the kitchen men said, "Maybe he's tellin' the truth, Roy."

"My ass he's tellin' the truth," Phil said. "And we got this young college gal here to prove it."

Pain still radiated up from Huggins' punch-damaged kidney. The sense of unreality was back again, too. This still had the dimensions and feel of a nightmare. Or of a terrible and cosmic practical joke.

The dark gods were working overtime today.

"You just go over there and sit down," Roy said, pointing to the counter. "And keep your mouth shut."

There was no point in arguing. Huggins did what he was told. The law would be here soon and this would all be over. He'd be on his way to Des Moines again.

He went over and sat down.

"Do you think I could use your bathroom?" Marcia Quinn said, really playing up her helpless-female routine.

"Sure, hon," Ellie said. "You think you can walk back there by yourself?"

"I think so," Marcia said.

Academy Award performance, Huggins thought bitterly.

The performance got even better when she stood up and walked to the rest room in the back.

She walked as if she'd been shot six or seven times. Or maybe eight.

"You don't think she's faking it at least a little?" Huggins said.

"Shut up," Phil said.

"Damn right shut up," Ellie said. "Or I'll get you in that choke hold again, you sonofabitch."

Marcia Quinn wasn't about to let down her fans.

When she reached the jukebox, she suddenly lurched to the right, clinging to the glass of the big music machine.

"Aw, hon," Ellie said, hurrying to the back to help her new friend.

"You sumbitch," Phil said. "Look what you done to that gal."

"Same thing he done to Charlene," Ellie said, " 'cept he didn't stab here."

"He would've," Phil said, "if she hadn't jumped out of his car."

Ellie got Marcia into the rest room. The poor dear

was probably going to need surgery, the way she was carrying on.

"I thought you called the police," Huggins said to Phil.

"You just stand there and shut up."

Huggins looked toward the small man who worked in the kitchen, the one who'd suggested that maybe Marcia Quinn wasn't telling the truth. He appeared to be Mexican. There were a lot of illegals in this part of the state because of the coming harvest.

"She's lying," Huggins said, knowing he sounded desperate. "She really is."

The kitchen man looked away. He obviously didn't want to be associated with Huggins. He probably regretted speaking up in the first place. Everybody in the café seemed absolutely certain that Marcia Quinn was telling the truth. Only a fool wanted to stand up against everybody that way.

"She really is lying," Huggins said.

"You get back in the kitchen, Juan."

"Yes, Miss Ellie."

This time Huggins heard the accent in the man's voice. A Mexican in this part of the country, he'd probably sympathized with Huggins' situation. Mexicans still didn't have many liberties out here. And right now, Huggins didn't either.

Juan disappeared into the kitchen.

Inside the rest room, the toilet flushed explosively. Then the sound of water pipes engaging could be heard.

Roy and Phil still stared hard at Huggins.

Where the hell was the local law? What was keeping them so long? They were Huggins' last hope. A good law officer would have a lot of questions for Marcia Quinn.

The rest room door opened. Marcia Quinn reappeared, and Ellie rushed to help her. Marcia was forgetting her acting continuity. This time she was limping on her left foot. She hadn't been limping before. Not that anybody seemed to notice. They were too busy glowering at Huggins.

Ellie and Quinn were just reseating themselves in the booth when Huggins heard the sound of a car in the parking lot.

The fog was so heavy, he couldn't see anything. Just heard a car door opening and chunking shut. New car. Had to be, the way the door closed so nice and tight.

Now everybody was looking at the front door.

A man in a khaki uniform filled it. Literally. He had to run six-three, six-four and weigh two-fifty.

He opened the door and came inside. He walked that kind of slant-walk, body at a slight angle, that most people associated with John Wayne. The rest of him suggested the Old West, too, the burning blue eyes beneath the heavy shelf of brow; the taut, hard line of mouth; and the large, wide jaw.

From his waist hung a Sam Browne belt packed tight with a large, holstered Magnum; a night stick that looked vicious enough to bring a deadly animal to heel; a small walkie-talkie; and enough fine, new shiny bullets to start a war.

He walked over to Roy and Phil and said, "I sure hope this was important, boys. You dragged me out of a town council meeting."

"Oh, it's important, all right, Rick," Phil said. Then nodded to Huggins.

Huggins said, "I want to bring charges against these men."

He knew how desperate and weak he sounded—almost hysterical—but he didn't care.

"Who's this?" Rick Shay said.

"Name's Huggins," Roy said. "Least that's what it says on his license."

"He tried to kill her," Ellie blurted from the booth. "Same as he killed Charlene."

With the mention of Charlene, Rick Shay's face got even tighter and he looked at Huggins with even harsher scrutiny.

"That true?" Shay said.

"No, it isn't true," Huggins said, still sounding desperate. "She's just mad because I wouldn't give her a ride. That's why she made all this up. To get back at me."

"A ride?"

"She was hitchhiking, officer."

This kind of guy, Huggins figured he'd wanted to be called "officer."

"But you didn't give her one?"

"No, I didn't."

"Why not?"

Huggins averted his eyes a moment. "This is going to sound stupid."

"Let me decide that."

Rick Shay sounded a lot smarter than he looked, thank God.

"Well, I'd usually give a woman a ride, especially on a nasty day like this one."

"So why didn't you?"

"Because she reminded me of Lavonne."

"Who's Lavonne?"

"My old college girlfriend."

"I see."

"Lavonne and I didn't end up on real friendly terms."

"She dump you?"

Huggins shrugged. "I guess you could say that."

"So you didn't pick her up, this girl Roy and Phil are talking about?"

"She's right here, Rick," Ellie said, nodding to Marcia, next to her in the booth.

"No, I didn't."

"She never got in your car?"

Thank God. These were the kinds of law-enforcement questions that Huggins had been wanting to hear.

"No, sir, officer, she didn't."

"All right, sir. You just wait right there."

"I want to say something else," Huggins said.

"Oh?"

"Roy and Phil. They hit me several times."

"Roy and Phil. These two?"

"Right," Huggins said, knowing he sounded more like wuss-of-the-year than ever. "Well, I mean technically, it was Phil who hit me."

"Technically?"

"Roy was giving the orders. Phil was carrying them out."

"He was trying to escape, Rick," Roy said.

"He sure was," Phil said.

"We were all afraid he was going to get violent," Ellie said.

"I'll get back to this later," Rick said. "Right now I want to talk to the girl. Ellie, how about you getting me a cup of coffee?"

Nice, cool, professional.

Huggins knew this wasn't over yet for sure. But he felt better now that a competent lawman was on the scene.

Rick slid into the booth across from Marcia Quinn. "Morning, ma'am."

"Morning," she said. "I'm real sorry for all this trouble."

Now she was playing the innocent schoolmarm in an old-fashioned Western.

He took out a small notebook he carried in the pocket behind his badge.

He then took out an expensive ballpoint and snicked it into action.

"Your name?"

"Marcia Quinn."

"Middle name?"

"Anne."

"Age?"

"Twenty-two."

"Occupation?"

"I'm a junior at Drake."

"In Des Moines?"

"Yes."

"And you were on your way back to school?"

"Yes."

"Do you normally hitchhike?"

"No. I was driving back with my boyfriend."

"And where is your boyfriend now?"

"Probably in Des Moines. We had an argument in the car."

"And he left you on the road?"

"It was as much my fault as his."

"I see."

"He's actually a very nice guy."

"I'm sure he is." He wrote something in his notebook, then looked up at Marcia. "Now I'll have to ask you some questions that'll probably make you uncomfortable."

"That's all right."

"You heard what he said. He said you didn't get in his car."

"That's not true. He pulled over to the side of the highway and"—she gulped, cast her eyes down to the table, as if it was all simply too-too much to remember—"I started to get in the car and he whipped out his knife and grabbed me and—"

"Just a moment, ma'am." Rick Shay looked over at Roy and Phil. "Did anybody search Mr. Huggins?"

"I did," Phil said proudly.

"You find anything?"

"No, I sure didn't, Rick."

"You search him carefully?"

"He did, Rick," Roy said. "I taught him how to search people the way I learned in the auxiliary police."

"And you didn't find anything, Phil?"

"Nothin'."

Ellie brought Rick Shay his coffee. Rick thanked her and then picked up the white cup in one massive hand.

"So he didn't let you get in the car?"

"No, because when I looked in and saw him. I decided not to take a ride after all."

"So you didn't get in the car?"

"Well, I think I started to sit down. I mean, I may've sat down on the seat but—"

Marcia teared up.

Huggins had to give it to her. She belonged in Hollywood.

No doubt about it.

"I don't remember exactly."

"But you do remember that he had a knife?"

"Yes."

"Do you know what kind of knife it was?"

"What kind?"

"The style, I mean."

"I'm not sure what you're talking about."

"Was it long?"

"I think so."

"Did it have a white handle or a black handle?"

"White, I think."

"Did he try and pull you in the car?"

"No, he didn't," Marcia Quinn said. "He jumped out at me. I guess he felt safe because of the fog."

"So he jumped out of the car and then what?"

"He got me on the ground."

"Was he hitting you?"

"Not really. But he was holding the knife to my throat."

"Was he touching you sexually?"

"Oh, yes. All over."

"Did he try to unzip your Levi's?"

"Yes."

"Were you fighting him?"

"As hard as I could. The knife really scared me."

"But you managed to get away from him?"

"Yes, sir," she said, shuddering. "Yes, sir, I did."

"Did he come after you?"

"I don't remember."

"Where did you go?"

"Just ran. I'm not sure where. I kept falling down.

Every time I did, I figured he'd catch up with me."

"But he didn't?"

"No. I didn't see him again after I ran away. Not until I got in here."

"In the café?"

"Yes."

He wrote a few more things in his notebook and said, "Anything you want to add?"

"I'd just like to get going."

"To Des Moines?"

"Yes."

"I don't blame you."

He looked over at Huggins. "Sounds like you've been a very busy boy, Mr. Huggins."

"She's lying."

"And you can prove that?"

"Yes, I can. You won't find any evidence of her being in my car. No fibers, no hairs."

"I see. Scientific evidence, you mean."

"Yes."

Huggins watched curiously as the lawman pushed himself to his feet, adjusted his Sam Browne, glanced back at Ellie, and said, "Good coffee, missy."

"Thanks, Rick."

"And I enjoyed meeting you, ma'am."

"Thank you."

He turned and faced Huggins fully. Then he took five very large steps, until he stood about two feet away.

"I guess they didn't tell you, huh?" he said.

"Tell me what?"

"They mention a little gal named Charlene?"

"Yeah, Ellie did. I guess that Highway Killer got her."

"Yeah," Rick said. "The Highway Killer."

He stared directly into Huggins' eyes as he spoke. "The Highway Killer. About the most chicken-shit creature I've ever heard about, you ask my opinion. Snatchin' gals that way, then cuttin' them up the way he does."

Huggins felt himself start to tremble. His bowels were doing cold and slithery and distasteful things. "I'm not the man you want, officer. I'm really not."

He felt claustrophobic again. Closed in by the fog. The café. The people who hated him so much.

"Guess they didn't tell you anything about me and Charlene, huh?" Rick Shay said.

"No; no, they didn't."

"We were going to be married three weeks after she died."

"Oh, God."

"I been waiting to meet you for a long time, you bastard."

With that, he pulled out his nightstick. It seemed to shine like Excalibur in the dusty light of the café.

"A long time," Rick Shay said.

He knew just how to do it, Rick Shay did. Just how to hit.

First the left knee, Huggins crying out and starting to sink to the floor. Then the elbow, right on the very tip of it, Huggins blind now with pain, grabbing at his elbow as he started to collapse. Then the shoulder. Right on the corner of it.

"Give it to him, Rick!" Ellie shouted. "Give it to him good!"

"Damn right," Phil said.

Rick Shay went to the right knee this time, cracking

the stick downward, at an expert angle, so the knee-cap felt as if it was exploding.

Huggins screamed. He no longer cared about looking like a wuss.

"No! Don't hit him anymore!"

Huggins was too busy with his pain to notice what was happening. He grabbed the edge of a chair and let himself sink downward.

"I made it all up!" Marcia Quinn said. "Honest to God. Officer Shay, this is all my fault."

Huggins looked up now, saw Marcia push herself out of the booth and past the formidable Ellie.

She came over to him and put her small white hand on his bruiser of an arm. The arm that yielded the nightstick.

"I was just mad that he wouldn't give me a ride," she said. "I just wanted to make him sweat a little. But it got out of hand so fast—"

She walked over to Huggins now. "I'm really sorry, Mr. Huggins. I really am. I don't blame you for being mad."

"Just get the hell out of my sight."

"I really don't blame you for hating me. I'd hate me, too."

"Just get the hell away from me."

"I really do apologize, Mr. Huggins. I really do."

Huggins, still very much in pain, said, "Every one of you in this café is going to be in a lot of trouble with the law. Including you, Shay. If you thought I was guilty, you should've taken me in. I wasn't resisting arrest at all. There wasn't any need to hit me."

"She was my fiancée," Rick Shay said. "What the hell did you expect me to do?"

Ellie came up and stood next to Marcia Quinn. "I

can't believe you lied to us this way. And about somethin' so important."

She didn't wait for Marcia to apologize or explain, Ellie didn't. She cocked her right hand back and drove a punch deep into the fetching face of the young woman. Blood burst from Marcia's nose. She immediately began sobbing.

"Little bitch," Phil said. "Kick her ass, Ellie. She's got it coming."

The irony wasn't lost on Huggins. They didn't much care who they pushed around. They were just as happy to start working Marcia Quinn over . . . and forget all about Huggins.

Much as he didn't want to, Huggins saw that he would have to help Marcia.

No way he was going to leave her here with these violent hayseeds.

"Leave her alone," Huggins said to Ellie.

"Punch her face in," Phil said.

"You're in one hell of a lot of trouble, young lady," Rick Shay said. "I'll tell you that much for sure."

Marcia Quinn was angry, humiliated, terrified. "Aren't you going to arrest her?" she demanded, putting napkins to her nose to stop the bleeding.

"I'll tell you who I *am* going to arrest," Rick Shay said. "And that's you."

"The hell you are," Huggins said, getting wearily to his feet.

His entire body ached. Every step was torture.

He walked over to Marcia Quinn and put his hand on her arm in a clearly possessive way.

"I'm going to make a deal with you folks," Huggins said, "and you'd damned well better take it." He didn't give them a chance to say anything. "I could bring serious charges against every one of you—just the way you could bring charges against Marcia. So we'll call it a draw. I'm going to forget about everything, and so are you. And right now Marcia and I are going to walk out that front door. Does everybody understand that?"

"I'm the law here," Rick Shay said.

"Not right now you're not." Huggins. said. "I've got a friend in the state attorney's office. Once he hears about your little example of hillbilly justice, you and all your 'auxiliary deputies' are going to be out of a job."

"Maybe he's right, Rick," Roy said. "Plus you've still got those brutality charges against you and—"

"Shut up," Rick said.

"So you won't bring any charges against anybody here?" Rick said.

"Not if you let Marcia and me walk out that door."

"She deserves to get her ass kicked," Ellie said.

"Yes, she does," Huggins said. "But not by you or Rick. Or Roy or Phil."

He nodded to the door. "Now we're going to walk out of here and nobody's going to try to stop us."

"I've got your word about not bringing any charges?" Rick Shay said.

"You've got my word," Huggins said. "Now I want to walk the hell out of here. And right now."

Rick Shay said, "You go right ahead, Mr. Huggins."

Shay glanced at the others. "Nobody's going to try to stop you, isn't that right, folks?"

They all nodded silently, sullenly.

All their fun was walking out the door.

Now they'd only have townspeople to beat up on.

Huggins gripped Marcia's arm, urging her to the door.

"You didn't have any right to hit me," Marcia said to Ellie.

"Slut," Ellie said.

Huggins pushed her forward.

Marcia finally got the message and started walking quickly to the front door.

Huggins grabbed the handle, yanked the door back, and half pushed her out to the parking lot.

"Hurry, dammit," he said.

"She didn't have any right to hit me," Marcia said.

"Just keep quiet."

The fog was thicker than before. Damp, slimy, wrapping and roiling around them.

"I can't even see your car," Marcia said.

Huggins led the way.

He found his car by running into its back fender.

He got the door open and pushed her inside.

"What the hell's the hurry?" she said.

"Before they change their minds," Huggins said. "Unless you want to spend some more time with them."

"I guess you're right."

Huggins slammed the passenger door then walked around and got in the driver's side.

She looked over at him and gave him a little smile. Not even a bloody nose could take the shine from her good looks. "I guess you ended up giving me a ride anyway."

"Yeah," he said. "I guess I did."

He started the engine.

"Will you be able to drive all right in this fog?"

"I'll just have to keep my headlights on and drive

very slowly," Huggins said. "I just want to get the hell away from here."

He started his foggy trek, moving at ten miles per hour. As they reached the road, the fog started to thin enough so that he could see the center line down the asphalt that led to the interstate.

"I don't blame you for hating me."

"You said that already."

"I just thought it'd be funny."

"Yeah. Hilarious."

"I didn't have any idea it'd get that far out of hand. Then I got afraid to speak up. Afraid they'd turn on me, you know?"

"Yeah," he said. "I know all about being afraid."

"I really am sorry."

"Right."

"Just imagine," she said, laughing just a little bit, obviously trying to calm herself down. "Just imagine if you'd really been carrying some kind of knife when Phil was searching you."

He leaned down so that his right hand could reach his shoe. People who searched you never thought to look in your shoes.

"You mean like this one?" Huggins said, bringing up the pearl-handled switchblade with the eight-inch blade.

"Oh, my God," she said. "The blade is serrated. Then you really are—"

"—the Highway Killer," he finished for her.

"Oh, my God," she said.

"Yes," Huggins said, at last finding some humor in this whole situation. "Oh, my God."

Rite of Passage

Soon enough, the tribe knew the truth about the boy.

Despite his six-foot-three; despite his taut, packed muscles; despite the long unruly hair he'd bleached with lime in warrior fashion; and despite his agility with javelin and broadsword alike—he was not a soldier.

There was nothing of the weakling about him, and this was what so confounded the leaders of this particular Celtic village. The boys who held the same interests of girls rarely showed Valerius' skill with weapons. Or his ability in appearing fearsome—slathering his naked body in the red and yellow clay and then donning a bronze helmet and then attacking viciously the various targets that had been set up for the warriors to practice on—he was all one could want in a warrior. He had strange powers, too. When he walked the sun-dappled forests, the animals would crowd round him and he would speak to them, and one had the excited sense that they were truly communicating with each other. And he could paint pictures on stone that shocked the eye with their clarity and precision—children and moons and sunsets he painted, and the comic faces of raccoons and rabbits and village puppies.

Valerius' father Corvinus was the king of this particular tribe and it was for his father that Valerius feigned interest in soldiering. He loved his father and did not want to humiliate him before the other warriors of the village. He even went along on three attacks on other villages with whom his own people were warring. He was thrilled to see the war-chariots in action, two Celts to a chariot, one man with the reins, the other hurling javelins at the enemy. He was equally thrilled to hear the legendary battle horns, those instruments that made sounds so harsh and discordant that some villages surrendered at the sound of them. This was particularly true of the Romans, who felt that the horns were literally of hell. But he could not kill, and that was the trouble. Fight, oh yes, he was magnificent to see—but kill? It was as if some invisible hand clamped his wrist at the last moment. Woman, child, man, animal—it didn't matter. Valerius could not bring himself to take another's life. It was as if he had been born crippled, crippled in the urge to kill.

All the villagers knew his real passion, and they did not begrudge him it, either. In addition to his ability to paint and speak with animals, Valerius had the most beautiful singing voice any of them had ever heard. On wedding nights, he would serenade the couple, and they would be so moved, they would lie in their marriage beds and weep with that ineluctable sorrow that made their joining all the sweeter. At village assemblies, he would sing tales of brave warriors, and not a single arm would be free of goose bumps. And at funerals—where the war-painted corpse of the warriors were nobly fed to the vultures, and diseased or elderly bodies were simply burned— he sang of the village itself, and how it had endured down the years, free of the enslavement that had claimed some of the other villages.

Valerius' singing was so beloved by the villagers that they did not care if he was a warrior. Let him sing and farm, they told his father King Corvinus. There will always be other warriors—but there will never be another with a voice like your son's.

By the time Valerius was seventeen summers, even King Corvinus had accepted the fate of his boy. Valerius was a good organizer and for the first time in the history of the village, the granary was always filled. Valerius saw to it.

In her nineteenth summer, Epona, so named after the Gallic horse goddess, told Valerius that soon they would have a child. Valerius was happy to be a father and spent far more time with his beautiful little girl than village elders thought appropriate. Was this manly? His relationship with Epona had made him look even weaker to the warriors of the tribe. Epona was of the old way—she thought that men and women alike should be faithful (many Celtic women were as unfaithful as their husbands) and she thought that husband and wife should not only share the same residence but share a variety of housely duties. He would be doing this while the other young men his age were off warring.

But he loved her and could not be without her and so he became the husband she wanted.

Shortly after Valerius' twenty-third summer, when Epona's stomach swelled for a third time, the Druid known as Taranis came to the village. There was a great myth about this man who cloaked himself in many layers of dark and coarse robes and whose eyes, shadowed by the cowl, burned with an unhealthy yellow light. Unlike most Druid priests who were judges and astronomers and doctors, it was said that Taranis could actually grant wishes.

Taranis spent two full days in the village. Everyone swarmed about him. Even the forest animals, apparently sensing divinity in the man, drew near the edges of the village. There were feasts and games and much drinking. Many villagers, emboldened by wine, asked Taranis if he would grant their wishes but he only shook his long, narrow, ugly, head and scattered them away with a flick of his bony hand. Despite all the ways the villagers had tried to please him, he was not a friendly man.

Near the end of the festivities, Valerius sang. Epona and their two children sat bathed golden in the light of the huge fire, watching him. Epona's eyes smiled with pride in her husband.

Taranis startled everyone by crying openly, especially when Valerius sang of the man who'd lost his wife and children to Roman attack.

When the night was done, and the moon rode into midnight, Taranis came over to Valerius and said, "Your song was how my own wife and children died. By the hands of the Romans. I need to be purged of my grief from time to time, and tonight you helped me. Now I would like to help you. I will grant you any wish I'm able to."

By this time, the center of the village, where festivities were held, was growing dark, the fire little more than embers, the moon behind heavy gray clouds portending more cold spring rains. Most people were already asleep in their circular thatched houses.

The shame Valerius carried—so many warriorly gifts, and yet not being a true warrior—came quickly to mind and he told Taranis of his dilemma.

"I'm surprised, my young friend," the old Druid said, and there was a note of sorrow in his voice. "I would have thought you'd have chosen something for your wife and children. Long lives, if nothing else."

"I love my wife and children very much," Valerius said. "But I want to be a warrior. I will never feel like a true man until I am a warrior. My body is ready but not my heart." He tapped his powerful chest. "It is in here I need to change."

The Druid stared at him from beneath the cowl. His pale yellow eyes seemed disembodied from the rest of the face, which was lost in shadow. "It is not mine to tell you what to wish for. But you must value the warrior's life very highly to give up what you have."

"To give up? I don't understand."

"To say yes to one thing is to say no to another," the priest said. The Druid hesitated. "But you will have to learn that for yourself."

Valerius had no idea what the old priest was talking about. And didn't care, either. "Grant me my wish, ancient Father. Please."

The old priest reached out with a twisted and be-grimed hand and touched a thumb to Valerius' fore-head. For a moment, the old man closed his eyes and spoke some words in a tongue Valerius had never heard before.

"Your wish is granted," the Druid said, and then sighed deeply. "I think I'll go to bed now. Sometimes I dream of my wife and children, and then my mind is at peace once more."

Valerius did not sleep well.

He was up before dawn gathering spear and knife and ax and heading into the deepest part of the forest. He spent the entire day hunting—and killing. At first, he wasn't certain that he could murder the doe who had been drinking by the clear blue pond. And yet he did it. And felt an undeniable sense of triumph as he knelt next to the dead thing that had once been a song of nature. And so the day went. He returned to the village laden with kills of every kind, deer, bird, fish. And he presented them to Epona as he would have presented a wedding dowry. And yet when he reached out to embrace her—so joyous in his pride—she only turned from him and began weeping while she clutched her enormous belly as if in pain.

Epona woke just after dawn to the cries and bel-lows of a raiding party. The straw mat next to her was empty. Her first thought was that Valerius, as he sometimes did, had gone into the forest to pick flow-ers for her. But then, as she remembered yesterday and the subtle but definite change she'd seen in her husband, a chill traversed her entire body. She went to the center of the village where the raiding party was just now ready to depart, huge horses striped with war colors, the men on their backs also painted up for battle. She could see the silver breath of horse and man alike. The air above them was a jungle of spears and lances black against the dawning umber sky. The chill air smelled of wine and sweat and horseshit. She did not see Valerius among these men. She felt great relief. He'd gone to the forest, after all.

But when she turned to go back to the hut, one of the village women, Ierna, a woman who had never liked her, came up and said, "Well, we'll see if that husband of yours is a man or not."

"I don't know what you're talking about."

Ierna smirked. "He does not take you into his confidence? A wife should beware when that happens. My husband tells me everything." Then, seeing that Epona still didn't know what she was talking about, the woman said,

"He left earlier this morning, with the first raiding party."

Valerius was gone sixteen days, in all. He knew immediately that the Druid's magic had worked. Instead of feeling revulsion at what he saw and participated in, he felt great joy and freedom. They were expert raiders and he was proud to be one of them. They would swoop down on an enemy village and immediately set fire to all the thatched huts. They would do all this while screaming and shouting and blowing the animal-headed horns—the noise alone overwhelming and terrifying the enemy into submission. And then the slaughter and rape began. The treasures most sought—those they could use as barter when they returned to their own village—were livestock, healthy women who could be sold as slaves, gold, and the severed heads of the village leaders. There were only two things that Valerius would not do, and that was kill children and rape women. None of the other raiders were troubled about murdering little ones but Valerius would not do it, and often, when his fellows weren't watching, he helped the little ones hide in the surrounding forest.

The raiders returned home late one night. Valerius found Epona asleep and crawled beneath the blanket. When she woke, she simply looked at him and said, "I can smell death on you, Valerius. Are you happy now that you're just like all the rest of them? You were unique once, and now you're no better than they are." She would not let him make love to her. In anger, he went to the hut where the new slave women were being kept. He raped one of them most savagely and then went home and slept next to his wife. He still loved her deeply and could not believe she had so spurned him.

In the next two years, Valerius went on many more raids, a number of them into lands that Caesar had claimed for Rome, far from the home village, into lands not on the Celtic maps. They enjoyed destroying with particular zeal anything owned by Caesar. Valerius adopted the wavy battle lance as his weapon of choice. The weapon was thrown, just as any other lance would be, but when it was pulled out, the wavy blade lacerated the wound, making death twice as gruesome and painful. The greatest pleasure came from storming a castle. So fearsome were the raiders in the clamor of their cries and horns and death songs, that the inhabits of the Castle Reis—whose prince, it was said, was a relative of Caesar himself—surrendered even before any blood had been spilled. They offered jewelry and gold and their daughters as slaves. The raiders accepted these bribes with grim amusement. They then set about their real business, which was killing. Trying to impress themselves, they tossed the quarters and halves of bloody bodies and arms and legs and heads and hands into an enormous pile right in front of the castle gate. They hoped that Caesar's men would arrive soon, when the body parts were still fresh. They would report what they'd found back to Caesar and the fame of the raiders would increase a hundredfold—as would the dread and terror they inspired, the Romans starting to see them now as almost supernatural beasts. But once again, Valerius would not participate in killing children. Indeed, he still had to look away when he saw a child about to be slaughtered. He thought of his own children then, and for the moment his loneliness for them was like a madness. He helped women whenever he could, too.

Winter came. Winter raids were the most debilitating. A number of raiders were lost to avalanches—they had gone up into the mountains where, it was rumored, there were other villages claimed by Caesar—and to an illness that started as a cough and ended with vomiting blood and hallucinations and death only a few days later.

It was spring before they returned home. They came in at night and saw a huge bonfire burning. The villagers celebrated spring in many ways. This was one of them, the entire village gathered round the campfire listening to—song. A handsome young man who looked somewhat familiar to Valerius stood on a flat stone singing songs such as Valerius once had. Songs of valor and love and loss. The villagers were enraptured, so enraptured that few of them greeted the raiders. Then one of the villagers saw Valerius and urged him to join the young man—who had been identified as Aruns, son of a villager Valerius knew well.

What power, these two singing together.

Valerius had not sung in over a year. He had been too busy. The warriors were suspicious of singing this refined, anyway. They liked coarse battle songs, not trilling odes to the moon and the intricate ways of the heart. He stood with Aruns on the flat stone and it was from there he caught his first glimpse of Epona. And saw the way she was looking at Aruns. She had looked at Valerius this way once—but not since he'd become a warrior. He sang but it was clear that the purest song had died in him somehow. Arms overwhelmed him with the clear soaring beauty of his voice. After one duet, the crowd asked that only Aruns sing.

In his hut, he found his two daughters sleeping. And next to their heads he found small flat stones upon which portraits had been painted. Stunning portraits, of the sort he'd once painted.

He was kneeling there, staring at the paintings, when Epona came into the hut.

"Who did these?" he demanded to know.

"Aruns did them," she said. "What're you so angry about? Is this a way to greet your wife?"

She had told him, after his first raid, that she could smell death on him.

And just so, he could now smell adultery on her.

His daughters were starting to stir. His anger had awakened them.

He left the hut, fled to the woods, which had always

been his solace, the animals there and the true pure voice of the river and the vast dreaming arc of sky. He walked for nearly an hour, and darker and denser the forest became, walked for nearly an hour, aware with each step that none of the animals were filling his head with thoughts, the way they'd once been able to silently communicate. His head was empty of all but rage and jealousy and despair.

He slept by the river, wrapped in his cloak. In the morning, he returned to the village. He was almost to his hut when Ierna came up to him. "You came home too late, Valerius. Your wife is in love with Aruns. And everybody in the village knows this but you." She feigned sorrow. "I say this as a friend."

Epona was gone. But the girls were there. The little one was too young to even remember him. The three-year-old said, "Aruns is going to take us swimming this afternoon."

"Do you know who I am?"

The little girl was hesitant. "I'm not sure."

He felt his heart stop. He had just died a death, seeing the blankness in her eyes, hearing the wariness in her voice. He had been on so many raids over the first three years of her life. Grief numbed him.

He started to tell her who he was but what was the point?

"If you see Aruns, would you tell him to hurry please?" his oldest daughter said. "We really want to go swimming."

He spent the next half hour searching the village for his wife. He took his broadsword with him. She was nowhere about. And then Ierna appeared again, eager to conjoin trouble. "If you look by the brook to

127

the west you may find them. They spend much time there."

And so it was he found them. He climbed a tree that overlooked the brook where the two lovers sat. She played the flute, and it was beautiful. And Aruns sang, it was more beautiful still.

He had to turn his head away when Aruns took Epona in his arms and kissed her. He could smell and taste and feel Epona in his own arms—as she had been when she loved him. A madness overtook him and he climbed down from the tree and drew his broadsword and started to walk through the long grasses to the bank of the brook.

And then stopped himself.

What would happen to the girls if he killed their mother and her lover? Who would take care of them?

He slid his broadsword back into its sheath and walked away from the brook, back into the forest once again, the sunlight glowing here and there on the huge boles of ancient trees, larksong and sweetwind momentarily cooling his anger. Aruns could talk to the beasts of the forest, he was sure of it.

Just as Aruns could paint and Aruns could sing and Aruns could make love to Epona. Aruns was who he used to be. And thinking that, not even larksong nor sweetwind could cool or solace him.

He went back to the bank of the brook and slew them both with his great slashing bloody sword. He beheaded Aruns and carried his head back to the village and nailed it to the front of Aruns' hut.

And was then fallen upon by the elders of the village, who locked him in a hut and prepared for trial.

*　　*　　*

Celtic law was strict and simple. You could not kill another simply because he had committed adultery with your mate. That was the law and on a sunny morning, the elders read the law as Valerius stood before them. The entire village was ringed behind, eager to know what punishment the elders would hand down. Executions were always fun to watch.

And it looked as if there might well be an execution until Brein, the most celebrated of all the village warriors, told of the toll that two ceaseless years of raiding took on the raiders themselves. While not all the elders appreciated the activities of the warriors, the elders had to admit that without them the village would be far poorer—and might not be able to exist.

The crowd found this a reasonable argument and began to chant for Valerius' freedom. The elders knew they dare not go against the crowd. The warriors had long wanted to pack the council with their own members and get rid of the elder tribunal and this—if they ordered Valerius' death—would be a fine opportunity.

The elders spent two hours in their hut and then emerged and announced that Valerius was free to rejoin the raiders again.

There was rejoicing for the rest of the day, led by Valerius' father, who made no secret of the fact that he was proud of his son for slaying both an unfaithful wife and an interloper like Aruns.

Valerius went to Semona, the woman who had volunteered to raise his daughters. He asked to see them but Semona said that they did not want to see him ever again. She saw his grief and took his arm and said in the way of wise older women that she felt someday their attitude would change, that they would

129

understand how a madness had fallen upon him and that he was sorry for what he had done. And it was then he realized—though of course he would not say this to Semona—that he did not feel sorry at all. Did not the true warrior right wrongs? And had this situation not been wrong for a true warrior to endure? He thanked her and went away.

A week later, Valerius was part of a raiding party that went deep into Caesar-held territory. He killed with a particular rage that day, and when a young girl ran in front of his horse, he bent down and cleaved her head off with his broadsword, and he did not feel half so bad as he'd imagined he would.

Masque

From a police report:

I found the nude body of Janice Hollister in a deep ravine. Some children who'd been playing in the neighborhood told me that they'd seen a dog with what appeared to be blood on his coat. The dog led me back to her. The first thing I noticed about the Hollister woman was the incredible way her body had been cut up. Her entire right breast had been ripped away.

"I've listed it as a car accident," Dr. Temple says.

They are in a room of white tiles and green walls and white cabinets and stainless steel sinks. The room smells of antiseptic and the white tile floor sparkles with hot September sunlight.

Dr. Temple is in his mid-fifties, balding, a lean jog-

131

ger in a white medical smock. He has very blue eyes and very pink skin. He is an old family friend.

"You've taken care of the records, then?" Mrs. Garth asks. She is sixty-eight and regal in a cold way, given to Dior suits and facelifts.

"Yes."

"There'll be no problem?"

"None. The record will show that he was transferred here two weeks ago following a car accident."

"A car accident?"

"That will account for the bandages. So many lacerations and contusions we had to cover his entire body." He makes a grim line of his mouth. "Very dramatic and very convincing to the eye. Almost theatrical."

"I see. Very good. I appreciate it."

"And we appreciate all you've done for the hospital, Ruth. Without your generosity, there'd be no cancer clinic."

She stands up and offers her delicate hand in such a way that the doctor fears for a terrified moment she actually expects him to kiss it.

From a police report:

I thought the dog might have attacked her after the killer fled. But then I saw that her anus and vagina had been torn up just the way the rest of her had and then I knew that it had to be him. The perpetrator, I mean. I checked the immediate vicinity for footprints and anything that might have fallen from his pockets. I found nothing that looked useful.

A new elevator, one more necessity her money has bought this hospital, takes her to the ninth floor.

She walks down a sunny corridor being polished by a dumpy, middle-aged black woman who has permitted her hose to bag about her knees. The woman, Mrs. Garth thinks, should have more respect for herself.

Mrs. Garth finds 909 and enters.

She takes no more than ten steps inside, around the edge of the bathroom, when she stops and looks in horror at him.

All she can think of are those silly movies about Egyptian mummies brought back to life.

Here sits Steve, his entire head and both arms swathed entirely in white bandages. All she can see of him are his face, his eyes, and his mouth.

"My Lord," she moans.

She edges closer to his hospital bed. The room is white and clean and lazy in the sunlight. Above, the TV set mounted to the wall plays a game show with two fat contestants jumping up and down on either side of the handsome host who cannot quite rid his eyes of boredom.

"Aren't you awfully hot inside there?" she asks.

He says nothing, but then at such times he never does.

She pulls up a chair and sits down.

"I am Zoser, founder of the third Dynasty," he says.

"Oh, you," she says. "Now's no time to joke. Anyway, I can barely understand you with all those bandages over your face."

"I am Senferu, the Warrior King."

"Oh, you," she says.

133

Ed Gorman

From a police report:

Her neck appears to have been broken. At least that was my first impression. The killer's strength must be incredible. To say nothing of how much he must hate women.

An hour after she arrives in the hospital room, she says, "An old man saw you."

Inside the mummy head, the blue eyes show panic.

"Don't worry," she continues. "He has vision trouble, so he's not a very credible witness. But he did describe you pretty accurately to the press. Fortunately, I told Dr. Temple that some drug dealers were looking for you. He seemed to accept my story."

She pats him on the arm. "Didn't that medication Dr. Gilroy gave you help? I had such high hopes for it. He said you wouldn't any longer want to . . . You know what I'm trying to say."

But now that he knows he's going to be safe, the panic dies in his blue eyes and he says, "I am King Tut."

"Oh, pooh. Can't you be serious?"

"I'm not serious. I'm King Tut."

She clucks.

They sit back and watch the Bugs Bunny cartoon he has on. He says, through his bandages, "I wish they'd show Porky."

"Porky?"

"Porky Pig."

"Oh, I see." My God, he's forty-six years old. She says, "In case there's any trouble, Dr. Temple is going to tell the police that you've been here two weeks and that the old man couldn't possibly identify you because even if you were out and about, you'd have been wearing bandages."

"They won't arrest Senferu the Warrior King, mother. They'd be afraid to."

"I thought after that trouble in Chicago you told me about—"

"There's Sylvester!" he exclaims.

And so there is: Sylvester the cat.

She lets him watch a long minute, the exasperated cat lisping and spitting and spraying. "You were very savage with this one," she says. "Very savage."

"I've seen this one before. This is where Tweety really gives it to Sylvester. Watch!"

She watches, and when she can endure it no more, she says, "Perhaps I made some mistakes with you."

"Oh, God, Sylvester—watch out for Tweety!"

"Perhaps, after your father died, I took certain liberties with you I shouldn't have." Pause. "Letting you sleep in my bed . . . Things happened and I don't suppose either one of us is to blame but nonetheless—"

"Great! Porky's coming on! Look, Mother, it's Porky!"

From a police report:

Down near the creek bed we found her breast. At first I wasn't sure what it was, but as I stared at it I started getting sick. By this time the first backup was arriving. They had to take over for me a few minutes. I wasn't feeling very well.

In the hospital room, sitting there in his mummy bandages, his mother at his side, Steve stares up at the TV set. There's a commercial on now. He hates commercials.

"Maybe Daffy Duck will be on next, Mother. God, wouldn't that be great?"

Now it's her turn for silence. She thinks of the girls in Chicago and Kansas City and Akron. So savage with them; so savage. She will never again believe him that everything's fine and that his medication has gotten him calmed down once and for all and that she should let him take a trip.

But of course this time he didn't even go anywhere. Most dangerous of all, he did it here at home.

Right here at home.

"Wouldn't it be great, Mother?" he asks, wanting her to share his enthusiasm. He loves those occasions when they share things.

She says, "I'm sorry, darling, my mind just wandered. Wouldn't what be great, dear?"

"If it was Daffy on next."

"Daffy?"

"Daffy Duck," he says from inside his mummy head. And then he does a Daffy Duck imitation right on the spot.

Not even the bandages can spoil it, she thinks. He's so clever. "Oh, yes, dear. That would be great if Daffy came on next."

He reaches over and touches her with his bandaged hand and for a horrible moment she almost believes he's been injured.

But then she sees the laughter in his blue blue eyes inside the mummy head.

She pats his bandaged hand. "You'll get a nice rest here for a few weeks and then we'll go home again, dear, and everything will be fine."

He lays his head back and sighs. "Fine." He repeats the word almost as if he doesn't know what it means. "Fiiiine." He seems to be staring at the ceiling. She hopes it's not another depression. They emerge so quickly and last so long.

But then abruptly he's sitting up again and clapping his bandaged hands together and staring up at the TV screen.

"It *is* Daffy, Mother. It *is* Daffy!"

"Yes, dear," she says. "It is Daffy, isn't it?"

Dark Muse

Hanratty came in that rainy Thursday afternoon and found what he'd dreaded he'd find.

Another song waiting for him on the battered Steinway that provided half the entertainment in Kenny's Lounge, the other half being Hanratty's cigarette-raspy forty-two-year-old voice. Hard to believe anything that rough-sounding had ever sung "Ave Maria" at St. Mallory's Catholic High back in Shaker Heights.

Another song.

He lit a cigarette and sat down at the Steinway and started playing the notes and singing the words that had been left there for him. This one was a ballad called "Without You" and it was so heartbreakingly good that even the janitor, turning the chairs back up and polishing the floors, stopped to listen. As did the bartender shining glasses.

When he finished, Hanratty's entire body was shaking and tears collected in silver drops in the corners of his blue eyes.

It wasn't just the song that had gotten to him— though God knew it was beautiful enough—it was the mystery behind the song.

For the past three months now Kenny's Lounge (if you were wealthy and inclined to cheat, then you knew all about Kenny's Lounge) had been enjoying standing-room-only business and it was exactly because of all the new songs that Richard Hanratty had been writing that the crowd wanted to hear.

There was only one trouble with all the adulation being bestowed on Hanratty. He didn't deserve it. Literally. Because he wasn't writing the songs.

Once a week he'd come into work, he was never sure which day it would be, and there on the Steinway up on the circular little stage with the baby blue spotlight that made him look a little less fleshy and a little more handsome than he in fact was . . . waiting for him there on the Steinway would be a brand new song all laid out in perfect form on sheet music in a very precise and knowing hand.

Hanratty had no idea who was leaving these songs for him.

Hanratty said, "You think over my offer?"

Kenny Bentley said, "You want a lot, Richard. Too much."

"You think they're coming here to see you—or hear me?"

Kenny Bentley sighed. He was forty-one, slender, and had apparently taken as his hero one of those gangster B-movie actors from the forties who seem never to be out of tuxedo or into daylight. He wore his dyed black hair slicked back and wore contacts so dark his eyes sparkled like black ice. He carried a gun in a shoulder rig in an obvious way. It added to the sense of danger he liked to create right down to the small jagged scar under his left eye which Hanratty felt sure Bentley had put there himself for effect. Bentley—even that was phony, Hanratty learning from the bartender that Bentley's real last name was Sullivan.

They were in Hanratty's dressing room. It smelled now of mildew and martini, the one drink Hanratty allowed himself before going on. The walls were covered with big black and white blowups of movie goddesses from the thirties and forties. Hanratty's favorite was of Rita Hayworth in a silky, sensual slip. He didn't think he'd ever seen a more erotic woman. The rest of the room was taken up by a couch, a full length dressing table with bubble lights encircling the mirror and various kinds of makeup strewn across the chipped and faded mahogany surface. Hanratty was secure enough in his masculinity that wearing makeup had never bothered him.

He said, taking a slightly defensive tone that sickened him to hear, "I'm just asking for my fair share, Kenny. Business has nearly tripled, but you're paying me the same."

"That another new song I heard out there?"

"Is that an answer to my question?"

Bentley smiled with startling white teeth a vampire could envy. "I still can't figure out where you got so much talent all of a sudden."

"Maybe my muse decided to pay me a visit."

"Your muse." Bentley bit the words off bitterly.

141

Ed Gorman

"You're a lounge piano player for twenty-some years who's had three bad marriages, ten cars that the finance company has all repossessed, and you've got a slight drinking problem. The few times you ever played your own compositions before, the whole crowd went to sleep and I had to force you to go back to playing standards. But then all of a sudden—" He took out an unfiltered cigarette from a silver case that cost as much as Hanratty's monthly rent. The smoke he exhaled was silver as the case itself. His hair shone dark as his eyes. He gazed suspiciously down at Hanratty. "Then all of a sudden, you start writing these beautiful, beautiful songs. I don't understand and something's damn funny about it. Damn funny."

"Maybe it just took time for my talent to bloom," Hanratty said. There was a note of irony in his voice. He was uncomfortable talking about the songs. They weren't, after all, his.

A knock sounded tentatively on the door just as Bentley was about to say something else.

Bentley went to the door, opened it.

She stood there, Sally Carson, looking as overwhelmingly voluptuous as ever—almost unreal in certain ways—spilling out of the tiny pirate's costume all the waitresses wore at Kenny's Lounge. She was six feet or better, with a breathtaking bust, and perfectly formed hips and legs. She also owned one of those tiny overbites that add just the right sexy bit of imperfection to a beautiful woman's face. Only one thing was wrong with Sally and that was all the makeup she wore around her right eye. It looked as if she'd put it on with a spade and Hanratty knew why.

She was Kenny Bentley's current girl friend and

Kenny Bentley, a man who brought new meaning to the term insanely jealous, had obviously worked her over again last night. If you looked carefully at Sally—as Hanratty did dreamily many times—you also noticed that her nose had been fractured right up on the bridge. Another memento from Kenny.

"What the hell is it?" Bentley demanded. "We're talking business."

Sally suddenly lost all her poise and confidence. She shied back and said, "You said to tell you when the Swansons arrived."

"Oh. Right. Thanks."

And with that, Bentley slammed the door in her face.

Hanratty said, "You shouldn't treat her like that, Kenny. She's a hell of a nice woman. Smart." He wanted to say *too smart for you* but he knew better.

Bentley stubbed out his cigarette. "I'll go half your demand, Hanratty. Half but no more."

Hanratty shrugged. "I'll have to think it over, Kenny."

"You do that." The suspicion was back in his eyes. "In the meantime, I'm going to find out what the hell's going on here."

"What's that supposed to mean?"

"It means that no broken-down lounge singer suddenly comes into talent. There's just no way, Hanratty, just no way." He started toward the door and paused. "In college did you read a book called *What Makes Sammy Run?*"

"As a matter of fact, I did."

"Well, you know how Sammy Glick steals that poor jerk's movie scripts and sells them as his own?"

Hanratty felt his face redden and his hands fold up naturally into fists.

"Well, something like that's going on here, Hanratty. Something very much like that."

With that, he was gone, the sound of the slamming door reverberating like a gunshot.

Hanratty had a cigarette, just one of the innumerable vices he'd never been able to give up, and tried to calm down. He thought of how ironic it was that he'd just become so self-righteous when Bentley had accused him of using somebody else's material. Wasn't that exactly what he was doing?

He thought again of the tentative call he'd made this morning to a New York song publisher. Inquiring about how you went about selling songs . . . But then he'd backed off and told the woman he'd call her back soon. Without knowing where the songs came from, it would be a dangerous thing to start peddling them . . . At the least it could lead to embarrassment, at the worst to prison.

He jabbed out his cigarette and went over to the walk-in closet to select one of four lamé dinner jackets. There was a green one, a red one, a blue one, a black one, festive and tacky at the same time, and just what you'd expect from somebody who had spent his life—despite big gaudy dreams of being a star in his own right—singing other people's material, tapping parasite-like into creativity not his own.

As usual, the smell of moth balls startled his senses as he pushed the sliding closet door back. It always reminded him of his parent's attic back in South Dakota. He reached in for the blue jacket and felt another familiar sensation—a slight draft, one whose source he'd never been sure of. It was inside the closet only occasionally and he'd never checked it out but tonight, with twenty minutes to go and no desire to sit at his dressing table and brood, he decided to get on his hands and knees and find out just where the draft came from somewhere in the darkness at the east end of the long closet.

He had just gotten down on his hands and knees and started to crawl into the closet, the draft becoming much stronger and colder the more deeply he went inside, when an abrupt knock came on his door. Instead of responding to the knock, he decided to go a few feet closer to the wall. He put his hand out and felt for the first time a piece of plywood about three feet by three feet that had been nailed against the wall itself. Given all the nailheads his fingers found there in the gloom, Hanratty could tell that the plywood should have been firmly affixed. But it wasn't. Not at all. It almost came off in his hands. He put fingers on either side of the plywood and felt an opening whose chill metal surface told him that it was a wide piece of duct work now closed off for some reason. He wondered where it led and why it had been closed off. Then, just as he sensed a sweet odor—perfume coming from duct work?—the knock on his door became adamant. He reaffixed the piece of plywood as well as he could, crawled backward out of the closet, and then went to answer the door.

There, in his standard white bartender's uniform, stood David Sullivan. David was twenty-four, a former second-string tackle for the Browns, and now a guy trying to get himself an MBA at the local state university while working nights here. Sullivan was big, as you might expect, and handsome in the way a somewhat forlorn St. Bernard is handsome. Hanratty knew why he was forlorn. Sullivan was in love with Sally Carson.

"Can I talk to you a minute, Richard?"

Sullivan was a good kid and Hanratty both liked him and felt sorry for him. "Sure. Come on in."

Sullivan did so, closing the doors. His brown eyes watched curiously as Hanratty wiped closet dust from his hands. Hanratty thought of explaining, then saw that Sullivan's business seemed to be a lot more urgent.

"What's going on?"

"You saw Sally?" Sullivan said. His voice was trembling.

"Yeah, kid, I did."

"That bastard. That's the third black eye in less than two months." He made a fist the size of a melon. "You know what I want to do—"

Hanratty lit a cigarette, exhaled smoke. "Look, kid, I don't mean to hurt your feelings, but remember the last time we had this conversation?"

"I remember, Richard. You told me that if she really wanted to get away from him she would."

"That's right."

"Not any more."

"Oh?"

"She snuck over to my place about dawn this morning and really broke down. Just laid on my couch and cried and cried. She was really scared."

"Of Bentley?"

"Right."

"Why doesn't she just leave him?"

Sullivan said, "She thinks he'll kill her."

Hanratty frowned. "Look, I take no back seat in my loathing of Kenny Bentley. I know he likes to cheat his employees every way he can, and I know he likes to harass and debase people every way he can, and I know that he gets some kind of sick kick from beating up his woman-of-the-moment. But I can't say that I see him as a killer. Not on purpose anyway."

"She thinks he may already have killed one of his women."

"What?"

"Two years ago. She ran into a waitress who used to work here and the waitress told her that there was this really gorgeous but very quiet waitress named Denise Ayles who worked here while she was going to the Harcourt Academy. She got involved with Kenny very briefly but started to back away once she saw what he was like. Only he wouldn't *let* her back away. He kept coming at her. Then she just vanished."

"Vanished?"

"Right. Vanished. The waitress said she called the police and had them look into it, but all they concluded was that Denise Ayles, for reasons of her own, just took off." He made the melon-sized fist again. "You know damn well what happened, Richard. He killed her and got rid of the body."

Hanratty's jaw muscles had begun to work. "I guess that wouldn't be out of the question, would it?"

"Not with Bentley."

"And the cops lost interest?"

"Bentley had an alibi. He was in Vegas."

"Then maybe he didn't kill her."

"You know Bentley's friends. He could buy an alibi with no problem."

"I guess that's true."

Big, shaggy Sullivan looked sorrowful again. "I don't know what to do about Sally."

"Just kind of ride with things, kid. See what happens."

"If he lays a hand on her again, I'll break his neck, Richard. That's a promise." The cold rage in his otherwise friendly gaze told Hanratty that this was no idle threat. Not at all.

Hanratty reached up and put his hand on Sullivan's shoulder and said, "Let's just see what happens, all right? I don't want to see you *or* Sally get into a jam, okay?"

Sullivan sighed, calmed down somewhat. He even offered a quick flash of smile. "I don't know why you stay here. Especially since you got hot as a songwriter the past few months. You ever thinking of selling your songs?"

Hanratty wanted to say: Kid, I'd love to. If they were really *my* songs."

He played the new song for them that night, "Without You," and you could sense how the audience liked it. Enough to set down their drinks; enough to quit copping cheap feels in the shadows; enough to quit shedding tears over lovers who were never going to leave their spouses. How intent they looked then, sleek pretty people in sleek pretty clothes, the sort of privileged people Hanratty had always wanted to be—and now, as always when he played one of the songs left so mysteriously for him—now they paid complete attention.

By the time he got to the payoff, his voice straining just a little to hit the final high notes, he could see their eyes shine with the sadness of the song itself.

The lyrics got to Hanratty himself, always did. Whoever was writing them knew the same kind of tortured loneliness Hanratty had felt all his life but had never been able to articulate, not even to himself. But it was there in the majestic melancholy of the music itself, and only reinforced by the words.

They applauded till their hands grew numb.

A few of the drunker ones even staggered to their feet and gave him an ovation.

And there was one more phenomenon Hanratty took note of—the certain look the women had been giving him. Not as if he were a too old, too chunky, too clichéd piano bar man but instead a very desirable piece of work. The same kind of looks the bartender David Sullivan was always getting.

Finished with "Without You," and realizing that he had now run through the six songs that had been left to him over the past few months, he sat down and began playing the standards Kenny Bentley insisted on, everything from Billy Joel to Barry Manilow, with a few Broadway tunes thrown in to give the proceedings a more mteropolitan air.

And he lost them then, as he always lost them then.

They started talking again, and grabbing cheap feels, and giggling and arguing.

Without the six original songs composed for him by the phantom composer, Richard Hanratty's act had gone back to what it had always been—background music.

Three hours later, finished for the night and sitting in his dressing room with a scotch and water and a filter cigarette, Hanratty stared at the six pieces of sheet music that he felt could secure him the sort of future he'd always wanted. If only he could be sure that once the songs became hits nobody would show up to claim them . . .

He got the chills, as happened many times after the show, because even playing ballads you worked up a sweat. He needed to get out of his jacket and shirt, wash up in the basin in the corner, and put on a turtleneck and regular tweed sportcoat.

He splashed water on his face and under his arms and then slapped on Brut and deodorant. Feeling much cleaner, he stepped to the closet and picked out the turtleneck he'd worn to the show tonight.

Because the club was so quiet—the unregistered aliens Bentley liked to hire for less than minimum wage sweeping up the floor now, David Sullivan preparing the bar for tomorrow—he was able to hear the whimper.

His first impression was that it belonged to an animal. A cat, perhaps, caught somewhere in the walls.

Then he remembered the piece of plywood over the duct opening in the closet wall. A cat lover, he wondered if a feline of some kind might not be caught down there.

He went over to the drawer and took out a long silver tube of flashlight and then went back to the closet and got down on his hands and knees and put his hand on the plywood rectangle again.

Still loose, it was easily pulled away from the nails mooring it.

He pushed the beam inside the wide mouth of metal duct and then poked his own head inside.

He saw what was down there instantly and just as instantly, he recoiled. His stomach knotted, he felt real nausea, and he banged the crown of his head pulling it from the duct.

He'd seen what had made the whimpering sound all right.

My God had he seen it.

After he had composed himself, and still armed with the flashlight, he replaced the piece of plywood, moved backward out of the closet, stood up, finished dressing, and then went out into the club to speak with David Sullivan.

"Bentley around?" Hanratty asked.

Sullivan sighed. "No, he and Sally split already."

"Good."

"What?"

"Oh. Nothing." Instinctively, Hanratty knew enough to keep what he'd seen to himself. "I'm going down to the basement."

Sullivan grinned. "It's okay, Richard. We've got a bathroom up here." Then, more seriously, "What's down in the basement?"

"A subbasement, if I remember right."

"Yes. We're close enough to the river that the sewer system runs right next to the subbasement, which used to be kind of a retaining wall before this part of the city burned down in the early part of the century."

Now it was Hanratty's turn to grin. "How do you know all this stuff, kid?"

Sullivan snapped his white bar towel like a whip. Hanratty had no doubt who the kid was whipping. "Well, when the woman you love spends all her time with a jerk like Bentley, you've got a lot of time to read." Then he shrugged. "Actually, I heard it on the news the other night. This whole area of the sewer system has become a refuge for some of the homeless who are wandering around."

"Poor bastards," Hanratty said. He nodded to the fifth of Chivas sitting next to the register. "How about a shot?"

"Sure." Sullivan poured and handed the shot glass to Hanratty. "It's on Bentley."

The first level of the basement was what you would expect to find—essentially a storehouse of supplies to keep the lounge running, everything from large cardboard boxes of napkins and paper plates to crates of glassed olives and cocktail cherries. The majority of the storage room, naturally enough, was taken up by tall and seemingly endless rows of brand name booze. The basement walls had been finished in imitation knotty pine and the floor had been given a perfunctory coat of green paint. Everything was tidy and dry and smelled of dust and the vapors of natural gas from the large furnace unit in the east corner.

Duct work of various types ran everywhere. It took Hanratty ten minutes to figure out which of the pieces of silver metal fed into his closet. Once he concluded that he'd found the right piece, he found its track along the ceiling over to the door to the subbasement, which was just where he suspected it would lead.

He had not forgotten what he'd seen in the duct work earlier. He would never forget.

It waited for him on the other side of the subbasement door. He could sense it.

He clicked on the flashlight, felt his stomach grab in anticipation, and put his hand on the door leading to the subbasement.

It was locked.

He spent the next five minutes trying everything from the edge of a chisel to a screwdriver—he found a tool kit in the corner—but nothing worked. The lock remained inviolate.

He raised his head, finally, and shone the light along the duct work leading over the door and beyond. He needed to find a section he could pry open.

This time from the tool kit he took a hammer and an even larger screwdriver. He went to work.

In all, it took twenty minutes. He cut his hands many times—he'd done sheet metal work two summers in college and it had always been a bitch—and he was soaked and cold with sweat.

His work complete, he two took cases of Cutty Sark, piled one on the other, and used them as a ladder.

Then he crawled up inside the duct work and started his inching passage down the angling metal cave till he reached its end.

His first reaction, once inside, was of claustrophobia. He thought of all those horror films he'd seen over the years about being buried alive. What if he never got out of here . . .

He moved forward, knowing that was his only hope.

Fortunately, the passage was straight, no sudden turns that would block or trap him.

After five minutes or so he began smelling more than dust and sheet metal and the rat droppings that he crushed beneath with his hands and knees. He began smelling—river water.

Then the duct ended abruptly and he let himself drop from it to a huge concrete tunnel that was obviously the sewer system. David Sullivan had been talking about. Everything smelled fetid. As he played the flashlight around on the walls, he saw red, blue, and yellow and green obscenities spray-painted on the filthy gray arching walls. Rats with burning, hungry eyes fed on the carcass of what had apparently been an opposum. Broken soda bottles, crushed cans, sticks with leaves that trailed like dead hair all floated in the foot of filthy water that ran down the curving floor of the sewer.

He spent the next few minutes getting oriented, moving the beam around, fascinated and sickened at what he saw. To think that people actually lived here . . .

Then he heard the whimpering again and when he wheeled around he saw, high up on this side of the wall, a ragged hole in the concrete.

The creature he had earlier glimpsed was, Hanratty was sure, inside that hole.

Steeling himself for his second glimpse of the thing, he walked through the dirty water until he was directly beneath the hole.

"Why don't you come down?"

Nothing.

"Why don't you come down?" Hanratty said, his voice reverberating off the peaked ceiling and the vast stretch of concrete cave. Still nothing.

"I won't hurt you. I want to help you." He paused. "You've been leaving those songs for me, haven't you?"

The whimpering sound—this time it was more like mewling—began again.

He stood on his tiptoes and played his light inside the dark hole a few feet above him. The opening made him think of a bird's nest. The reeking dampness choked him.

The opening was perhaps four feet deep and three feet high. Inside he saw a six pack of Coke, a loaf of Wonderbread, an open package of Oscar Meyer luncheon meat, several magazines including *Vogue* and *Harper*'s and then female clothes of all kinds, from undergarments to dresses and sweaters. Spread across the floor were several mismatched blankets. At this point he raised the beam and waved it in the rear of the opening, where it angled down sharply to meet the retaining wall behind.

This was where he found her.

This time her face wasn't deeply pitted with what appeared to be radiation burns of some kind. Nor was her head sleek and bald and likewise tufted with terrible burns. No, this time she wore a mask to cover her hideousness, a rubber Cinderella mask from the Disney version of the classic fairy tale.

She said something he could not understand. The mask made her words incomprehensible. She tried again and this time he heard, "Stay away."

"I want to help you. You're the one who writes the songs, aren't you?"

"Stay away."

If he hadn't seen her face without the mask, he would have taken the rest of her to be a quite beautiful woman with perfectly formed wrists, ankles and neck, and a pleasing swell of breast beneath her ragged man's work shirt and heavy blue cardigan and baggy jeans.

"You live down here, don't you?"

She cowered in the rear of the opening, covering the eye-holes in the mask as his beam bore in.

"Why would you live down here?"

But as soon as he'd spoken he knew exactly why she lived down here. Her face. That horribly scarred and boiled face.

"Would you come out of there so we can talk?"

She shook her head.

He went back to asking questions. "You work your way up the duct work and leave the songs on my piano in the middle of the night when nobody's there, don't you?"

Faintly, she nodded.

"But why? Why do you want me to have them?"

Once more she spoke and once more he had a difficult time understanding what she was trying to say. Finally, finally, he heard properly. "Turn out the light."

"Why?"

"I want to take this mask off so you can hear me more clearly."

"All right."

He clicked off the light, lowered the long silver tube of flashlight.

He heard the rumple of rubber being pulled off. The opening was now a black pit with no detail whatsoever.

From the gloom, she said, "At night I lie here and listen to you play the piano and sing. You have a very sad voice."

He laughed. " 'Sad as in pathetic."

"No, 'sad' as in troubled. Hopeless. And that's why I write the songs for you. Because you and I share the same kind of pain."

"You could make a fortune with your songs."

Now it was her turn to laugh, but when she did so

it sounded morose. "Yes, I suppose I could get my face on the cover of *People*."

"No, but—"

She sighed. "I write for my own pleasure—and yours, I hope."

"Believe me, I love your songs."

"You may have them."

"What?"

"I'm making a gift of them to you."

"But—"

"That's a very serious offer, Mr. Hanratty. Very serious. Now, I've talked enough and so have you."

"But I'd like to help you in some way."

She sighed once again, sounding old beyond imagining. "You can't help me, Mr. Hanratty. Only one man can. Only one man." She paused and said. "Now go, Mr. Hanratty. Please."

Her voice was resolute.

"I appreciate the songs."

"If they make you wealthy, Mr. Hanratty, promise me just one thing."

"What?"

"To never fall in love as foolishly as I did."

"But—"

"Leave now, Mr. Hanratty. Leave now."

He heard a rustling sound as the woman crawled to the back of her lair, lost utterly in the darkness.

He stared a moment longer at the wall of gloom keeping her hidden from him, and then he jumped down to the watery floor, and started his way back through the duct work and to Kenny's.

In the morning, he called New York and a music publisher who at first would not even take his call. But finally, adamant, he convinced the secretary to put him through to her boss, who turned out to be a woman with a somewhat mannered accent and a strongly cultivated hint of *ennui* in her voice.

He made the call from his small apartment cluttered as usual with scabrous cardboard circles from delivery pizza, beer cans and overflowing ashtrays. Grubby overcast light fell through the cracked window and fell on his lumpy unmade bed.

She was about to hang up when he said, "Listen, I'm sure you get thirty calls like this a week. But I really do have songs that could make both of us really wealthy. I really do."

"That will be all now," the woman said. "I'm quite busy and—"

"Two minutes."

"What?"

"I just want two minutes. I'm sitting at an upright piano and all I need to do is set the phone down and play you one of these songs for two minutes and—"

A frustrated sigh. "How old are you?"

"Huh?"

"I asked how old you are."

"Mid-forties. Why?"

Her laugh startled him. "Because you're like dealing with a little boy." She exhaled cigarette smoke. "All right, Mr. Hanratty, you've got two minutes."

So he played. With fingers that would never be envied by concert artists. With a voice that not even the raspiest rocker would want. But even given that, even given his hangover, even given the grubby winter light, even given the mess and muck of his apartment—even given all that there was beauty that morning in his apartment.

The beauty of the deformed woman's pain and yearnings and imprisonment in a face few could stand to gaze on.

He played much longer than two minutes and somehow he knew that the woman on the other end of the line wouldn't hang up. Because of the beauty of the melody and the poetry of the words.

By the time he finished the song, he'd forgotten where he was. He had given himself over completely to the music.

When he picked the receiver up again, he was sweating, trembling. "Well?" he said.

"How soon can you catch a flight to New York?"

"A couple of hours."

"I'll have a car waiting for you, Mr. Hanratty." As hard as she tried, she could not keep the tears from her voice. The tears the music had inspired.

Hanratty went to New York with a checking account of $437.42. He returned with a checking account of $50,437.42—and a contract that promised much, much more once Sylvia Hamilton, the music publisher, interested top recording artists in these properties. She was talking Streisand, for openers, and she was talking quite seriously.

As he deplaned, he caught the white swirling bite of the blizzard that had virtually shut the city down. He had to wait an hour for a taxi to take him directly to Kenny's. Bentley had not wanted him to leave in the first place and told him that if he took more than two days off, he'd be fired. In an expansive mood now, Hanratty planned to finish out the week at the lounge, and then head immediately back to New York where Sylvia (a not bad-looking older lady whom

Hanratty felt he was going to get to know a lot better) was already finding an apartment for him.

Coming in on the crosstown expressway was an excruciating crawl behind big yellow trucks spewing billions of sand particles beneath whirling yellow lights into the late afternoon gloom and watching the ditches where obviously overworked and weary city cops were checking to see that the people who'd slid off the road were all right. Fog only added to the air of claustrophobia Hanratty felt in the back seat of the cab that smelled of cigarette smoke and disinfectant.

He saw the red emergency lights a block before the Checker reached the lounge. They splashed through the blizzard like blood soaking through a very white sheet. His stomach tightened the way it always had when he'd been a little boy and feared that a siren meant that something had happened to one of his parents or to his brother or sister.

Something was wrong at Kenny's.

The police already had sawhorse barricades up, but in this kind of weather they were almost pointless. It was too bitterly cold to stand outside on a night like this and gawk at somebody else's misfortune.

He paid off the cabbie and fled the vehicle immediately.

A tall, uniformed officer tried to stop him from going into the brick-faced lounge but after Hanratty explained who he was, the cop waved him in.

"What happened?" Hanratty said, his voice tight.

"You better ask one of the detectives."

What surprised him, two steps across the threshold, was how strange the familiar place appeared. Violence had a way of doing that—of altering forever a setting one once took pleasure in.

From behind, a voice said, "May I be of any help?"

He turned to see a gray-haired detective in an expensive gray suit and a regimental striped tie step forward. He wore his ID tag pinned to his left lapel.

Hanratty once again explained who he was.

"You're the piano player."

"Yes," Hanratty said. "Why?"

"Sullivan said you'd vouch for him."

"David? The bartender?"

"Right. We've got him in custody."

"Custody."

The detective, who looked as much like a banker as a cop, nodded. "For killing the owner of this place, Kenny Bentley."

Hanratty felt a shock travel from his chest all the way out to the ends of his extremities. He could easily enough imagine the scenario Detective Keller (that being the name on the ID) had just sketched out. Sally Carson had come to work beaten up once again and David, unable to control himself, had grabbed Kenny and—

"Stabbed," the detective said. "In his office."

Hanratty was jarred back into reality. "You said stabbed?"

"Yes."

"No way."

"What?"

"David might beat him to death. Or choke him. But stab him—no way."

"You may be a great piano player, Mr. Hanratty, but I can't say that I put much stock in your abilities as a detective."

As he finished speaking, a white-coated man from

the crime lab came out of Kenny Bentley's private office and drew Keller aside.

Hanratty looked around again. The chairs had not been taken down from the tables. The lights behind the long, elegant bar had not been lit. The stage seemed ridiculously small and shabby. Even the Steinway lacked sheen.

"I need to go have one more look at the body, Mr. Hanratty," Keller said. "You'll excuse me."

Without quite knowing why, Hanratty said, "Mind if I go?"

Keller offered a bitter smile. "You hated him, too, and want to make sure he's dead?"

"Oh, I hated him. But that isn't why I want to go."

"No?"

"No. I just can't believe David is the killer."

Keller shrugged and exchanged an ironic glance with the crime lab man. "Well, if you enjoy looking at corpses, Mr. Hanratty, then I guess I can't see any harm in your coming along."

The office showed virtually no sign of struggle. The flocked red wallpaper and gaslight-style wall fixtures and huge leather-padded desk all suggested Kenny Bentley's fascination with the Barbary Coast of the 1900s.

Bentley sat in his tall leather desk chair, dumped face forward now on his desk. A common wooden-handled butcher knife protruded from the right side of his spine. It had not been pushed all the way in, a good three inches of metal blade still showing.

Hanratty said, "Even if David had stabbed him, you don't think he would have pushed the knife all the way in—with his strength and his anger?"

Keller's eyes narrowed. Obviously Hanratty had

made sense to him no matter how much he didn't want to admit it.

Hanratty moved around the desk. Kenny Bentley's body already smelled sourly of decay.

"Hey," Keller said, "don't touch anything."

"I won't."

Hanratty examined the proximity of a pencil to Bentley's right hand. Then he leaned over and stared at a single word scrawled in a dying man's clumsy script.

The word was Harcourt.

Keller must have caught Hanratty's surprised expression. "Something I might be interested in, Mr. Hanratty?"

Hanratty shook his head. "Guess not." He took his cigarettes from his trench coat and stuck one carefully between his lips. "Maybe I'll go have myself a drink."

Keller, no longer so unfriendly said, "Maybe seeing him dead proves you didn't hate him quite as much as you thought, huh?"

"Oh, no," Hanratty said. "It just proves that I hated him even *more* than I thought."

"What?" Keller said.

But Hanratty didn't answer. He just went out of the office and across the small dance floor to the bar where he had himself several good belts of Chivas while the police finished their work.

Two hours later, Keller came over and said, "Afraid we're going to have to throw you out, Mr. Hanratty. We're closing down for the night."

The ambulance people had come and gone, as had at least a dozen other people. Now Kenny Bentley was headed for the morgue.

Hanratty set down his drink and said, "Fine."

He went outside. The wind and snow whipped at him. Whatever kind of drunk he'd been building was quickly banished by the chill. He walked ten blocks, along a black wrought iron fence on the other side of which was the sprawling river, its pollutants frozen for the moment by ice.

When he figured he'd spent half an hour, he turned around and walked back the way he'd come, back to Kenny's place.

He had a key to the back door so getting in was no problem, even if the police signs warning of CRIME SCENE were ominous. Inside was shadowy and warm. He went to the dressing room. He took off his trench coat and went immediately to the closet where he lifted off the plywood rectangle that covered the duct.

This time, he made the trip in less than fifteen minutes.

When he'd constructed another jerry-rigged ladder and gotten up on it and clicked on the flashlight, he got a brief glimpse of her without the Cinderella mask. She must have been sleeping and he'd surprised her. The lair was the same as before, reminding him of an animal's cave.

This time he recognized the horrible raw burns for what they were. Not radiation but acid.

As she grappled on the mask, he said, "I know who you are."

"I knew you'd figure it out."

"You worked for Kenny Bentley two years ago and went to the Harcourt Academy, which is a music school for particularly gifted people. Kenny got jealous of you and threw acid on you and you were so ashamed of your looks that you took up living down here where nobody could see you."

"Please turn out the light."

"All right."

Once again, he spoke to her in darkness. The sewer system echoed with their voices. The amber eyes of rats flicked through the gloom.

"I went to doctors," she said. "But they couldn't help me."

"Why didn't you turn Kenny in?"

"Because I want my own kind of vengeance. Just seeing him go to prison wouldn't have satisfied me."

"They think somebody else killed him. A nice young kid named David Sullivan."

"I know. I crawled up the duct and heard the police talking and then arrest him." Pause. "Get ready to catch something, Mr. Hanratty."

From the blackness a small white oblong of paper drifted down to his hands.

"That's a complete confession, Mr. Hanratty. Your friend will be freed as soon as you hand it over to the police."

"I'm sorry," he said.

"You know something, Mr. Hanratty, I sincerely believe you are."

The gunshot came just after her words, deafening as the noise of it bounced off the walls of her small lair, acrid as the odor of gunpowder filled his nostrils.

"My God," he said. "My God."

He stood there on his rickety makeshift ladder for a long time, thinking of her hideous face and her beautiful songs.

When he jumped free of the boxes and stuffed the envelope into his trousers, he realized he was crying, the way he sometimes cried when he played her songs.

He paused for a moment and shone the flashlight up the wall and across the dark opening again.

Finally, he did the only thing he could do. He walked away, the sound of his footsteps softly splashing the fetid water loud inside the huge cave of the sewer.

He hadn't quit crying yet and he wondered if he ever would.

Synandra

"Our cosmology is a double exposure of two realities superimposed."

—Phillip K. Dick

And everywhere that Synandra went, death was sure to follow.

In 520 BC, Carthage was a city of nearly a million, spending all its attention upon the commerce of Negro slaves, ivory, metal, and precious stones. Yet despite all this prosperity, a famine took the city near the end of its reign, a famine that left men killing their own children to spare them the cruel death of starvation. An unnamed scribe from the time described how he one night saw "a beautiful woman wrapped in a mist of some kind, who walked the streets accompanied by a wolf whose fur was the color of swirling smoke and

167

whose eyes were redolent of midnight moons."

In 1348 AD the plague reached England and destroyed half the population; in Europe the toll rose to twenty-five million dead. A Dominican friar noted in his journal that "Every night I follow her, this woman so beautiful and terrifying, as she passes among the plague-dead and dying in the streets, trailed by the eerie wolf that calls her name in a human voice. 'Synandra! Synandra!' I saw her take a dying young man to her and kiss him with an eroticism that was sinful to behold. I did not realize, not until the young man fell to her feet, that she was not kissing him at all, but rather sucking his soul from him, and ingesting it herself."

In 1943 a Jew at the Belsen death camp confided to his journal that he had had nightmares for the past few months "of an astonishingly beautiful woman, her face and body obscured by some kind of mist, pushing my father's perambulator into one of the rooms where the cyanide killed as many as thirty at a time." A few days after this journal entry, the man saw exactly that, his father disappearing down a sloping ramp to the death chamber . . . pushed in his wheelchair by the woman who was in turn followed by a wolf "who was the color of 3:00 a.m. and who evoked in me a chill so terrible that I could not stop from trembling, and could not even cry out a warning to my poor frightened father."

The smells are what I can never get used to.

I've been timelining for half my life, thirty-seven years realtime, and no amount of preparatory drugging, no amount of inhalants can help me. I always spend the first few minutes in a new timezone letting my sinuses have their way with me—runny eyes, sneezing, a constricting throat. And the foulest smells imaginable stenching my olfactory system.

Today was no different. Fifteen minutes earlier I'd climbed through a hole in the air that was instantly sealed up behind me. I had in my hand a psychID card that identified me as Jason Parks, History Professor from timezone 2178. As part of my tenure, I'm granted three timetrips a year, usually to zones that I'm studying for discussion in my classes.

But this trip was different. This trip was an emergency. I had just reached timezone 2034 AD.

An early autumn dusk—mauve sky, cool and graying darkness, a sprawl of bright stars, the dying sounds of birds in leafy trees—took the world into night.

I stood on a street filled with buildings that looked about ready for demolition. The Timeline offices are usually hidden in neighborhoods like this one.

I checked the address in my hand and started down the street. Ragged, raw children of all ages bolted from an alley just ahead of me and descended on a newer car that had been crazy enough to come through this neighborhood. They swarmed over it, laughing, cursing, screaming, rending it like scavengers tearing a carcass. They started stripping it of everything that could possibly be resold. They let the elderly fat man driving it escape screaming down the block. They didn't shoot him until he was a few hundred yards away.

I hurried on.

A dozen women shouted out all the erotic things they wanted to do to me with their mouths. A beggar threw himself at my feet and beseeched me for money. A madman stood in the center of the sidewalk, slashing his left arm with a razor blade.

The number I wanted was 1204, a narrow building set between two wider buildings. I went up a steep dark staircase. The smells were overwhelming—vomit, blood, feces, street drugs.

Atop the landing was a long hallway with four office doors on each side. Timeline was on the right, three doors down.

Dirty, dim light shone behind the pebbled glass in the door. The door itself was ajar an inch or so.

Behind me, at the top of the stairs, footsteps sounded.

I ducked inside the Timeline door, closed it, clipped off the overhead light.

In the dusty fetid darkness of the building, a man walked down this corridor whistling an ancient love song. A Jerome Kern song, in fact, Kern being a popular composer I'd sometimes taught.

The whistling went past the door and on down the hall.

A door was opened with a key that had to be wiggled violently; door was opened, man walked heavily inside, door was closed behind him.

I clipped the light back on, ready to face the Timeline employee at the desk behind me. I'd caught only a momentary glimpse of him. He would certainly be wondering what the hell was going on here. My abrupt entrance had probably frightened him into silence.

So I turned around and faced him.

He was a young, fleshy man in a dirty white shirt and a pair of heavy black-rimmed glasses sitting behind a battered desk that contained a computer screen far too sophisticated and expensive for a building like this.

He was still silent, but it wasn't me who had silenced him. It was the blaster hole in the middle of his stomach that had done it. Now I was sure that all my suspicions were confirmed. My student assistant Thornburg had indeed stolen one of my timepasses and put dozens of hours on it figuring out where he could best intersect with the creature known as Synandra. I'd become aware of her by accident, by seeing that the same wraithlike woman was present at most of history's great tragedies. Who was she? What was she? I hadn't been able to find out, but I had the feeling that my assistant Thornburg knew.

He'd had to check in with the dead young man here to get instructions about this timezone—where to eat, what areas to avoid, any notable festivities or holidays coming up.

But after getting the information, Thornburg had killed him, wanting to erase his presence on this world so that the University would never learn what he was up to. And nobody could track Synandra through him, in case some other professor on some other timeline had also stumbled on to her mysterious existence.

I found another chair, pushed the dead man a few feet away, and spent the next twenty minutes on the computer.

The dead man had been nice enough to lay out an entire three-day vacation plan for Bob Thornburg, the finale of which was a day-long stay at a resort in the mountains. Thornburg had obviously passed himself off as a tourist.

But there was one address that didn't fit in with a

vacation plan, an address, according to the computer map, only a few blocks from here.

This was what Thornburg had really been after. This was where he would find Synandra. And so would I.

In addition to regular academic studies, the University specializes in developing weapons for the government. For instance, it was rumored—though as yet I'd never seen any evidence of it—that a mind-scrub unit no larger than a pistol was now in development. Mind-scrubbing was used on all revolutionaries and on many kinds of sex deviants. At its most powerful, the process utterly erased a person mentally and spiritually; not only was his memory taken away, so were all his instincts and proclivities.

There was rumored to be another type of police tool in development, too. But I knew this was more than a rumor. I held one in my hand. The scientists on the project called it a dissolver. It could break down molecular structures in a matter of moments.

I pointed it at the head of my friend the dead man and watched him vanish. The only trouble was the smell. They needed to work on that.

After I finished with him, I set to work on the computer, destroying it as well. When I got back to University, I'd let Timeline know that I'd wiped out all evidence of their existence in this particular timezone and that they'd have to set up a new office.

Ten minutes later, I walked down a narrow street filled with men and women who were falling to their knees and literally tearing off their clothes and ripping out their hair at the bloody roots. A man in flowing white robes and a crown of thorns stood on the back of a flatbed truck. In one hand he held a microphone and in the other a cigarette. He exhorted the people to go out and rob and steal and plunder and murder if necessary but bring back green American cash because wasn't the grand total of tonight's Christ-A-Thon looking particularly woeful. A mostly naked girl, who couldn't have been more than fifteen, shot her hip and pointed seductively to a flashing white sign that read $1,350. "We need a lot more fucking money than that, my friends," the guy in the white robes told them in a harsh voice. Meanwhile, the true believers continued to wail and moan and tear at themselves. I suspected that the good reverend had probably given them too much of whatever drug he used on them.

Then into gunfire darkness. A block where all the streetlights had been shot out. Where all the house-lights and apartment lights were dark. A block where the only illumination was the muzzle-flame of weapons firing back and forth across the street at each other. Some kind of ongoing feud.

I ran down the middle of the street, zigging and zagging, keeping my head down, anticipating the awful *thunk* of a bullet ripping into my flesh and tearing up my vital organs as it made its way out the other side.

The street, and the gunfire, fell away, and then I was on some kind of pier, vast black water tinged with moonlight, a lonely foghorn hooting in the midnight distance.

The pier had been on the computer map.

Not far now. Just a few blocks.

Freezing inside my own sweat, I ran along the pier, northward bound.

At one point the pier jogged left. Remembering the

map, I went right, now running down three or four
blocks of alleys where huge plump rats ate their way
down inside garbage cans, their pointed tails flicking
in the night like antenna.

Then I heard the mob.

There's maybe no other sound quite so terrifying.
A large group of people driven insane with drugs or
drink but most especially driven insane with hatred.
I've been to Nazi Germany and I've heard such mobs
first-hand. I've also seen blacks lynched in Missis-
sippi at the turn of the century. And elderly white
people kicked to death by young blacks in LA.

Mobs always sound the same. Always.

I drew to the head of the final alley and got my
first look at them. They carried ball-bats and lead
pipes and torches whose flames snapped in the wind.
They were rich and poor, young and old, black and
white. They flung rocks at the windows of the two
large Victorian-style houses that sat on the corner.
They also hurled an unceasing list of ugly names at
the people inside the houses, some of whom could be
seen in silhouette at the windows. Even from here,
you could tell how frail they were.

The plague had begun to spread in this timezone,
and these were the people singled out for blame.

The mob lunged as one toward the houses, their
voices thunderous beneath the same moon that had
witnessed Druid sacrifices and witches burned at Sa-
lem and American Japanese in prison camps during
World War II.

And once again, Synandra would be pleased. And
she would pass through this night, an angel of sorts,
eyes alight, sated for the moment by this misery and

treachery, her smokeghost wolf crying his pleasure, too.

I shouted for them to stop, but it was already too late. The houses were already in flames and soon enough would come the cries of the dying trapped within the walls.

"She'll really like this very much."

Somehow even above the din, I heard the voice, and knew who it belonged to even before I turned to face him.

Thornburg.

"I knew you'd catch on eventually," he said. Handsome, blond, and smirky, he looked at me with his usual disdain. "You think you know about her, Professor, but you don't. You think you understand this—" and here he indicated the mob as they set the second house afire, "—but you don't. You think it's about good and evil. But it's not. Not any more. That's where your scholarship is so pathetic, Professor. So pathetic."

Thornburg considered himself my superior in every way, including scholarship. "I'm going to tell you about her, Professor, so I hope you'll listen."

"It's hard to listen when people are dying in the background."

"They don't matter," he said. "That's what you don't understand." The smirk again. "Synandra is several million years old, Professor. The being that created the universe had two trusted allies, whom he'd also created, his son Clotho and his daughter Synandra. But Clotho was jealous of Synandra because he knew that her son would some day come to hold a very special place in the master's mind. And so Clotho found a being who could transform one thing into another, and he forever transformed Synandra's son into a wolf. And then, because he knew that suffering caused his sister such pain, he began destroying that half of the universe which the master had given her. Only reluctantly did she begin to retaliate—by destroying the worlds in Clotho's half of the universe. And after a time, so violent and all-consuming did her rage become, that she forgot all about sparing lives . . . and became just like Clotho himself. She took the same pleasure in destroying his worlds as he took in destroying hers—plagues and novas and asteroid attacks." The smirk. "She uses whatever whim strikes her fancy at the moment. This is the real nature of the universe, Professor, the battle between Synandra and her brother Clotho and it will continue a billion years into the future."

"I'm going to stop her," I said. "That's why I came here."

I thought he might respond to that with a joke, but instead, as if he'd heard a silent call, he angled his head to the right, and there, far down the alley, she stood, beautiful beyond description, radiant hair tumbling to naked shoulders, smokeghost wolf, her son, crying his pleasure at the sight of the houses burning.

I started to reach for my dissolver, but Thornburg put a hard hand on my arm. "Don't be a fool, Professor. You can't destroy her. She is a force you know nothing about." He smiled. "Anyway, in a few minutes, you won't even remember anything about her. I've taken her name out of all your computers. And now I'm going to take her name out of your memory."

From his pocket, he took a small silver pistol that looked like a miniature blaster. "You've heard about the mind-scrubber weapons? The tiny ones we're researching at University? Here's the prototype."

And just then, I heard the first sobs and pleas of the men inside the houses as the flames reached them. And I saw a man on fire climb out a third-story window and fall through the air. The mob gathered around him and kicked and stoned him to death.

And I saw Synandra, so beautiful inside the mist swirling about her—and I saw the smokeghost wolf— begin to walk away down the long, dark alley, satisfied now that their job was done.

They would stay long enough in this timezone to make sure that millions of other plague victims died in similar ways. And then it would be on to another timezone.

"You won't have to worry about her any more, Professor." Thornburg said, as I turned back to him. "I'm going to follow her from planet to planet, timezone to timezone. This is the only history that matters, Professor, the battle between Synandra and her brother Clotho."

"And the lives they destroy in their selfish little war?"

The smirk. "As I said, Professor, you won't have to worry about that any more."

He raised the prototype and shot me with it.

"Nice timetrip?"

"Very nice. Thank you."

His colleague Brendan stood in the doorway of his office.

"I was afraid something was wrong."

"Oh?" he said.

"You put in for an emergency timetrip."

He looked up from his computer, startled. "I did?"
"Uh-huh."

He shook his head. "Don't know why I did that. Just took a nice little trip was all. I must have punched the wrong access code. Hit emergency instead of vacation. All I did was relax."

That was not true, not exactly, because he wasn't sure what he'd done. He had no memory of the 48 hours he was gone. But all that could mean was that he hadn't done anything significant enough to remember, right? We like to think we're masters of timetripping, but we're not, he thought. People still have all sorts of strange reactions to going back and forth in time. He'd obviously just had a strange reaction himself.

The tone rang for class.

"Well, time to go share my wisdom with my students," Brendan said.

He smiled. "That shouldn't take long."

Brendan laughed, and left.

He turned back to his computer, checking messages he'd received while timetripping.

There was only one, from his assistant Bob Thornburg.

I know this is crazy, Professor Parks, the message began, *but I just couldn't stay away from my fiancée any longer. I've given up my scholarship. By the time you read this, I'll be living with Emmie in Portland. I've enjoyed working with you. I learned a whole lot.*

For a long time, he just stared at it. Something about his timetrip and Thornburg . . . some vague memory that teased him. . . .

But no, he thought, there's no connection. Just another odd reaction to timetripping itself. He looked back at the message and smiled. Who would have thought that such a smug academic as Bob Thornburg had it in him to give up his scholarship and run away for love?

But then, he thought, *there are a lot of things about this old universe we don't understand.*

Junior

The first thing my Pa did when we came to this town was kill a man. Actually, two men, if you're of a mind to count Indians.

Two years ago, it was.

This happened over at the livery stable, and it happened the way it always did with Pa—fast and pretty much unexpected. It was that temper of Pa's that always did it.

The livery man overcharged my Pa for some smithing work. Or my Pa said he did, anyway. He and Ma had been drinking some of that liquor my uncle puts up, and well Pa's kind of mean even when he ain't drunk so when he's got a snootful . . . The livery man and his Indian friend started arguing with my Pa and, being that they were both armed, my Pa saw no reason not to kill them. There were witnesses who testified to the Sheriff that it was all fair and legal, the way it always was when Pa killed people, at least most of the time.

What the livery man and the Indian didn't know is that they had just gone up against Earle C. Kenton, Sr.

But the town knew who'd they gone up against.

By the time our wagon drew up in front of the small house my Pa had bought along the creek, as many as twenty townspeople stood in our yard, bringing us all kinds of good gifts, everything from smoked meat to wine to tobacco. A lot of them stood under the big shade tree that Ma liked so much.

Earle C. Kenton, Sr., probably the most feared man in the entire Territory, was somebody you wanted to keep happy. Real happy. Even the Sheriff was there that day with some fresh cut flowers for Ma and a pint of sour mash for Pa, which, unfortunately, Ma snatched up before Pa could drink it. She likes to pour whiskey on boils. Her other favorite thing is to squeeze blackheads. She likes to make it hurt when she's squeezing. I got a lot of them on my back and she always says, "You're just like a little girl, you sissy," whenever I complain about her hurting me.

And so we became citizens of Alberne, Wyoming, pop. 2,104, every single one of them living in terror of displeasing my Pa, Earle C. Kenton, Sr.

This was in hot ripe September—September 4, 1886 if you want the exact date—right when school started.

My first morning there, nobody was especially friendly to me. I admit I've always been a little bit plump, and my eyeglasses are pretty darn thick when you come right down to it, and I always had had a certain problem with gas—but once the teacher introduced me—"Boys and girls, this is Earle C. Kenton, Jr."—they all looked at me in a whole new way.

They didn't have much choice.

Their daddies were afraid of my Pa; and so they were smart enough to be afraid of me.

I guess right here I should tell you some of the things that I did *not* do over the past two years of living here.

I did *not* set fire to the Lutheran church.

I did *not* stampede the Bar2's horses the night they trampled that Mex family that had been sleeping outdoors near the line shack.

I did *not* hang all six of Widow Barker's cats by their tails on the clothesline, and then set them on fire.

Now I admit that I have sometimes abused my position in this town. But tongues got so wild that they had me doing everything terrible that was ever done in the whole Territory.

I *did* set fire to that blind girl's braids that time, and the fire *did* get sort of out of control.

I *did* make Tom Wyman dive off the bridge but I didn't have any idea he'd strike his head on a rock and be paralyzed the rest of his life.

And I *did* switch tracks on that engine but I *didn't* have any idea that it would run into that other engine. And anyway, nobody was hurt all *that* bad, except for a couple of them.

Oh, and one other thing: I *did* do a little bit of fibbing that day when I told my Pa that my teacher Mr. O'Neill got mad at me and slapped me across the face. Actually, he didn't slap me, he just said, "Everybody else may be afraid of you, Earle, Jr., but I'm not. And if you don't have your homework in to-morrow, I'm going to give you an F." True, Mr. O'Neill *was* unarmed when my Pa killed him but I quick-like slipped a gun into his hand so that when the Sheriff saw him lying there, he looked up at Pa and said, "Sure looks like it was a fair fight to me, Mr. Kenton, sir."

I was sleeping when Ma got home last night. She'd gone with Pa to the next county to look at some land.

The liquor from the Silver Dollar had me sleeping pretty good. Technically, they aren't supposed to serve me because of me being only sixteen and all but they aren't about to argue. I didn't even hear Ma come in, or light the kerosene lantern, or pull the chair up to my bed. From what she said, I didn't even feel her shake me at first.

"Earle, Jr., you gotta wake up. It's terrible, it's terrible."

I didn't really want to wake up but I couldn't get back to sleep without knowing what she meant by "it's terrible" so I sat up on the edge of the bed and started rubbing sleep from my eyes. I stank of perfume and I knew it. I always cadge a free gal or two couple nights a week at Emma's red light house out on the edge of town. Emma doesn't really want to give her gals away for free but I always just kind of hint that my Pa, Earle, Sr., wouldn't be very happy if he knew she was hurting my feelings that way, and then she gives me pick of the litter.

"What's wrong?" I said.

The only light was moonlight; the only sound my Ma's cursing.

"You know what the dumb idiot did?"

She didn't really expect me to answer.

She just went right on.

"He seen this rattler by the side of the road and Pa was dead-ass drunk and he took his gun out and tried to kill the snake and then guess what?"

It was another one of those questions she liked to ask. Rhetorical, is what I think that sissy teacher Mr. O'Neill called them. Any time I ever answered one of them, she slapped me. So I knew to be quiet.

"The darned bullet hit a rock and ricocheted up and hit him right in the head."

"Hit Pa in the head?"

She slapped me hard across the mouth. "You stupid moron, that's what I said ain't it? Hit him right in the head. Now you come out and help me get him out of the wagon."

He was worse than she said.

I couldn't see his face, there was so much blood.

I got his shoulders and she got his legs and we carried him inside and laid him out on the bed.

She got a lantern lit and then stared down at his face and said, "I sure hope he don't die."

I nodded. "I sure hope so, too."

She looked up at me sharply. "He dies, this whole town's gonna turn on us, you know that, boy?"

"I know."

"No more free meat from the butcher for me," she said.

"And no more free cigars for me at Swenson's."

And no more gettin' all the bustles and bonnets I want from Freida's Lady's Shop."

"And no more shootin' free pool over at Spitzer's."

"And no more pickin' out free furniture down at Sondrol's."

"And no more gettin' free *Ned Buntlines* over at Nicholson's."

We both looked down at him at the same time and said the same mournful thing. "Doggone it, Pa, you miserable sonofagun, you *can't* die. You just can't!"

But he was worse in the morning. He wasn't even moaning much.

"You gonna get Doc over here?" I said.

"Junior, you always will be a damned idiot, won't you?"

"Huh?"

"If I get Doc over here," Ma said, "then he'll tell everybody in town that Pa is dyin'—and then they won't be afraid of us no more."

"Oh, right, guess I didn't think of that."

She leaned over the bed and checked him out. The blood was all crusted in his hair and down the side of his face. He was paler than the white sheet he laid on.

"He's just about gone," she said. "So we got to get started."

"Get started?"

She sighed one of those deep sighs of hers then slapped me a good one right across the face.

"Figure it out, boy. We got to get out of this town before people figure out Pa is dead, right?"

"Right."

"But we got somethin' else to do before we leave here, don't we?"

"We do?"

Another deep sigh. But at least this time she didn't slap me.

"We got to get everything we've been wantin' to

get, and do it in a real hurry—get it while we can still get it free."

I finally figured out what Ma was talking about.

Of course.

Nobody was gonna give us anything free once they knew that Pa was dead.

"I been wantin' that saddle," I said.

"And I been wantin' that real purty emerald ring."

"And I been wantin' that Remington rifle."

"And I been wantin' that high-necked blouse."

"And I been wantin' that lariat like the fella throws in the Wild West Show."

"And I been wantin' a prairie wolf robe like I seen in the Sears catalog."

"And I been wantin'—"

"Junior, we got to get busy and get all the stuff we want and bring it back here and load up the wagon and git out of town before they find him."

We took another look down at Pa, who looked sorrowful weak now. He could barely even moan.

"We got to get busy," Ma said.

In case you're interested, the saddle I wanted was a Texas style with Mexican hide on the seat and on the horn and cantle as well. And the fenders was extra wide.

Mr. Bulow, the saddlemaker, was just handing it over when Sheriff Lacy walked in.

"Morning," he said to both of us, standing in the sunlight streaming through the front window.

We both morninged him back.

"That's a right smart saddle," Sheriff Lacy said.

"Best one I got," Mr. Bulow said, and you could

see in his eyes he wasn't too happy about giving it to me for free.

"Puttin' it on the 'account', huh?" the Sheriff said. Bulow nodded, still looking unhappy.

"Oh, one more thing to put on the account, Mr. Bulow," I said. "You had a rawhide lariat in here the other day. I'd sure like to take that one home to Pa. He tole me just last night how much he'd like to have it."

Mr. Bulow frowned and said, "I sold the one you're talkin' about. I'll have to see if I've got another one back in the stock room. You can stop by a little later."

"I'll do that, Mr. Bulow," I said, and walked outside carrying my saddle.

"You're havin' a busy mornin'," Sheriff Lacy said walking along the board sidewalk, him nodding good morning to ladies in sunbonnets and men in Stetsons. "Every store I stop in, they tell me you just been there and put something on the account."

"Well, there was a whole bunch of stuff Pa told me to get for him today, so I guess I *have* been kind of busy."

Just then, Mr. Houseman from the general store opened his door and pushed a wheelbarrow full of stuff in front of us on the sidewalk.

"Here's all the things you wanted, Junior," he said. He sounded even unhappier than Mr. Bulow had when he'd handed me the saddle. I told Mr. Houseman to throw in a wheelbarrow so I'd have some way to get all the stuff home.

"That sure is a mighty impressive mountain of merchandise there," Sheriff Lacy said.

There were fancy shirts and leather boots and a couple of Colts and some ammunition and some Ned

Buntlines and two gold railroad watches and a Remington breech load and some duck calls for hunting next fall and a nice new fireman's lantern and then on top of it all—the brand new saddle.

Sheriff Lacy looked at the merchandise and then looked at Mr. Houseman and said, "Sure wish *I* could afford all this stuff."

"Sure wish I could, too," Mr. Houseman said, still mighty unhappy as he wiped his hands on his denim store apron.

"Well," I said, just to remind them of why I was getting all this merchandise free of charge, "I'd better get this on home to Pa. We sure wouldn't want to get him in a bad mood now, would we?"

I said a good morning real nice and polite, and then relieved Mr. Houseman of the wheelbarrow.

When I got home, Ma was loading the wagon. It was damned near three-quarters full and none of the stuff was old, either. She was only taking the items she'd gotten that morning. There were dresses and fancy lamps and huge picture hats and parasols and high-button shoes and leather traveling bags and two trunks and a steroscopic camera and even the stove she'd always fancied down at Semple's.

"How'd you get all this home?" I said.

"Oh, they helped me, Junior. I just told them that Pa was on a drinkin' jag and in a real terrible mood." She grinned. "They always help me real nice and polite whenever I tell 'em that."

After we loaded everything up, we went inside to pay our last respects.

Pa was dead.

Ma slapped him a lot and I kicked him three times

in the ribs and he didn't make even a peep so we knew for sure he was dead. Pa would've killed us for abusing him that way if he hadn't been dead.

Ma glanced around the house and said, "We had a nice good life here, Junior. But now it's time to skee-daddle."

Just as she said that, I heard heavy footsteps on the front porch, and then the door was flung inward and there stood Sheriff Lacy with his badge and his carbine.

"I don't want neither of you to move," he said.

Behind him, out on the lawn, I could see a whole crowd of people, maybe thirty or forty. A lot of them were the merchants we'd been visiting this morning.

"He's gonna kill you for bargin' in here like that," Ma said. "Kill you right in your tracks."

"Where is he?" Sheriff Lacy said.

"He's sleepin' off a drunk," Ma said.

When Sheriff Lacy walked past us, two men took his place in the doorway: Mr. Houseman from the general store and Mr. Semple from the hardware store where Ma got the stove.

They both had carbines.

I looked at Ma and she looked at me.

She had one of those expressions where I knew she wanted to slap somebody and slap him real hard and for a real long time.

Sheriff Lacy came back and said to Mr. Houseman and Mr. Semple, "Just what we suspected, gentlemen. They were piling up the merchandise before they got out of town. Earle C. Kenton, Sr. is in there, dead."

Mr. Houseman turned in the doorway and shouted to the crowd. "Earle Kenton, Sr.'s dead! Did you hear that everybody? Earle Kenton, Sr.'s dead!"

Not even at a baseball game where the home team just hit a home run had I ever heard such cheering.

Sheriff Lacy pointed his carbine at us and said, "Outside, you two. And now."

I guess I expected them to be cursing at us, or maybe even throwing stuff at us, but all that crowd did was stand in a semi-circle under the big shade tree and watch us.

And then one man stepped from the crowd and it was Mr. Bulow the saddlemaker and he stepped up to me and said, "You know that rawhide lariat you wanted, Junior? Well, here it is."

They hanged Ma first, and then it was my turn.

Lover Boy

Ted and I caught the squeal, and it was the kind that makes for good war stories later in cop bars.

"You're not going to believe what happened," he said, laughing.

And when he told me, I laughed, too.

"Captain wants us to interview her," Ted said. "She's skimming back with him, then we'll meet her in the Pentathol room."

I sat there looking at the place, all the dazzling lights out front, all the sexy throbbing music filling the ears. Places like this were all over the city now, and there were bound to be victims.

Humorous as the situation was, the woman who'd just been arrested had been a victim, for sure. Even knowing the little I knew, I felt kind of sorry for her.

* * *

"Name?"

"Vanessa Conway."

"Age?"

"Thirty-six."

"Married?"

"You know I am."

"We have to make it official, ma'am, for the record, I mean."

Sigh. "Yes, married."

"Husband's name?"

"Robert Conway."

"Children?"

"Two."

"Ages?"

"Six and eight."

I looked over at Ted. The Captain likes us to interview certain people because he says we have the common touch. We don't have the kind of handsome faces you see on the cop vids, but we do have the kind of faces most people seem to trust.

"Have you consulted counsel about what happened tonight?"

"Not yet."

"Do you prefer human or android counsel?"

She looked at Ted. She had huge beautiful eyes. "Human."

"Note that at 10:42 P.M., suspect was offered counsel."

"The hormones."

"Ma'am?" I said.

"That's when they changed."

"When what changed, ma'am?"

After everything that had happened in the past few hours, I didn't expect her to be completely lucid.

She'd had a couple jolts of Pentathol. That can make them fuzzy, too.

"When the parlors changed."

"I see."

"When they started with the hormones."

Ted looked at me.

It was unlikely we'd ever forget the time when the hormones were introduced to the cybersex parlors. Wealthy people can keep their diversions and perversions private in their homes. But for most people who want cybersex, it means going to the bars. And renting the kind of fullbody data suits the wealthy have at home. Then the rich folks discovered that cybersex is even better if you do it in conjunction with hormones that are laced with steroids. These days, the people who go to the bars don't get hooked just on the cybersex. They get hooked on the drugs, too.

"Why did you go there tonight, Vanessa?"

"Because I couldn't take it any more."

"Take what, Vanessa?"

"The way he was."

"The way your husband was?"

"Right."

Ted said, "How was he, Vanessa?"

"Cold. Angry. Or indifferent. The indifference was the hardest thing to take."

"What do you think made him this way?" Ted said.

"What do I think—" She stopped herself. Smiled sadly. Shook her head. "The cybersex parlors were bad enough. I mean, he'd come home after spending time there and he'd want me to perform all these gymnastics. And I couldn't. And I didn't want to anyway. I mean, I *love* my husband. And I want sex to

195

be a part of that love. I don't want sex—"

She paused and looked at me with those gorgeous lost eyes of hers. "I want sex to have some meaning for me other than a simple orgasm."

"So the parlors got in the way of your home life?" I said.

"Got in the way?" She shook her head again. "He started spending half our income on the parlors. He also started spending half his *time* in the parlors."

She started crying, then. Just that abruptly. Put her sweet little face in her hands and just started sobbing.

Ted and I looked at each other. Now it was our turn to shake our heads.

I saw a survey once that said that there were almost as many women as men addicted to the cybersex parlors. The image you see on the newsies every night is of some horned-up urban male leaving one of the parlors all bow-legged and dewy-eyed from the incredible sexual experience he's just had.

But every night we checked out the parlors, we saw more than our share of women. And they looked every bit as bow-legged and dewy-eyed as the males.

This was back before the hormones. The hormones sort of tipped the balance. After the hormones, the whole thing got a lot more dangerous. And a lot more male.

"Then we tried a separation."

"When was this, Vanessa?"

"Six months ago."

"How did that go?"

"Well, for a little while, I had a lot of hope. Even to the point where I let him move back with us."

"He gave up the parlors?"

"He said he did. He even convinced the counselor he had."

"Counselor?"

"A head shrinker."

"I see."

She smiled at Ted. "He was a roid and very good at his job."

Ted smiled back.

"But then one night this old friend of his stopped by our house and started talking about the hormones and—I could see it in his eyes."

"His eyes?"

"My husband's eyes."

"Oh."

"I could see how much he wanted to try it out for himself. His friend kept saying that he'd never had cybersex unless he'd had it with the hormones."

The first couple of times, you needed to take the hormones eight days in advance for them to really work when you got to your cybersex parlor.

But after they'd been in your system for a sufficient time, all you had to do was take a pill when you got to the parlor and you'd be all set.

Shortly after the hormones were introduced, the federal government tried to get them taken off the market, but by then nobody was listening. The FDA had screwed up, but it was too late to put the genie back in the bottle.

The parlors changed, too. The hormones increased cybersex pleasure a thousand times over, according to users; but they also increased the psychotic episodes. And these didn't have to do with bliss. These had to do with rage.

For the first time, the parlors got violent. The users started attacking each other. Murder was not unheard of.

But no matter how dangerous they got, the number of users increased twenty percent a month.

Unfortunately, the users didn't leave their violence at the parlors, either. They brought it home with them.

"I remember the first night he beat me."

"You want to tell us about it?"

"I was asleep and he came in to our bedroom and woke me up. He had just gotten back from the parlor. He wanted to have sex. Very rough sex. I tried to be cooperative, but he was really hurting me. And the less cooperative I got, the more violent *he* got. He beat me up pretty badly."

"Did you call the police?"

"Not that time. Later on. I did. But the beatings weren't the worst part, anyway."

Ted said, "What was the worst part, Vanessa?"

"When he fell in love with her."

"Her?"

"The woman in the holo at the cybersex parlor."

"The wo—But they're just images," Ted said. "They're not real people."

Ted hadn't been keeping up on his newsies. This was a phenomenon that a lot of head shrinkers were deeply worried about, the parlor customers starting to prefer the reality of holographic women to the reality of their wives and lovers. Fullbody data suits—and you could jack into a reality far more "real" than the real world.

"He started sending her flowers and wine and little trinkets—having them delivered to the parlor, if you can believe it." Vanessa said. "He even started pretending he was going to leave me for her. One night, he came home and said, 'I've got to be honest with you, honey. I've fallen in love with Angie.' 'Who's Angie?' I said. 'The woman at the parlor. The woman I see all the time.' I couldn't help myself. I laughed. He looked so earnest and pathetic, like this little boy with his head filled with fantasies. And when I laughed—he took me in the bedroom and raped me. And broke my arm in the process."

"Did you move out again?"

"That's what I was in the process of doing tonight," she said. "I skimmed home after work to pick up the kids—but when I got there, the doors were padlocked and the kids were gone. There was a note. He'd taken them to his mother's and didn't want me to bother them. He said he was going to divorce me and get custody. And that Angie was moving in with him over this weekend. And that was when—"

"You went to the parlor tonight?"

"Yes. And walked straight to see Angie—"

She was silent then, staring at the wall.

"Did I really do it?"

"Yes, I'm afraid you did."

"With a scissors?"

"Yes."

"They can . . . reattach things like that, can't they?"

"He's at the hospital now."

She raised her head. Looked at me. "You know what I did afterward? While he was still lying there bleeding?" Shook her head. "I put the headset on and had a look at Angie for myself. God, she's not even that pretty. She looks kind of cheap, in fact. It must be the hormones."

"Right. The hormones." Then I said: "Vanessa?"

"Yes."

"I've read you your rights. But you've just given us a confession in effect—without counsel being present."

She shrugged. "Oh, I did it. I'm not trying to deny that."

"So you're making this confession voluntarily?"

"Yes, voluntarily. And you know the worst thing?"

"What?"

"I'm not even sorry I did it. Not right now, anyway. I mean, later on maybe I'll be sorry. But not right now."

As we were winding up for the night, Ted said. "I feel sorry for her."

"Yeah, so do I."

"Hard to imagine that a man would prefer a holo to a nice sweet woman like that."

"Yeah," I said.

We said good night as we walked out to our personal skimmers.

"See you tomorrow," Ted said.

I was about halfway home when I watched as my hand reached for the communicator and punched the "Home" button.

"How's my big strong policeman doing tonight?" my wife's face said on the tiny screen.

"Fine. But very tired. And they're making me work overtime again."

I saw the disappointment in her face. "But I thought

tonight—Well, it's been a while since we've had—oh what did I used to call them?"

"Romantic interludes."

"Oh, right," she laughed. "It's been a while. I even chilled a bottle of wine for us."

"Give me a freaking break, will you?" I shouted at the communicator. "I'm busting my ass off on overtime—and all you can do is whine about it."

I heard the violence in my words and was shocked. Buddy, the guy who got me the hormes, said I had to be careful of sudden temper flare-ups. He wasn't kidding.

"I'm sorry, honey."

"I'll just see you when you get here," she said, and broke communication. She sounded forlorn and confused.

"One hour ticket," I said to the man at the booth in the front lobby of the parlor.

"And your lady?"

"Alison."

"Alison, it is," he said, and took my credit card and made the necessary arrangements. When he handed it back, he said, "She's a very popular lady."

This was the third night running he'd said that to me. And it was funny, every time he said it, I felt a strange hot surge of jealousy.

Then I went in to see my Alison.

The Monster Parade

1

Quite an honor, to be the only senator standing next to the president on the reviewing platform. Senator Loomis's political consultants were ecstatic. More than three billion people would see their man on trivid this morning.

This occasion had come to be called the Monster Parade by the press.

The last rocket had brought back some real eye-poppers from the deserted alien space station.

Frank Loomis was the senator in charge of the space program, and as such he belonged here on the reviewing stand, which had been built in front of 1600 Pennsylvania Avenue.

Both men waved to the endless stream of marching bands strutting past them, and long after each had passed, the music of drum and trumpet still rang in their ears. Both men were dressed similarly in old-fashioned homburgs; old-fashioned black overcoats. The holo people had insisted on something photogenic.

The temperature was six below zero.

Crowds of black and white, rich and poor, young and old stood waving at the passing parade.

The president leaned over to Loomis and whispered, "I don't know about you, but my nuts are freezing off."

Loomis leaned back and whispered, "My nuts went a long time ago. It's my cock I'm worried about now."

Their faces were deadpan, betraying not the slightest amusement.

And so it went.

Two solid hours of warm-up before the president and Loomis got to see what all three billion people wanted to see: the monsters.

Pennsylvania Avenue was lined for miles. The citizens didn't even seem to notice the cold. All they wanted was a good long look at the creatures the astronauts had taken from the alien space station that had been sent into this solar system as a scouting party to determine if Earth was sufficiently vulnerable to attack. But the Kraken had encountered some kind of virus that had killed most of them. Only twenty or so remained, and these had been brought down to Earth at the rate of three per year. The survivors indicated that their home planet would soon be dispatching other scout stations and that eventually Earth would be not only invaded but conquered.

And then, at long last, the first one appeared, right

behind a float celebrating "The American Farmer," with a tractor and a bunch of bathing beauties honoring this most sacred of institutions.

Loomis leaned over and whispered, "Back when I was a farm boy, we sure didn't have any girls who looked like that."

The President whispered right back, "I do believe that those girls just unfroze my balls."

A pause of maybe a minute or so and—

There was the first one.

Big, clear, cagelike box.

Sitting right inside.

You could hardly stand to look at it.

Most of the monsters that came back were humanoid, in that they had two arms, two legs, and walked erect. But all resemblance ended there. The only thing Loomis had ever been able to compare these pitiful creatures to was the infamous Elephant Man, a grim parody of what a normal human being should look like.

This first one had baseball-sized blisters all over its scaly blue skin, with one obliterating even half of its only eye.

Loomis spent the next few minutes experiencing all the feelings pertinent to such a slight: repulsion, fear, anxiety, pity, and then an abiding curiosity.

Then Loomis started wondering about Major Davidson. Where was the army investigator the Space Oversight Committee was using to follow up on the strange letter they had received from a woman in Oaxaca? They hadn't heard from him in two weeks. He had disappeared in that mysterious region in the dark and ancient mountains of Mexico's Sierra Madre del Sur.

At first, Loomis and the other senators had almost totally discounted the letter. Every nutcase on the planet sent the Space Oversight Committee letters or tapes hinting that some terrible conspiracy was going on. This was a routine part of the committee's job: to sift through and evaluate all this correspondence. Less than one percent of the letters proved worthy of the slightest scrutiny.

But the letter was so outlandish it had a perverse kind of truth to it. Who could make such stuff up? Loomis went to the army, which resented all the funding the space program received from Congress. The army, in the person of Major Davidson, was only too happy to investigate the letter's allegations.

Senator Loomis pulled his white silk scarf more tightly against his throat. Freezing his ass off out here.

As more monsters passed—they always padded out the parade with monsters that had been seen in previous years—two blue rockets thundered across the sky in a salute from the space program.

The president, ever a hambone, saluted dramatically right back.

Loomis found himself saluting, too. But he wondered again about Davidson.

What the hell was going on?

2

Major Kenneth Davidson wasn't going to die.

Ever since the security team from the space program had shot him, two weeks before, he'd lived with the assumption that he was dying.

He was back in business, his laser pistol filling his

right hand as he made his way through the heavy undergrowth.

But two weeks before . . .

The charge had entered his left shoulder and had spread poison throughout his body. He had been following a tip from one of the villagers about a strange concrete block building in the steamy overgrown lowlands . . . and then, hearing something behind him, he'd turned to see two Americans in the buff blue uniforms of the Space Corps fire on him with laser rifles.

He was never sure who had dragged him away to safety. A few days later, his fever having broken, his delirium having quieted, he woke alone in a small tin shack, where some kind of stew was boiling in a kettle over an open fire.

The wound had been cleaned and treated and wrapped in faded but clean cotton.

He made the mistake of trying to stand, landing on his face for his trouble, hitting his nose against the dirt floor sharply enough to draw blood.

A few hours later, just at dusk, he'd rallied sufficiently to try standing again.

This time he made it to the door of the shack and looked out.

In a foggy valley below, on a dirt road as twisted as a coiling snake, he saw women with heavy burdens of firewood strapped to their backs. Behind them came a shepherd boy with his goats.

Even at this distance, he could recognize the people's race: Mixtec, the crossbreed of Mexican and Indians indigenous to this region.

But who had cleaned his wound?

He soon lost strength and went back to his blankets on the dirt floor, next to the fire and the boiling stew.

He drifted into a troubled sleep. When he awoke again, the door was filled with blue sky and green leafy trees. Gone was dusk, and fog.

"My friend the Americano," said a male voice somewhere behind him.

He stood up and walked over so Davidson could see him without moving.

The man was older, in his sixties perhaps, with one of those tanned leathery faces that assume the shape and texture of mask. He wore a vast straw sombrero, a festive red shirt, and dirty jeans. He smoked hand-rolled cigarettes that were so crooked Davidson was impressed that smoke could even pass through them.

"I had the dream again, my friend."

The dream? Who was this man and what was he talking about?

The man smiled. "You are confused, eh?"

"Yes. I'm afraid I am."

"I'm the man who helped you with your wounds."

"You saved my life."

"Perhaps. But we should not make too much of it. I was raised by nuns. They taught me things about medicine. There was a war going on—over land or something equally silly, I forget—and so they showed me how to treat wounds."

"But laser wounds—"

"Even laser wounds. The nuns knew their medicine."

Davidson pushed himself to a sitting position. "That stew smells good."

"Another good sign." He patted his belly. "Your appetite, I mean. Let me serve you."

The man produced not only a wooden bowl and spoon but a half loaf of bread, which he dropped in Davidson's lap.

As Davidson ate, the man said, "I must tell you the truth."

Davidson stopped eating, just looked at him.

"I am not as selfless as I would seem, *señor*. No. I didn't save your life simply for your sake."

"Why, then?"

The man stared at his callused hands, then balled them into loose fists. "Even now, the rage—Forgive me if I begin to cry."

"Of course."

"My rage is about the *Americanos*—"

"The *Americanos?*"

The man nodded, his vast sombrero bobbing up and down. "The ones in the blue uniforms."

For the first time, Davidson began to suspect that there might be a connection between this man's troubles and his own.

"The ones who shot you," the man said. "They are the same ones who did unspeakable things to . . ."

Davidson, who had finished eating, set his bowl down on the dirt floor and said, "Why don't you tell me about it?"

The man nodded. "I would be most appreciative if you would hear my story—and do your best to believe it."

"I'll do my best," Davidson said.

And so the man had told his tale.

3

The Space Corps floats came between the two displays of monsters. The men and women in their handsome blue uniforms moved with ease and precision past the reviewing stand, saluting the President as they walked by.

"You think the next batch'll be any uglier than the first?" the president whispered to Senator Loomis.

The senator almost smiled. The president was just a kid when it came to monsters. He loved being scared and sickened.

But if the president knew what Loomis and a few others suspected . . .

"I'm told they've got some real doozies this year," the senator whispered back.

The monsters all looked different because the virus seemed to affect each individual Kraken differently. Some were almost humorous in a sad way, their deformities as much comic as grotesque.

But some . . .

The one with the eye on the shoulder . . .

Davidson's name came to Loomis's mind again.

Out of contact now for more than two weeks. What could possibly be going on down there? Was Davidson even alive now? Should Loomis send someone else?

"You have your differences with the Space Program, I know that, Senator. But you have to give them one thing."

"What's that, sir?"

"They put on a good show."

"They certainly do that, sir."

"These monsters—they're wonderful. I hope I can get my son some good color holos of them. The way I did last year."

"That shouldn't be any problem, sir."

"He loves those things. He still hauls them out at least once a day."

"I'll see that he gets some good ones, sir."

"I'd appreciate that, Senator. I really would."

More dark blue rockets streaked across the buff blue sky.

Two of the marching bands began playing patriotic songs. At moments like this, patriotism became a palpable thing. It really did.

"Here come some more monsters," the president said, sounding like a kid again.

"Yes, indeed," Senator Loomis said. "That's what we need more of: more monsters."

The president looked as if he did not quite know how to interpret the senator's remark.

4

Luis Lopez Cruz, the man who had saved Davidson's life, now led Davidson through the jungle, wanting to show him the way into the compound Luis had been describing over the past two days.

Lopez had even obtained laser pistols for them. He had had to travel three days on the back of a burro to the city where none of the old ways were honored, where girls as young as eight sold themselves to the *turistas*, and where the boys roamed in packs, like wolves. But he got the guns.

They traveled half a day before Davidson had to rest. He lay next to a jungle stream. Lopez took out his machete and beat the bushes to scare away snakes so that Davidson would not be troubled by them.

Lopez sat down with him. "Even now, I think of my son, *señor*. He is all I can think of."

"I'm sorry about him, Lopez."

The tale Lopez had told him a few days before had been simple enough. *Americanos* had built a small fortress in the mountains here six years ago. Over the past five years, young Mixtec men had started vanishing, Lopez's eldest son among them. But the eighteen-year-old had somehow managed to escape, find his father, and tell him what was going on.

Lopez found it difficult to believe such a story. He felt that his son must be delirious.

The men in the blue uniforms appeared within hours of the boy reaching home. They took him back at rifle point. Lopez never saw his son again.

"Perhaps I am the one who is *loco, señor*," Lopez said. "Sometimes when I think about it all . . . It is like a bad dream, you know?"

"Well, we'll soon find out."

An hour later they stood on a dirt trail on the downslope of a snow-peaked mountain. Far up the road was a compound fenced off and patrolled by guards in the uniform of the Space Corps. They would certainly not gain entrance this way, Davidson thought.

"You said there was a cave?"

"Yes, *señor*."

"And it leads into the compound?"

"Yes. Two centuries ago there was a pagan movement in this land. The priests and the nuns did not approve of it and so the pagans held their ceremonies in caves. One of the caves leads into the center of the compound but the officials there do not know it."

Davidson gripped his laser rifle. "Let's go, Lopez. While I still have the strength."

5

Following the parade, there was a reception at the White House and, as always, the First Lady had had too much to drink, a fact that all did their best to overlook.

"I'll bet the president wouldn't mind sending her up to Jupiter," said a Space Corps colonel who had managed to corner Loomis.

"I have a brother who's that way," Loomis said, "so I suppose I have a little more compassion for her than you do."

The colonel flushed. "I wasn't making fun of—"

"I know you weren't, Colonel, I know you weren't." But Loomis had enjoyed making the pompous military man uneasy. "Now, why don't you save us both a little time and tell me how much money you need and what you need it for?"

This particular colonel had a brother-in-law who worked as a vice president at one of the major space and defense contractors. The VP and his staff were always coming up with new and better ways for the taxpayers to spend their money.

For the next twenty minutes, the colonel gave the senator a slide show without slides. The project dealt with a "mule" the company had designed, a craft for hauling heavy things on the planets the Space Corps had targeted for the near future.

"All we need is a little bit of an investment to build a prototype," the colonel said.

And then went into the second part of his pitch.

Loomis let the military man talk but didn't pay much attention.

In fact, he began to glance around the glittering room to see who was there.

When he saw two army generals laughing over cocktails, Loomis started thinking about Davidson again.

Where the hell was he, anyway? And what the hell was he up to?

And why the hell hadn't he reported back yet?

6

They got lost three times.

Davidson began to wonder if this whole excursion wasn't the fever dream of a grief-stricken father.

They walked, they stooped, they crawled between rough and winding cave walls that stank of fetid water and almost unimaginable age. Occasionally, David saw strange symbols that looked vaguely Mayan in nature.

But finally one leg of the cave led to an opening that connected with a wide, round drainage pipe that trickled water like silver snakes.

"This will lead us to the compound," Lopez said. "It is how my son escaped."

Davidson tried not to think of all the rats and snakes that probably awaited them inside the huge pipe.

They set off on hands and knees.

Lopez talked a great deal as they made their way through the pipe. Several times Davidson thought of telling him to shut up but then realized he would miss the old man's voice.

The water was chill and filthy; the pipe itself rough on hands and knees. Davidson killed two rats and a snake with his Bowie knife, the second rat spraying blood all over Davidson's hands, arms, and face.

At last they reached a ladder.

"This will take us up to a sewer lid," Lopez said. "And then we can go and search the compound."

Davidson wanted to warn Lopez about the odds they'd be facing. The Space Corps had likely stocked the compound with several dozen troops and enough firepower to start a major war. Two men wandering around the compound would be very vulnerable.

Davidson went up the ladder first.

He pushed up the lid and peered out.

Mercury vapor lights. Electrified fencing. The backsides of three two-story buildings with darkened windows. Three sentries marching smartly to the east.

Davidson closed the lid.

"I hope you realize what we're up against."

"I just think of my son, *señor*, and what happened to him. The rest does not matter. My life is nothing."

"Just as long as you understand."

Davidson unholstered his laser pistol, lifted the sewer lid once again, shoved it quickly to the right, and then hoisted himself up through the opening.

Lopez did not come so fast, and when he got near the top, his hand slipped from the ladder rung above him and he almost fell back into the filth of the drain.

Davidson reached down and grabbed Lopez by the wrist, holding him until the old man could secure himself on the ladder once again.

Heat. The smell of the jungle. Mosquitoes that felt like swords as they bore into human flesh.

Lopez was up, then, and Davidson sliding the lid back in place.

"Hey! You!" someone shouted.

Davidson spun around and dropped to one knee as the lone guard sighted his laser rifle.

Davidson shot the young man in the face; flesh and bone melted so quickly that there was no time to scream.

Davidson beckoned for Lopez to follow.

He ran to one of the darkened buildings and slipped inside.

7

General Holcroft, the senior Senate liaison for the Space Corps, came over to Senator Loomis and said, "You don't look very happy these days, Senator."

"That may be because I'm *not* very happy these days, General."

"The report I gave you?"

Loomis nodded. "The report you gave me. It was all bullshit and you know it."

Two men from the State Department caught Loomis's harsh tone and frowned. In the world of diplomacy, such frankness was not permitted.

"I resent that," the general said.

"But not very much, you don't. Because you know as well as I do that every word in the report was a lie."

Two months earlier, Loomis had demanded that the general and his staff prepare a report on the origins of the creatures aboard the deserted space platform. Even then, Loomis had suspected the truth. The report had come in three weeks ago, two days before

Loomis, in great rage, had dispatched Davidson to Mexico.

"I don't know what you could reasonably expect, Senator. We don't know much about them. We suspect that they're from this galaxy but we can't be sure. We're studying them night and day to learn as much as we can."

"You know where they come from and so do I," Loomis said.

"And where would that be, Senator?"

Loomis smirked. "A strange and wondrous planet named Mexico."

8

Davidson and Lopez stayed in the first building for more than an hour. They found nothing but rooms filled with surgical centers where the operations were performed. They found none of the people involved.

They stood at a window looking out.

Davidson said, "That building over there looks more promising."

"Yes," Lopez said, "and more dangerous."

Getting into the next building required some skill. There were two sentries. Only when both were on the far side of the building could Davidson and Lopez get into the building.

They had just reached a main hallway when they heard boots marching toward them. They found a closet and hid inside.

Davidson felt dizzy and weak. The exertion and the fear were taking their toll.

Lopez said, "We should rest here for a time, my friend."

Ed Gorman

"Yes, I think you're right."

There were times when Davidson liked to play the brave and macho man. This was not one of them. He did not have the strength.

One hour and twenty-three minutes later, Davidson and Lopez crept into a shadowy ward where an even dozen men and women slept in high white beds.

Davidson studied their faces in moonlight.

No rapid eye movement. No twitch of nose or mouth. No rolling from side to side.

They lay like zombies, faceup, unmoving.

He checked their skin.

Perfectly human.

Twenty-eight minutes after sneaking into the first ward, they crept into the second.

Twelve more men and women.

Facing up.

Sleeping like zombies.

But their skin—

In the moonlight, he could see the rough scales that had encrusted their otherwise human forms.

This was the ward where the process started.

Just as they were about to enter the third ward, they heard footsteps again.

No closets to hide in this time.

They had to duck into the room and crawl beneath the beds.

Faster footsteps. Guards whispering to each other.

Flashlights in the ward now, guards searching.

Davidson and Lopez head beneath facing beds,

their breath coming in gasps, sweat hot on their trembling limbs.

After the guards had left, they waited ten more minutes before crawling out from under the beds.

Davidson began inspecting the zombies.

It was in this ward that the first results of surgery could be seen, the once-human faces ripped and slashed into the visages of creatures neither human nor humane.

The lights came on.

This time the two guards had brought backups.

There must have been ten of them, all with laser rifles.

"We've been expecting you, Captain Davidson," said the first guard. "Our commander is very eager to speak to you."

9

At home that night, in his smoking jacket, a goblet of brandy in his right hand, a copy of a political thriller in his left, Loomis cursed when the phone rang.

He set down his book and his brandy and picked up the phone. He was a widower and the ringing phone sounded very lonely echoing in the large colonial-style house in Georgetown.

"Hello?"

"I want to tell you about your man Davidson."

"You bastard. You've captured him, haven't you, General Holcroft?"

"Yes. Along with a man named Lopez."

"I know what you're up to and by tomorrow so will everybody else in Washington. Those aren't monsters in your parades—they're Mexicans you turned into monsters with chemicals and surgery."

"You're correct, of course. What can I say?"

"You want the public to think that the Space Corps is actually accomplishing something or otherwise your funding would be cut and used on something more important—such as poverty."

"Poverty is a very real concern, Senator. But then so is a meteor strike."

"Meteor strike? What the hell are you talking about?"

10

The doctors wasted no time with Davidson and Lopez.

Word had come from General Holcroft to rush these two through the entire process as quickly as possible. He wanted them turned into monsters within forty-eight hours.

The doctors weren't sure they could do it but they were certainly going to try.

They started on Lopez first, tearing away his nose and his lips and half his jaw line.

They were amazed at how efficient they could be under all this pressure.

Very efficient. They next took out his left eyeball and caved in the eye cavity.

11

"My God," Loomis said. "I had no idea."

"We have so many problems in this country that the citizens don't want to spend any money on the space program. The president doesn't want to tell them about the meteor strike that's going to destroy this planet in two and a half years because there would be panic and lawlessness. But some people have to get off this planet before the strike comes. And that means we've got to continue the space program so that we can perfect the craft of traveling great distances in space. If we don't, our entire species will die right here on Earth."

"So you created the monsters?"

"Right. Monsters they can understand. An alien invasion they can understand. That's why they keep giving us money through their elected representatives." General Holcroft sighed. "So now you know."

"I'm sorry, General. Here I thought you were a bastard and—"

"That's all right, Senator. No apology necessary. All I can ask is that you keep this to yourself. Fewer than twenty people know the real secret."

Now it was the senator's turn to sigh as he thought of his two sons and his grandchildren and the prospect of a meteor strike. "Two and a half years?"

"Yes," General Holcroft said. "Two and a half years."

12

Three-hundred-and-sixty-five days later, the creature that had been Lopez sat inside a transparent cage that was being transported down Pennsylvania Avenue. He was followed by another cage, inside of which was the creature that had been Davidson.

Up on the reviewing platform, standing right next to the president, Senator Loomis watched the monster

Ed Gorman

parade with a melancholy that had his friends and assistants worried.

The senator was just not himself these days; not himself at all.

The Face

The war was going badly. In the past month, more than sixty men had disgraced the Confederacy by deserting, and now the order was to shoot deserters on sight. This was in other camps and other regiments. Fortunately, none of our men had deserted at all.

As a young doctor, I knew even better than our leaders just how hopeless our war had become. The public knew General Lee had been forced to cross the Potomac with ten thousand men who lacked shoes, hats and who at night had to sleep on the ground without blankets. But I knew—in the first six months in this post—that our men suffered from influenza, diphtheria, smallpox, yellow fever and even cholera; ravages from which they would never recover; ravages more costly than bullets and the advancing armies of the Yankees. Worse, because toilet and bathing facilities were practically nil, virtually every man suffered from ticks and mites and many suffered from scurvy, their bodies on fire. Occasionally, you would see a man go mad, do crazed dances in the moonlight trying to get the bugs off him. Soon enough he would be dead.

This was the war in the spring and while I have here referred to our troops as "men," in fact they were mostly boys, some as young as thirteen. In the night, freezing and sometimes wounded, they cried out for their mothers, and it was not uncommon to hear one or two of them sob while they prayed aloud.

I tell you this so you will have some idea of how horrible things had become for our beloved Confederacy. But even given the suffering and madness and despair I'd seen for the past two years as a military doctor, nothing had prepared me for the appearance of the Virginia man in our midst.

On the day he was brought in on a buckboard, I was working with some troops, teaching them how to garden. If we did not get vegetables and fruit into our diets soon, all of us would have scurvy. I also appreciated the respite that working in the warm sun gave me from surgery. In the past week alone, I'd amputated three legs, two arms and numerous hands and fingers. None had gone well, conditions were so filthy.

Every amputation had ended in death except one and this man—boy; he was fourteen—pleaded with me to kill him every time I checked on him. He'd suffered a head wound and I'd had to relieve the pressure by trepanning into his skull. Beneath the blood and pus in the hole I'd dug, I could see his brain squirming. There was no anesthetic, of course, except whiskey and that provided little comfort against the violence of my bone saw. It was one of those periods when I could not get the tart odor of blood from my nostrils, nor its feel from my skin. Sometimes, standing at the surgery table, my boots would become soaked with it and I would squish around in them all day.

The buckboard was parked in front of the General's tent. The driver jumped down, ground-tied the horses, and went quickly inside.

He returned a few moments later with General Sullivan, the commander. Three men in familiar gray uniforms followed the General.

The entourage walked around to the rear of the wagon. The driver, an enlisted man, pointed to something in the buckboard. The General, a fleshy, bald man of fifty-some years, leaned over the wagon and peered downward.

Quickly, the General's head snapped back and then his whole body followed. It was as if he'd been stung by something coiled and waiting for him in the buckboard.

The General shook his head and said, "I want this man's entire body covered. Especially his face."

"But, General," the driver said. "He's not dead. We shouldn't cover his face."

"You heard what I said!" General Sullivan snapped. And with that, he strutted back into his tent, his men following.

I was curious, of course, about the man in the back of the wagon. I wondered what could have made the General start the way he had. He'd looked almost frightened.

I wasn't to know till later that night.

*   *   *

My rounds made me late for dinner in the vast tent used for the officers' mess. I always felt badly about the inequity of officers having beef stew while the men had, at best, hardtack and salt pork. Not so bad that I refused to eat it, of course, which made me feel hypocritical on top of being sorry for the enlisted men.

Not once in my time here had I ever dined with General Sullivan. I was told on my first day here that the General, an extremely superstitious man, considered doctors bad luck. Many people feel this way. Befriend a doctor and you'll soon enough find need of his services.

So I was surprised when General Sullivan, carrying a cup of steaming coffee in a huge, battered tin cup, sat down across from the table where I ate alone, my usual companions long ago gone back to their duties.

"Good evening, Doctor."

"Good evening, General."

"A little warmer tonight."

"Yes."

He smiled dourly. "Something's got to go our way, I suppose."

I returned his smile. "I suppose." I felt like a child trying to act properly for the sake of an adult. The General frightened me.

The General took out a stogie, clipped off the end, sniffed it, licked it, then put it between his lips and fired it. He did all this with a ritualistic satisfaction that made me think of better times in my home city of Charleston, of my father and uncles handling their smoking in just the same way.

"A man was brought into camp this afternoon," he said.

"Yes," I said. "In a buckboard."

He eyed me suspiciously. "You've seen him up close?"

"No. I just saw him delivered to your tent." I had to be careful of how I put my next statement. I did not want the General to think I was challenging his reasoning. "I'm told he was not taken to any of the hospital tents."

"No, he wasn't." The General wasn't going to help me.

"I'm told he was put under quarantine in a tent of his own."

"Yes."

"May I ask why?"

He blew two plump white perfect rings of smoke toward the ceiling. "Go have a look at him, then join me in my tent."

"You're afraid he may have some contagious disease?"

The General considered the length of his cigar. "Just go have a look at him, Doctor. Then we'll talk."

With that, the General stood up, his familiar brusque self once again, and was gone.

The guard set down his rifle when he saw me. "Good evenin', Doctor."

"Good evening."

He nodded to the tent behind him. "You seen him yet?"

"No; not yet."

He was young. He shook his head. "Never seen anything like it. Neither has the priest. He's in there with him now."

In the chill, crimson dusk I tried to get a look at

the guard's face. I couldn't. My only clue to his mood was the tone of his voice—one of great sorrow.

I lifted the tent flap and went in.

A lamp guttered in the far corner of the small tent, casting huge and playful shadows across the walls. A hospital cot took up most of the space. A man's body lay beneath the covers. A sheer cloth had been draped across his face. You could see it billowing with the man's faint breath. Next to the cot stood Father Lynott. He was silver-haired and chunky. His black cassock showed months of dust and grime. Like most of us, he was rarely able to get hot water for necessities.

At first, he didn't seem to hear me. He stood over the cot torturing black rosary beads through his fingers. He stared directly down at the cloth draped on the man's face.

Only when I stood next to him did Father Lynott look up. "Good evening, Father."

"Good evening, Doctor."

"The General wanted me to look at this man."

He stared at me. "You haven't seen him, then?"

"No."

"Nothing can prepare you."

"I'm afraid I don't understand."

He looked at me out of his tired cleric's face. "You'll see soon enough. Why don't you come over to the officers' tent afterwards? I'll be there drinking my nightly coffee."

He nodded, glanced down once more at the man on the cot, and then left, dropping the tent flap behind him.

I don't know how long I stood there before I could bring myself to remove the cloth from the man's face. By now, enough people had warned me of what I would see that I was both curious and apprehensive. There is a myth about doctors not being shocked by certain terrible wounds and injuries. Of course we are but we must get past that shock—or, more honestly, put it aside for a time—so that we can help the patient.

Close by, I could hear the feet of the guard in the damp grass, pacing back and forth in front of the tent. A barn owl and then a distant dog joined the sounds the guard made. Even more distant, there was cannon fire, the war never ceasing. The sky would flare silver like summer lightning. Men would suffer and die.

I reached down and took the cloth from the man's face.

"What do you suppose could have done that to his face, Father?" I asked the priest twenty minutes later.

We were having coffee. I smoked a cigar. The guttering candles smelled sweet and waxy.

"I'm not sure," the priest said.

"Have you ever seen anything like it?"

"Never."

I knew what I was about to say would surprise the priest. "He has no wounds."

"What?"

"I examined him thoroughly. There are no wounds anywhere on his body."

"But his face—"

I drew on my cigar, watched the expelled smoke move like a storm cloud across the flickering candle flame. "That's why I asked you if you'd ever seen anything like it."

"My God," the priest said, as if speaking to himself. "No wounds."

*   *   *

In the dream I was back on the battlefield on that frosty March morning two years ago when all my medical training had deserted me. Hundreds of corpses covered the ground where the battle had gone on for two days and two nights. You could see cannons mired in mud, the horses unable to pull them out.

You could see the grass littered with dishes and pans and kettles, and a blizzard of playing cards—all exploded across the battlefield when the Union army had made its final advance. But mostly there were the bodies—so young and so many—and many of them with mutilated faces. During this time of the war, both sides had begun to commit atrocities. The Yankees favored disfiguring Confederate dead and so they moved across the battlefield with Bowie knives that had been fashioned by sharpening with large files. They put deep gashes in the faces of the young men, tearing out eyes sometimes, even sawing off noses. In the woods that day we'd found a group of our soldiers who'd been mortally wounded but who'd lived for a time after the Yankees had left. Each corpse held in its hand some memento of the loved ones they'd left behind—a photograph, a letter, a lock of blonde hair. Their last sight had been of some homely yet profound endearment from the people they'd loved most.

This was the dream—nightmare, really—and I'd suffered it ever since I'd searched for survivors on that battlefield two years previous.

I was still in this dream-state when I heard the bugle announce the morning. I stumbled from my cot and went down to the creek to wash and shave. The day had begun.

Casualties were many that morning. I stood in the hospital tent watching as one stretcher after another bore man after man to the operating table. Most suffered from wounds inflicted by minie balls, fired from guns that could kill a man nearly a mile away.

By noon, my boots were again soaked with blood dripping from the table.

During the long day, I heard whispers of the man General Sullivan had quarantined from others. Apparently, the man had assumed the celebrity and fascination of a carnival sideshow. From the whispers, I gathered the guards were letting men in for quick looks at him, and the lookers came away shaken and frightened. These stories had the same impact as tales of spectres told around midnight campfires. Except this was daylight and the men—even the youngest of them—hardened soldiers. They should not have been so afraid but they were.

I couldn't get the sight of the man out of my mind, either. It haunted me no less than the battlefield I'd seen two years earlier.

During the afternoon, I went down to the creek and washed. I then went to the officers' tent and had stew and coffee. My arms were weary from surgery but I knew I would be working long into the night.

The General surprised me once again by joining me. "You've seen the soldier from Virginia?"

"Yes, sir."

"What do you make of him?"

I shrugged. "Shock, I suppose."

231

"But his face—"

"This is a war, General, and a damned bloody one. Not all men are like you. Not all men have iron constitutions."

He took my words as flattery, of course, as a military man would. I hadn't necessarily meant them that way. Military men could also be grossly vain and egotistical and insensitive beyond belief.

"Meaning what, exactly, Doctor?"

"Meaning that the soldier from Virginia may have become so horrified by what he saw that his face—" I shook my head. "You can see too much, too much death, General, and it can make you go insane."

"Are you saying he's insane?"

I shook my head. "I'm trying to find some explanation for his expression, General."

"You say there's no injury?"

"None that I can find."

"Yet he's not conscious."

"That's why I think of shock."

I was about to explain how shock works on the body—and how it could feasibly effect an expression like the one on the Virginia soldier's face—when a lieutenant rushed up to the General and breathlessly said, "You'd best come, sir. The tent where the soldier's quarantined—there's trouble!"

When we reached there, we found half the camp's soldiers surrounding the tent. Three and four deep, they were, and milling around idly. Not the sort of thing you wanted to see your men doing when there was a war going on. There were duties to perform and none of them were getting done.

A young soldier—thirteen or fourteen at most—stepped from the line and hurled his rifle at the General. The young soldier had tears running down his cheeks. "I don't want to fight any more, General."

The General slammed the butt of the rifle into the soldier's stomach. "Get hold of yourself, young man. You seem to forget we're fighting to save the Confederacy."

We went on down the line of glowering faces, to where two armed guards struggled to keep soldiers from looking into the tent. I was reminded again of a sideshow—some irresistible spectacle everybody wanted to see.

The soldiers knew enough to open an avenue for the General. He strode inside the tent. The priest sat on a stool next to the cot. He had removed the cloth from the Virginia soldier's face and was staring fixedly at it.

The General pushed the priest aside, took up the cloth used as a covering, and started to drop it across the soldier's face—then stopped abruptly. Even General Sullivan, in his rage, was moved by what he saw. He jerked back momentarily, his eyes unable to lift from the soldier's face. He handed the cloth to the priest. "You cover his face now, Father. And you keep it covered. I hereby forbid any man in this camp to look at this soldier's face ever again. Do you understand?"

Then he stormed from the tent.

The priest reluctantly obliged.

Then he angled his head up to me. "It won't be the same any more, Doctor."

"What won't?"

"The camp. Every man in here has now seen his face." He nodded back to the soldier on the cot. "They'll never be the same again. I promise you."

*   *   *

In the evening, I ate stew and biscuits, and sipped at a small glass of wine. I was, as usual, in the officers' tent when the priest came and found me.

For a time, he said nothing beyond his greeting. Simply watched me at my meal, and then stared out the open flap at the camp preparing for evening, the fires in the center of the encampment, the weary men bedding down. Many of them, healed now, would be back in the battle within two days or less.

"I spent an hour with him this afternoon," the priest said.

"The quarantined man?"

"Yes." The priest nodded. "Do you know some of the men have visited him five or six times?"

The way the priest spoke, I sensed he was gloating over the fact that the men were disobeying the General's orders. "Why don't the guards stop them?"

"The guards are in visiting him, too."

"The man says nothing. How can it be a visit?"

"He says nothing with his tongue. He says a great deal with his face." He paused, eyed me levelly. "I need to tell you something. You're the only man in this camp who will believe me." He sounded frantic. I almost felt sorry for him.

"Tell me what?"

"The man—he's not what we think."

"No?"

"No; his face—" He shook his head. "It's God's face."

"I see."

The priest smiled. "I know how I must sound."

"You've seen a great deal of suffering, Father. It wears on a person."

"It's God's face. I had a dream last night. The man's face shows us God's displeasure with the war. That's why the men are so moved when they see the man." He sighed, seeing he was not convincing me. "You say yourself he hasn't been wounded."

"That's true."

"And that all his vital signs seem normal."

"True enough, Father."

"Yet he's in some kind of shock."

"That seems to be his problem, yes."

The priest shook his head. "No, his real problem is that he's become overwhelmed by the suffering he's seen in this war—what both sides have done to the other. All the pain. That's why there's so much sorrow on his face—and that's what the men are responding to. The grief on his face is the same grief they feel in their hearts. God's face."

"Once we get him to a real field hospital—"

And it was then we heard the rifle shots.

The periphery of the encampment was heavily protected, we'd never heard firing this close.

The priest and I ran outside.

General Sullivan stood next to a group of young men with weapons. Several yards ahead, near the edge of the camp, lay three bodies, shadowy in the light of the campfire. One of the fallen men moaned. All three men wore our own gray uniforms.

Sullivan glowered at me. "Deserters."

"But you shot them in the back," I said.

"Perhaps you didn't hear me, Doctor. The men were deserting. They'd packed their belongings and were heading out."

One of the young men who'd done the shooting said, "It was the man's face, sir."

Sullivan wheeled on him. "It was what?"

"The quarantined man, sir. His face. These men said it made them sad and they had to see families back in Missouri, and that they were just going to leave no matter what."

"Poppycock," Sullivan said. "They left because they were cowards."

I left to take care of the fallen man who was crying out for help.

In the middle of the night, I heard more guns being fired. I lay on my cot, knowing it wasn't Yankees being fired at. It was our own deserters.

I dressed and went over to the tent where the quarantined man lay. Two young farm boys in ill-fitting gray uniforms stood over him. They might have been mourners standing over a coffin. They said nothing. Just stared at the man.

In the dim lamplight, I knelt down next to him. His vitals still seemed good, his heartbeat especially. I stood up, next to the two boys, and looked down on him myself. There was nothing remarkable about his face. He could have been any of thousands of men serving on either side.

Except for the grief.

This time I felt the tug of it myself, heard in my mind the cries of the dying I'd been unable to save, saw the families and farms and homes destroyed as the war moved across the countryside, heard children crying out for dead parents, and parents sobbing over the bodies of their dead children. It was all there in his face, perfectly reflected, and I thought then of what the priest had said, that this was God's face, God's sorrow and displeasure with us.

The explosion came, then.

While the two soldiers next to me didn't seem to hear it at all, I rushed from the tent to the center of camp.

Several young soldiers stood near the ammunition cache. Someone had set fire to it. Ammunition was exploding everywhere, flares of red and yellow and gas-jet blue against the night. Men everywhere ducked for cover behind wagons and trees and boulders.

Into this scene, seemingly unafraid and looking like the lead actor in a stage production of King Lear I'd once seen, strode General Sullivan, still tugging on his heavy uniform jacket.

He went over to two soldiers who stood, seemingly unfazed, before the ammunition cache. Between explosions I could hear him shouting, "Did you set this fire?"

And they nodded.

Sullivan, as much in bafflement as anger, shook his head. He signaled for the guards to come and arrest these men.

As the soldiers were passing by me, I heard one of them say to a guard, "After I saw his face, I knew I had to do this. I had to stop the war."

Within an hour, the flames died and the explosions ceased. The night was almost ominously quiet. There were a few hours before dawn, so I tried to sleep some more.

I dreamed of Charleston, green Charleston in the spring, and the creek where I'd fished as a boy, and how the sun had felt on my back and arms and head. There was no surgical table in my dream, nor were my shoes soaked with blood.

Around dawn somebody began shaking me. It was Sullivan's personal lieutenant. "The priest has been shot. Come quickly, Doctor."

I didn't even dress fully, just pulled on my trousers over the legs of my long underwear.

A dozen soldiers stood outside the tent looking confused and defeated and sad. I went inside.

The priest lay in his tent. His cassock had been torn away. A bloody hole made a target-like circle on his stomach.

Above his cot stood General Sullivan, a pistol in his hand.

I knelt next to the cot and examined the priest. His vital signs were faint and growing fainter. He had at most a few minutes to live.

I looked up at the General. "What happened?"

The General nodded for the lieutenant to leave. The man saluted and then went out into the gray dawn.

"I had to shoot him," General Sullivan said.

I stood up. "You had to shoot a priest?"

"He was trying to stop me."

"From what?"

Then I noticed for the first time the knife scabbard on the General's belt. Blood streaked its sides. The hilt of the knife was sticky with blood. So were the General's hands. I thought of how Yankee troops had begun disfiguring the faces of our dead on the battlefield.

He said, "I have a war to fight, Doctor. The men—the way they were reacting to the man's face—" He paused and touched the bloody hilt of the knife. "I took care of him. And the priest came in while I was doing it and went insane. He started hitting me, trying to stop me and—" He looked down at the priest. "I didn't have any choice, Doctor. I hope you believe me."

A few minutes later, the priest died.

I started to leave the tent. General Sullivan put a hand on my shoulder. "I know you don't care very much for me, Doctor, but I hope you understand me at least a little. I can't win a war when men desert and blow up ammunition dumps and start questioning the worthiness of the war itself. I had to do what I did. I hope someday you'll understand."

I went out into the dawn. The air smelled of campfires and coffee. Now the men were busy scurrying around, preparing for war. The way they had been before the man had been brought here in the buckboard.

I went over to the tent where he was kept and asked the guard to let me inside. "The General said nobody's allowed inside, Doctor."

I shoved the boy aside and strode into the tent.

The cloth was still over his face, only now it was soaked with blood. I raised the cloth and looked at him. Even for a doctor, the sight was horrible. The General had ripped out his eyes and sawed off his nose. His cheeks carried deep gullies where the knife had been dug in deep.

He was dead. The shock of the defacement had killed him.

Sickened, I looked away.

The flap was thrown back, then, and there stood General Sullivan. "We're going to bury him now, Doctor."

In minutes, the dead soldier was inside a pine box borne up a hill of long grass waving in a chill wind.

The rains came, hard rains, before they'd turned even two shovelfuls of earth.

Then, from a distance over the hill, came the thunder of cannon and the cry of the dying.

The face that reminded us of what we were doing to each other was no more. It had been made ugly, robbed of its sorrowful beauty.

He was buried quickly and without benefit of clergy—the priest himself having been buried an hour earlier—and when the ceremony was finished, we returned to camp and war.

The Broker

Every six months or so Rick Marner puts his ass on a plane and flies out to Vegas. Not that he doesn't like Chicago. Just he needs some *fresh* every once in a while. Fresh pussy. Fresh faces around the poker table. Fresh dinners on the menus.

Marner is one of those guys you always see in the supper clubs of rich and important people. The Marners never quite look as if they belong. Not even Armani suits can disguise them. Not even proper English can disguise them. Not even all the courtesy and polish in the world can disguise them. They weren't born to this life and it will always show. Like a nasty facial scar or the wrong color skin.

They're in these places, the Marners of the world, because the wealthy and affluent people need them to get certain things for them, merchandise of all kinds. The Marners never approach the important people.

The important people have to approach the Marners before any kind of conversation is struck. These are the rules, and the Marners of the world better damn well understand them or the wealthy will just go and get themselves new Marners.

Tonight, Marner is feeling pretty good about himself as he sits at the bar of a pricey Loop restaurant and watches himself in the mirror running behind the cash register. When he was a little kid, he never had any trouble recognizing himself. He was always Marner and life was uncomplicated. Now he doesn't know who he is any more. The body a mite fleshy. The hair a mite gray. The handsomeness soft, no longer weapon-sharp. The eyes are what's most distressing. They aren't his eyes. They really aren't. They don't even look like his color any more. This is a masquerade of some kind. It really isn't Marner at all. Someday, he's going to tear this middle-aging mask off his face and find the boy inside him again.

This morning, he sent his seventeen-year-old daughter a birthday present and he feels good about it. The good parent and all that. She lives with her mother in San Diego. Marner hasn't seen her in six years. He doesn't really want to see her. She'd put on a lot of weight the last time he'd visited. He'd been embarrassed about walking down the street with her. She was that fat. Marner tries always to put on a sleek and knowing front. This English teacher he was balling one summer (she liked dangerous men), she taught him proper grammar. She also taught him a little bit about literature. He listened to *The Great Gatsby* on audio tape. He identifies with Jay Gatsby. She also took him to the art museum. Now when books are brought up at a high-tone dinner table, he talks about Gatsby. Or, if the subject is art, Modigliani. So you have a guy in Armani who knows about Scott Fitzgerald and modern art, do you really want to see him walking down the street with some wallowing fat kid? No. It just doesn't reflect well. It doesn't mean he doesn't love Doris (though he's never been crazy about her name) or that he isn't proud of the fact that she's an A-student. It's just that a guy has a certain image of himself—and the people who should be around him—and Doris just doesn't fit.

He senses somebody near him. He has this kind of radar. Somebody near him he doesn't want near him. And he turns. And there's this guy and at first he doesn't recognize him.

"You sonofabitch," the guy says. And when he says this, the bartender, who is maybe ten feet away, looks up.

Dawson, the guy's name is. Peter Dawson. But my God. That was forty pounds ago. The deep raccoon-black circles under the eyes. The uncertain gait. The vampire-pale skin. Even the once-glossy black hair is now a dirty white.

"You want to talk to me," Marner says, "we'll go get a table." He tells the bartender to bring them two scotches straight up.

Dawson looks as if he's going to collapse before he makes it to the table. He moves jerkily, a bad imitation of a Romero zombie. When he sits down, he sighs deeply, as if he's just climbed a mountain. Marner thinks back, not all that long ago, when Dawson had been a jaunty, arrogant man bored with his wife and his girlfriends. He was all yacht club and country club and Gold Coast condo, all cold hard de-

Ed Gorman

mand. Not that long ago. Now, he is emaciated and very drunk.

The table sits in a shadowy corner. A jungle of trendy ferns form a partial wall around them, making the section even more private. Dawson starts to talk but Marner says, "Shut up."

"What?"

"Wait till he gets our drinks."

The bartender brings two things: drinks and a very suspicious gaze. He sets the liquor down and leaves. But his gaze lingers. Marner knows he's lost a couple of points with this bartender tonight. Doesn't do you any good to have people who look like Dawson come in and walk up to you. It sure doesn't.

Dawson says, "You sonofabitch, you didn't tell me what I was getting into."

"Yes, I did. I told you there might be a downside."

"Might be—" Dawson shakes his head. "I've been to every doctor in this town. I even spent a week at the Mayo clinic. They've run every test they can. And they can't find anything. Nothing." His eyes suddenly glisten with tears. "But I'm dying. They give me three months at the outside. And I've got a family, a wife and two kids. Do you understand that, you sonofabitch? I've got a family!"

"Maybe you should've thought of that."

Dawson is done with theatrics, at least for now. His breath is coming in small gasps. He seems to be getting paler right before Marner's eyes. "You should've told me what she was."

For a moment, Marner allows himself a moment of sentiment. "I'm sorry it happened, pal. I really am. But I did warn you. Two or three times, I said that there could be a downside to this babe. But you weren't listening. You'd just heard all the stories about her and wanted some of it for your own. 'The Wildest Fuck In The Windy City.' That's what you said about her, remember, after you'd been with her a couple of times. You didn't have any complaints, then."

"No, not back then. But after a couple of months—"

Marner takes a drink. "I told you that, too, if you think back. I said, you should move on to something else but if you don't, there can be trouble if you're with her too many times. But you didn't listen to that, either." Marner is practiced at this kind of situation, however uncomfortable it makes him sometimes, his customers complaining about the merchandise he's obtained for them. Rich people are like anybody else, they don't like to spend any more money than they absolutely have to. How Marner obtains his merchandise is something they don't want to know. That's his business. He's brokered items as various as a Mercedes-Benz limousine, a summer cottage, mink coats, expensive watches, and even famous pieces of jewelry. For a price, no questions asked. And sometimes he handles women, too. Not your everyday hookers, God forbid. Not even the undernourished beauties who model during the day and put out for big bucks at night. No, he went for the exotic. The extremely special ones.

"You've got to help me," Dawson says, sounding sick again.

"I can't. If I could I would."

"Who is she?"

"I don't know."

"What the hell does that mean?"

"She just appeared one night. In this bar."

"She just appeared? Just walked up to you?"

"Right. I was sort of pre-occupied, and she walked up to me told me her name was Nadia."

"Nadia what?"

"Nadia nothing. She's never given me a last name."

"And what'd she say?"

"She told me about herself. That she was special. And that she understood that maybe I could help her and that we could both make some money."

"Money, of course. It's always money."

"I wasn't born wealthy, the way you were. I have to make a living."

The sick man looks embarrassed. "I'm sorry. Go on."

"So I set her up in the penthouse and things have gone well ever since." He is understating; Nadia is the single most profitable item he has ever offered his clientele.

"Oh, yes, very well. Look at me, Marner. I'm dying and the doctors can't even tell me why. I'd turn you both in if it wouldn't cause my family a scandal."

Marner stares at him a moment. "This has only happened a few times. The way you got sick and everything. Whatever she does . . . it only affects a few people."

"And one of them, unfortunately, is me." He puts his elbow on the table and his head in his hand. He begins quietly crying.

Marner glances around, seeing if anybody is watching. "This isn't the place," he says. A man in his position, a man who brokers things the way he does, a man like him can't afford to cause scenes.

"Then just where the fuck is the place, Mr. Marner?"

This time, no doubt, half the restaurant hears Dawson. Marner freezes in place, so many people staring. They will think that Marner has himself a very unhappy customer, which can't be a good advertisement for his business.

"Then just where is the place, Marner?"

"We're going now, Mr. Dawson."

"You put a hand on me, I'll kill you. And you'd better understand that."

"You're going to walk out of here quietly, Mr. Dawson, or I'm going right to that phone and call your wife and tell her everything."

"You would, wouldn't you, you bastard?"

"Yes, I would."

"You sonofabitch."

"You need to get some new insults, Mr. Dawson. You've called me that several times already tonight."

"You don't give a shit that I'm dying, do you?"

"I'm sorry you're dying, Mr. Dawson. But I warned you about the risk of going back and back and back."

"But she addicts you, don't you understand that?"

"Just a few people is all, the ones she addicts. Just a few."

It takes Marner twenty minutes to get Dawson out of the place. By then, Marner knows that he can never again come in here. If he doubts that, all he has to do is look at the bartender, at that cold superior sneer on his face.

Marner spills Dawson into his Bently and then walks away. Even when he gets to the other end of the parking lot, he can hear Dawson in his car, weeping.

*   *   *

Seven months ago, after he realized just how much money Nadia was going to make him, just how many men wanted to spend time with her, Marner laid out the bread for a beautiful condo just off Lake Shore Drive. An A-location. Underground parking garage. Smiling uniformed doorman at the front door. The swiftest of elevators to the ninth floor. Room 907. Marner has the key, of course. And lets himself in.

Darkness. The only light is in the full window where a quarter moon and stars look down upon the city. This is Thursday night, collection night. Nadia never keeps any of the money. She puts it in an envelope for him on the coffee table in the well-appointed living room.

Thursday is her down night. He never makes any appointments for her on Thursday. She says she needs her rest. One time, and only one time, he opened her bedroom door and peeked in. And still wishes he hadn't. Even in the briefest of glances, she is ghastly, a squid-like thing on the bed, the pus-bag center section rising and falling with each breath, the noise a frantic rasping. The stench is even worse. He clamped his hand over his mouth and quickly closed the door.

How something like this could turn itself into beautiful Nadia, The Wildest Fuck in The Windy City, he doesn't know. And doesn't want to know. All he wants is what he has now, his envelope with all that lovely money in it.

As the elevator falls quickly and certainly to the ground level, he finds himself thinking about his daughter again. God, he wishes she'd lose some weight. It'd be so nice to have a good-looking young daughter on his arm to show off to people. It would be so damn nice.

The Long Sunset

The afternoon it all started, Sean and I were playing basketball. Or rather, Sean was playing basketball, and I was trying to keep up with him. Sean was the star athlete of Woodrow Wilson High. I was the basketball team manager, thanks to his influence. I played like a team manager, too.

It was just after the season had ended. There were still patches of dirty April snow on the playground asphalt. The wind was warm and hinted of apple blossoms and the first sputtering sounds of lawn mowers and Saturday afternoons, of little kids with their wobbly kites and adults with their frisbees and happy dogs. Just a few weeks away now.

Ken Michaels pulled his red Kawasaki motorcycle right up to where we were playing and whipped off his helmet. "Hey, you hear about Jenna?"

"Jenna?" I said, knowing instantly that something terrible had happened to her.

"Downtown," Ken said. "A car hit her."

"Oh, God," I said.

"Is she alive?" Sean asked.

"Yeah. But she's in pretty bad shape."

A minute later Sean and I jumped on his motorcycle and headed for St. Mary's Hospital. Jenna, Sean, and I had grown up in the poor section of our little town of Black River Falls, Iowa. The Knolls they call it, up in the hills above where the great factories used to roar before all the manufacturing went first down South, and then to Mexico. We were inseparable friends. We were bright and ambitious, too, and determined not to stay in the Knolls (or Black River Falls, for that matter) any longer than we had to. There was only one problem. Jenna was in love with Sean, and I was in love with Jenna. And Sean was in love with the princess of Woodrow Wilson High, Kim Westcott.

The good news was that Jenna wasn't as death-threatened as Ken Michaels had led us to believe. The bad news was that her right leg was so badly smashed by the car—the driver a local guy with two previous drunk driving arrests—that the doctor told her folks that she would probably always limp. They hadn't mentioned any of this to Jenna. This wasn't the time.

I stayed until they kicked me out around seven o'clock. Jenna, pale, pretty, scared, was obviously happy I was there. But she was even happier that Sean was. But after four o'clock, which was when he left to get ready for his date with Kim, Jenna didn't look so happy again. She chit-chatted with her folks and then chit-chatted with me while they were down in the cafeteria having dinner. But she kept staring longingly at the empty doorway, as if she thought Sean might magically reappear for her.

She stayed in the hospital almost three weeks. The tests and examinations were intense. They told her about the limp. She took it so badly, they put her on one of those psychoactive drugs for depression.

She made it back to school just in time for graduation. Sean wasn't around much, spending every possible moment with Kim and her friends. Knolls people like Jenna and I weren't invited.

The first time I ever saw her drunk was graduation night. She'd asked if she could ride to the ceremony with me. When I went to pick her up, her mother came to the door and whispered, "Jenna went somewhere this afternoon and got drunk. You weren't with her, were you?" I assured her I wasn't. "We've been pouring coffee into her for the last couple of hours."

Her father brought her down. She looked sweet in her cap and gown. She made it about halfway across the tiny living room and dropped straight down, unconscious. No graduation ceremony for Jenna.

"She was afraid of walking across the stage to get her diploma," her father said, "everybody staring at her. You know, her crutches and cast and everything."

"But she's so pretty," I said. "Nobody cares about that."

"*She* cares," her mother said. "And that's all that matters."

The first time she was arrested for driving while intoxicated, I was the one the Chief of Police called. Jenna's parents were out of town visiting relatives. He wanted $350 in bail money. I had about $3,000 in the bank, my savings toward college. Iowa City was less than an hour away. I was taking three classes a semester and working at a supermarket the rest of the time. I'd been planning to go full-time, but then there was a downturn in the agricultural market. Since my father sold big-ticket farm implements, we didn't have much money.

This was two years after graduating high school. Jenna hadn't gone to college at all. The problem wasn't money. It was alcohol. Jenna had become a serious alcoholic very quickly. A lot of public scenes, slapping people in bars, drunken crying jags at parties, a couple of half-assed suicide attempts. She worked at the mall sometimes. The job had been regular at first. But then her uncle, who had a caramel-corn concession out there, just let her come in when she wanted to. He was her godfather and didn't know what else to do.

The first time I bailed her out wasn't so bad. She was contrite and full of resolve never to take a drink again. We ended up sitting in my car in her darkened driveway for almost three hours. She cried a lot. She even let me kiss her a few times. It was heady, and I'm not kidding. This girl I'd loved since I was a little kid . . . at last in my arms.

Over the next year, I bailed her out twice more. One time she was belligerent. Fucking cops. Fucking stupid laws. She'd been *walking*, for God's sake. Not driving. And since when could fucking stupid cops pick you up for fucking *walking*. Public intoxication, I said gently. Oh, you're so fucking full of shit, I can't believe it, she said and slammed out of the car.

The next time she was really sick. She opened the door and threw up twice before I even got her home.

I guess it was around this time—to be honest, I didn't have any reason to pay this kind of thing any particular attention—that a few farmers started calling the local radio station and newspaper with stories of spaceships hovering over their houses late at night. And not long after that, some of the same people started talking about being abducted by creatures from those very same spaceships, little aliens with tear-shaped heads and glowing emerald-colored eyes. At the time I remember thinking, sure, whatever.

Sean didn't get back to town until he was twenty-eight. By then, he'd spent three years as an All-American at Ohio State and four years as the star quarterback of the Bears, his career ending when his throwing hand was crushed in a riding mower accident. He'd invested his enormous salary, though, and was rich.

He came back to town with his high school princess and three gorgeous blonde daughters in tow. He built a house that cost almost as much as our library had six years earlier, and bought a horse ranch that provided the stud services for two thoroughbreds that had come very close to winning the Derby. He drove around town in a big Mercedes-Benz convertible the color of a misty dawn.

As for the princess, she took over the Junior League, the country club, all the charities that could get her on TV, and the major party scene, such as it was. Fluttering about her at all times was a group of smirking empty-headed gossips whose husbands were this generation's city fathers. Giggle giggle giggle; whisper whisper whisper.

Jenna and I watched him and his life the way you

would a movie. Parts made us laugh, parts made us mad, parts made us sad. He hadn't forgotten us entirely. Jenna and I hung out at a tavern called Dudley Do-Right's. Every so often Sean's Mercedes would sweep into a parking lot filled with Harleys and pick-up trucks, and he would come inside and have a few beers with us. The men inside tended to fawn over him when he walked in. They always asked for the inside scoop on this player or that coach, and he gave them enough tidbits to make him forever popular there.

One rainy August night, the rain hotter than the day itself had been, he came in late. Jenna had already gone home. She was working her way back to de-tox. Her pattern was always the same. A month or so after de-tox, she'd start hanging around Dudley's again. She'd start out with just Diet Pepsi. A week later, it was beer. Alcoholics will always argue that beer doesn't really count. A week after that, she'd be back on the hard stuff. Then it was a matter of five, six months. She'd lose another job, have another lousy affair, sleep with Dudley a few times so he'd forgive her bar tab, and then start calling me in the middle of the night to cry over Sean. She was still in love with him; she would *always* be in love with him.

Not that my own life was any better. A two-year marriage gone bust. A job out at the mall hawking computers. Watching my parents slowly fade and die. I was long over loving Jenna. But instead of relief, all I felt was emptiness.

I was always eager to see Sean because he represented a life I'd never have. Not just the big car or the horse ranch or the investments but the wife and daughters. Unlike my life or Jenna's, his had a defin-able and discernible *meaning*.

Or so I thought till that rainy August night.

He said, "I envy your life, Randy."

He said, "Man, it was so fucking wonderful on Sunday afternoons. All those fans screaming and shouting and applauding. And my life'll never be like that again. Not ever again."

He said, "You know how many women I've slept with in the last year? Over fifty. And you know what? I didn't come with any of them. I can't have an or-gasm anymore. I used to think it'd be so great, to be able to go all night, literally *all night* if you wanted to. But it's a curse, man. Believe me, it's a curse. And the fucking doctors can't seem to find any way to help me."

He said, "You know what I've been thinking lately? I've been thinking maybe I married the wrong woman. Maybe I should've married Jenna. Maybe I've been in love with Jenna all along and didn't know it. All that society bullshit my wife is into. I hate it. Jenna isn't like that at all."

He didn't say all these things in sequence, of course. He said them over the course of several hours, both of us getting drunker and drunker. In between, we talked a little town gossip, a little local politics, a little nostalgia. He was once again the Sean I'd grown up with.

But he was going to destroy Jenna. He wanted an easy answer to what he saw as the torpor of his life, and he was going to try anything that was at hand. He didn't care if an affair was good for Jenna. All he knew was that it would be good for him. At least temporarily.

He disagreed, of course, when I brought it up.

"You didn't hear what I said, Randy. I said I think I *love* her. Not just that I want to hop in the sack with her. That I *love* her." He brought his fist down on the booth table so hard that everybody looked in our direction.

I knew then that there was nothing I could do to stop it. Jenna was finally going to have that love affair with Sean she'd wanted since we were all little kids growing up poor and sad in the Knolls.

Jenna bloomed. She even cut her drinking way back. Sean was able to provide what the de-tox clinics hadn't been able to. She went to work regularly and bought herself a lot of new clothes. Her drab apartment became festive with new paint, new curtains, a new couch. On the nights when Sean couldn't make it over, and I didn't have a sex date with one of my waitresses or mall clerks (a bad marriage can scare you off romance for a long time), Jenna'd have me over so she could tell me all about how wonderful it was to be in love with Sean, and to have Sean in love with her. He'd leave his wife, and they'd be married. They'd build a new house, a huge masterpiece of a house, out on the edge of Hartson Woods, where they'd raise themselves some gleaming children.

Sean was just as taken with Jenna. I'd never seen him vulnerable to anybody before. It made him human in a way he'd never quite been. He'd grin like a kid when he talked about her; and stare off with great grave melancholy when he recalled certain tender things they'd said to each other. Even the swagger vanished. He was just a simple man in simple love.

It lasted longer than I thought it would. Four-and-a-half months. I've never been sure exactly how he met Kristin, but suddenly she was there—she'd moved here from Cedar Rapids to take over a small real estate firm—and suddenly Jenna was in my apartment sobbing and frantically throwing back straight scotches.

I slept with her. I knew I was taking advantage, but I didn't care. I no longer loved her, not romantically anyway, but I'd always been curious about sex with her. The first time, she was so drunk she had to excuse herself in the middle of it to hurry into the bathroom and throw up. The second time, she was so drunk she passed out beneath me. But the third time . . . she was sweet and sad and tender and it was the best sex I'd ever had, her hair fragrant as flowers, her voice gentle and even poignant at times, and her slender body a marvel of surprising richness. The only time she got spooked was when she was naked in any kind of light. The limp. The crushed leg. She was so ashamed of it. For a while I was afraid I was going to fall in love with her again. But it didn't happen, and a part of me was sad about it. It had been a long time since I'd burned with that searing fever that takes over your whole life. And I wanted it again. But she was gone from me now, we truly were just friends now, and so the best I could do for her—or for myself—was hold her when she wept, and make timid, cautionary remarks about how her drinking was getting out of hand again. I knew I was wasting my time. She was drinking harder than she ever had.

There were scenes. She drove drunkenly out to his horse ranch and slapped him and started sobbing. And then she accosted him in a bar one night and spat in

Kristin's face. And then she called Sean's wife and they commiserated on what a shit he was and (at least according to Jenna's drunken retelling) they became friends for life on the basis of that single phone call.

I didn't see Sean for a while. He had his shiny New One to spend time with. The night I did run into him in one of the local pubs, I was drunk enough to follow him out the door—he and the bartender were sick of me telling him what an asshole he was—and hit him hard in the mouth. Hard enough to split his lip. It felt great. Then he hit me three or four times and not only bloodied my lip but my nose as well.

He went back in and got a six-pack and we sat in his Benz convertible polishing off the beers and listening to blue Miles Davis jazz low on the CD player and talking about the old days in the Knoll and how he was sorry he'd hurt Jenna and would do anything he could to help her, including picking up the tab for this special de-tox clinic he'd heard of just outside St. Paul. We used the alley as our chamber pot. We sat there two hours and in the course of it I was able to gauge just how much he'd changed. Or maybe he'd always been like this and I just hadn't been observant enough to understand it. The kindness, the concern was there to make him palatable to his fellow humans. He was a good actor. But he didn't really give a shit about Jenna or his wife or his kids or me. He was even waffling on Kristin, her no longer being "quite as interesting" as she'd once seemed. There was a new New One, it seemed. . . .

When I got home, Jenna was asleep in my bed. I slipped in beside her. In the morning we made quick love and then took a shower together. She said she'd make some breakfast while I got ready for work. The breakfast was Cheerios and orange juice out of a can. And, for Jenna, a generous glass of my whiskey. . . .

I guess it was about four or five weeks later that she called me and asked me to come over. She sounded strange—distracted and distant—and I wondered if she was thinking about suicide or something. The tone of her voice made me nervous as hell.

She was sober. That was the first thing I noticed. And she had this velvet painting of a forlorn Jesus sitting on her dining room table, a dinner candle burning in front of it like a votive candle in a Catholic church. Jenna was a Methodist.

She was better kept than I'd seen her in a long time. Scrubbed, short dark hair combed forward to flatter the elegant bones of her small face, white blouse and designer jeans clean and freshly pressed.

"Pepsi all right?"

"Fine," I said.

"I haven't had a drink in three weeks."

"Great. I'm proud of you. AA again?"

Shook her head. "On my own."

"Wow."

She disappeared into the kitchen, returned with glasses heavy with ice and dark with Pepsi. "Diet was all I had."

"No problem. I prefer it, actually."

She sat on the couch, pulled her legs up under her wonderful buttocks. She made me horny and sad at the same time. She said, "You're the first one I'm telling."

"All right."

"And I know you're going to be skeptical. And think that this happened when I was drunk. And that it was just a dream or something. That's why I mentioned the drinking. The first time, I *was* drunk, and I'll admit it. But that's why I mentioned about not having a drink for three weeks."

"I see."

"I want to tell you, but I'm afraid to tell you."

"All right."

"Just please don't laugh, Randy."

"I promise."

"Or smirk."

"Scout's Honor."

"Or ask me to see a shrink or anything like that."

I smiled. "You ever going to tell me what it is?"

She hesitated. "All these people who say they were abducted by aliens?"

"Uh-huh."

"They're telling the truth. At least, the majority of them are."

No laughing. No smirking. No asking her to see a shrink. Those were the ground rules. My body did tighten up, though. Nothing I could do about that.

"All right."

"Is that a smirk?"

"Nope."

"You know what I'm going to tell you, don't you?"

"That you were abducted?"

"That's right. I was. Three times, in fact."

"Two of them sober."

"Two of them sober." She hesitated again. "So what do you think?"

"I guess I take your word for it."

"It happened. It really did."

"And I believe you believe that."

She laughed, but there was more sadness than joy

in the sound. "That's what most people around here'll say when they hear it. Stuff like that. I don't think they hate me, actually. They just feel sorry for me. The booze and all. And this'll be one more step up to the mental hospital door. Permanent residence, this time. Die in there at the ripe old age of 103."

"Maybe you shouldn't tell anybody."

"In other words, you don't believe me."

"No," I said. "Not that at all. It's just that I know how people respond to things like this."

"Come over here."

"Over there?"

"Yes. The couch. Next to me."

"You sure?"

"I'm sure."

"I thought we agreed not to—"

"I don't want sex. I just want you to hold me."

"I charge by the hour."

"How much?"

"A nickel."

"I *think* I can swing that."

We ended up in bed, of course. Slow, sweet love. I couldn't ever recall sex being so tender or innocent. And she must have found it the same way because after we were done, we lay next to each other holding hands and talking about when we were little kids up in the Knolls, the good stuff, not the bad stuff, the good sweet innocent times, kittens and puppies and TV shows and movies we loved and funny things happening at school and how much we'd loved our now-dead folks, a sweet sadness coming on with that, and when it was time to go, I realized that something had crept up on me: happiness. Usually, I spent my time looking back at all the bad things that had hap-

pened to me. But being with Jenna this snowy afternoon—I was so exultant, I left my car and walked
home. I stopped and helped a little girl build her
snowman, giving her my brand new fedora for the
snowman's hat; I got in a friendly snowball fight with
some high school kids; and I stopped in a Catholic
church and said a few Presbyterian prayers; and at the
comic book shop, I bought thirty dollars worth of *Bat-
mans* and *Daredevils* from the late seventies and early
eighties and took them home and had a great grand
night reading them. I was high out of my mind. But
it wasn't drugs. Drugs had never come close to making me feel euphoric. It was something else: it was
Jenna. I was high on Jenna.

The next day, I started calling her as soon as I got
off work. Her line was busy. It stayed busy. I called
the operator. She told me there was apparently trouble
on the line. I was getting kind of desperate. All I'd
been able to think about all day long was how good
I'd felt after being with her. It wasn't the sex, though
that had been great; and it wasn't that I'd fallen in
love with her again, which I hadn't. It was just the
mental state she'd somehow put me in. For several
hours after leaving her, I'd been able to transcend all
my petty human problems. While I'd been raised
poor, I'd been a pretty happy kid. And I'd been kid-
happy again last night, after being with Jenna.

I spent another useless hour trying to contact her
on the phone. Still busy. I drove over there.

There was a group out in front of her shabby old
apartment house. People of all ages, colors, social stations. Maybe fifteen in all. A couple of the older
women held candles, as if this was a religious service.

Nobody seemed to mind the cold night. Or the snowfall.

"What's going on?" I said.

They all just looked at me. Said nothing.

Their eyes told me how much they resented me.

I pushed past them and went inside.

A few residents were in the hall. "You see any cops out there yet?" a black man asked me.

"No."

"The bastards. I wish they'd hurry up."

"What's going on?" I said.

A heavy man shook his head. "They think she's some kind of angel or something."

"Who is?"

"Your friend," the black man said. "Jenna."

"They're all outside because of Jenna?"

The heavy man nodded. "The cops ran them off earlier tonight. But now they're back again."

"Is Jenna upstairs?"

"Far as we know," the black man said.

We'd long ago swapped apartment keys. I went upstairs and knocked softly. No answer. Stained wallpaper hung loose from the hallway walls. A country-western CD competed with the rap CD across the hall. Ancient steam heat radiators clanged and banged busily.

I let myself in. Darkness.

She said, "Close the door. And please don't turn on the light."

I sat down on the couch next to her.

"You all right?"

"Sure. I love having mobs of people out on my lawn waiting for me."

"What happened?"

"I don't know." She sighed. "That ship. The spaceship or whatever it was. I know you don't believe me—"

"I believe you now."

"You do?"

"Yeah. Something really did happen to you on that ship." I told her about the bliss I'd felt last night.

"Well, they must've felt it, too."

"Who are they?"

"Oh, you know, just people I met today. The guy in the expensive topcoat and the homburg—he's my banker. The woman in the wheelchair runs the cash register at the beauty shop. The teenager is a bag boy at the supermarket. I somehow gave them the same kind of euphoria I gave you. And now they want more of it. They're addicts. I was just trying to be nice, was all."

I went to the window and looked out. A police car had just arrived. Two cops got out and made their way up the snowy walk to the apartment house. Took a while, but they managed to break up the people who stood dumbly staring up at Jenna's apartment window.

"Can I stay at your place?" she said. "I'm afraid to be here alone."

I got blissed out every night.

By the fourth night, I didn't want to get up and go to work. I just wanted her to focus on me, find that spiritual part of myself that made me happy (thinking of my boyhood never failed), and then make me euphoric. It was kind of like telepathy, I guess, her ability to read you and find the aspect of memory that

264

released all that lovely happiness. And it wasn't even illegal.

The people she'd blissed out the other day had taken to quieting down. In their fervor, they'd managed to alienate a lot of their friends. The town was uncomfortable enough with all this talk about alien abductions. The prospect of an alcoholic woman who could work emotional miracles was downright embarrassing.

I knew better, and so did she. Several times, she tried to describe what had happened to her when she'd been taken aboard the ship. Unlike the experiences of most people, she reported a gentle and lovely time, not unlike those reported in many near-death experiences, when a soft, foggy atmosphere was filled with a warmth and security that imbued not only her body but her mind and soul as well. And during her fourth abduction, she returned from the ship carrying the blissful state with her. And sharing it with anyone she had the time to concentrate on. Not passing strangers, but people she spent at least a few minutes with. When she focused, Jenna relieved them temporarily from all their anxiety and apprehension, filling them with tender and exultant feelings.

I wouldn't have believed any of this if I hadn't experienced it myself. I would have said that she was back on the bottle again and into fantasy and self-delusion.

But I knew better.

She kept me pretty well blissed out. I rented a lot of Abbott & Costello movies, and we watched a lot of late night old movies, and ate a lot of pizza, and kept ourselves happy. I had to go to work, but it was difficult to concentrate. Several times the boss ragged on me. I wasn't exactly his favorite, anyway. That dubious honor belonged to Kenny Wayman, who did everything except wash and wax the boss man's car.

I couldn't wait to get home, to disappear inside that cocoon of well-being she created.

I was whistling as I came through the door. Usually, I heard the sound of the TV or the CD player as I came into the apartment. But now there was only silence. Suddenly a brief burst of light in the sky visible through my kitchen window caught my attention. My first thought was of the ship, the aliens she had talked about. But that was ridiculous. As quickly as it had appeared, the light was gone, and I gave it no more thought.

I stood on the threshold, knowing something was wrong. It was more than just the silence. It was the *absence*. Jenna's beatific presence had changed the air. It really had. There was a freshness, the way the air is fresh and clean after a rain. But now the air was just air, apartment air, with faint food smells and the homey scent of furniture polish.

No note. No message on the phone machine. She was gone. I sat in the dark for many hours. The pizza got cold. I opened a couple of beers but didn't finish either of them. I fell asleep on the couch. The two cats slept on my back.

Around nine AM, somebody pounded on the door. Two guys in moving uniforms.

"We're supposed to pick up some stuff that belongs to Jenna McKay."

I'd trekked over to Jenna's apartment during her stay here and had brought back a considerable number of her things. This is what they were picking up. I asked where they were delivering her things. They said they weren't supposed to tell me.

It wasn't much of a weekend. I cruised past Jenna's place at least twenty times, hoping she'd show up there. She didn't.

I used my car phone to check my home machine every twenty minutes in case she'd called. She hadn't.

I even drove out to the company the movers worked for. The place was locked up.

I didn't sleep well either Saturday or Sunday night. I couldn't bring myself to lie in the bed where we'd made love. Too lonely. The cats got to use my couch-prone body as a mattress again.

Monday night, just after work, she called.

She said, "How you doing, Randy?"

So, I told her how I was doing, and I wasn't very nice about telling her.

She waited until I finished and then she said, "It's going to happen, Randy. Finally." I'd never heard her this happy.

"What is?"

"He's going to get a divorce and marry me."

I didn't need to ask her who "he" was.

"When did this happen?"

"He stopped by to see you last week, and I was there. And we just started talking—and he said he wanted to set me up in my own place—a real nice place. And that'd give him time to think of how he was going to handle the divorce. He doesn't want to hurt his wife."

Dumping his wife for another woman. Now how would that hurt his wife? "Yeah, he's a real sensitive guy."

"C'mon, Randy. We all grew up together. You should be happy for us."

"Remember what happened the last time he dumped you? Remember how bad you got?"

It was kind of funny. Even though I was no longer in love with her—and I wasn't—I had this proprietary feeling about her. She was like my kid sister now. I wanted to protect her. "You know how he is. He's fickle. He wants everything. And he figures he deserves it, too. You have to be very careful, Jenna."

"He loves me."

"That's the only dangerous part of you being blissed out. You've taken your guard down. You used to be very protective of yourself. And with Sean, you need to be."

"I know love when I see it, Randy. And he loves me. He really does."

What was the point of arguing? And how could I be sure that he *didn't* really love her? Maybe he'd changed. I've lived long enough to know that some people really *do* change.

"I'm happy for you, Jenna."

"Oh, thanks for saying that, Randy. It means a lot to me."

"I hope it all works out."

"I should've left a note or something. I just didn't know what to say. It all happened so fast."

"No problem. But let's keep in touch."

"Of course we will."

A few days later, I was eating lunch at The Big Table when I saw Sean's Mercedes pull up outside. He appeared to be headed to the bank down the street. I threw a five and my lunch bill on the counter and hurried out the door. I caught him at a red light.

He didn't seem happy to see me. "I'd appreciate it if you wouldn't talk to Jenna anymore."

"She called me, Sean."

"Oh, yeah. I guess that's right." He nodded to a diner. "Let's have some coffee." After we'd been served, and were sitting at a window table watching all the bundled-up people hurrying red-nosed and red-cheeked through the sunny Midwestern winter, he said, "I don't want anything to upset her."

I was shocked. I couldn't ever recall Sean saying anything like that before, being so protective of somebody else. I was not only impressed; I was moved. Maybe Jenna was right, after all. Maybe this time, he really was going to marry her.

"I mean, I don't know if all that UFO bullshit actually happened to her," he said. "But something did." He looked around and then spoke in a half-whisper. "The happiness stuff. She said she did it to you."

"Yeah," I said, "she did." I wondered if she'd told him we'd slept together. I hoped not.

"I haven't felt this good since I scored that thirty-yard touchdown pass against the 49ers in the playoffs. Won the fucking game," he said. The way he said it, I could tell he'd been with her pretty recently. He was still blissed.

But he was also something else, something far more recognizable: he was selfish. He was already addicted to the state of bliss she infused in him and he meant to keep her all to himself.

He said, "I'm just afraid she'll lose it somehow."

"Maybe it's religious."

"What is?"

"You know, her power. Maybe the things on that ship are religious beings. Maybe they showed her how to key in on her own innocence and to share it with other people."

"That's the dumbest fucking thing I've ever heard of."

"Thank you."

He smiled. "I'm sorry. That came out harsher than I'd intended. I just mean it sounds like some dipshit sci-fi show or something."

Actually, it was. A similar idea had been done on an invasion-from-outer-space anthology show called *Beings*.

"Well, she developed this power somehow."

He shook his head. "How she got it doesn't matter. It's keeping it that counts. That's why I'm taking good, good care of her. I'm putting her somewhere nobody knows about. I've convinced her there're these rumors all over town about her power and that she'll be treated like a freak if she ever walks the streets. That scares her. She *wants* to hide out."

"She says you're going to leave your wife and marry her." I wanted to see how he'd respond.

He smiled. It was close to a smirk. "Well, you know how the ladies are, Randy. They like you to whisper sweet things in their ear."

"Even if the sweet things aren't true."

The famous Sean temper was there instantly. "What the fuck are you? Her lawyer or something?"

"I just don't want to see her hurt again, Sean. I don't think she could handle it. The last time, she ended up in de-tox."

"Her choice, my man. Her choice entirely. Lots of people get dumped and don't end up in de-tox."

He was absolving himself of all guilt. He didn't have time for guilt.

"And if she loses her gift, you'll dump her again."

"You think I don't care for her, Randy? I do. I really do. She's a sweet, sweet girl. A lot of problems, but very sweet nonetheless. And you know what? She loves this idea of being hidden away. She picked the house and the furnishings—everything. It's a hideout for her. She's never been able to deal with people anyway. And now she doesn't have to." The smile again. Not a hint of smirkiness this time. Just the coldness that was always there. "She gets what she wants, I get what I want. I've cornered the market on bliss."

Every once in a while during the next month, I'd run into one of the people I'd seen standing on Jenna's lawn that night. They come up and grab my arm and plead with me to tell them where she was. Sad people. Junkies, really. Bliss junkies. I didn't feel superior to them. I had a physical ache in the pit of my stomach; I wanted the bliss, too. I don't think they believed me when I said I didn't know where she was. Our conversations were held in whispers. They didn't want the town to think they were still pursuing their wild claims.

A lot of nights, I'd sit home and watch TV and stare at the phone, kind of willing it to ring. And one night, it did. She spoke quickly, in a whisper. "I need to get out of here."

"Then leave."

"I'm—afraid."

"Where are you?"

She told me. She said he was upstairs, sleeping. "If I leave, he'll just come after me."

"He can't hold you against your will."

"Yes, he can. In this town, he can."

I told her I'd pick her up in half an hour. She said she'd be ready.

The house was a chalet-style affair in the center of a tree-encircled meadow. No mailbox out front to announce it, and a road that would be impassable for most vehicles in deep winter.

She was out on the road, looking anxiously around, when I arrived. Winter dusk had rouged the sky the color of pink salmon. A quarter moon was crisply outlined against the night.

I didn't notice it right away, her walking to the car. Only when she was three or four feet away did I realize what was different about her.

When she got in, I said, "You're not limping."

She looked over at me and grinned. A kid-grin, it was, and it was gorgeous. "Yeah, isn't it great?"

"What happened?"

"I don't know. It just went away."

I smiled. "You must've 'blissed' it away."

"I know you're making a joke. But I think that's actually what happened."

By the time we got to my apartment, she'd told me all about it. Sean was quite literally hooked on being blissed out. That's all he wanted, the bliss. He rarely went to work. He rarely even watched TV or read a newspaper. He'd demand that she bliss him up and then he'd go lie on his *Playboy*-style round bed and lie there for hours until the blissful mind-state had finally faded. Then he'd be at her again, demanding that she bliss him again. If she didn't do it, he'd get violent with her. He was smart enough not to bruise her face, she said. But her body was covered with cuts and bruises. Power had made Sean's already considerable temper even worse. She was now really afraid of him. He kept demanding that she could put him in an even higher state of bliss, if only she'd concentrate more. New, Improved Bliss—more potent than ever. Jenna said she feared for his sanity.

The first twenty-four hours were nice. It being a weekend, I didn't have to go to work. I rented some videos and ordered in some pizza. I watched her slowly relax. She blissed me, but it was incidental. She said she hadn't even tried. But her own joy and purity just naturally worked its way into me. I spent a couple of hours reliving some of the great times with my younger brother and sister whom, I learned in retrospect, I should have been a whole lot nicer to. But there were great memories nonetheless, good enough in fact to streak my cheeks with tears. She held me while I cried.

Toward dawn, she said, "I still love him."

"I know."

"Really?"

"Sure. It's in your voice. Even when you're angry with him, there's a kind of melancholy in your tone."

"He scares me."

"He scares me, too."

We didn't say anything for a long time. Then, "Maybe if he actually gets a divorce, and we have a chance to live a normal life, maybe he won't be so hung up on being blissed out as you call it."

It didn't make much sense to me either, what she'd just said—I mean, she'd run to me because she was scared of him; now she was talking about going back with him—but I let it drift away, her words like wisps of smoke, and let myself slide into sleep.

*   *   *

I don't know what time the door-pounding started. I jerked awake at the first heavy thud.

Jenna whispered, "It's him."

"Sean?"

"Yeah."

"I'll take care of him."

"No; I've been thinking." Her tone of voice said it all. "I've been awake all night. I love him, Randy. I really do. I can help him through this thing. I really can. Being so hung up on being blissed out, I mean."

The pounding kept on.

She slipped from the bed and opened the door.

He did a Rhett Butler. They didn't say a word to each other. He just swept her up in his arms, her mussed in my ancient blue threadbare KMart bathrobe, and carried her out to his Mercedes. Then they were gone.

I guess the rest of it, you pretty much know. You do if you watch TV or read the papers, anyway.

She called me the night before it happened, one of her frantic whispered calls. "I've got to get out of here. I think this phone is tapped. He doesn't want me to talk to anybody he doesn't know about. He's afraid somebody's going to take me from him. I want my own life, Randy. He doesn't love me. He just wants to stay blissed out. I can see that now. And that makes it easier for me. I just want to get out of town, so he can't find me."

The phone line clicked a few times: a phone tap, as she'd said. Then the connection went dead. I doubted she'd hung up. Someone had broken the connection for her.

I drove out to their eyrie that night. No lights. No

cars in the driveway. I parked up on a ridge for a couple of hours with a pair of field glasses. I didn't see anything moving inside the house. Not even shadows.

He was sitting on my couch in the darkness when I got back home around midnight. He scared the hell out of me when he spoke. I hadn't known he was in there.

He said, "Don't turn the light on."

"It's my place, Sean. I can do what I want."

"I—want to wash up first." He hesitated. "I've got blood all over my hands and shirt."

"You sonofabitch."

I started to lunge at him. But then moonlight outlined the pistol he raised and pointed at me. "No heroics, Randy. I don't want to kill you, too."

"We grew up together. The three of us."

"I know."

"We were as close as you could get without being kin."

"She was going to leave me."

"You didn't give a shit about her. It was being blissed out you were worried about."

He didn't say anything. "I'm never going to have it again. Being high like that."

"Maybe you should've thought of that before you killed her."

"She was going to leave me." he said, "I couldn't let her go."

"Well, I guess you stopped her, all right."

"Take me down to the police station, will you?"

I sighed. "Maybe I better call your lawyer first."

"I don't give a shit about lawyers. Just take me to the station, all right?"

I took him to the station. I knew the night man and told him everything that had happened and how Sean was out in the car. The night man called the Chief and, after spending a full minute apologizing for wrestling the Chief from his beauty sleep, told him what was going on. Then he hung up.

"We better go get your friend," the night man said.

I had just started to open the front door of the station when the gunshot sounded. Just one. Ordinarily, a 9mm wouldn't make that much noise, but it was late and the streets were empty and quiet, and Sean had the window rolled down because of the heat. It was still in the eighties and it was after midnight.

The car was a mess. I guess I focused on that so I wouldn't have to focus on the dead man in my front seat or the dead woman he'd left back at his eyrie. They took an ambulance a while later and got her.

Sean's wife came down to the station after half an hour. I hadn't seen her in years. She didn't seem as icy as I remembered her. She hadn't aged especially well—three kids and all the despair over Sean's affairs had taken their toll—and when she saw me, she came over and hugged me and started crying. I thought of all the times this girl had snubbed me when we'd been growing up. But then I realized how petty I was being and held her tenderly and let her cry. I even told her I'd help any way I could with the funeral arrangements.

I tried to cry myself that night. I guess I've learned the male syndrome too well. Boys don't cry. It's funny. I see movies and TV shows all the time that make me cry. But when it's something personal—I tried but I couldn't cry. And then the hot raw dawn broke and I slept fitfully.

*   *   *

A couple of months after Jenna was murdered, I heard the first rumor. Somebody told me there was a Jenna Internet site. I logged on and looked it over. Seems Jenna hadn't really been murdered. That was just a cover story for the aliens who'd taken her back up to the mother ship where she was now residing.

I went out there one Indian summer night, out to the meadow where the people said they saw the ship every once in a while. There was a crowd of thirty or so. I recognized some of them. They were the people who'd stood in her yard that time hoping to see her again to get high on the joy merely seeing her brought them.

I suppose I felt superior to them. My mind wasn't filled with all their delusions; I was brave enough to face reality. There had been no ship, no abduction. She was simply one of those people who'd developed a power to make people feel better. Such people were celebrated throughout history. Jesus was certainly one of them. And Jesus did not come from a spaceship.

But late that night, in the darkness of my bed, I didn't feel superior to them at all. I envied them. On our trip through the universe, the lonely and unknowable universe, they had something to cling to, anyway. I didn't have anything at all.

To Fit the Crime

1

I never would've done it if Alison had kept her word.
I know that sounds as if I'm blaming her, but—

She was working at that new cybersex bar over on
Kensington Avenue, and she was supposed to meet
me on the corner afterward. Much as the customers
like the cybersex booths, they always like to see a
little *real* female flesh around, too.

Female flesh doesn't get much nicer than Alison's,
believe me.

We were going to take her car up the river tonight
and celebrate our three year anniversary. It hadn't exactly been a smooth relationship—especially with the
accident and all—but I figured it was an important
date to celebrate if I was ever going to convince Alison to marry me.

She wasn't there.

I waited twenty-five minutes on the corner, and when she didn't show up, I went inside.

I actually hate it inside.

You see all these young guys with a lot of money peacocking around, thinking they're something very special, and really treating the girls as if they were sluts. Alison was always calling one of the guards to throw somebody out for practically raping her.

I couldn't watch it. I got too mad. One night I got into it with one of Alison's customers and just about got Alison fired.

The place was packed, of course. This was Friday night.

There were two or three guys outside every booth, waiting their turn to get in.

This was one of the bars that had a permit to sell camphin, the steroid derivative that increases all your sensations when you wire yourself up to the body suit before beaming yourself into VR mode. That's why this bar is so expensive. Drugs aren't cheap.

She wasn't there either.

The guards didn't tell me squat, and one of them even got a little threatening. He went seven feet and weighed three hundred pounds and sounded like an answering machine when he spoke. All he needed to do was hit me once, and I'd end up in ER.

I worked on some of the girls. It was easy to see that they were being loyal to Alison. It was also easy to see that they were keeping something from me.

I was just leaving when Darla came over and said, "Buy me a blackout."

Blackouts were the drink of choice these days, a concoction of drambuie, vodka, and a liquid that was allegedly being shipped in from some place exotic.

We pushed and shoved our way through the noisy, sweaty crowd and finally found a small space at the bar, where I ordered two blackouts.

She looked at me curiously when I ordered one for myself. She knew about the accident and my probation. Guy in my circumstances probably shouldn't be drinking anything stronger than water.

She said, above the din, "She has a fella."

"A fella?"

"Boyfriend."

"No. No way."

She shrugged appealingly bare shoulders. She was a nicely set-up brunette. From time to time, I'd had idle fantasies about her. But I'd never been unfaithful to Alison. Not once.

"Goddammit." I said.

"I'm sorry." Then, "Maybe you better not drink that, Sam. You know, what with the accident and all."

"Who is he?"

"One of the bartenders here."

"She never mentioned a word about him."

"She was afraid to tell you. She likes you, Sam. She really does. She was sorry she had to hurt you."

I felt sick, weak. I felt rage, humiliation. I wanted to be old, and through with love and lust.

I wanted Alison.

"Where is she?"

"They took her car to NewChi."

NewChi. That's where we'd been going to get married last year. Before the accident.

"I need to talk to her."

"It won't do any good, Sam. They're—getting married next week."

"Married?"

I shouted it so loud people started staring at me. I could be heard even above the din.

"Why don't you let me take that?" she said, reaching for my blackout.

I stared at my drink and then decided she was right. Drinking or drugging would only make my problems worse.

I pushed the drink to her along the bar.

"You feel like a little sex?" she said. "You think that'd help?"

I shook my head. "I never really got into the cyber stuff."

"Not cyber, Sam. Me. Maybe a little sex would ease the pain for a while. You're a nice guy, Sam. It'd be my pleasure."

She was a sweetie, she really was. I looked at those full breasts and that small waist and I could imagine what she'd be like. Any other time, I'd have a difficult time saying no. But not now.

I was dead inside.

"I appreciate the offer, Darla. I really do."

I turned around, looked toward the front of the place.

"Where'll you go, Sam?"

I shook my head again. "I don't know. But I gotta get out of here."

She touched my arm. "Just don't get in trouble, Sam. You know, what with the accident and all—"

I pulled her close to me and gave her a wild kiss on the mouth. For a moment, my groin stirred and I reconsidered her offer. But no, by the time we got to one of the rooms upstairs, my desire would have waned again, and I would be left with not only my grief but embarrassment as well.

"I'll be fine," I said.

"Call me tomorrow."

I nodded, and started pushing my way through the crowd.

2

The next few hours, I spent walking. Couldn't tell you where. Couldn't tell you why.

I must have passed several dozen blackout bars where the music and laughter were high and inviting. I must've passed a hundred car rental lots. I felt like getting in one and just taking off.

Of course, the law wouldn't look too kindly on it.

And then I ran out of places to walk to.

Found myself on a long pier jutting out into the diamond-black ocean, with the full golden eye of the midnight moon peering down at me.

Alone.

I listened to the waves lap the shore. I listened to the distant cry of the city behind me. I looked out and saw the endless number of drivers out for an evening's entertainment.

And I listened to all the letters that my mind was composing to Alison. Bitter, angry letters, some of them, while others were weak and pleading letters.

I don't know how long I stayed on that isolated pier, staring out at the ocean.

But at some very late point in the night. I turned around and headed back to the city, knowing exactly what I was going to do.

I wasn't even going to try and stop myself.

I really didn't care any more about stopping myself.

I went into the first blackout bar I could find. I walked up to the bar and laid down cash and the bartender was soon sliding my blackout to me.

I told myself there was just going to be one. I told myself that I was going to make this last all night. I told myself that I would then, sensible fellow, go back to my apartment and pack it in for the night.

I must have had five or six blackouts at that first bar. And then I was in a group, and one of the people had a car, and then we were hitting some of the more expensive blackout bars in the cities.

I can recall being insanely happy for the first part of the night, as if all the drinks had inoculated me against the illness known as Alison.

There were a couple of nice looking gals in the group and they seemed to find me as appealing as I found them. I took turns dancing with them. More than once. I felt an erection surging in my pants, and I felt little-boy proud of myself.

Life without Alison was going to be all right, after all.

I don't remember much about stealing the car.

I do recall being the only one at the table—all the others were up dancing—and seeing the key; the car owner had left it sitting next to his drink.

After that, things really get murky.

I was arguing with the parking lot attendant that I was plenty fine to drive. He was calling the cops, which gave me the few moments I needed to dive in the car and take off.

And then I was on my way, and really liking it. I

hadn't driven for more than a year, ever since the accident.

I felt more confident than ever that Alison was going to take me back and that everything would be all right between us.

I kinda did that all night, swung back and forth between thinking that it was over with Alison and that I could handle it, and thinking that she'd take me back and that we'd soon be married.

I remember wanting to see just how fast this car could go. And so I gave it max power.

And then I heard—

a crashing sound.

And screams.

It was like my memories of the accident.

And then the sirens.

Cops.

And then—

They kept me twenty-four hours in detox, strapped down to an unyielding cot in a gray windowless little room.

A nurse came in every few hours and gave me injections. I had no idea what they were giving me. I was in no position to complain.

This was jail. No doubt about it.

At the time of the accident, I'd been put in a room very much like this one. And strapped down in a similar fashion.

Did that mean—

I didn't know what it meant.

I wasn't able to reconstruct much of last night.

I was talking to Darla. I was drinking blackouts

with my new friends. I was driving a stolen car. And—

The door slid back.

A tall, thin man with slicked-down black hair and a pockmocked face said, "I'm Enrique Ramirez. The court has appointed me as your attorney."

"But my attorney's Fred—"

"Fred Wilson. Yes. The court contacted him, but he declined to represent you this time."

"Declined? What the hell are you talking about?"

He drew himself up inside his black three-piece suit and gray shirt and red necktie. The contempt in his eyes was unmistakable.

"Do you remember what you did last night?"

"Just had a few drinks. Just had a few laughs."

This was every blackout drinker's worst moment. When he couldn't put the previous night together, and when somebody somberly offered to tell him about it.

Cold sweat covered me, and inside my straps, I was trembling.

"You killed a woman and her two little boys," Enrique Ramirez said.

"Oh, bullshit."

"Not bullshit. Would you like to see the accident film? One of the boys, the four-year-old, was decapitated. Your car broadsided them. At max speed."

For the first time, I'd started to panic inside my straps. I had to work myself free. Had to escape this jail.

These people were telling lies about me.

Had to get with my real friends. Who would protect me.

Had to get back to reality.

"I recommend that you plead guilty," Enrique Ramirez said. "Plead for mercy. I think we can make the case that you're a blackout junkie and can't help yourself. I'm afraid that's about all we've got going for us at this juncture."

He looked at me a long moment and said, "At least your last accident, you didn't kill any kids. Just that old man."

Two car accidents in one year.

"This can't be true."

"It is true," he said. "And now you need to listen very carefully to your options. There are three."

I listened.

"One, we can go to court, and have you plead for mercy, as I just said. Or two, you can go on 'Execution Night' and try your luck there."

With the overcrowding of prisons. Death Row prisoners were now allowed to go on a TV show called "Execution Night," where they were tried by a jury of average citizens. About one out of every twenty prisoners was found innocent. There were rumors that the TV producers "fixed" these innocent verdicts so that the show would have surprise and suspense. The guilty were taken to a soundproof booth, strapped to a gurney, and given a lethal injection as the TV host stood just outside the booth and described what was going on inside.

"God, they get so bloodthirsty, those jurors."

"It's an option to consider, anyway."

"You said there were three."

"Legal experts have been experimenting with this one in secret for some time now. It's still in the early stages, but they *are* making it available to everyone now."

"All right. What is it?"

"A fortune teller will come and see you. And if you meet the requirements, you will be free to walk out of here."

"A fortune teller? What kind of crazy bullshit is that?"

"I'm not allowed to tell you any more than that at this point."

"All I do is see a fortune teller, and then I can walk out of here?"

"If the fortune teller says you qualify."

"This sounds crazy."

"Yes, it does. But the law enforcement people seem to think it has merit."

He stared at me for a long moment, not trying to hide his contempt. I suppose he had children of his own, and was thinking about them when he saw the pictures of last night's accident.

"You don't feel any regret at all, do you?" he said.

"Right now, I don't know what I feel. I'm miserable with this frigging hangover, and I can't remember much about last night and—"

"I need your answer now." He checked his watch. "I've got to be back at the office in twenty minutes. Your answer please."

"I have to decide right now?"

"Right now."

"This fortune-telling thing—"

He smirked. "I knew you would choose that one. I knew it."

He walked over to the door and pressed a button for the android guard to let him out.

"If I qualify, I just walk right out of here?" I said anxiously.

"Right out of here," he said.

And then he smirked again.

3

They kept me for two more days before the fortune teller came.

I guess I expected some gypsy lady with a kerchief on her head and a crystal ball in her hands.

This particular fortune teller was nothing like that at all.

She was tall, blonde, patrician, and wore a fitted gray business suit with a very frilly white blouse.

The guard didn't just let her into my cell, as he had with Enrique Ramirez, he stayed with the young woman.

"My name's Heather Cosgrove," she said, offering a slender hand.

Yesterday, they'd unstrapped me. This morning, I'd been allowed to shower and put on a new jail uniform.

I sat on the edge of my cell, watching her.

"Has anybody explained to you what I'm going to do this morning?"

"Not really."

"I'm going to hold your hand, palm up, and then I'm going to start moving a sensor around on your palm."

"A sensor?"

She reached crisply into her tiny jacket pocket and brought out a small black device about the size of a cigarette. Its tip glowed alternately red and blue. "This is the sensor."

"And it does what exactly?"

Ed Gorman

"Exactly? I'm not sure. But it does help me form a better mental picture of you."

"And you're trying to determine what?"

She smiled. "That part I can't discuss with you right now. If you pass the test, *then* we discuss what I've learned. Are you ready?"

It really wasn't a whole hell of a lot, as far as tests go. There was nothing painful about it. Or nothing dramatic. Or nothing even very interesting.

She stared at me for a few minutes. I had the sense that she was seeing something in or around me that I'd never been aware of.

Auras, that's all I could come up with.

She was seeing my aura.

She spent a few minutes with the sensor, crisscrossing my palm several times. She paused only once to go back over a certain area. Then, seeming to be satisfied with what she picked up the second time, she went back to her rather rapid crisscrossing.

"There," she said, "all done."

"That's it?"

"That's it."

"They said you were a fortune teller?"

She laughed. "Well, I guess you could call me that in a way."

"And you'll get back to me?"

She let me have her slender hand again.

Touching her reminded me of Alison, and thinking of Alison made me angry.

I wouldn't have gotten drunk and killed those little kids if only Alison had been decent to me.

"You'll be hearing from me very soon," she said.

The guard opened the door for her and let her out.

* * *

290

Two days later, the guard took me for a ride on the elevator. Walking down the hall, there was a window. I wanted to stay there and just look out at the countryside. It was October, and all the trees were ablaze, and the sky was a beautiful cloudless blue.

The guard took me into a long, narrow gray room. Two men in suits sat at the far end of the table.

The guard closed the door behind me.

The man with the white crewcut said, "They buried the two little boys this morning."

"I'm very sorry," I said.

"Spare us the bullshit," said the man with the dark crewcut. "You don't give any more of a damn about those two little boys than we give a damn about you."

I didn't know what to say.

"In about five minutes," said the calmer man, the one with the white crewcut, "the guard will take you to the ground level, where you'll be given street clothes and set free."

I couldn't believe what he was saying. I was going to be released—

"The woman you saw the other day," black crewcut said, "was a seer. They used to be called fortune tellers. The government is experimenting with these people for a variety of purposes. This particular seer has a specialty."

"A speciality?"

White crewcut said, "She can predict the day a man or woman is going to die."

"That's impossible," I said.

White crewcut went on as if I hadn't said anything: "We feel that the worst punishment a man can have is to know the exact time of his death. Especially when the day is very near. No matter what he does,

291

no matter where he goes, he can't escape his destiny. There's an old Arab parable about it, in fact. One night a rider sees another man riding frantically toward Damascus. The rider asks the man where he's going in such a fury. The man says 'I'm trying to escape Death, so I'm riding to Damascus to hide. He'll never find me there.' The man rides off. A little later the rider sees Death astride a horse. Death stops and the rider says, 'Where are you going in such a hurry?' And Death replies. 'I have an appointment in Damascus.' "

"In other words," black crewcut said. "You can't escape the fate our seer envisions for you."

"You're going to die the day after tomorrow, at just before two o'clock in the afternoon."

I smiled. "That's what she told you?"

"That's what she told us," white crewcut said. "And she hasn't been wrong yet."

"She's predicted other deaths?"

"Yours will be the fifteenth," said black crewcut.

"And you let every one of them go?"

White crewcut shook his head. "Only those whose death is very near. To give a man twenty years of freedom before his death—that's hardly punishment. But if his death is at hand and he knows the exact time—that's the worst punishment of all. To know that there's no place to run, no place to hide—"

"Your very own appointment in Damascus," the black crewcut said. He offered me a cold smile.

"So I'm free to do whatever I like?"

"Whatever you like, as long as you don't violate any laws," white crewcut said.

"And go wherever I like?"

"Go see the sunny tropics," black crewcut said.

"But you'd better hurry. You're going to be dead in a day and a half."

"I am, huh?" I said.

My smile was just as cold as his had been.

White crewcut pressed a button. The door shot open, and the guard stepped in.

"Take him downstairs," white crewcut said.

"Yes," black crewcut said, scowling at me. "Get him the hell out of here. He stinks the place up."

4

I stood on the street corner down from the city jail for a good twenty minutes, taking in the air, the sight of fellow human beings, and the bumper-to-bumper traffic that made the city streets all but impassable.

I started walking across the bridge. I was about halfway across when I got a jolt. I saw a young woman, her blonde hair trailing in the soft autumnal breeze. Alison.

I started running after her, calling her name.

But when I got there—

"Alison! Alison!" I said, coming up behind her, putting a hand on her shoulder.

The woman, not-Alison, turned and glared at me. "Take your hand off my shoulder right now."

"I'm sorry, miss. I really am."

She turned around and finished walking across the bridge.

An even more dangerous impulse came as I reached the far end of the bridge. I saw a blackout bar and my whole nervous system went into self-destruct mode.

God, I wanted a blackout. My entire body was trembling, sweating.

But I forced myself to push on past, even though the laughter and the glimpse of beautiful young women through the front windows tried to pull me back.

A few minutes later, I jumped in a cab that was waiting at the stand and went back to my apartment.

The place was dingy and depressing as always. Most of the time I'd spent at Alison's, so I hadn't bothered to fix up this place. It smelled of mildew and cold dead air.

There was no food, and for some reason I couldn't even get the TV to play the news. In a rage, I picked the damned thing up off its pedestal and smashed it against the wall. It made a satisfying smashing sound as it fell against the floor.

Every few minutes, I'd think of the seer. I didn't believe that kind of thing at all. But they sure as hell must have had confidence in her—or else they wouldn't have set me free.

A day and a half, that's what I had left to live according to her.

I managed to grub up enough coffee beans and hot water to grind out a cup of coffee.

I stood at the window looking at evening settle on the city. The coffee tasted good. It was my only pleasant experience this entire day.

Somewhere out there, Alison and her new boyfriend were in the sack together. I could hear their whispers. She'd say all the same things to him that she'd said to me. And do the same things to him, too.

I ended up smashing my coffee cup against the wall.

Night settled on the city.

I didn't want to turn on a light.

I was hiding in the dark.

For some reason, the seer's prediction had started to seem a lot more likely to me.

I always came back to the same thought: if her predictions hadn't been borne out in the past, then they never would have used her. Never would have set me free.

I had to get out of here. Really hide out someplace until the day and a half had passed.

I couldn't let myself believe this junk. I'd go crazy if I did.

Two minutes later, the phone rang.

"It's good to hear you," Darla said.

"You heard what happened? The two kids?"

"I heard. But it could've happened to anybody. We all have a little too much to drink sometimes."

Not until this very moment did I realize that Darla was in love with me. But anybody who could excuse what I'd done so quickly—well, only love could blind her to the kind of problems I had.

"You're not working tonight?"

"No. It's wonderful. I have some sick days coming. So I'm free the next three days."

"You up for a guest for a couple of days?"

"I am if that guest happens to be you."

"How about an hour?"

"Make it two. I want to pick up the apartment a little and then take a nice, long shower."

"See you then."

Cabs being as busy as they were this time of night, it was three hours before I got to her place.

Darla lived in one of those hundred-floor condos.

295

Her apartment was on the eighty-sixth floor.

When she opened the door, she was wearing nothing more than a very diaphanous thigh-length shirt. She had a wonderful body.

She had a table set with fancy china and two flickering candles.

She helped me out of my coat, guided me to the table, sat me down in one of the two chairs, and then proceeded to feed me some of the best cuisine I'd had in years. Vegetarian lasagna was the main course, and it was sumptuous.

Afterward, we sprawled out on the floor of her living room and watched some erotic videos. She'd known just how to ensure my sexual interest—good food, a relaxing massage, and sexy images of people making love.

I took her twice right there on the floor. The third time I carried her into the bedroom. Not until I was starting on my fourth round did I realize that she'd slipped some kind of sex drug in my food. But I wasn't complaining. I needed a workout like this. You know how it is when a bad love affair ends. The sex usually isn't great. It had been a long time since I'd been this heated up.

5

The next twenty-four hours were a repeat of the first couple of hours.

She made three complete meals, she massaged every inch of my body (just as I massaged every inch of hers), and we did a good job of working through every single position in the *Kama Sutra*.

And then I made my big mistake.

We were just finishing up another round in bed, and I was nearing the frenzy of release, when I kissed her on the forehead and said, "This is great, Alison. This is great."

She froze.

She knew what I'd said and I knew what I'd said. Alison.

She slapped me several times across the face, and then bit down into my naked shoulder until she drew blood.

I shrank away from her. She slipped out of bed, ran into the bathroom. Slammed the door.

Wept.

I knocked.

"Go away."

"Please let me come in and talk to you."

"I've worked so hard to make this so good. And then you can't even remember my name."

"It was a mistake, Darla. It doesn't mean anything."

"It means that you're still thinking about her."

"Of course I'm still thinking about her. Sometimes. But not very often." I hesitated. "It's going to work out for us. You'll see. A few more weeks, and I won't be thinking about her at all." I paused. "If I'm still alive."

She didn't want to get sucked in to responding but she couldn't help herself. "What's that supposed to mean? If you're still alive?"

"You haven't asked me why they let me out of jail."

"I just assumed you were out on bail."

"Uh-uh. Free and clear. All charges dropped."

"But why?"

"Because they think I'm going to die tomorrow afternoon."

"That's crazy."

"Let me in, and I'll explain."

There's nothing like a tiny little bathroom for wooing a woman: she's sitting on the toilet lid and you've got your bottom parked on the sink.

I told her about the seer and her predictions, and how both white crewcut and black crewcut were obviously convinced that she knew what she was talking about.

"You don't believe it, do you?" Darla asked.

"Not really," I said. "But why take any chances? If you don't mind. I'd just as soon hang around here until tomorrow night. Out of harm's way. Then I'll take you out, and we'll really have a celebration."

She just stared at me and shook her head. "God, I wish I knew why I love you so much."

I smiled. "I'm just glad you do." Then I pointed to my shoulder. "Now how about patching up the teeth marks?"

She reached out and took my hand. "That's one thing you should know about me. I'm insanely jealous. My last boyfriend broke up with me because I pulled a gun on him when he came home late from work one night."

"Just please don't ever try that on me."

She said, quite seriously, "Then don't ever call me Alison again."

Fifteen minutes later, we were making love again.

6

In the morning, I watched some of the quiz shows (they were now giving away cyber sex weekends to keep audiences interested), and helped Darla clean up.

I didn't notice how fast my pulse rate was until I stood up abruptly from picking up a stack of magazines.

I was dizzy. I pitched forward to the couch.

Darla saw me fall. She screamed and ran over to me.

My heart was hammering, and I was having a hard time getting my breath.

"What is it? What's wrong?" she said, daubing my sweaty brow with her hand.

"Oh, I'm just falling for their trap."

"Trap?"

"The seer's prediction. It's working on me subconsciously. I'm getting scared, and that's why I'm starting to hyperventilate this way."

"It's not going to come true, darling. It really isn't. They were just trying to scare you."

"Exactly."

"You're perfectly safe here. It's completely security-proof. Nobody can get in here unless I let them in."

I was starting to relax. "And tonight—"

She smiled. "Tonight, we have ourselves a ball."

I spent the next hour sitting in a recliner watching the TV.

Darla brought me a cold chicken sandwich and a glass of decaf ice tea.

I tried not to keep watching the clock, but I couldn't help myself.

Twelve became twelve-fifteen, and twelve forty-five became one.

And one became one-thirty.

That's about when I started sweating and twitching again. Thoughts of death started filling my brain.

Utter extinction. I guess that's the part I could never get used to. No matter who you were—a king or a homeless person—it didn't matter. Eventually, time erased all evidence that you ever existed.

Utter extinction.

One-forty.

"How you doing, hon?" Darla called from the kitchen.

"Fine," I said, putting on my dulcet he-man voice.

"You're going to be fine."

"I know. And thanks for being so sweet about everything."

One forty-five.

The heart started again. BAM BAM BAM.

I could feel my throat tightening up.

And then I smiled.

Right in the middle of this whole seizure-type thing, I actually smiled.

Because I suddenly realized how those other people had come to die at the time the seer had predicted.

There'd been a sociological study I read somewhere about banished tribesmen in Africa. If the witch doctor felt you were unfit to be part of the clan, he sent you into the jungle to die. So real was the threat of the witch doctor's words that the banished person did exactly that—went in the jungle and died. The banished man had literally been scared to death.

That's what was happening here. I was going to make her prediction come true by bringing on my own coronary arrest.

Mind over matter.

I started gasping, then, unable to breathe.

Choking.

I tried to cry out, but I didn't even have the strength to do that.

I pushed myself up from the chair, stumbled across the living room and into the kitchen.

Darla was at the sink, shining a long silver knife.

At first, she didn't see me.

I did my best to call out to her. "Alison!" I cried. "Alison!"

This she heard.

She turned to me with such fury, bringing the knife up as she did so.

She came at me, arcing the knife up in the air. "You bastard! You bastard!"

I had no choice but to try and run away—even though I could barely breathe. She was so angry, she couldn't see that I was dying.

So the seer was right after all. I'd gone to Darla's, thinking I could escape the death the seer had seen. What I hadn't understood was that Darla herself would be the instrument of my demise.

She came shrieking through the living room, following me all the way to the door.

Somehow, I managed to stagger into the hall and lope down to the elevator.

My fear of Darla and her knife had suspended my psychosomatic fears. I was breathing all right again.

Now I just needed to get away from Darla.

She tried to jump on the elevator car, but I managed to get the doors closed just as she was about to leap forward.

I could hear her screaming at me for at least ten floors. Then there was just the faint hum of the elevator itself. I was dropping eighty-six floors.

On the ground floor, some of the nattier tenants gave me a displeased glance. I hadn't shaved in two days and my clothes were pretty wrinkled.

But I didn't give a damn.

I glanced up at the lobby clock.

One forty-eight.

Darla had been the instrument of my demise.

And I'd managed to elude her.

I gathered myself up to a height of great dignity, and then proceeded to walk through the lobby, and out to the sidewalk.

I was just walking over to read the newspaper headlines in the vending display when the car jumped the curb and slammed into me. The last thing I felt was my neck tearing from my shoulders.

Cages

He knows the bad thing will happen, the way it always happens, his father coming home late and all dreamdusted up and his mother shrieking and screaming how he spent all the money on the dreamdust and then the—

He knows when to put the pillow over his head so he will not hear when his father slams his mother into the wall and starts hitting her.

Sometimes he tries to stop it but it never does any good. He is three foot six and has only the one arm and is no match at all for his father.

Then in the room next to his, in the darkness, after the hitting and the screaming, there are other sounds now on the bed, grunts and sighs and whimpers and then.

Sleep.

A dream.

His mother and father and himself in a new car riding down the street. People pointing at them. Envious. Such a nice family. The envious people do not even seem to notice his bald head or his lone shriveled arm or the way the sticky stuff runs from his ear and

Awake.

Late night.

Sirens.

Laser blasts.

Coppers hunting down dreamduster gangs.

He wants to kill the man who invented dreamdust. All the misery it causes. Mrs. Caruso's daughter letting all those men stick themselves up the slit between her legs. Mr. Feinmann smashing his wife's head in with a bottle because she wouldn't give him the tips from her waitress job. Little Betty Malloy being killed by the dreamduster who put a broomhandle up her backside and then cut her up with a butcher knife.

Night.

Hot.

Goes out on the fire escape.

Tomorrow it will just start again. The argument about you fucking cunt where'd all the money go? and her shrieking you dreamdust fucker you dreamdust fucker!

Always: money money money.

And then he remembers the commercial on the vid. Seen that commercial a lot the last five six weeks. And always has the same thought.

$

$

$

flashing on the screen and this real loud guy telling you how you can collect them.

All you gotta do see is

Be so easy.

So fucking easy.

And then they'd have plenty of $.

No more fights.

No more hitting.

He lies out on the fire escape thinking about tomorrow morning. His mother will be gone to work and so will he.

No trouble going in the closet where

And getting a sack

And

Going down to the place it says in the commercial

And

He can see all those fuckers who pick on him and hit him and call him faggot and mutant and all that shit

He can see them standing enviously on the corner when he cruises by in the back seat of his parents' new car

Fuck you

You're the faggot

You're the mutant

Not me

Fuckers

And yes yes won't they be sorry and yes yes won't they be envious

He wishes it was tomorrow morning already

Bitch can't even fix me any fuckin breakfast? you know how fuckin hard I work on that fuckin dock you cunt?

Early morning battle

Father slamming out heading for the choppy dark waters on this muggy overcast day

Mother not long behind him

Coming in and leaning down to his bed and giving him this wet perfume kiss and still crying from the early morning battle and because she got clipped a good one on the right cheekbone even a little bruise there

And him going fitfully back to sleep

And dreaming the car dream again

And dreaming about going to see this doctor who fixes him up so he looks just like the fuckers who pick on him all the time

Hey Quasimodo they say sometimes

Hey hunchbacka Notre Dame you little faggot

And is awake now

And in the bathroom taking down the underwear his mother always washes out at night him only having the one pair but no amount of washing taking the brown stains from the back or the yellow from the front

And then moving fast

Afraid one of them might pop back in and see what he's doing and

With his sack he hurries from the apartment.

Horns and exhaust fumes and perfume and farts and fat people and skinny people and people talking to themselves and dreamdusters and gangs and whores and faggots and

And he's hurrying fast as he can down his little street carrying his little sack and he makes it no more than half a block when he sees Ernie that fucking Ernie wouldn't you know

And nigger Ernie steps in front of him and says, What shit you got there in that sack?

Is scared. Isn't sure what to say. Ernie is real real tall with gold teeth and knuckles that feel like sharp rocks when they hit your skull.

Takin back some popsies. You know get the refund.

Popsies shit. That ain't popsies in that sack, you little fuckin mutant.

Then Gil then Bob then Mike are there all friends of Ernie two of them be white but no matter they're every bit as mean as Ernie hisself

And Mike grabs for the sack and says gimme it you little faggot

Hunchbacka Notre Dame Bob says.

You heard him Ernie says give it to him

Just a plain brown sack but you can see stains on the sides of it now damned thing leaking from inside

Thinks he's gonna get a clear run for it starts to weave and wobble between them

But then Gil and Mike grab him by the shoulders and throw him up against the building and

Ernie grabs the sack from him

And smiles with his gold teeth

And holds the sack teasing up real high

And says you can have it faggot if you can jump this high

And he starts to cry but stops himself knowing that will only make it worse

Fuckin Ernie anyway

Nigger Ernie

Hey asshole Mike says look inside

So Ernie does

Turns away

And holds the sack down
And opens it up
Holy shit
What's wrong?
Man, you gotta see what's in this sack, man.

So Gil takes a look. And he makes the same kinda sick face that Ernie did. Aw God. I wanna puke.

He's afraid they'll do something to it. He keeps thinking of the place he saw on the commercial. He wants to be there now. Getting his money.

You just bring 'em right down here for more cash $$$$ than you ever seen in your life. You just ask for Smilin Bob. That's me.

And reaches out to snatch the sack back.

And gets hit fullfist by Mike.

Please c'mon you guys please.

Doesn't want to start crying.

And then they start throwing the sack back and forth over their heads.

Fuckers you fuckers he cries running back and forth between them.

And then he sees the cop, an android, not a real person, android coppers being the only kind they'll send to a shithole like this one.

And the android senses something wrong so he comes over.

And of course Ernie and the others split because androids always want to ask a lot of questions being programmed to just that and all, and people like Ernie and Gil always having something to hide and never wanting to answer questions.

They drop his sack on the ground and take off running.

He bends and picks it up and then he starts running,

too. He doesn't like androids any better than Ernie does.

He keeps his sack pulled tight.

By the time he gets to Smilin' Bob's, the rain has started, dirty hot city rain summer rain dirty summer rain, and he's drenched.

And there's a line all the way out the front door and all the way down the block.

People of all ages and descriptions holding boxes and sacks and bags. And the things inside them making all kinds of squeals and groans and moans and grunts and cries. And smelling so bad sometimes he thinks he's gonna puke or pass out.

And then this guy dressed all in yellow with this big-ass laser gun dangling from the same hand bearing the fat sparkly pinkie ring, he keeps walking up and down the long line saying, If you got somethin' dangerous, you let us know in advance, folks, cause otherwise we'll just have to kill the thing right on the spot unless you warn us about it. He says this in both English and Spanish. And then just keeps walking up and down up and down saying it over and over and over again.

All the time raining its ass off.

All the time getting bumped and pushed and kicked because he's so little.

All the time his sack wiggling and wriggling trying to get free.

There's a lot of talk in line:

How this one guy heard about this other guy who brought this little sack to Smilin' Bob's and two days later the fucker was a millionaire.

How this one guy heard about this other guy he's waitin' in line here just like now ('cept it ain't rainin' in this here particular story) and this fuckin' thing comes right up outta this other guy's sack and kills the first guy right on the spot, goes right for his throat and tears it right out.

How this one guy heard about this other guy said that he had two of them once that ate each other— just like cannibals you know what I'm sayin'—but then they'd puke each other back up whole and start all over again. No shit. I swear onna stack of Bibles and my pappy's grave. True facts. Puked each other up and started all over again . . .

Finally finally finally the rain still raining and the thing in his sack still crying, he reaches the head of the line and goes inside.

First one this fat girl, they say no.

What you do inside is stand in another line and when you're first up they take your sack or your box from you and carry it inside this room that's bright with a special kind of lighting and they half-close the door and they talk among themselves except Smilin' Bob himself who stands at the head of the line sayin You folks jes relax we're getting to ya fast as we can. He's got up just like on TV big-ass ten-gallon hat and western-style shirt and string tie and downhome accent.

And when they're done with the fat girl's bag this tall pale guy comes out and shakes his head and says sorry ma'am just won't do us no good.

Fucker you fucker you know how bad I need this money? she shrieks.

But Smilin' Bob jes kinda leans back and says No call for talkin' that way to Butch here' no call at all.

And the fat girl goes away.

And a black kid steps up and they take his box and they go inside the blinding bright room and lights flash and male voices mutter and they come back out and hand him the box and the tall pale one is wiggling and waggling his hand sayin that little fucker bit me you want me to I'll kill him for you kid. We got an easy way of doin it kid won't hurt the little fucker at all.

But the kid snatches the box back and takes off all huffy and pissed because there's no money in it for him.

And next and next and next and next and finally.

His turn.

Is scared.

Knows they're not going to take it.

Knows he won't get no money.

Knows that his dad'll beat the shit out of his mom tonight soon as they start arguin' about money and dreamdust and shit like that.

Smilin' Bob takes the sack and peeks inside and makes the same face Ernie did and says Well well well and my my my and I'll be jiggered I'll just be jiggered and then hands the sack over to the tall pale assistant.

Who takes it inside the bright room and starts all the usual stuff lights flashing meters clicking voices mumbling and muttering and

Holy shit

That's what the guy inside says:

Holy shit. Lookit that friggin meter.

Smilin' Bob he hears it too and he looks back over his shoulder and then back at him and winks.

Maybe you dun brung Smilin' Bob somethin special.

Ed Gorman

I sure hope so Smilin' Bob.

And Smilin' Bob smiles and says: I give you a lotta money, what y'all gonna do with it anyways?

Give it to my dad and mom.

Well ain't that sweet.

He's a dreamduster and they fight all the time and I'm scared some night he's gonna kill her and maybe if I get enough money and give it to my mom maybe they won't have to argue any more and

The door opens

Tall pale guy comes out

Walks right over to Smilin' Bob and whispers something in his ear

And Smilin' Bob real solemn like nods and then comes over and puts his hand on his shoulder and leads him away from the line

You know how much we're gonna give you? Smilin' Bob asks.

He's excited: How much?

$500!

$$$$$$$$

Just like on the commercial.

That's all he can think of

$$$$$$$$

How happy his Mom will be

How proud his Mom will be

No more arguments

No more beatings for anybody

$$$$$$$

Oh thank you Smilin' Bob thank you

One hour and twenty-eight minutes later he's on his way home. No sweat with Ernie and those fuckers. Rainin too hard. They're inside.

Wants to beat Mom home.
Wants to be sittin there this big grin on his face
And all this money sittin right on the table.
And wants to see her face.
See her smile.
And say oh honey oh honey now me'n your dad
we won't have to argue no more
Oh honey
Which is just where he is when she comes through
the door
Right at the table
And which is just what he's doing
Counting out the money so she's sure to see it
$$$$$$
And at first she's so tired she don't even notice it
Just comes in all weary and all sighs and says think
I gotta lay down hon I'm just bushed
And starts draggin herself past him into the little
living room with all the smashed-up furniture from
the last couple of fights
And then she notices
Out of the corner of her eye
Says: Hey, what's that?
Money
Aw shit honey them cops they'll beat you sure as
shit they catch you stealin like that
Didn't steal it ma honest
Comes closer to the table and sees just how much
is there: Aw honey where'd you ever get this much
money?
And he tells her
And she says: You what?
Sold it
Sold it! It ain't an "it" for one thing it's your sister

Ain't my sister he says (but already he's feeling hot and panicky and kinda sick; not turnin out the way he planned not at all) ain't nobody's sister she's just this little—

And she slaps him

And he can't believe how terrible and rotten everything has turned out

Where's her smile?

Where's her sayin they won't argue no more?

Where's her sayin what a good boy he is?

She fuckin slaps him

Slaps him the way the old man always slaps him

And after he did so good too

Gettin the money and all

Slaps him!

Then she's really on him

Shakin him and slappin him even harder

Where is she? Where is she?

Smilin Bob's got her he says

Who's Smilin Bob

He's this guy on TV ma

SHE'S YOUR SISTER YOU STUPID LITTLE BASTARD! CAN'T YOU UNDERSTAND THAT SHE'S YOUR OWN FLESH AND BLOOD! Now you take me to this Smilin' Bob

Never seen her like this

Not even when the old man beats her

All crazy screamin and fidgetin and cryin

Grabs him and pulls him up from the chair and says: Take me to this Smilin Bob and right now

And so they stumble out into the early night

And

On the way she explains things again even though he can't seem to understand them: Sixty years ago bad people put bad things into the river and ever since then some of the babies have been strange and sad and sometimes even frightening creatures, some babies (like his sister) being born so ugly that they had to hide them from the government, which is why they kept his little sister in the spare room because word would get around the neighborhood and government agents might find out and would kill the little girl.

But she isn't a little girl he says she don't even look like a little girl

(His mother hurrying down the streets now, hurrying and jerking him along)

And these Smilin' Bob fuckers (she says) what they do is they take in these babies and the ones they think are telepathic (or something else worth studying) they sell to the government or private labs to study. They wouldn'ta paid you no $500 unless they thought she was gonna bring em a lot back.

The rain has stopped. Night has come. A chill night. The neon streets shine blue and yellow and green with neons. The freaks and the geeks are back panhandling.

As she hurries hurries

And (she says) You was lucky and don't you ever forget it. You was lucky, the way you was born I mean, you wasn't normal but you wasn't like your sister. Nobody wouldn'ta taken you away like they woulda her.

And then she starts crying again

Which is the weird thing as they hurry along

How she keeps shifting in and out of sobbing and tears and curses

One minute she'll be all right talking to him and then she just goes crazy again

You shouldnt'a fuckin done it you shouldnt'a
fuckin done it over and over and over again

Without the long lines (and in the night) Smilin'
Bob's looks very different long shadows and soft
street light hiding the worst of the graffiti
And
You show me the door you went in
Right there ma
And she goes up and peers inside
And then goes crazy again
Banging and kicking on the door
And screaming you gimme my little girl back you
fuckers you gimme my little girl back
And is crying again of course
Sobbing screaming keening
And banging and kicking and banging and kicking
and
Just the darkness inside
Just the silence
You gimme my little girl back
And then
She runs around back and all he can do is follow
Alley very dark smelling awful as they pass a
Dumpster
She opens the dumpster lid and peeks inside and
Screams
Freaks and geeks of every kind inside the rejects
that they thought they could sell but couldn't
half-cat half-baby things things with one cyclopean
eye in the middle of their forehead things with a
flipper-like little arm sticking out of their sternums
things that are doll-like little replicas of human beings

except in the open eyes (even dead) you can see their stone madness

And every one of them had been hidden by their mothers till some stupid family member decided to earn some extra money by coming down to Smilin' Bob's or some place just like it and sell off the family shame

And you didn't have to be legal age because the Smilin' Bobs all got together in Washington and had a bill passed sayin' any family member at all of any age could bring in these mutants and

They lay like fish piled high in a net these Dumpster mutants moonlight glistening on their bloody faces and limbs and the stench

Then she runs to the back door which doesn't even have a window to peer in and starts banging and kicking again

You fuckers you fuckers

And him going up to her now and sayin

Ma I'm sorry ma please don't be like this it scares me when you get like this

And she turns on him and shrieks

She's your little sister! Can't you understand that!

And then she turns back to the doors and starts banging and kicking again

And then something startling happens

Door opens

And Smilin' Bob is standin there and

Evenin ma'am he says (in his Texas way) help you ma'am?

You bought my little girl today. You give my boy here $500. I wanna give it back to you and take my little girl home

And Smilin' Bob takin off his white ten-gallon hat

and scratchin' his head says Well now, lemme get a better look at this young 'un here

And he opens the door and looks down and says 'fraid not ma'am 'fraid I never did see this here kid before and I'd certainly remember if I had, givin him $500 Yankee cash and all like you said

Tell him (she says) tell him

And so he tells him

How he waited so long in line

How everybody ahead of him got turned down

How he got $500

But Smilin' Bob he just looks down at him and nods his head and says, Oh yeah, now I remember you. You brung that teeny-tiny girl with three eyes.

She pushes the money at him.

Please take it.

'fraid I can't ma'am. Deal's a deal, least where I come from.

I just want her back

'fraid she's gone ma'am.

Gone?

Lab guy, he just happened to pop by and we showed her to him and—Well, he took her.

You liar.

No call for that kinda language, ma'am.

You fuckin *fuckin* liar is what you are. She's in there ain't she?

And suddenly hurls herself at Smilin' Bob and tries to get past him

And he flings himself at her tryin to get her off Smilin' Bob but as he grabs out he feels Smilin' Bob's arm and

Smilin' Bob is an android!

But Smilin' Bob is also somethin else besides—a

very pissed off citizen hitting an alarm button to the right of the door

She just keeps trying to get inside

Kickin scratchin hittin even bitin (but with an android flesh bitin don't matter much)

And then footfalls in the night

Jackboots

Two three four of them maybe.

Comin real fast

And then surrounding them there in the alley.

Four android coppers, lasers pulled and ready to blast and

Two of the coppers go up and pull her off Smilin' Bob

Sure glad you boys got here

She hurt you Smilin' Bob?

Little lady like that? Not likely (Smilin' Bob smilin about it all) But sure would appreciate it if you'd get her out of here so I could get some work done

You bet we will Smilin' Bob (and some kind of look exchanged some kind of murky android look that no human could ever understand) and the coppers pull her even further away from the door as Smilin' Bob goes back inside

She your ma (one of the coppers says)

Uh-huh.

Then we're gonna put her in your custody. You understand?

Yessir.

We're gonna give you a pill.

A pill?

(Android nods) She gets all crazy again, you give her this. You understand?

Yessir.

'cause if there's any more trouble she's gonna be in deep shit.

Yessir.

You think you can handle this?

Yessir.

We already gave her a little juice with a stun needle.

Yessir.

So she's calmer now. But if she should happen to get—

Yessir. This here pill.

The coppers nod and leave.

Halfway home the rain starts up again but this time it's just a mist and the black streets shine with blue neon and red neon and yellow neon and in the shabby little rooms and holes and hallways you can hear the human music of conversation and laughter and crying and sex.

His mother walks in silence

The stun needle having curbed her tongue

Her fingers touching her stomach

Remembering what it was like to have the little girl in her womb

And not until it is too late does he realize that as they've been walking

His mother has been letting the filthy useless money fly from her hands

And leave a trail of dollars behind them

In the long sad night

The long sad night

Emma Baxter's Boy

The night rain didn't slow them down any. Sheriff Dan Gray had his lantern, and his breed deputy had his own lantern, too.

They had gone through the house, and now they were searching the outbuildings: barn, silo, chicken house. In the barn, you could hear the restless horses above the hiss of cold November rain.

Joel Baxter and his wife Emma stood on the porch of the farmhouse, just beneath the dripping overhang, watching the lawmen set about their work.

Joel was a scrawny man in his late twenties. He shaved only once a week, which left him with a heavy growth of dark, gristly stubble. He had guilty, frightened blue eyes and more of a tic than a smile. He wore bibs and a flannel shirt and a corn cob pipe was stuck in the corner of his mouth.

Emma was twenty-five. She'd been pretty but went

early to fat. Her prettiness was hidden now in her fleshy cheeks. She wore a gingham dress, a soiled apron, and a red woolen shawl. The temperature could be no more than thirty. When they talked, their breath was silver.

The Baxter farm was on the outskirts of Dade Township, which was a small community of merchants that served the surrounding agricultural areas. The sheriff and the breed worked out of there.

Joel watched as the sheriff and the breed came together in front of the silo. They were talking, their words lost in the sibilance of the rain. There being no moonlight, their expressions were hard to read. They both wore ponchos heavily oiled for just such a downpour, ponchos and wide-brimmed Texas hats.

Emma said, "Maybe they'll want to search the house again."

"It'll be all right."

"But what if they do?"

"They won't, Emma. Don't get all excited now." Emma had a tendency to do that, to get all excited whenever the root cellar was threatened. Nobody knew about the root cellar but her and her husband. She meant to keep it that way. She had lost two babies to miscarriage. She didn't plan to lose this one to anything.

The sheriff and the breed came over and stood below them on the ground.

"You wouldn't have any coffee, would you, Emma?" the sheriff said.

Joel looked at her. He knew what she was thinking. Let them in for coffee, they just might start searching the house again. This time, they might just find the trap-door to the root cellar.

"Sure we do," Joel said. It would look funny, turning the sheriff down.

A few minutes later, the three men sat at the kitchen table, the large kerosene lamp casting off smoky illumination. On the counter beneath the three-shelved cupboard a large piece of pork soaked in brine. Also on the counter was a bottle of New England rum, which Joel had bought for Emma in town earlier that day. She used it to wash her hair with, which kept it clean and free of prairie mites. The pride she'd once had in her face and body, she now had in her auburn tresses.

She brought them steaming hot coffee.

The breed said, "Thank you very much, ma'am." The breed was always polite. The priests had educated him. He was clean, too, and never looked insolent the way most breeds did.

She went into the bedroom to sew. Women were not welcome when men were talking. She kept the door open, though, so she could hear them.

"There's a child out here, somewhere," the sheriff said. "I don't see no reason to keep bullshittin' us about it, Joel. You've got a kid of some kind on these premises." The sheriff was a fleshy, white-haired man whose white beard was stained a chestnut color around the mouth from chewing tobacco. He had a bad pair of store boughts that clicked and clattered when he talked too fast, so he made a point of speaking slowly and distinctly which strangers mistook for him being wise and deliberate in his words.

"Mrs. Calherne drove by up on the hill in her buggy the other day," the sheriff went on, "and she seen Emma and a kid playin' in the yard here. She was too far away to see what the kid looked like. But it was a kid, all right."

"She must have bad eyesight, Sheriff, that's all I can figure."

"Bad eyesight?" the lawman said. The breed never talked except to say thank you. "Then we must have a lot of people around Dade Township with bad eyesight because this is about the tenth, eleventh party to see a kid in your yard."

Emma had to be more careful about where she took the kid out. He'd have to remind her of that again.

"One of the other ones who saw the kid, saw him a couple of times, matter of fact," the sheriff said, "was my deputy, Frank Sullivan. He was real curious about why somebody would want to keep their kid hidden the way you folks do."

The sheriff looked over at the breed. "Then one day Sullivan, he told me he was going to come out here and look around when he knew you folks was in town. Well, he did that, Joel, two weeks ago it was, and nobody's seen him since. He come out here and then he disappeared. Now what the hell's that all about, and why are you keepin' this kid of yours a secret, anyway?"

Joel said, "I don't know what happened to your deputy, Sheriff."

The sheriff looked at the breed again, then back at Joel. "Where's the kid, Joel?"

"What kid?"

"You know what kid. The kid a whole lot of people have seen from a distance, but you won't admit to."

"There isn't any kid," Emma said, as she entered the kitchen.

She stood next to the stove, watching the men. "I

don't know what those folks think they're seeing but it isn't a kid. I guess I'd know if I had a kid or not, wouldn't I?"

The sheriff sighed. "He's here somewhere. I'm sure of it."

"You looked everywhere," Joel said.

"Maybe not everywhere," the sheriff said. "Maybe you've got a secret place, something like that."

"No secret place," Joel said. "Where would there be a secret place?"

Thunder rattled the farmhouse windows. In the lightning that followed, Sheriff Gray's face looked lined, old, dead.

"Guess we have searched it pretty good," he said. He sounded too tired to move. He sighed. "Maybe we'll push on back to town," he said to the breed. The breed nodded. "I appreciate the coffee, Emma."

"Yes, thank you," the breed said. The priests on the reservation had done a good job of educating him. He sounded a lot whiter than most white men.

They stood up and shrugged into their ponchos and shoved their hats down heavy on their heads and said a few more good nights, and then pushed on into the cold, slashing rain.

When they were sixty seconds gone, Emma said softly, "My heart was in my throat. The breed, he kept looking over there by the stove."

"I think you're imagining things, Emma. I didn't see him looking over there once."

Her reaction was immediate, angry. "You don't give a damn about your own son, do you? *You* want them to find him, don't you? You know what they'd do to him, don't you? They'd kill him? They'd take one look at him and then they'd kill him, and you wouldn't give a damn, would you, Joel? Your own son and you wouldn't give a damn at tall."

"They're not gonna quit lookin' for their deputy," he said quietly. "They're gonna come back here, and they're gonna keep comin' back."

"That all you got to say?"

"That's all I got to say."

"I don't suppose you're gonna go down there with me and say good night to him and say his good night prayers with me. That'd be askin' too much, wouldn't it?"

"Yes," he said. "Yes, it would."

She took the lamp and walked over by the stove and lifted up the small hooked rug and bent down and lifted the metal ring on the trapdoor.

The root cellar stank of dirt and cold. They'd kept vegetables fresh down there, but the coldness muted all the other odors. His grave would smell like that, Joel knew, dirt and cold. This was the smell of eternity. Darkness, rot, nothingness.

She went down the steps quickly, pulling the trapdoor closed behind her.

Joel stood there, listening to the noises the child in the cellar always made. He had never heard anything like these noises, a very low keening followed by a kind of sucking sound.

Without the lamp, the house was dark now, a lonely, empty dark.

Joel went into the bedroom and stripped to his long johns and lay down and listened to the rain thrum on the roof. He wished he could pray. He wished he still believed. He didn't know what they were going to do about the root cellar.

He rolled over and went to sleep. There was no

sense waiting up for her. Sometimes, she stayed down there till dawn.

Sound woke him.

What kind of sound?

He sat up, listened, reaching for the Navy Colt on the floor next to the bed.

Kitchen. Table. Somebody bumping against it.

Hiss of rain.

It could be Emma, but instinct told him otherwise.

He eased himself out of bed, tiptoed to the bedroom doorway that looked out upon the one large room that was both living space and kitchen. He glanced out the window. A lone horse was ground-tied by the silo.

The trapdoor. Somebody crouching there. Opening the door six inches to peer into the dank darkness below, the keening sound louder suddenly, agitated. Lamplight flickering up from the cellar.

"Joel?" Emma said from the root cellar. "Is that you up there?"

The crouching man heard him then. Started to turn, started to stand.

"Better come up here, Emma," Joel said.

"What's wrong?" Emma called.

"The breed came back."

"The breed? I tole you, Joel. I tole you."

The keening sound became mournful then, the way it always did when Emma left the root cellar and came back upstairs, mournful and frightened and impossibly lonely.

She came up, bringing light in the form of the lamp.

The breed stood next to the stove.

"You saw it, didn't you, when you were looking

down there, in the lamplight I mean," Joel said.

"I didn't see anything," the breed said in his perfect English. His poncho and his hat stank of rain.

"Maybe he didn't see, Joel," Emma said hopefully.

"Oh, he saw, all right," Joel said. "He saw all right." Then, "Where's the sheriff?"

"He's outside waiting for me. I don't come out pretty soon, he'll come in here."

"Oh, my Lord," Emma said. "What're we gonna do, Joel?" In Emma's voice, he could hear her fears: Now her third child would be taken from her, too. Emma Baxter, it seemed, was never to be blessed with a child she could keep.

"You're lying," Joel said. "The sheriff ain't out there."

"Oh? And how would you know that?"

"Because there's only one horse out there."

"That doesn't prove anything."

"It proves it to me," Joel said. Then, "Come over here."

"What?"

"Step away from the wall."

"Why would I want to do that?"

"Because I told you to."

"I only take orders from the sheriff."

Joel decided to get it over with. He crossed the floor in three steps and brought the barrel of his gun down hard on the breed's right temple.

The breed looked startled for a moment. Then he sank to the floor, unconscious.

"Oh, my God, Joel, what're we gonna do?" Emma said. "What're we gonna do?"

But Joel didn't say anything. He just got the rope

and tied the breed up, wrists and ankles, then dragged him over to the corner.

"We got to put him down there," Emma said twenty minutes later.

The trapdoor was shut. She had poured them both coffee. The breed was still unconscious.

"Emma," Joel said, "you know what we got to do." He sounded sad as Emma looked.

"Oh, no, Joel, oh, no. You don't do that to our son. He's your own flesh and blood."

"Part of him is my flesh and blood," Joel said. "Part of him is somethin' else."

He still recalled the night it happened, a steamy August night, him waking to find the bed empty, Emma gone off somewhere. Him scared. Where had she gone? And then her coming back, telling him she'd heard this strange sound in the sky, and then seen this explosion over the hills in the woods, something falling from the sky. And then her going out there to see what it was. And finding the fire and next to the fire the odd bubbling muck—like quicksand, she kept saying, like quicksand—and then her stumbling and falling into it, and grasping and gasping to be free of it, the thing boiling and bubbling and sucking her down, sucking her down, and her free finally, finally free.

She'd vomited several times that night. And run a fever so hot Joel was sure she was going to die right there in their wedding bed. But in the morning, she was not only alive, she rolled over when the rooster crowed and shook him gently and whispered, "I'm going to have a baby again, Joel. I'm going to have a baby again."

Ed Gorman

Her fever was gone, and no more vomiting.

Joel himself went over the hill to the woods that morning. He could see where a fire had burned an area of the forest, a scorched black circle as if a fiery disk had fallen from the sky, but there was no evidence of the bubbling hole she'd described, no evidence at all, though on her dress he could see strange mauve stains, and knew she was telling the truth.

Winter came, and the child was born, and when the midwife delivered it, she screamed and tried to run from the room. But it was too late. Joel buried what was left of her, her flesh so shredded and torn, up in the hills by the deep stand of hardwoods. She was the first person to die because of what had been birthed between Emma's legs. If they killed the breed, he would be the fourth.

"I got to, Emma," he said. "I got to. We just can't go on killing people this way. They'll figure it out and they'll hang us. They'll hang us right down in Tompkins Square the way they did those two breeds last spring."

"He's our son."

"No he ain't, Emma," Joel said gently, "and I think deep down you know that."

"He come from my womb."

"Yeah, but it wasn't me that put him there, and you know it."

She looked at him. He'd expected tears, argument. All she said was, "Then I'll do it, the breed I mean."

He shook his head. "Emma, listen, the breed wakes up, I'm gonna take him into town, and we're gonna talk to the sheriff, and I'm gonna explain everything, how none of this was our fault, and how we want to stop it now before it gets any worse. That's the only thing we can do, Emma. The only thing."

No reaction this time either. She just watched him. She didn't even look angry any more. Just watched him.

The breed moaned. He was coming around.

"I love you, Emma," Joel said. "I want a good life for us. It wasn't our fault what happened. I think Sheriff Gray'll understand that. He seems to be a good man."

"What is that thing, anyway?" the breed said. You could hear pain in his voice. Joel had cracked him pretty darned good on the side of the head.

"You shut up, breed," Emma said. "That's our son is what that thing is. And we're proud he's our son. Very proud."

Now she was crying, crying hard. "You don't call him a 'thing,' either, you understand that?" Emma said.

"C'mon, Emma," Joel said gently, touching her hand. "I'm gonna let the breed go and then we'll ride into town, all right?"

But all she did was weep. Weep.

Joel, more tired suddenly than he'd ever been in his life, stood up and walked over to Emma on the other side of the table and kissed the top of her head, the way he'd do with a child. "It'll be better once we tell the sheriff, Emma. It really will."

Then he went over and crouched down and started undoing the ropes binding the breed.

And that was when the breed shouted, "Watch out, Joel!"

All Joel had time to see was the carving knife coming down in an arc, the huge and terrible blade gleaming in the lamplight, coming down, down, down.

And then the pain in his shoulder, then the pain all over the upper part of his body.

When she was all finished with the knife, Emma dragged Joel over to the trapdoor and pushed him down into the root cellar. His body made a big noise when it collided with the dirt floor.

She did the breed the same way. He was even bloodier than Joel had been. She'd gotten the breed to admit that he'd been lying. He'd come back here after riding back to town with the sheriff.

She gave the breed an extra hard push through the opening.

Then she closed the trapdoor and left her son to his business.

An hour later, Emma hefted the large metal trunk on to the back of the buckboard. Her son would be safe and dry in there, especially after she threw the blanket over it and fastened it down with rope.

Then she climbed abroad and took the reins and set off. The roads were muddy, but at least the rain had let up. She wasn't quite sure where she was going. She just needed to get to another part of the Territory as fast as possible.

She thought about Joel, and that first spring she'd met him, and how he'd courted her with his big, wide, country boy grin. He'd been so nice back then, nice all the time right up to the night when their son was born. And then he hadn't been nice at all. Then he'd changed so much he wasn't like Joel at all.

By sunrise, they had reached the stage road. The rain hadn't been so bad over here. The going was easier, much easier.

Survival

1

A lot of people in the hospital were still mad at me about last night . . .

. . . but then they'd been mad at me before and they'd be mad at me again . . .

. . . the problem was, what got them mad, was that he was more crazed than dangerous, the dreamduster who'd broken into the supply area on the first floor. He was also nine years old. They'd wanted me to kill him but I'd declined the honor and handed my .38 auto Colt to Young Doctor Pelham and said, you want him killed, you kill him yourself. Pelham just muttered some bullshit about the Hippocratic oath and gave me my weapon back.

What I ended up doing with the little bastard was

putting a chute on him and then taking him up on a skymobile and pushing him out somewhere over Zone 1. He'd be lucky to survive forty-eight hours. There was some new kind of influenza taking hold there. It had already buried something like 2,000 people in less than a week. Maybe I would've done him a favor killing him quick the way Pelham wanted me to. Being a dreamduster, his life was over anyway. . . .

After dumping the kid, I went back to the hospital and walked the ten flights up to my room. There's an elevator but since all our power comes from the emergency generators Pelham figured out how to soup-up, we use the elevators only when it's absolutely necessary.

My little place is on the same floor as the mutants that our two resident bio-engineers are studying with the belief that one of the pathetic wretches will someday yield a vaccine useful to what remains of the human race. Tuesday, March 6, 2009—six long years ago now—the Fascist-Christian party got their hands on several nuclear warheads (helped considerably by several Pentagon Generals who were also part of the plot) and proceeded to purify our entire planet of its sins and sinners. What the Christers in all their wisdom didn't understand was that twenty of the warheads also carried some pretty wild germ warfare devices, devices that had killed many of the workers who'd helped create them.

Tenth floor of the hospital used to be the psych ward. Each patient had his own room with a heavy door and a glass observation square built in.

I used to hurry past the doors on the way to my

room but now I stopped most times and peered in through the squares.

They're pretty repulsive looking, no doubt about that, none older than five years old, none resembling a real human being in more than a passing way, not unless you consider three arms and no vertebrae—or a completely spherical body with a head the size and shape of a pin-cushion—or a squid-like creature with heartbreaking little hand-flippers—definitely not the kind of folk you'd like to see at your next family reunion.

They were used to seeing me now and as I waggled my fingers and smiled at them, they made these sad frantic little noises, the way puppies do when they want to be picked up. So, exhausted as I was, I spent a few minutes with each of them. By now I was not only used to looking at them, I was also used to smelling them. Poor little bastards, they can't help it.

I went to my room and got some sleep.

What I am, you see, is what they call an Outrider. Back in the Old West, this was a person who rode on ahead of the wagon train to make sure everything was safe.

A year ago, after my wife and two daughters died from one of the variant strains of flu that had claimed half the people in Fort Waukegan, I tried to kill myself with my trusty .38 auto Colt. Oh, the bullet went in all right but it managed to traverse the exterior of my skull without doing serious or permanent damage.

A scout from Fort Glencoe found me out on the periphery of Zone 2 and brought me back to the hospital. Once they had me on my feet again, they asked me what I'd done before the Christers got their bright idea of "purifying" the planet. When I told them I'd been a homicide detective, they asked me how I'd like to stay in Fort Glencoe permanently, as an Outrider—scouting Zones 1 through 5 surrounding Fort Glencoe and making sure no bands of warriors were headed here—and doubling as a hospital security guard. Dreamdusters, the junkies who got off on synthetic powder that was cheap to make and more powerfully addictive than any heroin ever concocted— were always breaking into hospital supply rooms in search of toxins and vaccines that would give them the ultimate kick 'til they got some real dreamdust.

They kept telling me how lucky I was to be alive. I wasn't sure about that.

But I stayed on as their Outrider and Security man and it was in that role that I first heard of Paineaters, even though I didn't quite believe in them, at least not as described by my boss and nemesis, Young Doc Pelham.

Troubled sleep. But then it usually is. I dream of Joan and the girls and I wake up with a terrible sadness upon me. Usually I throw my legs off the side of the bed and sit there with my head in my hands remembering faces and voices and touches and laughter.

Then there's the nightmare. It started a few months back when I—well when I got in some trouble with the staff here . . .

Today, though, there wasn't any time for reveries.

Not with somebody pounding, pounding, pounding on my door.

"Yeah?" I said, rolling, still mostly asleep, from bed.

She didn't say anything. Just came through the door.

Nurse Polly. Coppery hair; big brown melancholy eyes; sweet little wrists and ankles; and a kind of childlike faith that everything will always work out.

"Pelham."

"Oh, great," I said.

"Emergency, he says."

"Isn't it always?"

She gave me a look I couldn't quite read. "You slept through it."

"Slept through what?"

I stood up, giving her a good look at my hairy legs in boxer shorts. (Nurse Polly and I had made love several times in a conveniently located storage closet on the third floor. We always did it standing up. She was very good, sexy and tender at the same time. She seemed to sense that I always felt guilty about it. "You're thinking about your wife, aren't you?" "Yeah; guess I am." "That's all right." "It is?" "Sure. I'm thinking about my husband. He died pretty much the same way." And then we'd just hold each other, two lonely animals needing comfort and solace.)

"We had two people die in surgery last night. He couldn't operate because—Well, you know."

"God."

"We've got three operations scheduled today and no Paineater."

"I won't go alone. I want somebody to go with me."

"I'll go."

"Really?"

"Uh-huh."

"I don't know."

"Why?"

"Polly, you've got a great big heart. And you can get so involved with them . . ." I shook my head. "You know what happened to me, what I did."

I didn't know if she felt like being held by a hairy guy in white boxer shorts with red hearts on them but I figured I'd give it a try.

I held her and she seemed glad I did, snuggling into me and putting her arms around my waist.

Then she took my hand. "C'mon. Let's go see Pelham."

But I held back. "You know what I did—he shouldn't send me out to get a new one." I was getting spooked. I didn't want to go through it all again.

She looked at me and shook her head. "You want me to take you down and show you the patients waiting for surgery? One of them had his eyes cut out by a dreamduster."

"Shit," I said.

2

Young Doctor Pelham might not be so bad under normal circumstances—where a doctor had the staff and facilities to do his best work—but here he's always stressed out and usually angry. I might be that way myself if I was losing 60% of my patients on the table.

A day or two after the Christers dropped the bombs, the looting and raping and murdering began. I hate to be cynical about it but the human beast was a much darker one than I'd ever imagined. Made me regret all the times I'd been civilized about it and spoken up against the death penalty.

A couple of things became clear to all citizens good and true, man and woman, white and black, Christian and Jew, straight and gay—that there were a whole lot of really terrible people out there meaning them great malice. The good folk would have to band together. The concept of a fortress came along soon after.

Most Forts comprise five or six miles inside a wall of junk cars. The walls are patrolled twenty-four hours by mean humans and even meaner dogs. Zoners, those living in the outer areas, sometimes sneak through but most of them end up as little more than blood and flesh gleaming on the teeth of the Dobermans.

Most Forts are also built around hospitals. The good citizens had to quickly decide which was the most important of all buildings. Police station? Courthouse? Hospital? Indeed. With the bioengineered warheads continuing to do their work, life was a constant struggle not only against violence—once every three months or so a small army of Zoners would take a run at the various Forts and inflict great casualties—but also disease.

Inside the walls of scrap metal, the citizens lived in any sort of shelter they could find. Houses, garages, schools, roller rinks—it didn't matter. You lived where you could find room for you and your family.

Then there was the hospital. I know how you probably imagine it ten floors of the various units that all modern hospitals have—maternity, pediatric, surgical, psychiatric, intermediate care, intensive care—all staffed by crisply garbed interns and residents and registered nurses and practical nurses and nurses aides, many of whom spend their time walking between the pharmacy, the central service department, the food service and the laboratories.

But forget it.

This hospital is ten floors of smashed windows and bullet-riddled walls and blood-stained floors. Before the Fortress wall could be erected, some roving Zoners staged a six-day battle that cost a thousand people their lives, and nearly resulted in the Zoners taking over the hospital.

Patients are brought in on the average of fourteen a day. On average, eight of those are buried within twenty-four hours.

"There isn't any time for your usual bullshit," Young Doctor Pelham told me when I stood before his desk. "In case you want to give me any, I mean."

The glamorous Dr. Sullivan, dark of hair and eye, red of mouth, supple and ample of figure, sat in a chair across the room, listening. Everybody knew two things about the good doctors Pelham and Sullivan. That they'd once been lovers. And that they now hated each other and that Sullivan wanted Pelham's job. She was always telling jokes about him behind his back.

"They're kids," I said, wishing Polly had stayed. Her presence would have made Pelham less harsh. She had that effect on people.

"I know they're kids."

"Little kids."

"Little kids. Right. But I don't have a lot of choice in the matter. I have to do right by my patients."

Much as I dislike him, Pelham's arguments about the Paineaters are probably sound. Ethically, he had to weigh the welfare of his patients against the welfare of the Paineaters. He had to choose his patients.

He sat behind his desk, a trim man in a white medical smock that had lost its dignity to spatters of human blood and other fluids. He looked up at me with tired brown eyes and a face that would have been handsome if it didn't look quite so petulant most of the time. "I've got what he wants."

He reached down behind his desk and lifted up a leather briefcase. He set it on the desk.

"It's a shame we have to deal with people like that," Dr. Sullivan said.

"Do you have a better idea, Susan?" Pelham snapped.

"No, I guess I don't."

"Then I'd thank you to stay out of this."

She really was twice as beautiful when she was angry. She got up and left the room.

"I want one understanding," I said.

"Here we go," he said, "you and your fucking understandings."

"I won't bodyguard her. Don't forget what happened last time."

The brown eyes turned hostile. "You think I could forget what you did, Congreve? You think any of us could *ever* forget what you did?"

"I was thinking of her."

"Sure you were, Congreve, because you're such a noble sonofabitch." He shook his head. "You did it because you couldn't take it anymore. Because you weren't tough enough."

He pushed the briefcase across to me.

"We need one right away. I've got seven patients ready for surgery. They're going to die if I don't get to them in just a few hours."

I picked up the briefcase. "Just so we understand each other, Doc. I won't bodyguard her."

He smiled that smirky aggravating smile of his. "It's not something you have to worry about, Congreve. You think after what you did, we'd even *want* you to guard her?" I guess he probably had it right. Who the hell would want me to guard her?

I went outside and got in my skymobile.

3

Polly was in the passenger seat. She'd changed into a green blouse and jeans and a brown suede jacket.

"I don't remember inviting you."

"C'mon, Congreve. I won't be any trouble."

"I get downed somewhere and surrounded by a gang of Zoners and you won't be any trouble? Then I have to worry about you as well as myself."

She brought an impressive silver Ruger from somewhere inside her jacket. "I think I can take care of myself."

If you've ever seen photographs or film of Berlin right after World War II, you have some sense of what Chicago looks like these days, skyscrapers toppled, entire neighborhoods reduced to ragged brick and jagged glass and dusty heaps of stone. With no sanitation, no electricity, no official order of any kind, you can pretty well imagine what's happened: the predators have taken over. Warlords divided up various parts of each Zone. You do what they say or they kill you. Very simple.

We were headed for the eastern sector of Zone 2, which had once been the inner-city.

"I disappointed you today, didn't I?" Polly said.

"A little, I suppose."

"I know how you feel about Paineaters."

"I can't help it. I just keep seeing my own daughters."

"We don't have any choice, Congreve. You have to understand that."

"I'll take your word for it."

"You can really be an asshole sometimes."

"But Pelham can't?"

"We weren't talking about Pelham."

"I was. Pelham and all the other Pelhams who run these Fortresses and use Paineaters."

"You should see the patients who—"

"I've seen the patients," I said, "that's the only reason I'm doing this. Because I don't have the stomach or balls or whatever it takes to see all those people lying there and suffering. Otherwise I wouldn't help at all."

She leaned over and touched my hand. "I shouldn't have called you an asshole."

I smiled at her. "Oh, what should you have called me?"

She smiled right back. "A prick is what I should have called you."

"I guess that's a promotion of sorts, anyway."

"Of sorts," she said.

Sometimes when you're up there, you can forget everything that's happened in the last six years. Dawn and sunset are especially beautiful and you can feel some of the old comfort and security you knew; and that awe you found in the beauty of natural things. That's why I took the skymobile every chance

I got . . . because if I didn't look down I could pretend that the world was the same as it had always been . . .

The last twenty miles, we went in low. That's when you get a sense of the daily carnage, going low like that.

Bodies and body parts strewn all over the bomb-blasted Interstate. And not just warriors, either, children, women, family pets. Families try to leave a Zone area when there's a war going on. Too often they make the mistake of following the Interstate where bandits wait. These are not the gentlemen bandits of Robin Hood fame. A doc told me once he'd seen a ten-year-old girl that ten adult bandits had gang raped. I'd kill all of them if I got a chance.

Originally, Jackson Heights had been a nice little shopping area for upscale folks. But those upscale folks who didn't get killed by the Christers' bombs got their throats slashed by the Zoners who took the place over and renamed it after one of their old time leaders.

There was a block of two-story brick buildings. On the roofs you could see warriors with powerful binoculars and even more powerful auto-shotguns. I imagined, if I looked hard enough, I'd also find some grenade launchers.

Six black men raised their shotguns.

"God," Polly said, "are they just going to shoot us down?"

"Hopefully, one of them will recognize the mobile here and realize it's me."

"Yeah," she said anxiously, "hopefully."

I circled the roofs one more time and in the middle of the circle the shotguns lowered and two of the men started waving at us. Somebody had radio'd headquarters and described our skymobile and headquarters had okayed us.

"Feel better?" I said.

"Sorry I was such a candy ass. I was just scared there for a minute."

"So was I."

Hoolihan is a black man.

I know, I know—his name is Irish; as is his pug nose, his freckled and light-skinned face; his reddish curly hair; and his startling blue eyes. But he's Negro—which you can tell, somehow, when you see him.

Hoolihan, by my estimation, has personally killed more than two thousand people.

I reach this conclusion by simple mathematics:

$$365 \times 6 = 2190$$

He's been the warlord of East Zone 1 for the past six years. I figure, probably conservatively, that he's killed one person each day. As I say, simple math.

This day Hoolihan sent his own personal vehicle for us, an ancient Army jeep painted camel-shit green with a big red H stenciled on the back panel. He uses the H the way cattle barons used to use their brands.

Hoolihan lives in a rambling two-story red brick house. Easy enough to imagine a couple of Saabs in the drive, a game of badminton going on in the backyard, steaks smelling wonderful on the outdoor grill. Suburban bliss. The effect is spoiled somewhat, however, by the cyclone fencing, the barely controllable

Dobermans, and the armed guards in faded Army khaki.

In case none of that deters you, there's one other surprise: a front door that detonates a tiny bomb just big enough to render the visitor into several chunks if he doesn't know the password.

The guard knew the password. "Your Mama," he said.

Hoolihan had a nasty sense of humor.

The door was buzzed open and we walked in.

What Hoolihan's done with the interior of his house is pretty amazing. He's turned it into a time travel exhibit: the world as it was before the Christers got hold of it. Sore sad eyes can gaze at length upon parqueted floors and comfortable couches sewn in rich rose damask and Victorian antiques and prints by Chagall and Vermeer; and sore sad ears, long accustomed to the cries of the dying, can be solaced with the strains of Debussy and Vivaldi and Bach.

Hoolihan, whatever else he is, is no fool.

He made us wait five minutes.

He enjoys being fashionably late.

He also enjoys looking like a stage fop in a Restoration comedy. Today he swept in wearing a paisely dressing gown, and his usual icy smirk. Oh, yes, and the black eyepatch. Dramatic as hell until you realize that it keeps shifting eyes. Some days it's on his right eye and some days—

"Nice," he said, referring to Polly. "I don't suppose she's for sale."

"I don't suppose she is," Polly said.

"Too bad. I know people who'd pay a lot of money for you."

That was another thing about Hoolihan. He had a sophomore's need to shock.

"Martini?" he said.

"Beer would be fine," I said.

"The lady?"

"Beer," she said.

He nodded to a white-haired man in some sort of African ceremonial robe. The man went into the next room.

"We found a supermarket that had been contaminated so long people gave up on it," Hoolihan said. "I sent some men in last week. And now we have enough beer to last us for a long, long time."

"The land of opportunity," I said.

He said, "The palm of my hand is starting to itch."

I had to smile. He was a melodramatic sonofabitch but he had the brains to kid himself, too.

"I wonder what that means," I said.

"It means my right hand wants to just walk over there and grab that brief case."

"We need to cut a deal first."

"I take it you don't want drugs, little girls or boys for sex, or the latest in weaponry my men took from that National Guard Armory in Cleveland last month."

"None of the above. Why don't we just cut the bullshit and you tell me if you've got one for sale."

The elderly man with the intelligent dark eyes returned with our beers. I've never been much for servants. I felt funny accepting it from him, as if I should apologize.

"Please," Hoolihan said, "let's sit down and make this all very civilized. We're not making some back-alley deal here."

We sat. But I'm not sure how civilized it was. Not considering what the product happened to be.

"I've got five on hand at the moment," he said from his throne-sized leather chair across the room from where Polly and I sat on the edge of an elegant couch.

"We need one right away."

"I've got them out in a shed."

Polly muttered something nasty under her breath.

Hoolihan smirked. He'd aggravated her and he loved it. "Don't worry, pretty one. It's a perfectly civilized shed. Clean, dry and protected not only from the elements but from Zoners. They're much better off in my shed than they would be wandering free."

With that I couldn't argue.

"Now how much is in that briefcase?"

"$100,000. It's all yours as long as you don't dicker."

"$100,000," he said. "My, my, my, my. I wish my poor old broken-down nigger daddy could see me now."

That's the funny thing about the warlords. Even though they know that the currency is absolutely worthless, they still revel in getting it.

Hoolihan's father had served three terms in prison for minor crimes and had never known a day's happiness or pride in his entire life. Hoolihan had told me all this one night when he'd been coasting on whiskey and drugs. And he'd broken down and cried half way through. He was bitter and angry about his father, whom he felt had never had a serious chance at leading a decent life.

He was probably right.

His old man would have been damned proud of his one and only son.

One hundred thousand was now his. Didn't matter that it was worthless. It still had an echo, a resonance, money did, at least to those of us who could remember how everything used to be before the Christers went and screwed it all up.

A tear rolled down Hoolihan's cheek. "I miss that old fucker, you know?"

Not even Polly, who obviously didn't care much for Hoolihan, could deny him this moment. Her own eyes teared up now.

"Let's go get her," I said, "before it gets dark."

Kerosene torches lit the blooming gloom of dusk; a chill started creeping up my arms and legs and back; a dog barked, lonely. You could smell and taste the autumn night, and then smell the decay of bodies that hadn't been buried properly. Even though you couldn't see them, their stench told you how many of them there were. And how close.

The shed was a quarter mile through a sparsely wooded area that a dog—maybe the same one barking—had mined with plump squishy turds.

Two guards in khaki stood guard in front of the small garage that Hoolihan called the shed. Hoolihan, by the way, had traded his foppish robe for an even more foppish military uniform. He had epaulets big enough to land helicopters on.

The guards saluted when they saw Hoolihan. He saluted them, crisply, right back.

"C'mon in and you can pick one," he said merrily enough, as if he were inviting us on to a used car lot.

We went inside. He'd been telling the truth about the tidiness of the place. Newly whitewashed walls. Handsomely carpeted floor. Six neat single beds with ample sheets and blankets. At the back was a table where food was taken. The place even smelled pretty good.

There were four of them and they sat on their beds watching us, their outsize heads tottering as they gaped at us. For some reason I don't understand—this sort of thing I leave to Young Doctor Pelham—their necks won't properly support their heads. They were all female and they all wore little aqua-colored jumpsuits that resembled pajamas. They're mute, or most of them are anyway, but they make noises in their throat that manage to be both touching and disgusting. They were little and frail, too, pale and delicate, with tiny hands that were always reaching out for another human hand to hold.

"Where the hell's the dark-haired one?" Hoolihan said.

The guard got this awful expression on his face as his eyes quickly counted the little girls.

Four.

There were supposed to be five.

"Where the hell did she go?" Hoolihan said.

The children couldn't answer him; they couldn't talk.

And the guards were no help. They'd somehow managed to let one get away.

Hoolihan walked over to a window at the back of the garage. A small wooden box had been placed directly under it.

Hoolihan put pressure on the base of the window. It pushed outward. It was unlocked.

The kid had gone out the window.

As he was turning around to face us all again, Hoolihan took a wicked-looking hand gun from his belt and shot the guards in the face.

Nothing fancy. No big deal.

One moment they were human beings, the next they were corpses.

Anxiety started working through me—surprise, shock, anger, fear that he might do the same to me— and then, as I looked at the children, I felt the turmoil begin to wane.

They stared at us.

They said nothing.

They started doing their jobs.

A few moments later, the worst of the feelings all gone, we followed Hoolihan out into the dark, chilly night.

"We're going to find that little bitch," Hoolihan said.

4

Well, we found her all right, but it took two hours, a lot of crawling around on hands and knees in dark and tangled undergrowth, and a lot of cursing on Hoolihan's part.

The little kid was a quarter mile away hiding in a culvert.

When we found her, got the jostling beam of the flashlight playing across her soiled aqua jumpsuit, she was doing a most peculiar thing: petting a rat.

This was a big rat, too, seven, eight pounds, with a pinched evil face and a pair of gleaming red eyes. He probably carried a thousand kinds of diseases and an appetite for carrion that would give a flock of crows pause. After the Fascist-Christians had their way with the world, rats became major enemies again.

But there he sat on the little girl's lap just the way a kitten would. And the little girl's tiny white hand was stroking his back.

There was some semblance of intelligence in the girl's eyes. That was the first thing that struck me. Usually the saucer-shaped eyes are big and blank. But she seemed to have a pretty good idea of who and what we were.

Then Hoolihan shot the rat and the little girl went berserk.

The rat exploded into three chunks of meat and bone and gristle, each covered with blood-soaked flesh.

The keening sound came up in the little girl's throat and she quickly got on all fours and started crawling down the culvert as fast as she could.

Hoolihan thought it was all great, grand farce.

I wanted to kill him—or at least damage him in some serious way—but I knew better. He had too many men eager to kill anybody white. With Hoolihan gone, Polly and I would never get out of here.

Polly went after the kid.

I was still trying to forget the kid's terrible expression. They establish some kind of telepathic link with their subject, that's what the kids do, and so the relation becomes intimate beyond our understanding. Rat and little girl had become one. So then Hoolihan goes and kills it.

"You look pissed, man," Hoolihan said.

"You're scum, Hoolihan."

"Just having a little fun."

"Right."

"I like it when you get all judgemental and pontifical on me, Congreve. Kinda sexy, actually."

"You knew what the little girl was doing."

"Sure. Linking up." The smirk. "But maybe I have so much respect for her I didn't want her to link up with some fucking rat, you ever think of that?"

I grabbed his flashlight.

He started at me, as if he was going to put a good hard right hand on my face, but my scowl seemed to dissuade him.

I didn't find Polly and the girl for another fifteen minutes and I probably wouldn't have found them then if it hadn't been for the dog.

He was some kind of alley mutt, half-boxer and half-collie if you can imagine that, and he stood on the old railroad siding barking his ass off at the lone boxcar that stood on the tracks that shone silver in the moonlight.

I could hear her now, the kid, the mewling deep in her throat. She was still terrified of the rat exploding.

I climbed up inside. In the darkness the old box car smelled of wood and grease and piss. A lot of people had slept in this, no doubt.

Polly was in the corner, the kid in her lap.

Polly was sort of rocking the kid back and forth and humming to her.

I went over and sat down next to her and put my hand to the kid's cheek. It was soft and warm and sweet. And I thought of my own daughters when they were about this age, how I'd see their mother rocking them at night and humming the old lullabies they loved so much.

I thought of this and started crying. I couldn't help it. I just sat there and felt gutted and dead.

And then Polly said, "Why don't you take her for a little while? She's calming down. But my legs are going to sleep. I need to walk around."

I took her. And rocked her. And sang some of the old lullabies and it was kind of funny because when my voice got just so loud, the mutt outside would join in and kind of bark along.

Polly jumped down from the boxcar. I imagined she needed to pee, in addition to stretching her legs.

When she came back, she stood in the open door, the night sky starry behind her, and the smell of clean fresh rushing night on the air, and said, "God, that'd make a sweet picture, Congreve, you and that little kid in your arms that way."

And then I got mad.

I put the kid down—I didn't hurt her but I wasn't especially gentle, either—and then I stalked to the open door and said: "No fucking way am I going to go through this again, Polly. I don't want anything to do with this kid, you understand? Not a thing."

She knew better than to argue.

She went back and picked up the kid.

She came back to the open door.

I'd jumped down and stood there waiting to lead the way back to Hoolihan.

Polly was pissed. "You think you could hold the kid long enough for me to jump down?"

"Don't start on me, Polly. You know what I went through."

"I love it when you whine."

"Just hand the kid down and get off my back."

She handed the kid down.

I took her, held her, numbed myself to her as much as possible. It wasn't going to happen again.

Polly jumped down. "That Hoolihan is some piece of work."

"Dreamdust."

"That's an excuse and you know it. He would've done that if he was straight. It's his nature."

"Nothing like a bigot."

"I'm not a bigot, Congreve. There're lots of white people just like him. I'm starting to think it's genetic."

"Here's the kid."

She didn't take her right away but put her hand on my arm. "I know how hard it is for you, Congreve, after what happened and all, with the little one here I mean."

"I appreciate you understanding, Polly. I really don't want to go through it again."

"I'll take care of her."

"I appreciate it."

"We're saving lives, Congreve. That's how you have to look at it."

"I hope I can remember that."

Now she took the kid. Cuddled her. Looked down at her. Started talking baby talk.

It was sweet and I wanted to hold them both in the brisk night winds, and then sleep warm next to them in a good clean bed.

When I got Polly and the kid in the skymobile, Hoolihan said, "I heard about what you did."

"Yeah, well, it happens."

"You're a crazy fucker."

"Look who's talking."

"Yeah but I got an excuse. I'm a warlord. I got to act crazy or people won't be afraid of me."

"I guess that's a good point."

He nodded to the kid inside the bubble dome. "You think you'll do it again?"

"This time I won't have anything to do with her."

"I'd still like to buy that chick."

"No, you wouldn't. She's too tough for you. You want somebody you can beat into submission. You couldn't beat her into submission in twenty years."

He laughed. "She sounds like a lot of fun, man. I love a challenge."

I got in the skymobile.

He leaned in and looked at Polly who was completely captivated by the small child in her arms.

"I'll see you both soon," he said, wanting to get one more shock in. "You know them little ones never last very long."

5

Young Doctor Pelham and his number two Dr. Sullivan put her right to work.

Polly gave her the name Sarah and fixed her up a nice cozy little room and then proceeded to wait on her with an almost ferocious need.

She also dressed her differently, in jeans and sweatshirts and a pair of sneakers that Polly had dug up somewhere in the basement.

Pelham started Sarah on the most needful ones first, which only made sense. He knew not to ever yell at her or push her—as I'd seen him do with a couple of them—but he was never tender with her, either. To Pelham, she was just another employee.

Polly, Sarah and I started taking meals together in the staff mess on the lower level.

Polly fussed with everything. Made sure Sarah's

food was heated just-so. Made sure her drinking glasses were spotlessly clean. Made sure that with each meal—which was usually some variation on chili—there was at least a small piece of dessert for Sarah.

In that respect, Sarah was a pretty typical kid. She lusted after sweets.

But that was the only way Sarah was typical. Autism is the closest thing I can liken her condition to. She was with us in body but not in spirit. She would sit staring off at distances we couldn't see. And then she would start making a kind of sad music in her throat, apparently responding to things far beyond our ken.

She hadn't been used much before we'd gotten her because she didn't exhibit any of the usual symptoms of deterioration. They start with the twitches and then graduate to the shakes and finally they end up clasping their heads between their hands, as if trying to fight a crushing headache.

After that, they're not much good to anybody.

And after that . . .

I didn't see much of Polly for the next few weeks. Not that I didn't go up to her room. Two or three times a day, I went up to her room. But she was always busy with the kid. Bathing the kid. Fixing the kid's hair in some new pretty way. Singing to the kid. Reading to the kid . . .

A few times I tried it real late at night, hoping that she'd want to lean against the wall with me the way she sometimes did.

But she always said the same thing. "I wouldn't

feel right about it, Congreve. You know, with Sarah in the room and all."

I just kept thinking of what had happened to me with the kid before this one. . . .

How fast you can get attached . . .

I felt responsible for Polly: I never should have taken her along to Hoolihan's. . . .

"Pelham says we can have a holiday party."

"Good old Pelham," I said. "What a great guy."

"You don't give him his due, Congreve. Maybe you'd be more like him if you were responsible for this whole hospital."

"Maybe I would."

She stood in my doorway, natty as always in her nurse whites.

"You know why I brought up the holiday?" she said.

"Huh-uh."

"Because we need a Santa."

"Aw, shit."

"Somebody found an old costume up on the sixth floor."

"Aw, shit."

"You said that."

"I don't want to play Santa."

"That nice little beer belly of yours, you'd be perfect."

"You haven't seen me naked lately; my little beer belly is even littler now."

I said it in a kidding fashion but I think she knew that there was some loneliness, and maybe even a bit of anger in it, too.

In the three months since Sarah had been here, I'd seen increasingly little of Polly.

No more standing-up lovemaking.

Not even the occasional hugs we used to give each other.

Sarah was her priority now.

"I'm sorry we haven't gotten together lately, Congreve."

"It's all right."

"No it isn't and you know it. It's just that between my two shifts and taking care of Sarah—"

"I understand."

"I know you think I'm foolish. About her, I mean."

I shrugged. "You do what you think's best."

"You think I'll get too attached to her, don't you?"

I looked at her. "You know how much you can handle."

"She's not going to be like the others."

"She's not?"

"No." She shook her coppery hair. I wanted to put my hands in it. "I think I've figured out a way to let her rest up between the visits she makes. I think that's what happened to the others."

"That doesn't sound real scientific."

"Simple observation. I saw how she was when Pelham was scheduling her. She started to twitch and shake and do all the things the others did. But two weeks ago I convinced Pelham to let me make up her schedule—and you wouldn't believe the difference."

I saw how excited and happy she looked. She was one damn dear woman, I'll tell you.

"I'm happy for you, Polly. I hope this works out for you."

"She isn't going to end up like the others. That I can promise you."

I stood up and went over to her. I wanted to make it friendly and not sexual at all but I guess I couldn't help it. I slid my arm around her shoulder and held her to me and felt her warm tears on my face. "You'll do just fine with her, Polly. You really will."

We stood like that for a time, kind of swaying back and forth with some animal rhythm coupling us fast, and then she said, sort of laughing, "You know, we never have tried it lying down the way most people do, have we?"

"You know," I said. "I think you're right."

And so we tried it and I have to admit I liked it fine, just fine.

6

A few days after all this, I saw a miracle take place: I was walking down a dusty hall, half the wall hoved in from a Christian-Fascist bomb, when I saw Young Doctor Pelham break a smile.

Now understand, this was not a toothpaste commercial smile. Nor was it a smile that was going to blind anybody.

But it was a) a real smile and b) it was being smiled by Young Doctor Pelham.

He was talking to Nurse Ellen, on whom I'd suspected he'd long had some designs, and when he saw me the smile vanished, as if I'd caught him at something dirty.

By the time I reached the nurse, Pelham was gone.

"I think I just had a hallucination."

"Pelham smiling?"

"Yeah."

"You should have been here a minute earlier. He slid his arm around my waist and invited me up to his room tonight. It's the kid."

"The kid?"

She nodded her short-cropped blonde head. "The Paineater."

"Oh."

"She's the best one we've ever had."

"Really?"

"Absolutely. She did three patients last night in less than two hours. Then she went into surgery with them this morning." She angled her tiny wrist for a glimpse of her watch. "In fact, that's where I'm headed now. Somebody got caught by some Dobermans. He's a mess. I'm not sure we can save him. They've been prepping him for the last ten minutes."

"The kid going to be in there?"

"Sure. She's already in there. Trying to calm him down."

"Guess I'll go take a look at her."

I started to turn away but she grabbed my arm. "I want to say something to you, Congreve, and I'm going to say it in terms you'll understand."

"All right."

"You're full of shit about Doctor Pelham."

"You're right. Those are terms I can understand."

"He works his ass off here. He's the only surgeon in the whole Fortress. He suffers from depression because he loses so many and when he can't sleep he spends time with all the wounded and injured. That's why he needs the Paineaters, Congreve. Because he doesn't have anybody else to help him and because he's so damned worried about his patients." She was quickly getting angry. "So I want you to knock off the bullshit with him, all right? The only reason he was mad about what you did was because of the bind you left him in with the patients. Or can't you understand that?"

The funny thing was, I did understand it and for the first time, what Young Doctor Pelham was all about. I guess I considered him cold and arrogant but what I missed seeing was that he was just a very vulnerable and overworked guy doing an almost impossible job. And it took Nurse Ellen to make me see it.

"He isn't so bad, is he?" I said.

"No, he isn't."

"And he isn't just using those Paineaters because he likes to see them suffer, is he?"

"No, he's not."

"Maybe he feels sorrier for them than I do."

"You're a stupid fucker, Congreve. You know the first three of them we ever had in here?"

"Yeah."

"When they—Well, after they died, he took each one of them out and buried her."

There wasn't much I could say.

"So knock off the 'Young Doctor Pelham' bullshit, all right?"

"All right."

"And one more thing."

"What's that?"

Now she gave me a great big smile of her own. "He's not so bad in the sack, either."

On my way back down the hall, I saw Dr. Sullivan and one of the nurses laughing in a secretive sort of way. They were probably telling jokes about Sullivan's boss, Pelham. It almost made me feel sorry for him.

I borrowed a book from Pelham's library once on the history of surgery. Pretty interesting, especially when you consider that the first operations were done as far back as the Stone Age. Using a piece of stone, the first surgeons cut holes in the skulls of their patients so that they could release evil spirits thought to cause headaches and other ailments.

But over the centuries, doctors had gotten used to slightly more sophisticated methods and equipment, x-rays and CAT scans and scalpels and clamps and retractors and sutures and hemostats and sponges and inverts among them.

And anesthesia.

Before 1842, when anesthesia came into use, all doctors could give patients was whiskey or compounds heavy with opium. And then the operations couldn't last too long, the sedative effects of the booze and opium wearing off pretty fast.

These days, Pelham and all the other doctors in all the other Fortresses faced some of the old problems. Anesthesia was hard to come by.

A few years back, a sociologist named Allan Berkowitz was out making note of all the mutated species he found in the various zones, when he was shot in the arm by a Zoner who robbed him and ran away.

Berkowitz figured he was pretty much dead. The blood loss would kill him if he didn't get to a doc. And the pain was quickly becoming intolerable. The blood loss had also disoriented him slightly. He spent a full half day wandering around in a very small circle.

He collapsed next to a polluted creek, figuring he might as well partake of some polluted waters, when he noticed a strange looking little girl standing above him. His first thought, given the size and shape of her head, was that she was just another helpless mutant turned away by her parents. You found a lot of freaks in the Zone, just waiting for roaming packs of Dobermans or genetics to take them from their misery.

This little girl made strange sad sounds in her throat. She seemed to be looking at Berkowitz and yet seeing beyond him, too. The effect was unsettling, like staring at someone you suddenly suspect is blind.

He dragged himself over to her. A fine and decent man, Berkowitz decided to forget his own miseries for the time and concentrate on hers. Maybe there was something he could do for her.

He took her little hand and said, "Hi, honey, do you have a name?"

And realized again that somehow she saw him yet didn't see him. The autism analogy came to mind.

And realized, also, that she couldn't talk. The strange sad noises in her throat seemed to be the extent of her vocabulary.

He wasn't strong enough to stand, so he gently pulled her down next to him, all the time keeping hold of her hand.

And then he started to feel it.

The cessation of his pain, of his fear, even of a generalized anxiety he'd known all his life.

His first reaction was that this was some physiological trick associated with heavy loss of blood. Maybe the same kind of well-being people noted in near-death experiences, the body releasing certain protective chemicals that instill a sense of well-being.

But he was wrong.

He sat next to the girl for more than three hours and in the course of it, they made a telepathic link and she purged him of all his grief and terror.

He knew this was real because each time he opened his eyes from his revery-like state, he saw animals nearby doing their ordinary animal things—a squirrel furiously digging a buried acorn from the grass; a meek little mutt peeing against a tree; a racoon lying on his back and eating a piece of bread he'd scrounged from some human encampment.

The wound didn't go away—she didn't heal him—but he felt so pacified, so whole and complete and good unto himself, that his spiritual strength gave him physical strength, and allowed him to find his way out of the Zone and back to his Fortress in Glencoe.

He brought the girl with him.

He took her straight to the doctor at the hospital and told the doctor what had happened and, skeptical as the doctor was, the little girl was allowed to audition, as it were.

They put her in the ER with a man whose arm had been torn off. You could hear his screams as far up as the sixth floor. They were prepping him for surgery.

The girl sat down and took the man's lone good hand.

He was in so much pain, he didn't even seem to notice her at first.

Nothing happened right away.

The strapped-down man went on writhing and screaming.

But then the writhing lessened.

And then the screaming softened.

And the doctor watched the rest of it, bedazzled.

Berkowitz's discovery made it possible for hospitals to keep on functioning. All they had to do was hire Outriders, men and women willing to take the chance of searching the Zones for more youngsters who looked and acted like this one. And while they were out there, like the Outriders of old, they could also note any gangs of people who seemed headed for the Fortress to inflict great bodily harm.

To date, these were a few observed truths about the Paineaters as they'd come to be called:

- Generally between the ages of 3–6
- Generally put out to die by their families because of their mutation
- Unable to speak or see (as we understand seeing)
- Generally useful for only a three-to-four month period
- Afterward, must be sent to Zone 4 for further study. At this stage, dementia has usually set in.

They could be used up, like a disposable cigarette lighter. They could absorb only so much of other people's pain and then that was it. A form of dementia set in. Fortress Northwestern had a group of doctors studying the used-up ones. By doing so, they hoped to increase the chances for longer use. There was a finite number of these children and they were extremely important to the survival of all Fortress hospitals. There were two other observations I should note:

- Extended proximity to these children has been known to make human beings overly protective of them, leading to difficulties with hospital efficiencies
- Extended proximity to these children has led to difficulties with normal human relationships.

I thought of all this as I stood in the observation balcony and watched the operation proceed.

The man who'd been attacked by the Dobermans was a mess, a meaty, bloody, flesh-ripped mess.

There would have to be a lot of plastic surgery afterward and even then, he would always be rather ghastly looking, a D-movie version of Frankenstein.

There were six people, including Pelham, on the surgery team. Even though he didn't have the equipment he needed—or in truth, the ability to completely sterilize the equipment he did have—Pelham tried to make this as much like his old surgery days as possible. There was the large table for instruments; the small table for instruments; and the operating table itself.

Above the line of her surgical mask, I could see Dr. Sullivan's beautiful eyes. Disapproving eyes. She obviously felt she should be in charge here, not Pelham.

They started cleansing the man's wounds, the surgical team, with Pelham pitching in. Surgeons were no longer stars. They had to do the same kind of work as nurses now.

The kid sat in a chair next to the operating table, holding the hand of the patient.

He was utterly tranquil, the man.

The kid had been working with him for some time now. The kid and the patient faced me, as did the surgery team.

I spotted Polly right away, behind her green surgical mask. She was supposed to be helping with the cleansing but she spent most of her time glancing at the kid.

You really do get hooked into them, some kind of dependence that you ultimately come to regret.

But then she was snapped back to the reality of the operating table when another nurse nudged her roughly and nodded to the patient.

Polly needed to clean a shoulder wound.

She set to work.

And just as she pulled her attention away, I saw the kid do it.

Go into a spasm, a violent shudder ugly to see.

And then I knew how foolish all Polly's talk had been about resting the kid so she didn't ever get used-up the way all the other ones did.

I got out of there.

I didn't want to be there when Polly noticed the kid go into a spasm, and realize that all her hopes had come to nothing.

7

The argument came three days later. Even two floors up, you could hear it.

I was walking up the stairs to my own room when I heard the yelling and then heard a door slamming shut.

Eighth floor, two down; eighth floor being Polly's. I decided I needed to check it out.

Pelham was in front of Polly's door. So was Nurse Ellen. They were speaking in low voices so nobody except Polly could hear them. Then Dr. Sullivan appeared, swank even in her dusty medical smock.

"What's going on?" I said.

Pelham frowned and shook his head. Of late I'd been nicer to him and was surprised to find that he'd been nicer to me, too.

He walked me down the hall, away from the door, to where a small mountain of rubble lay beneath the smashed-out windows.

Dr. Sullivan and Nurse Ellen stayed by Polly's door.

"Have you talked to her lately?"

"Not for a couple of days. She keeps pretty much to herself."

"That's the trouble. Herself—and the kid."

"I know."

"The same way you got, Congreve." For once there was sympathy in his voice, not condemnation. "Have you seen the little room she fixed up for the kid?"

"Huh-uh."

"It'll break your heart. Polly's convinced herself that she's the kid's mother."

"What's wrong with that? We're all pretty lonely here."

The frown again. But the dark eyes were sad, understanding. "She won't let us use the kid."

"Oh, man. Then she really is gone on her."

"Far gone. Maybe you can help."

"Not if she's this far along. You get hooked in."

"The same way you did."

I nodded. "The same way I did."

Nurse Ellen was getting mad. Raising her voice.

"Polly, we've got a ten-year-old boy down there who was shot by some Zoner. We have to operate right away. We need her, Polly. Desperately. Can't you understand that?"

"Let us in," Dr. Sullivan said in a voice that implied she expected to be obeyed immediately.

But the door didn't open.

And Polly didn't respond in any way at all.

"She said the kid has started twitching," Pelham said. "You know what that means."

By now, Nurse Ellen was shrieking. "Polly, we have to have the kid and we have to have her now!"

"C'mon, Congreve," Pelham said. "Try your luck. Please."

"Then you three go back downstairs."

"We don't have long. The boy's lost a lot of blood."

"I'll do what I can as soon as you two leave."

He wasted no time. He collected Ellen and Dr. Sullivan, went to the EXIT door and disappeared.

"They're gone, Polly."

"You can't talk me into it, Congreve."

"Polly, you're not being rational."

"And you are?"

"There's a little boy downstairs dying."

"Well, there's a little girl in here who's dying, too, and nobody seems to give a shit about that."

"She won't die. She's got a long way to go."

"You know better than that. You know how they are after they start twitching. And getting headaches."

"She'll be all right."

"I can't believe you're talking like this, Congreve. After what you did and all."

"They don't have any choice, Polly. They'll come and take her from you."

"I've got a gun in here."

"Polly, please, please start thinking clearly, will you?"

Three of them came through the EXIT door now, two men and a woman. The men were nurses. The woman was an intern. They all carried shotguns.

They were in a hurry.

They swept up to me and forced me to stand aside.

They meant to get Polly's attention and they did.

No warning. No words at all.

Two of them just opened fire. Pumped several noisy echoing powder-smelling rounds into the door.

Polly screamed.

The kid was making frantic animal noises.

"You going to bring her out?" one of the male nurses shouted.

"No!" Polly shouted back.

This time they must have pumped twenty rounds in there. They beat up the door pretty good.

"We're coming in, Polly!" the second nurse shouted.

Pretty obviously, she didn't have a gun. Or she would have used it.

Because now they went in. Booted in the door. Dove inside the room. Trained all three shotguns right on her.

She had pushed herself back against the corner in the precious pink room that she had turned into a wonderful bedroom for a little girl.

The girl was in her arms, holding tight, all the gunfire and shouting having terrified her.

Polly was sobbing. "Please, don't take her. Please don't take her."

She said it over and over.

But take her they did, and without any grace, either. The moment Polly showed the slightest resistance—held the kid tight so they couldn't snatch her—one of the nurses chunked Polly on the side of his head with the butt of his rifle.

I grabbed him, spun him around, put a fist deep into his solar plexus.

Not that it mattered.

While I was playing macho, the other two grabbed the kid and ran out of the room with her.

I dragged the lone nurse to the door and threw him down the hall.

Then I went back and sat on the small pink single bed where Polly was sprawled now, sobbing.

I sat on the bed and let her hold on to me as if I were her Daddy and knew all the answers to all the griefs of the world.

I was sitting up in my room, cleaning and oiling all the weapons, when Pelham showed up, knocked courteously—I told you we were trying to be nice to each other these days, Nurse Ellen's irate words taking their toll on me—and said, "Polly took the kid in the middle of the night and left."

This was two days after the incident at Polly's door.

"Maybe they just went out for a while."

"She took food, two guns and some cash."

"Shit."

"I've got a woman downstairs who won't see to-night if I don't get that kid back."

"Damn."

"I know how much you like Polly, Congreve. I like her, too. But I have to—"

"—think of the patients."

"I'm sorry if you get tired of hearing it."

I sighed and stood up. "I'll go get her."

"She tried to start the skymobile. Smashed in the window and then tried to hotwire it."

"She isn't real mechanical. On foot, she won't be hard to find. Unless something's happened to her already."

I tried not to think about that.

"You have to hurry, Congreve. Please."

Took me two hours.

She was up near the wall in what had formerly been a public rest stop. There were three semis turned on their sides in the drive, the result of the initial bombing, and they looked like big sad clumsy animals that couldn't get to their feet again.

Apparently, the rest stop had been pretty busy at the time of the bombing because from up here you could see the skeletons of maybe a dozen people, including that of a family—mother, father, two kids.

When I first spotted her, she was sitting on a hill, resting, with the kid sitting next to her.

She heard me about the same time as I saw her.

She stood up, wiped off her bottom from the grass, picked up the kid like a football and started running.

There was a deep stand of scrub pines but they weren't deep enough to hide her for long. I waited 'til she came running out of the trees and then I put the skymobile down not far away and started running after her.

She was in much better shape than I was. Even

holding the kid, she was able to stay ahead of me for a good half mile. I stumbled twice. She didn't stumble at all.

We were working up the side of a grassy hill when her legs and her wind gave out.

She just dropped straight down, as if she'd been shot in the head, straight down with the kid still tucked in her arms, straight down and sobbing wildly.

I stood several feet away and said nothing. There wasn't anything to say, anyway.

Pelham took the kid away from her and then put Polly up in one of the observation rooms in a straitjacket. He wouldn't let me see her for a couple of days.

By the time I got up there, she was a mess. She had a black eye from me having to wrestle her into the skymobile, and her coppery hair was shot through with twigs and dead flowers and her face was streaked with dirt. It was as if she'd been buried alive.

I took a straightbacked chair and sat next to her.

"You fucker."

"I'm sorry, Polly."

"You fucker."

But there was no power in her voice. She was just mouthing words.

"I'm sorry I got you involved in this. I never should have taken you along to Hoolihan's that day. I was being selfish."

"I don't want to live without her."

"You have to stop thinking that way, Polly. Pelham doesn't have any choice. He has to use Sarah for the sake of the patients."

"She's near the end."

"You need to get on with your life."

At one time, this room had been small and white and bright. Now it was small and dirty. The only brightness came from the kerosene lantern I carried, its flame throwing flickering shadows across Polly's face, making her look even more insane.

"Pelham's a fucker and Ellen's a fucker and you're a fucker. You're killing that little girl and none of you give a damn."

A knock. Just once. Curt.

The door opened and Pelham came in. He walked noisily across the glass-littered floor.

He stood next to me and looked at Polly in her chair and her straitjacket.

"You're doing better today, Polly. You're verbalizing much more."

"You're killing that little girl, doesn't that matter to you?"

This time her voice was heartbreaking. No curses. No anger. Just a terrible pleading.

"Another few days and maybe we'll be able to take off the straitjacket."

He was breaking her, the way cowboys used to break horses. By keeping her in this room long enough, in the straitjacket long enough, alone long enough, she would eventually become more compliant. She would never again be the fiery Polly of yore. But she would be a Polly who was no longer a threat to the hospital.

At least that was Pelham's hope.

"Would you like some Jello, Polly?"

But her head was down.

She was no longer willing to verbalize, to use Pelham's five-dollar word.

He nodded for me to follow him out.

"You get some sleep, Polly," Pelham said. "Sleep is your friend."

I took a last look at her.

No matter how long Pelham kept her in here, she would never forgive me and I wasn't sure I blamed her.

I followed him out.

9

That afternoon, over coffee, Pelham made me talk about it again and I resented it but I also understood that he was simply trying to help Polly and I was the nearest equivalent to Polly in the hospital.

Eight months ago, the hospital in need of another Paineater, I'd taken the skymobile over to Hoolihan's and bought myself a kid.

I got hooked. I wasn't even aware of it at first. The simplest explanation is that the kid became a substitute for my daughters. When she'd get back from downstairs, from consuming the pain of the patients that day, I'd find myself rocking her to sleep with tears in my eyes.

Soon enough, I saw her start to twitch. And then the headaches came. And night after night she made those same muffled screaming noises in her throat.

And Pelham, it seemed, was always at the door, always saying, "We need her again. I'm sorry."

And all I could do was watch her deteriorate.

"I know you hated me," Pelham said. "And I'm sorry."

I nodded. "You didn't have much choice."

He sipped his coffee. "So what finally made you decide to do it?"

"I guess when you started talking about her future and everything. How she'd be studied and tested so that we could get a better grasp on how to make the future ones last longer. 'New, Improved' models I guess you'd call them."

"Unless things change a whole hell of a lot, Congreve, we're going to need even more Paineaters in the future. And better ones."

"I guess that's what I was against. I don't think we have the right to use anybody that way. We get so fucking callous we forget they're human beings, and incredibly vulnerable ones."

"So you killed her."

"So I killed her."

That's what the nightmares were all about. Seeing little Michelle sleeping in my bed and creeping up to her and putting the gun to her chest and pulling the trigger and—

"I loved her," I said. "I felt it was the right thing. At least at the time. Now, I guess, I can see both sides."

"I really am going to let Polly go free in the next week or so. I just hope she's as rational as you are."

I sighed. "I hope so, too. For everybody's sake."

"We're doing the right thing, Congreve. The goddamned Christians took out half of Russia and China. We have to rebuild the species, what with all the mutation taking place. We normals have to survive. I don't like what we're doing with Paineaters but we don't have any choice. It's just survival is all."

He clapped me on the shoulder and went back to work. He looked exhausted but then he always looked exhausted.

10

She didn't get out in one week or two weeks or three weeks. It took four weeks before Pelham thought she was ready.

Mostly, she stayed in her room. They brought her food because she didn't go down to the mess. She was not allowed to see Sarah.

I stopped by several times and knocked. I always identified myself and always heard her moving about in there. But she would not acknowledge me in any way.

One day I waited three hours at the opposite end of the hall. I knew she had to come out eventually. But she didn't.

Another day I found her room empty. She was down the hall in the bathroom, apparently.

I hid in her room.

When she came back, I surprised her. Her face showed no response whatsoever. But her hand did. From a small holster attached to the back of her belt, she pulled out a small .45 and pointed it at me. I left.

A week after this she went berserk. This happened down in the mess. She was walking by and saw people staring at her and she went in and starting upending tables and hurling glasses and plates against the walls. She wasn't very big and she wasn't very mighty but she scared people. She wandered, sobbing and cursing, from the mess and went back upstairs to her room. After a while, Pelham went up to see her. He decided against confining her again.

11

"She's near the end. The spasms—I can barely stand to look at her. She won't last past another couple patients."

This was Pelham in his office two weeks after the incident with Polly in the mess.

Dr. Sullivan, lean, hungry and gorgeous as ever, sat to the left of Pelham, watching.

"Can you get ahold of Hoolihan?"

"Sure. Why?"

"Get another one lined up."

"She's that close to burning out, huh?"

Dr. Sullivan said, "Dr. Pelham is right. A few more patients at most. Sarah takes on trauma and grief and despair and frenzy as her own. She is a very small vessel. She can't hold much more. The situation is actually much more urgent than Dr. Pelham is letting on."

A deep, bellowing horn-like alarm that signals Pelham that ER has a patient very near death rumbled through the ground floor of the hospital.

Pelham and Sullivan were off running even before I got out of my chair. I followed.

"Used some kind of power saw on him," one of the techs said as the three of us reached the ER area.

Indeed. His neck, chest and arms showed deep ruts where some kind of saw had ripped through his flesh right to the bone. He wasn't screaming. He was unconscious.

Ed Gorman

"Get surgery set up!" Pelham shouted after one quick look at the man on the gurney.

"Things are just about ready to go," the tech said.

"We need the Paineater, then," Pelham said.

"She's in there, too," the tech said, "but she's not doing real well. You know how they get near the end—all the shaking and shit."

Five minutes later, we were all in surgery. One of the techs was sick today and I was asked to assist, as I did on occasion.

Operating table and instruments and staff were prepared as well as could be expected under these frantic conditions.

And Sarah was in place.

She sat, staring off at nothing, holding the bloody hand of the man on the table. Her entire body shook and trembled—and then went into violent seizures that would lift her out of her chair.

The screams in her throat kept dying.

"Your job is to watch her, make sure she stays linked to the patient," Pelham told me.

I went over and sat next to her. Just as she held the patient's hand, I held her free one. I kept cooing her name, trying to keep her calm.

She'd peed all over herself. The deep sobbing continued.

The operation started.

The patient was totally satisfied. You could see the pleasure on his face. Sarah was cleansing him not only of his physical pain but of all the grief and anxiety of his entire life. No wonder he looked beatific, like one of those old paintings that depicted mortal men looking on the face of an angel.

One thing you had to say for them, Pelham and Sullivan worked well together—quickly, efficiently, artfully. You'd never know they hated each other.

They had started doing the heavy-duty stitching when the rear door of the operating room slammed open.

I looked up and saw her there. Polly. With an auto-rifle. Face crazed and streaked with tears.

"You're killing her and you don't even care!" she screamed.

She worked left to right, which meant that Pelham was the first to die and then all the staffers standing next to him. This gave Sullivan and a few others the chance to hide behind the far side of the operating table.

By now I had my gun out and was crouched behind a small cabinet.

She kept on firing, trying to hit Sullivan and the others where they were hiding.

"Polly! Please drop your gun!"

If she heard me, she didn't let on. She just kept pumping rounds at the operating table, hoping to hit at least a few of them.

I started to stand up from my crouch.

She must have caught this peripherally because she suddenly turned in my direction, still firing, as one with her weapon.

"Polly!" I screamed. "Put it down!"

But she didn't put it down, of course, and then I had no choice. I put a bullet into the middle of her forehead.

She managed to squeeze off a few more shots but then her gun clattered to the floor, and soon enough she followed it.

Ed Gorman

Silence.

And then Sarah was up and tottering over to the fallen body of Polly's.

Sarah knelt next to her and made the awful mewling noises in her throat—the saddest sound in her entire repertoire—and then she was touching Polly's face reverently with her tiny white hands.

We all stood around and watched because we had never seen this before. Paineaters took on all the physical and psychic pain of others. Here was a Paineater who had to take on her own pain.

After a time, Sarah still kneeling there rocking back and forth and twitching so violently I was afraid she might start breaking her own bones, I went over and picked her up and carried her out of the room.

12

There was a funeral for Polly the next day. Some fine, sincere and very moving things were said.

Nurse Ellen announced that Dr. Sullivan would now be in charge of the hospital and that people should now come to her with any questions they had.

Afterward, I put Sarah in the skymobile and got ready to take off.

Dr. Sullivan came over to say goodbye. "The doctors at the school will be very interested in this one especially. Studying the effects of her own trauma. With Polly."

Sarah had made no sound since I'd carried her from the operating room yesterday. She just sat there in the throes of her shaking and jerking and trembling.

"I appreciate you doing this," Dr. Sullivan said. "I

know you don't think we should prolong their lives or their suffering. But it's necessary if we're to survive."

"That's what Pelham said."

She smiled her beautiful icy smile. "Well, at least he was right about something."

It took three hours to find the school, a rugged stone castle-like building that had once been a monastery sitting in the middle of deep woods.

"Well, this is going to be your home for a while, Sarah," I said. I'd tried not to look at her. The spasms were really getting to me.

Survival, Pelham had said.

I started circling for my landing, finding a good open area near the west wing to put the machine down.

And that's when the cry came up in her throat and her hand reached over and grabbed mine.

She shook so violently that I couldn't keep my hand around hers. Tears filled her dead eyes.

By now a couple of the docs below had come out and were waving to me. They knew who I was and what cargo I brought.

I waved back—or started to.

I pulled the machine up from the landing I'd started and swung away abruptly from the school.

I could hear them shouting below.

That night, in the mess, Dr. Sullivan came over and sat by me. "I really appreciate you taking her over there this afternoon."

"No problem."

"You doing all right?"

"Doing fine."

"I'm looking forward to working with you, Congreve."

"Same goes for me."

"Thanks."

Then she was off to do some more PR work with other people she felt vital to her new post as boss.

Being tired, I turned in early.

Being tired, I slept at once and slept fine and fast, too, until that time in the middle of the night when everything is shifting shadows and faint, disturbing echoes. I was awake and that meant I'd think back to this afternoon.

I'd tried to do it fast. I'd landed and carried her out of the skymobile and set her down on the grass and put one bullet quick and clean into the back of her skull. And then I held her for a long time and cried but the funny thing was I wasn't sure why I was crying. For her. For me. For Polly. For Pelham. For the whole crazy fucking world, maybe.

And then I buried her and stood over the little grave and said some prayers and a fiesty little mutt from the forest came along and played in the fresh dirt for a time. And I thought maybe she'd have liked that, little Sarah, the way the puppy was playing and all. And Polly would probably have liked it, too.

Darkness. Shadow. My own coarse breathing. I didn't want to think about this afternoon anymore. I just wanted sleep.

"You look tired," Dr. Sullivan said cheerfully at mess next morning.

"Guess I am kind of."

"You're going to see Hoolihan today, aren't you?"

"Uh-huh."

She looked at me hard then. I hadn't been properly enthusiastic when she brought the subject up. "You know how important this is, don't you, Congreve? I mean, for the whole species. Just the way Pelham said."

"Right," I said, "just the way Pelham said."

Three hours later I fired up the old machine and flew over to see Hoolihan.

Story Notes

"Yesterday's Dreams." A long, long time ago I saw a Canadian documentary about paranormal powers. It took as its premise the Russian notion that such powers are strong only in children and adolescents. One loses them as one gets older. I planned to write a novel about this someday but somehow it never came together. I decided to try it as a novelette and see where it got me. Kris Rusch bought it for *The Magazine of Fantasy & Science Fiction*, which was a particular kick for me because it's always been *the* class act of the science fiction-fantasy field.

"Different Kinds of Dead" was one of those stories I didn't think much of when I wrote it. You do the best you can and move on. But over the years, it's been reprinted six times, has appeared on two audio tapes, and has been optioned twice as a TV project. I also got a fair number of letters about it from men and women who spend lonely lives on the road. I was one such person when I worked for a year and a half in syndicated TV. I felt as isolated and weary as the protagonist. The late Karl Edward Wagner wrote and told me he thought it was "a very powerful story about loneliness" and asked me if he could reprint it. He then started telling me about his life and I sadly saw why he identified with it.

"Of the Fog" was inspired by the time I was fifteen and falsely accused of grand larceny. I was pretty much a street kid with some minor skirmishes with the law on my record but this was the big time. The cops didn't ask me if I'd taken the money; they *told* me I'd taken it. Even the lawyer my folks hired suggested I plead guilty. Turns out I'd innocently walked into a trap meant for somebody else—film noir stuff like that actually happens—and it took one detective a month to break down the guy he really suspected of setting the whole thing up. He was the only one of four cops who'd believed me. Thank God. The incident changed my life. I cleaned up my act, and just in time. A few months later my best friend started running with some very bad guys and got caught up in a gas station robbery in which the poor attendant was killed with a shotgun. None of this was much like *The Blackboard Jungle* or any of the American juvenile-delinquent movies. Truffaut got my version of lawlessness (and fear and loneliness) down forever in *The 400 Blows*, a picture you really should rent one of these days.

"Rite of Passage." As much as I like literature, I also like old-fashioned pulp—including Robert E. Howard, whom I've always enjoyed. When I finally got a chance to write a Howardian story, I said yes immediately. "Rite of Passage" is Howard with my own spin on it, questioning, I suppose, the basic ethic of the entire sword-and-sorcery subgenre. A side note: one of the most frightening scenes I've ever wanted to look away from was the opening raid in the first *Conan* picture. The pure terror of that kind of hand-to-hand combat has never been better filmed. I tried to get some of that into my story.

"Masque." This was done as work-for-hire. The Random House editor in charge of the anthology called up and said he desperately needed a "dark" story with a mummy theme and could I come up with something in seventy-two hours? Thus was born "Masque," a story line I lifted from TV. I'd been channel surfing and saw a soap opera where some wuss with his face bandaged was having a heart-to-heart with his mom. I thought, Gosh, a guy like that sure looks like a mummy. . . .

"Dark Muse" is my homage to all those brooding-young-composer melodramas I saw in second-run movie houses in the forties and then later on TV. This is one of the many assignments my best friend Marty Greenberg was nice enough to give me over the years, and I had a good time writing it. I picture John Cassavetes in the lead. He looked brooding even when he was asleep.

"Synandra" is a fragment of a nightmare that darkened my sleep when I was a teenager. I had no idea what it meant then. I've tried to give it shape and meaning in the story. I've always believed that there is some level of existence where cosmic battles are fought out—I hope all those Henry Kuttner–C. L. Moore adventure novels are true—and this is my contribution to that subgenre of pulp fiction.

Ed Gorman

Technically, being a Western, "Junior" doesn't belong in this collection. Ah, but it's a very special Western. It's an EC Comics Western. A while back a small publisher wanted to do a modern version of EC suspense/horror stories and asked me to come up with a story line. The comic book never appeared, so I translated it into prose. I think the Crypt-Keeper might have liked this one.

"The Monster Parade" was written after I went on a weeklong binge reading a small box of science fiction magazines. It's horror-sf but the style and tone owe a great deal to the great good writers of that decade. The short fiction of that era holds up very, very well. Better perhaps than the fiction of any other decade.

"The Face" I did after watching a PBS program about Civil War doctors. It was one of those stories I did in one long sitting. Earlier I'd come across notes by a Confederate surgeon and I incorporated some of these into the piece as well. The faces of the dead and dying on that PBS show are something I'll always—alas—remember.

"The Broker" is my contribution to shock-horror. While I generally like what I call mainstream horror, every once in a while I like a literary kick in the stomach. This one I wrote to give you a bit of a jolt, and I hope I succeeded.

"The Long Sunset" is one of my small-town stories fused with a horror/science fiction element. Small towns are filled with such stories. *Jules and Jim*, the famous French picture of the fifties, has always appealed to me—two men in love with the same woman—as has William L. Temple's ironic science fiction take on the same theme, *The Four-Sided Tri-*

angle. This is *my* version of both pieces.

"To Fit the Crime" got a TV option two weeks after it was published. It's horror-sf-noir, the kind of spiritual landscape I love as both writer and reader. It's one of the few times I've ever used an outright anti-hero as a protagonist (something done fairly often in the fifties), and it was an interesting project for me to face every day at the word processor.

"Cages" sat on the editorial desk of a long-esteemed magazine for six months. Finally the editor, who'd fought the good fight, said that the publisher said, "If we publish this, we'll lose five thousand subscribers." It's proved one of my most controversial pieces, finally ending up in the great British sf magazine *Interzone*. It's probably the most Philip K. Dickian pieces I've ever written—again, horror-sf—and one of my favorites.

"Emma Baxter's Boy." I once saw a *National Geographic* special about a lioness who refused to accept the fact that one of her cubs was dead. She carried him and protected him for several days—a corpse. I was so moved by this I knew I wanted to write a story about how tenacious mother love can be. And thus this tale.

"Survival." Horror-sf again. Someday I hope to expand "Survival" into a full-length novel. I like the metaphor of how we burden—and sometimes destroy—our children with our own problems . . . and I like the glimpse I give of this particular world. It's been optioned twice as a feature, and twice scripted. But neither draft was very good, I thought. A younger Robert Duvall would have been great for the role of the narrator.

ONE RAINY NIGHT

RICHARD LAYMON

"If you've missed Laymon, you've missed a treat."
—Stephen King

The strange black rain falls like a shroud on the small town of Bixby. It comes down in torrents, warm and unnatural. And as it falls, the town changes. One by one, the inhabitants fall prey to its horrifying effect. One by one, they become filled with hate and rage . . . and the need to kill. Formerly friendly neighbors turn to crazed maniacs. A stranger at a gas station shoves a nozzle down a customer's throat and pulls the trigger. A soaking-wet line of movie-goers smashes its way into a theater to slaughter the people inside. A loving wife attacks her husband, still beating his head against the floor long after he's dead. As the rain falls, blood flows in the gutters—and terror runs through the streets.

"No one writes like Laymon, and you're going to have a good time with anything he writes."
—Dean Koontz

NAILED
BY
THE
HEART

SIMON
CLARK

"One of the year's most gripping horror novels . . . Truly terrifying." —*Today* (UK)

The Stainforth family—Chris, Ruth and their young son, David—move into the ancient sea-fort in a nice little coastal town to begin a new life, to start fresh. At the time it seems like the perfect place to do it, so quiet, so secluded. But they have no way of knowing that they've moved into what was once a sacred site of an old religion. And that the old god is not dead—only waiting. Already the god's dark power has begun to spread, changing and polluting all that it touches. A hideous evil pervades the small town. Soon the dead no longer stay dead. When the power awakens the rotting crew of a ship that sank decades earlier, a nightmare of bloodshed and violence begins for the Stainforths, a nightmare that can end only with the ultimate sacrifice—death.

___4713-6 $5.99 US/$6.99 CAN

THE DAWNING

HUGH B. CAVE

In the all-too-immediate future, the day has finally come when crime, drugs, and pollution have made the cities of the world virtually uninhabitable. Gangs roam the streets at will, the police have nearly surrendered, and the air and water are slowly killing the residents who remain. But one small group of survivors has decided to escape the madness. Packing what they can carry, they head off to what they hope will be the unspoiled wilderness of northern Canada, intent on making a new start, a new life. But nature isn't that forgiving. For far too long mankind has destroyed the planet, ravaging the landscape and slaughtering the animals. At long last, nature has had enough. Now the Earth is ready to fight back, to rid itself of its abusers. A new day has come. But will anyone survive . . . the Dawning.

BLACK RIVER FALLS
ED GORMAN

"Gorman's writing is strong, fast and sleek as a
bullet. He's one of the best."
—Dean Koontz

Who would want to kill a beautiful young woman like
Alison...and why? But whatever happens, nineteen-year-old
Ben Tyler swears that he will protect her. It hasn't been easy
for Ben—the boy the other kids always picked on. But then
Ben finds Alison and at last things are going his way...Until
one day he learns a secret so ugly that his entire life is
changed forever. A secret that threatens to destroy everyone
he loves. A secret as dark and dangerous as the tumbling
waters of Black River Falls.

"Gorman has a way of getting into his characters and
they have a way of getting into you."
—Robert Block, author of *Psycho*

——4265-7 $4.99 US/$5.99 CAN

Dorchester Publishing Co., Inc.
P.O. Box 6640
Wayne, PA 19087-8640

Please add $1.75 for shipping and handling for the first book and
$.50 for each book thereafter. NY, NYC, and PA residents,
please add appropriate sales tax. No cash, stamps, or C.O.D.s. All
orders shipped within 6 weeks via postal service book rate.
Canadian orders require $2.00 extra postage and must be paid in
U.S. dollars through a U.S. banking facility.

Name_____
Address_____
City_____ State_____ Zip_____
I have enclosed $_____ in payment for the checked book(s).
Payment <u>must</u> accompany all orders. ❏ Please send a free catalog.

P(THE)OKER
CLUB
ED GORMAN

It all starts so innocently. It is just a group of buddies meeting for a weekly poker game. No harm done—until the night an intruder breaks in while they are playing. They don't mean to kill him, that is an accident. They think if they throw the body in the river no one will ever know. That's where they are wrong. The intruder hasn't come alone. His friend is waiting for him outside the house and he sees it all. Suddenly the game has changed. What starts out as a simple poker game now becomes a game of cat and mouse. The stakes are raised too—to life and death. And it looks like the attacker in the shadows holds all the cards.

___4683-0 $5.99 US/$6.99 CAN

SHADOW GAMES

ED GORMAN

Cobey Daniels had it all. He was rich, he was young, and he was the hottest star in the country. Then there was that messy business with the teenage girl . . . and it all went to hell for Cobey. But that was a few years ago. Now Cobey's pulled his life together, they're letting him out of the hospital, and he's ready for his big comeback. But the past is still out there, waiting for him. Waiting to show Cobey a hell much more terrifying than he ever could have imagined.

___4515-X $5.50 US/$6.50 CAN

Cold Blue Midnight

Ed Gorman

In Indiana the condemned die at midnight—killers like Peter Tapley, a twisted man who lives in his mother's shadow and takes his hatred out on trusting young women. Six years after Tapley's execution, his ex-wife Jill is trying to live down his crimes. But somewhere in the chilly nights someone won't let her forget. Someone who still blames her for her husband's hideous deeds. Someone who plans to make her pay . . . in blood.

___4417-X $4.99 US/$5.99 CAN